ROAD TO PURGATORY

wm

WILLIAM MORROW

An Imprint of HarperCollins*Publishers*

MAX ALLAN COLLINS

ROAD TO PURGATORY

This book is a work of fiction. References to real people, events, establishments, organizations, or locales are intended only to provide a sense of authenticity, and are used fictitiously. All other characters, and all incidents and dialogue, are drawn from the author's imagination and are not to be construed as real.

HarperCollins books may be purchased for educational, business, or sales promotional use. For information please write: Special Markets Department, HarperCollins Publishers Inc., 10 East 53rd Street, New York, NY 10022.

FIRST EDITION

DESIGNED BY JUDITH STAGNITTO ABBATE

Printed on acid-free paper

Library of Congress Cataloging-in-Publication Data

Collins, Max Allan.
    Road to purgatory / Max A. Collins.
        p. cm.
    ISBN 0-06-054027-3 (acid-free paper)
        1. World War, 1939–1945—Veterans—Fiction.
2. Irish Americans—Fiction. 3. Organized crime—
Fiction. 4. Chicago (Ill.)—Fiction. 5. Criminals—
Fiction. 6. Adoptees—Fiction. 7. Revenge—Fiction.
I. Title.

PS3553.O4753R63 2004
813'.54—dc22   2004042562

04 05 06 07 08 JTC/RRD 10 9 8 7 6 5 4 3 2 1

FOR DANIEL OSTROFF—

who launched the O'Sullivans

on the Hollywood road

WE WHO WALK THE DEMON'S PATH ARE NO LONGER ORDINARY MEN.

Kazuo Koike

WE'RE THE BATTLING BASTARDS OF BATAAN; NO MOMMA, NO POPPA, NO UNCLE SAM.

War correspondent Frank Hewlett

ONE IS LEFT WITH THE HORRIBLE FEELING THAT WAR SETTLES NOTHING; THAT TO WIN A WAR IS AS DISASTROUS AS TO LOSE ONE.

Agatha Christie

PROLOGUE

Bataan, the Philippines

March 1942

EVEN BEFORE THE BANZAI ATTACK, the young corporal who Captain Arthur Wermuth had taken under his wing, some months ago, was already something of a legend on the peninsula.

Michael Satariano of DeKalb, Illinois, had seemed so slight, such a child at twenty, that Wermuth had given in to protective feelings about his charge which were not wise in war. The boy was about five ten and slender, his tanned skin due not to an Italian heritage but the tropical sun that they all endured; his hair and eyes were dark brown, his face blessed with such an angelic innocence that the Filipino Scouts— who were so impressed with the lad's exploits—had taken to calling him *un Demonio Angelico*.

Any affection the captain nurtured for the soft-spoken, taciturn lad—any fatherly concern he might harbor—was off-set by the deadpan ferocity Satariano brought to combat. The boy's battlefield commission reflected his bravery during the withdrawal from Luzon to Bataan; Satariano—his behavior emblematic of General MacArthur's "stand and fight, fall back and dynamite" strategy—had waited until the last moment to dynamite a key bridge.

Cut off from the demolition experts of the Engineers, Wermuth had dispatched the young man to do his best, and witnessed from a safe distance images he would never forget: the little yellow men in brown uniforms halfway across the rickety, rotting suspension bridge, and the kid firing into the pile of leafy-branch-camouflaged wooden boxes (red-stenciled: DYNAMITE—DUPONT), followed by a thundering plume of orange and white and gray, wires snapping, planks flying like knocked-out teeth, enemy soldiers tumbling, those still alive screaming, arms windmilling, as they fell the fifty feet into a patiently waiting riverbed.

And the boy turning to trot back and rejoin the Scouts with an expression as coldly bland as a chilled glass of milk.

Wermuth—a heavy-set dark-haired man of thirty-three whose nondescript features and tiny twitchy mustache masked a grizzled combat veteran, his 1918-vintage tin helmet worn rakishly to one side—led the 57th Filipino Scouts, also known as the Snipers. The boy from Illinois was the only other white in the 57th, which was not unusual on Bataan, where the American forces numbered around five thousand to thirty-some thousand Filipinos, about half of which were the well-trained Scouts, the rest rather hopeless untrained native recruits.

A two-man sprinkling of khaki amid the coarse blue fatigues of the Filipinos, Wermuth and his young sidekick supervised the Snipers, their usual mission reflected by their name, Satariano the keenest shot of them all, captain included. Of late their duty had shifted, as General Wainwright had sent them out on patrol in the no-man's land extending across the breadth of Bataan, scouting for signs of enemy build-up or imminent attack.

Twenty-five miles long, twenty miles across, the peninsula of Bataan jutted into Manila Bay like a mini-Florida, its tip pointing to the nearby looming island fortress of Corregidor, MacArthur's HQ. Like twin spinal cords, two mountain ranges thick with jungle ran the peninsula's length—between them lay a narrow valley crisscrossed by streams, ravines and gullies . . . on either side, narrow coastal plains.

To Captain Wermuth, Bataan seemed a primitive sort of paradise in which to be fighting a modern war. The peninsula had its share of vividly glorious vistas—terraced rice fields, shimmering blue rivers, purple-peaked mountains—with civilization represented by the occasional village of thatched-roof nipa huts on stilts, dogs sharing the interior, pigs snoozing below. Boys chased chickens around and around just within the stone-wall periphery of such villages, a thigh-high barricade that wouldn't keep a monkey out, much less the Japanese.

The jungles through which Wermuth, his sidekick Satariano and their Scouts patrolled were snarls of palms, ferns, snake-like vines and brush, a steamy hot hell. But just when the rugged terrain was at its most unforgiving—the temperature and exhaustion and mosquitoes and hunger combining to test the limits of endurance—a cool stream could rush down out of the mountains, to make it up to you.

Such had been the case that muggy afternoon, and the captain instructed his dozen Scouts to catch some chow and some rest. They would take off their tin helmets and splash the refreshing stuff on their faces and arms and hands and drink as greedily as a desert wayfarer who discovered a mirage really was an oasis. Even as they ate, however, many of the Scouts at least half-reclined, their eyes on the trees . . .

. . . not enjoying the glimmering green tropical beauty, rather keeping an eye out for the glint of a rifle barrel amid high branches. As snipers themselves, they had a practical paranoia.

These Filipinos had been in their nation's army for years, virtually signing up for life. Well-equipped with M-1 rifles, gas masks, web gear, bed rolls and fine leather shoes, they could all muster at least a reasonable English dialect. Their worst sin, Wermuth knew, was a lack of initiative—in their culture, a guy couldn't get in trouble for something he *didn't* do. But with guidance, they could deliver merry hell on the enemy.

The Scouts were the best soldiers on the peninsula, American and Japanese included.

"Fellas," the captain said, as his men lolled back luxuriously, savoring their three-eighths ration of rice beside the babbling brook, "we should be within spitting distance of the perimeter defense line."

With a nod toward the trees, Satariano said, "Light machine gun position up that way."

"The corporal and me'll just drop by and say hello," the captain said. He pointed. "Take your latrine off that away. . . . Heading out, we'll try 'n' remember not to walk there."

This was an old joke among these warriors; nonetheless, the Scouts all laughed at the thought of stepping in their own mess. They were easily amused.

Wermuth and his corporal stayed together, almost side by side, as they moved through the jungle, Satariano hacking with a Filipino bolo; despite the blade, big branches and vines slapped the faces of the men for their rude intrusion. Staying close was a necessity in such thick underbrush, visibility often less than a yard. The occasional scurry of animals was probably small monkeys and lizards, who moved as if word had spread that the rations-shy GIs were eating them; the jungles were said to be home to wild pigs, pheasant and quail, too, but you couldn't prove that by Wermuth or just about any soldier on the peninsula. They did find the occasional water buffalo in a mud hole, though the flavor was about the same whether you ate the beast or the mud.

Satariano wore a shoulder-slung Thompson submachine gun with a black asbestos protective glove on his left hand; the weapon was like something out of a Cagney picture, the spare pair of round ammo drums like mini-canteens on his webbing belt. The kid had a sidearm as well, a .45 Army Colt that had been his father's in the last war. Neither soldier carried grenades, because such a high percentage were duds, and depending on them was more dangerous than not having them. Wermuth, like his Scouts, carried an M-1 and his sidearm was also a .45 Colt, dating to the "Great" War.

Wermuth wondered what it could be in the boy's background to give him such a capacity for killing. Smalltown kid Satariano had been one of the first group of recruits to arrive in the Philippines, back in April of '41, and even trained here. He'd been a standout on the target range—obviously, somebody in the boy's past had taught him to shoot; maybe he'd spent time on a farm.

Not long ago, the life of a G.I. on the Philippines had been damn near idyllic, training till noon with afternoons free (including an hour for siestas), and plenty of nightlife. American bucks went a long way—food was cheap, a bottle of gin thirty cents! The people were friendly, and this included the females. Then after Pearl Harbor the soldier's life of wine, women and song ran headlong into the reality of what they'd been training for. . . .

That the Filipino Scouts could adjust to war came as no surprise, considering the violent history of the Philippines; it was harder on the American boys . . . though Satariano seemed an exception. Wermuth was well aware that the toughest thing about combat was learning to control your emotions. Fear and panic were bigger hazards than anything the enemy could throw at you.

And emotional control included getting over the psychological hurdle of learning to take lives in combat; killing another human being required an adjustment that most people could never make in the civilian world, and thankfully never had to.

How this kid, fresh out of high school, had developed that ability . . . from whence the boy had summoned it . . . Wermuth had no idea. The boy did not seem to be a psychopath; he had no meanness in him—he was, if anything, a sweet, quiet, generous kid, albeit one to keep to himself.

The only exception to that solitary streak was the corporal's devotion to his captain. Strange that this kid who was such a loner behind the lines made the perfect sidekick at the front. But Satariano seemed to crave someone he could look up to. Someone he could please. And Wermuth fit that bill.

In less than ten minutes, Wermuth and Satariano had reached a small semblance of a clearing; whether the brush had been cut away or trampled into submission or cleared by mortar fire, Wermuth couldn't venture a guess. Whatever the case, anyone who stepped out of the jungle into the relief of this open air would make an excellent target.

As if to confirm the captain's opinion, a foxhole had been

dug at the edge of the clearing between the flange-like roots of a banyan, home to a trio of Scouts manning a light machine gun. Wermuth knew the three men well—they were under his command—and he was smiling as he approached the position, a greeting on his lips . . .

. . . which froze into a grotesque grin as he and Satariano looked down into the foxhole, the three Scouts flung to its earthen floor, their bodies battered and ruptured from the butts of rifles, blue fatigues blood-soaked. Their heads were off and had rolled here and there, billiard balls unsuccessfully seeking a pocket.

Hardened combat veteran that he was, Wermuth was nonetheless horror-struck; his mind shouted *Goddamn samurai swords!* But the words did not emerge.

Across from him, at the foxhole's other edge, Satariano looked up sharply at the captain. "Fresh."

Wermuth gazed down with new eyes, seeing the still-red blood, summoned from the gaping vacant necks, which spilled scarlet like kicked-over paint cans.

The boy's face under the tin helmet was void of emotion, but a tightness around the eyes spoke volumes.

All the corporal said, in a whisper that was little more than lip movement, was, "Not a shot fired."

Satariano glanced toward the clearing, then back at his captain, and their eyes locked in shared understanding: the Nips had killed these sentries without firing a shot, to avoid attracting attention. Why? To take full advantage of that inviting clearing. . . .

Meaning, they'd be back—*soon.*

Satariano was the first to climb down into the foxhole, ducking below its lip; and then so did Wermuth, finding a spot between corpses, though the wetness of blood leached unsettlingly through his khakis.

The crunching of footsteps on beaten-down brush was followed by the sounds of laughter and conversation in that distinctive foreign tongue. When Wermuth risked a peek above the foxhole rim, he saw a sea of brown uniforms—at least twenty of them—as the enemy soldiers . . . in helmets, a few in puttees, most with bayonets at their side, some with shoulder-slung machine guns . . . relaxed and joked and smoked.

Ducking back down, Wermuth looked at Satariano, who whispered, "Turkey shoot."

And there was no time for discussion, no chance to express a contrary opinion much less for Wermuth to exert his rank. The kid jack-in-the-boxed to a shooting posture and let rip with the tommy gun.

As Satariano's machine gun thundered, Wermuth aimed his M-1; but the captain held his fire momentarily, as every potential target seemed to be busy taking the boy's bullets, doing an awful dance for an unseen puppeteer. Spurts of blood, like ribbons flung in celebration, slashed the green landscape and streaked wrapping-paper brown uniforms with scarlet, and cries of agony and surprise made dissonant music in a jungle otherwise gone silent.

Toward the rear, the Nips were running for the jungle and Wermuth finally began to shoot, picking off one, two, three of them. A hot spent shell bounced off Wermuth's cheek as the blank-faced boy went about his business.

It took a full minute for the corporal to deplete the drum of .45 cartridges, and the captain fired rapidly with the M-1 while Satariano plucked another round magazine of slugs off the webbed belt. But then the clearing was empty of the living, though around twenty of the dead lagged behind. They lay in various awkward postures, snipped puppets now, and the smell of cordite singed the muggy air.

The two men exchanged glances.

Was that all of them? Was it over?

"Cover me," Satariano said.

The captain followed the corporal's order, as the boy rose from the grave-like foxhole to thread through the scattered corpses, making sure no living surprises awaited among the dead. The boy made a thorough job of it, occasionally bending over a body to check, and each time Wermuth felt his guts tighten.

Satisfied, the boy began back, moving across the corpse-cluttered clearing in a cautious, circling-around manner, tommy gun ready, managing not to trip over any of the fallen. He was almost half-way when the jungle began to bleed brown uniforms.

Dozens of Nips poured out between the trees, on the run, guns blasting, rifles, sidearms, some with swords upraised, shrill cries cutting the air like verbal blades, shrieking the all-too-familiar "*Banzai!*"

Wermuth instinctively sprang to his feet and began firing the rifle at the onslaught and when the bullet slammed through his chest and out his back, he tumbled back down into the foxhole, where he damn well should have stayed. He wasn't in much pain, but couldn't seem to get his hands to work, couldn't get himself in place to offer supportive fire to his corporal, out there in the midst of the banzai attack.

But the boy did have that hot tommy, and his cool head, and, at the rim of the foxhole, Wermuth watched in amazement as Satariano methodically mowed down the men, turning in ever so slow a pirouette to catch them as they came from all directions. There the young soldier stood, bullets flying all around him, carving into trees, ruffling fronds, lead bees zinging but not quite stinging, the corporal as yet unhit. Somehow Wermuth got his arms working and positioned himself and was taking aim when Satariano, finally, fell, dropping alongside an enemy corpse.

Dread rose like bile in the wounded captain, who nonetheless noted the almost comical sight as the twenty or more Nips momentarily froze, their eyes wide with their adversary's apparent death.

And then Satariano rose up, firing—he'd only been out of ammo, and reloading!—and once again the enemy was toppling like dominoes, the choppy roar of the tommy gun echoing through the clearing, drowning out cries of war and pain.

Wermuth picked off a few with the M-1, but it was his corporal who continued to rain death on the horde. When the second drum was empty, the boy calmly drew his .45 automatic—by this time only half a dozen enemy remained—and when that was spent, he unsheathed the Filipino sword from his webbing belt, and met a Samurai-wielding foe blade for blade.

The would-be Samurai, however, did not know his way around the sword and missed Satariano in the most clumsy fashion. When the American swung around with the bolo, the blade met the enemy's neck and the soldier's head went flying like a coconut shook from a tree.

The corpse stood there for a moment, a geyser of blood rising to the gods; the dead man weaved, as if trying to decide what to do next, and then made the obvious choice by toppling.

The remaining three fled toward the trees, but Wermuth got one of them with the rifle.

The sight of the boy standing in the midst of the corpse-strewn battlefield, Wermuth would not soon forget—unless of course the captain died right there in the foxhole. Corporal Satariano made a slow circle, while his machine-gun barrel traced a smoky question mark in the air, and—as casual and methodical as a merchant auditing his inventory—he again threaded through looking for fakers.

Then the corporal trotted over to his captain's position, checked the wound, said, "You'll live," and hoisted the bigger man up onto his shoulders and hauled him into the thickness of jungle.

"I'll . . . I'll put you up for the Medal of Honor for this, lad," Wermuth said.

"Let's get back alive, first," the boy said.

Wermuth passed out, shortly thereafter, but he learned from his Scouts that *un Demonio Angelico* had refused to let any of them relieve him, personally carrying his captain to the aid station.

THE NEXT MORNING—A BLISTERING, MUGGY REPLICA OF the day before—Major General Jonathan Wainwright, commander of the U.S. Army Forces on Bataan, paid a visit to the recuperating Captain Arthur Wermuth at Base Hospital #2.

A tall, lanky fifty-nine (his friends called him "Skinny"), the general ought to have cut an unprepossessing figure—weak-chinned, beady-eyed, jug-eared, long-necked, stoop-shouldered, cueball-bald. His khaki uniform had long since faded and shrunk, the pants of the high-water variety, his knobby knees bulging. An old knee injury from falling off a horse prompted the use of a cane—in Bataan, a carved bamboo stick.

And yet the impression this man gave his troops was one of cool strength—strength of character, and even physical power.

An Old School cavalryman, Major General Wainwright of Walla Walla, Washington, never ordered his men to do anything he would not himself attempt. His near-daily trips to the front had made him beloved among the troops (though stationed on nearby Corregidor, General MacArthur had set foot on Bataan exactly once, and was widely known among the men as "Dugout Doug"). Wainwright fought side by side with the enlisted men, and he and Marco, his trusty Filipino driver, had once rushed and knocked out a Japanese rifle position.

But the soft-spoken general did not consider himself in any way a hero. He had the same job as his men: to fight.

Wainwright's field headquarters were concentrated in Little Baguio, a flat area in the hills bordered by otherworldly trees with enormous trunks and vines extending from their tops to the earth. From Little Baguio, supplies, munitions, clothes and food (such as there was) were distributed to the front line. The nearby small town of Cabcaben consisted of two palm-lined dusty streets leading to a bay-front stone jetty frequented by supply barges; this was the southeastern tip of Bataan, the beach smooth and low, barbed-wire stretching out into the shallow water like nasty seaweed.

The laying of this barbed wire Wainwright had personally supervised; for all his apparent reserve, the general within himself was a restless, anxious commander who felt the need to check on every detail of his defensive position. He preferred to be at the front with his men, not weighed down under reports and memos behind the lines.

The general made the short trip—the hospital was just behind Cabcaben—in his command car driven by a temporary driver, a

Filipino who drove so timidly, so slowly, Wainwright thought he would go mad.

The hospital was a mammoth open-air ward of some three thousand beds under a tin roof; foxholes had been dug under most of the beds, a practical notion Wainwright applauded—on two occasions, bombs had fallen nearby. The patients ranged from the badly wounded—arms and legs missing, one man with half his face gone—to sufferers of malaria and malnutrition . . . though many a man with either (or both) of those maladies remained at the front.

A hatchet-faced fortyish nurse in Regular Army khaki shirt and pants led the general to the captain's bedside; the scent of disinfectant in the open-air ward made Wainwright's nostrils twitch. The general took his time, acknowledging every solider he passed with a smile and a comment. Finally, mid-ward, he was deposited at Captain Wermuth's bedside.

His chest heavily bandaged, the gauze spotted scarlet, Wermuth was prone—the beds did now allow a sitting position, nor for that matter did the captain's wound; but the dapperly mustached patient managed a chipper salute just the same.

"I hear you're a lucky man," Wainwright said, pulling up a metal chair, taking off his cap to reveal the brown egg of his skull. "If you have an extra rabbit's foot, I'll take it."

"Skinny," Wermuth said to his old friend, "if there was one spare rabbit's foot on *this* hellhole, it'd be eaten."

Wainwright smiled slightly, then said, "What's the prognosis?"

"Well, as I guess you know, slug missed my lung and went out the back, clean as a whistle. Should be getting my boys in mischief again in a week, maybe less."

"That your opinion or the medic's?"

"We're still . . . haggling."

Wainwright let out air in what was part laugh, part sigh. "Quite a story going around, you and your corporal in that clearing. Never thought you fellas would top your antisniper-detail score."

Last month Wermuth and his Scouts had cleaned out three hundred Nips who'd infiltrated the lines.

"Afraid we only got fifty-eight, this time, Skinny. Personally, I only got eight. But my corporal bagged an even fifty his own self."

"Fifty? Who is this boy—Jack the Giant Killer?"

"Michael the avenging angel's more like it," Wermuth said, and told the tale, which required no embellishment.

Wainwright whistled long and low. "He deserves a DSC."

"Distinguished service doesn't cover it, Skinny. I want to put the lad in for a Medal of Honor."

Wainwright's eyes tightened. "Perhaps we should, at that. That might well prove the first of this war, if it goes through."

Wermuth smiled, savoring the favorable response. "Can I ask another favor, sir?"

"I get nervous when you don't call me 'Skinny' . . . but, of course. Ask away."

"Don't send the boy out without me. I'll only be a few days. Find something for him to do, till then."

Wainwright chuckled. "Arthur, this boy sounds like he can take of himself."

"I know. Better than two old gravel crunchers like us. Just that . . . kid and me've been together through this whole damn campaign. We're kind of each *other's* rabbit foots. Feet."

After a moment, the general said, "Despite it all, ill-advised as it is, you do form bonds in a war." He nodded across the ward. "*My* next stop's my driver."

"Marco? He's checked into this hotel, too?"

"Yes. And no, we didn't crash or wind up in a ditch—simple dysentery." Wainwright reached out and patted the patient's arm. "Tell you what, Captain—I'll take Corporal Satariano on as my driver for the next few days. My current replacement's a Nervous Nellie whose goal seems to be driving slow enough to make a good target."

Wermuth chuckled, but his face was quite serious as he said, "I appreciate this, Skinny. Owe you one."

Arching an eyebrow, the general said, "Who's counting?"

With some effort, Wermuth rolled to his side. His voice soft, to keep the conversation private, he asked, "What do you hear?"

All of the implications of those four simple words were immensely clear to Wainwright. A few weeks before, he'd been confident of victory; but now his command was running out of food, medicine and even bullets—so hope was in short supply, as well.

The general said, sotto voce, "There's a strong sentiment stateside that MacArthur should not be permitted to remain on the Rock."

Wermuth's face retained its bland expression, but his eyes died a little.

Wainwright chose his words carefully. "If America's greatest hero were to be captured or killed, the home-front would take a terrible hit."

The propaganda value of a defeated MacArthur would be enormous—another indication, post-Pearl Harbor, that the Japanese were indeed invincible.

"But if he withdraws . . ." Wermuth began.

The captain did not complete the thought; he didn't have to— both men knew that MacArthur leaving would be a clear signal to the Philippines garrison . . . and to the entire world . . . that the USA's commitment to the islands was over.

"We'll know more soon," Wainwright said, rising. "The Old Man wants to see me tomorrow."

"Tell him we can still win this."

"You know I will. . . . Now, where can I find this corporal of yours?"

THE FOLLOWING MORNING—CLEAR AND HOT, TYPICAL March Bataan weather—General Wainwright broke in his new driver, who'd been summoned to him from the bivouac of the Scouts.

"You come highly recommended by Captain Wermuth," the general told the corporal, as they stood beside the open scout car. "And you'll be back in action as soon as he is."

"Good to hear, sir," the boy said in a clear second tenor.

So this was the one the Filipino Scouts called *un Demonio An-*

gelico. My God but he was young-looking! Satariano—what was that, Sicilian?

"This isn't a tommy gun," the general said, handing his personal Garand rifle to the boy, "but I know it will be in good hands. And so will I."

"Thank you, sir."

Accompanying the general were his aides, Lieutenant Colonel John Pugh and Major Tom Dooley. Pugh, black-haired with close-set eyes and a spade-shaped face with perpetual five-o'clock shadow, rode in back with Wainwright. Dooley—whose keen dark eyes in his narrow handsome face seemed to miss nothing—rode in front with the young driver. The Garand rifle leaned between them.

Dooley said to Satariano, "Keep an eye on the sky. It's a perfect day for strafing."

"Yes, sir," the corporal said, and slipped on sunglasses.

In back, Pugh said to the general, "Do we know what MacArthur wants?"

"No clue."

The drive to Mariveles—home to the naval base, or anyway the remnants thereof—should take an hour-and-a-half, or would with a driver not afraid of his own shadow. The general was pleased the boy, taking the trip at a good clip, seemed an experienced wheelman.

The first leg took them along a single-track road down the rather bare hillside, and the lower they went, the thicker the underbrush, which seemed to swallow the great naked trees. Before long the command car pulled onto the main road.

As usual, Wainwright passed the time quizzing his two aides on cavalry tactics and military strategy. The war felt far away, distant firing punctuating the conversation, and giving weight to the points the general made.

The last leg of the journey took the open vehicle under a cooling canopy of foliage so thick, the sun was blotted out. Military traffic was light this morning, but the leaves nonetheless wore a coating of dust, as did the vines and bushes, reflecting the heavy use this main highway received.

"I will speak frankly," the general was saying, "if I may have all of your discretion."

Everyone but the driver, apparently not listening, nodded.

"Ranking officers failing to visit troops at the front lines," Wainwright said, "is a blunder."

The general did not have to mention MacArthur by name.

"All we have to offer our people right now is morale," Wainwright continued, the vehicle finally exiting from under the canopy of foliage into bright sunlight.

General Wainwright's lecture had the attention of everyone in the car, with the exception of Michael Satariano, who was looking directly at the sun through squinting eyes and tinted glasses.

The corporal, though he said nothing, had noticed a black speck on the sun, like a blemish on its fiery surface.

But then that speck grew larger, ever larger, as it hurtled down out of the blazing ball into the blue and—growing wings, which dipped from side to side—bore in on them.

Satariano said, "Brace yourselves!"

The brakes screamed, and the vehicle jerked to a stop, each man flung forward but restrained by his safety strap.

"Out of the car!" the driver yelled. "Now!"

For a split second, the general and his aides were frozen in shock.

As the engine/propeller thrum grew to a roar, Satariano turned and in a blur of motion unfastened the safety strap across the general's seat and seized the man by the arm and pulled him from the car like a fireman's rescue in a burning building. Locked in their sudden embrace, the corporal and general rolled down a ditch into a thorny bush.

Dooley and Pugh followed unceremoniously, diving in for cover just as machine-gun chatter joined the thrum and swoop, and the percussive music of bullets chewing up metal and shattering glass told the story of an empty vehicle receiving a welcome meant for all of them.

As the officers clung to the bushes, Satariano, rifle in hand, ran up and out of the ditch and into the road.

"Corporal!" Pugh yelled. "It's coming back."

"I know," Satariano said, positioning himself just behind the shot-up car, taking aim.

And down the Jap Zero came, for another strafing pass, so close the Rising Suns on the wings and its retracted landing gear were vividly apparent, and bullets danced down the road, making powdery impressions.

Satariano stood his ground, aiming, and the plane was about at treetop level when the corporal fired three times and the Zero fired many more than that, chewing up the car. Then, behind spiderwebbed blood-spattered glass, the pilot slumped forward, swooping by.

This was a sight the general and his aides could see very well, from their front-row position.

The plane slammed hard to earth nose-first, just to the right of the roadside at the edge of a cane field, the crash both sickening and satisfying as metal met the ground, a sound that disappeared within the larger explosion as orange flame and billowing smoke marked the spot.

The general—giddy with the thrill of having survived this assault and witnessing a remarkable feat of courage—strode out of the ditch with his aides bringing up the rear.

But the boy was no longer standing.

Satariano remained in the road, near the bullet-riddled vehicle, though on his knees now, head down, in a posture that might have been prayer, or a man weeping. The "tears" that fell to the pavement, however, were red.

The general helped the corporal to his feet. The boy looked at him with one eye; shrapnel had removed the other one, leaving a torn, bloody socket.

"Got him, sir," the boy said, and grinned, and passed out in Wainwright's arms.

WITHIN HOURS, THE GENERAL WAS AGAIN AT A BEDSIDE, this time in the hospital tunnel on Malinta Hill on Corregidor.

18

Limping along in the shot-up vehicle until help met them half-way, they had brought Corporal Satariano—Pugh had performed first aid—to Mariveles and then, on the army's appropriated Elco cabin cruiser, to the hospital on the Rock.

Save for the heavily bandaged side of his face, the boy looked his typical angelic self. He was coherent, despite morphine.

"No one was hurt, sir?" the boy asked.

"No one but you, son." He placed a hand on the boy's arm. "I won't insult you by pulling any punches—you've lost an eye, Corporal. Your left."

Satariano said nothing; neither did his expression.

The general summoned a smile. "You've got the Hollywood wound, son—a ticket stateside. You weren't in this war long, but you already did your share."

The bandaged head shook, slowly. "Nobody's getting off Bataan, General. No matter how badly wounded."

"You're already off Bataan, aren't you? This is Corregidor."

The patient rose up on an elbow; the remaining brown eye was wide. "I can shoot with one eye. You sight with one eye closed, anyway, right, sir? I'm not through here!"

"Actually, you are. We can't send you back into combat. You'd be a danger to yourself, and to others, much too vulnerable on your left side and anyway, it's a matter of regulations. . . . No discussion on this point, son."

". . . Yes, sir."

"But you'll serve your country just the same."

The exposed eye seemed slightly woozy, and the boy was clearly fighting the morphine's effects, trying to stay focused and not float away. "How can I do that, sir?"

"You already have. You're going to be a hero."

For the first time, Satariano grimaced, as if pain had finally registered. "What?"

"I'm recommending you for the Medal of Honor for that little dust-up in the jungle. You'll have to settle for a DSC for the more minor matter of saving my life. . . . Having a hero come off this peninsula right now'll mean a lot to a lot of people."

"You make it sound like . . . like I'm . . ."

"You're going home, son. You *are* going home. . . . You see, I've just met with General MacArthur. He and his staff are heading out to Australia tomorrow tonight, and we're taking advantage of that to get you to a better medical facility, and off Bataan."

The boy, startled by this news, sat bolt upright. "MacArthur? Leaving?"

Wainwright did his best not to reveal his own bitter disappointment; taking over a command could hardly have felt worse. "Yes. It's a direct order from the President."

"But . . . the men. . . ."

"The general's determined to come back with reinforcements and air support. I'm afraid that's not your concern now. If you want to undertake another mission for me, then by God be the one ordinary G.I. who got off Bataan to tell our story . . . and make sure we aren't forgotten."

"All . . . all right, sir."

With an arm pat, the general said, "Now—get some rest, and get ready for a PT boat ride."

Satariano nodded, the eye half-lidded.

The general rose. He nodded toward the Garand rifle, leaned against the metal nightstand. "You did well with my rifle, Corporal."

"Thank you, sir."

"I want you to take that rifle home with you as a souvenir."

"But General, it's ordnance issue . . ."

"To hell with the pencil pushers back in Washington—it's yours. Take it in thanks for spotting that plane. He'd have gotten us all, if you hadn't seen him coming in out of the sun. We counted seventy-two bullet holes in that scout car, you know."

Wainwright removed a small notebook from a pocket and jotted down the words: "To Michael P. Satariano, Corporal United States Army, for saving my life in a strafing attack by a Japanese Zero fight on Bataan March 10, 1942. General Jonathan M. Wainright."

"Put these words under that gun," the general said, placing the slip of paper on the small metal bedside table," and hang that

Garand over your fireplace, for your kids and grandkids to see. Promise me you'll do it, son."

"... I promise. Would you ... do me another favor, General?"

"Name it."

"Say goodbye to Captain Wermuth for me. And tell him this is not my fault."

"Of course it's not your fault," the general began.

But the corporal had fallen asleep, his right eye fluttering till it closed, leaving the white gauze patch to stare accusingly at General Wainwright.

ON MARCH 17, AFTER A HARROWING JOURNEY, GENERAL MacArthur, his family and staff arrived safely in Australia by way of Mindanao. With them was the only American soldier to get off Bataan, the first Congressional Medal of Honor winner of the Second World War.

Michael Satariano of DeKalb, Illinois.

BOOK TWO

HOMEFRONT WAR

DeKalb and Chicago, Illinois

Miami, Florida

July 1942

———

1

PATSY ANN O'HARA, UNQUESTION-
ably the prettiest coed on the Northern
State Teachers' College campus, did not
have a date for the Fourth of July.

Apple-cheeked, strawberry blonde,
her heart-shaped face blessed with Shirley
Temple dimples, a beauty mark near her
full lips, her big long-lashed dark blue eyes
accented by full dark (cautiously plucked)
eyebrows, her five-foot-five figure one
that Lana Turner would find familiar,
Patsy Ann had been a stunning beauty for
so many years, she never thought about it
really, other than to carefully maintain this
gift from God.

The former Homecoming Queen of
DeKalb Township High (class of '38) considered herself more conscientious than

vain—meticulous about her grooming, maintaining an exercise regimen, avoiding excess sweets and too much sun, her selection of clothing as exacting as a five-star chef choosing just the right ingredients for a gourmet meal (before shortages, anyway).

Today she had selected an appropriately patriotic red-and-white-checked cotton sundress, its ruffled trim at both bodice and skirt accentuating her just-full-enough bosom and her Grable-esque gams, further set off by red-white-and-blue open-toed wedge-heeled sandals. The outfit perhaps seemed a trifle young—she was, after all, twenty-one . . .

. . . but she *wanted* to look like a high school girl today, or at least invoke one, even if doing so risked occasional askance glances or even envious ridicule from females who never had looked this good, not even *in* high school.

Anyway, the men would like it . . . though she only cared about the reaction of one specific man sure to be at the festivities today. . . .

None of the panting males at Northern State Teachers' College had even bothered to ask Patsy Ann out for the Fourth. This had nothing to do with a shortage of men—fully half the enrollment was male, ranging from 4-F's to guys waiting for Uncle Sam's inevitable "greetings," as well as a number who'd received deferments. They had long since stopped trying, knowing she was "taken."

The first several years at Northern, she'd been dating her high school boyfriend; and ever since her guy had joined the army and gone off to fight in the Philippines, Patsy Ann had been steadfastly true, a college woman wearing the high-school class ring of her overseas beau. Frustrated as some of the guys at Northern might be, they admired her for this loyalty—so did even the cattiest females on campus.

No one but Patsy Ann's young sister—little Betty, who was a high school senior already!—knew the truth; not even Mom and Dad. No one but Betty knew that Mike had broken it off with Patsy Ann before he went away, that he had kissed her tenderly and told her not to wait for him.

"Forget about me," he said.

"You can't be *serious*, Michael. . . ."

But he was almost always serious.

"A war's coming," he said. "I'm not going to put you in that position."

She'd felt flushed with emotion, some of it anger. "Doesn't my opinion count in this?"

"No," he said.

But she knew he didn't mean that. She knew he was *trying* to get her mad at him, to help break it off. . . .

She'd penned a letter to him every day. He had not sent a single reply, or at least none had made it back to her. And yet month upon month, she wrote to Mike, staring at his framed Senior picture, suffering in stoic, noble silence, an English Lit major wholly unaware that her love of romantic literature was influencing her behavior.

When she learned of Mike's breathtaking heroism, and that he was coming home, Patsy Ann had gone to Pasquale's Spaghetti House to see if Papa and Mama Satariano had an address for him. They did—their son was at St. Elizabeth's Hospital near Washington, D.C.

When he didn't reply to her stateside letters, either, she dismissed it—after all, Michael was recuperating, receiving therapy. And then, a few months later, the local paper was full of Papa and Mama Satariano taking the train to D.C. to attend the presentation by President Roosevelt of the Congressional Medal of Honor—the first of the war!

How Patsy Ann wished she could have been there, standing next to Michael in the White House Executive Office as General Eisenhower lowered the looped ribbon with the golden star over his head. . . .

For several weeks Michael had toured the East Coast, making speeches (she could hardly believe that, shy as he was!) and promoting the sale of war bonds and stamps. Banquets, dinners, receptions, receiving the keys to cities, shaking hands with mayors and governors and senators . . . how thrilling it would have been, to be at his side. Michael, though, probably detested all of it. . . .

Yesterday, in Chicago, Michael had been flown into Municipal Airport and whisked away for a ticker tape parade down packed State Street. The key-to-the-city ceremony had been at City Hall, with Mayor Kelly and various dignitaries lavishing praise on this "heroic native son of Illinois."

Michael gave a speech, his voice soft and uninflected; but even Patsy Ann, listening on the radio, would have to admit the talk was not a memorable one, sounding nothing like Michael: "There are many who speak of giving their all, but are they willing to allocate ten percent of their earnings for war bonds?"

Still, as she curled beside the console, feeling like a schoolgirl, heart beating like a triphammer, she cherished the sound of his voice.

Had she done the right thing, she wondered, not going in to the city? Waiting for today, for what she hoped and prayed would be just the right moment?

Last night, she and her sister had sat in their loose-fitting man-tailored pj's in the upstairs bedroom they still shared (Patsy Ann lived at home and had rebuffed any attempt by sororities to rush her).

Betty, dark-haired and cute, had been painting her nails cherry red as she said, "I don't get it, Sis. I mean, I can understand him wanting to break it off before he went over there and everything."

Patsy Ann, seated at the dresser mirror brushing her hair, said, "I know. He was being noble. The far-far-better-thing-I-do-than-I-have-ever-done-before bit."

"I saw that movie," Betty said, moving to the next toe.

"It's a book, too, not that you'd ever know it."

"You don't have to get short. Not my fault he hasn't called or written."

Patsy Ann put the brush down with a clunk. "No need to be 'noble' now—papers say, 'cause of his eye, he won't see any more action. Why hasn't he *called*? What's *wrong* with him?"

Betty shrugged. "Maybe it *is* his eye. Maybe he's scarred and stuff, and doesn't wanna make the woman he loves marry a freak."

"What an awful thing to say! . . . But you could be right."

"He's probably home right now. At his folks'. Phone line runs both ways, you know."

"You think I should call him?"

"Why not? You're a modern woman, aren't you?"

Patsy Ann studied her face in the mirror, as if girding herself for combat. ". . . I won't do that. I won't try to see him until tomorrow . . . at the Fourth. I'll just be this, this . . . *vision* in the crowd!"

Betty nodded. "Yeah—that should work. These soldiers are really horny when they come home."

"Where do you *get* that language?"

Another shrug. "It's a brave new world, Sis."

"That's also a book, y'know."

Betty frowned. "What is?"

The first wartime Fourth of July in a quarter-century fell on a Saturday, the perfect day to set the stage for a weekend celebration of independence. The radio and papers, however, were filled with governmental caution—fireworks and large gatherings could attract air raids and saboteurs. On the East and West Coasts, celebrations had been banned in some cities.

Not in the Midwest, not in a heartland city like DeKalb whose principal exports were barbed wire and hybrid corn. The city fathers scheduled fireworks along with baseball, horseshoes and archery, with musical programs all day long. Homes were draped red, white and blue (materials available gratis at the City Recorder's) and when the Fourth dawned warm, not humid, a trifle breezy, flags flapped all over town.

Patsy Ann accompanied her mother, Maureen, a plump, plainer version of herself, to the parade Saturday morning; her rugged, handsome father, William, was driving the mayor and his wife—as owner of the local Buick dealership, Daddy always provided a number of vehicles.

Every float or vehicle draped in red-white-and-blue crepe, each band blaring military marches, created a near hysterical uproar in the crowd, applause, whistles, cheers. And when a vehicle would roll by with sailors or soldiers or Marines, Patsy Ann could always spot in the midst of this frenzied fun a mother or two or three weeping.

The Grand Marshal of the parade was Sergeant Michael Satariano (he'd been promoted by the Secretary of War at the Medal of Honor presentation). Patsy Ann had abandoned her mother to work her way to the curb, positioning herself prominently.

Seated up on the back of the convertible, in his crisp khaki uniform, Medal of Honor around his neck, Michael wore a small frozen smile as he raised a hand in a barely discernible wave. Despite how little he gave the crowd, they gave him back plenty; occasionally he would nod, and look from one side of the packed street to the other, a shy and retiring conqueror.

If he saw her, Patsy Ann could see no sign—not of pleasure or displeasure or even recognition. In her little red and white sun dress, Patsy Ann had surely been noticed by every other healthy redblooded American male here. Then, as the Buick rolled by, she could see the scarring around his left eye—not disfiguring, but there—and realized she'd picked the wrong side of the street to stand on.

And then he was gone, and she thought, *That's all it was—his bad eye. . . . He just didn't see me. . . .*

That afternoon at Huntley Park, on the south side of town, the boulder-and-concrete bandshell, its red-tiled roof bannered with WELCOME HOME, MIKE!, showcased various dignitaries and the guest of honor. The mayor introduced Governor Green—imagine the governor choosing DeKalb for the Fourth, over Chicago or Springfield!—who introduced "Illinois's own Michael Satariano."

Pasty Ann sat between her parents in the front row—folding chairs had been provided to supplement stone benches—and they, like everyone, stood and clapped and cheered. Professional-looking photographers were snapping photos of both Michael and the crowd—later Patsy Ann learned that the *Trib* and the *Sun-Times* had sent teams, but even more exciting, so had *Life* and *Look*. On the sidelines stood another soldier, an officer.

Michael finally raised a hand to silence the audience. His

voice was firm, though not loud, and the microphone picked him up fine; anyway, you could have heard a pin drop.

First, Mike acknowledged his parents, who stood in the front row to warmly receive applause. Both of the elder Satarianos were portly, much shorter than their son; in truth, Patsy Ann had never seen any resemblance between her boyfriend and his balding, white-mustached bulbous-nosed father Pasquale and the sweet but barrel-shaped and downright homely Sophia.

After all the build-up, what followed was a repeat of yesterday's unmemorable "buy bonds" pitch. Mike's unimpassioned rendition of what was obviously a speech prepared by others undercut whatever power it might have had. Still, the crowd did not seem to notice, hanging on every word as if hearing the Gettysburg Address.

Then after a conclusion that tepidly wished the crowd a happy Fourth, Michael's voice rose, and Patsy sat up, recognizing a familiar edge.

"While you're celebrating your independence," Michael said, "setting off firecrackers, wolfing down a hot dog, tossing back a beer . . . please remember, and say a prayer for, our boys on Bataan."

A thrill went through her: Michael meant these words; these were all his!

"The men I fought beside don't enjoy freedom—this very moment they're in Japanese prison camps. Don't forget them! Back to Bataan! Back to Bataan!"

And the crowd was on its feet again, fists in the air, echoing him: "Back to Bataan! Back to Bataan! Back to Bataan!"

Patsy Ann noticed something peculiar: the army officer was not chanting along; he stood with arms folded, wearing a sour expression. A rather handsome man, about forty, in a business suit and fedora stood next to him—smiling.

Then Michael came down and shook thousands of hands and signed autographs and Patsy Ann waited alone, seated on a stone bench, her parents wandering off to watch the baseball tourney.

Almost two hours had passed before the crowd dissipated. The governor and mayor were long gone; even the proud parents, Pasquale and Sophia Satariano, had moved along. Finally only Michael and the army officer remained, speaking to Mike, in a curt, even harsh manner, though Patsy Ann did not hear what was said.

But she could understand Mike, as he told the officer, "I have my own ride."

And then Michael Satariano, in his Medal of Honor and crisp khakis, walked right over to the stone bench where she sat. The army officer, shaking his head, stalked off.

Michael stood before her. Loomed over her. His face was expressionless; his real eye seemed as lifeless as the glass one in the scarred socket.

Hands folded in her lap, feeling very much a little girl suited to her silly sun dress, Patsy Ann trembled, on the verge of tears. What terrible thing was Michael going to say?

"Captain's mad at me," Mike said, casually.

Then he sat down next to her on the bench, slumped forward a little; his good eye was next to her. It was as if they were still in high school and he'd caught up with her between classes.

"Why?" she managed.

He shrugged. "You heard that phony spiel they made me give. I've been doin' that all up and down the East Coast. And every time, I mention the boys on Bataan. My forgotten comrades."

"What's wrong with that?"

He turned to look at her and the half-smile was so wonderfully familiar. "I'm not supposed to talk about them. We left them there to rot, and I'm not supposed to remind anybody about them. . . . Yesterday, in Chicago?"

"I heard you on the radio."

"Well, you didn't hear all of it. The captain had warned them about me, and the broadcast engineer cut me off before I said my Bataan piece."

"That's terrible."

"Newsreel guys got it, though, and the reporters. A couple of big magazines heard me today. We'll see if they print it. . . . Guys dying for freedom, over there, and the military muzzles somebody like me, for telling the truth."

"That's just awful!"

He shrugged. "Ah, it's not so bad. Got its bright side."

"How is that possible?"

Another half-smile. "I just got fired. I'm done. On inactive duty. No more bond rallies; no more rubber chicken."

She laughed a little. "Public speaking, putting yourself on display . . . that must be torture for you."

"Well, there's torture and then there's torture. But I *would* rather be back on Bataan." Any hint of a smile disappeared. "I really would. . . ."

"I . . . I kinda thought maybe you'd prefer being here, with me."

"Of course." But he wasn't looking at her.

". . . You feel guilty, don't you?"

Mike turned to her, sharply—not angry, more like . . . alarmed.

She pressed on: "You're the only American soldier who got off that island, except for General MacArthur and his brass hats, right? So you feel like you abandoned your 'boys.' "

The faintest smile traced his lips; warmth filled the remaining brown eye. "You always were smart."

"You didn't do anything wrong, Mike. You were brave. . . . I read all about it. Everybody has. We need some heroes right about now."

"Well, I don't want to be one."

"What *do* you want to be?"

His eyebrows arched. "I wanna be in the backseat of one your daddy's Buicks . . . with you."

Her lips pursed into a smile. "Well . . . you might get your wish. But a girl likes to be kissed, first."

He did not respond to this cue.

Instead, he slumped again, his hands locked. He was staring at the grass. "You want a guy who threw you over to kiss you? Who didn't even bother writing you back?"

"You didn't throw me over for a girl. You threw me over for a war. . . . My letters—you read them?"

"Every one."

"That's all I wanted. Just you to read them."

He gazed at her, steadily, studying her. "You don't have a guy?"

"I have a guy."

Now he looked away. ". . . That's fine. I told you not to wait."

"*You*, Dumbo."

He took that like a punch; then he laughed—no sound came out, but it was a laugh, all right.

And finally she was in his arms and he was kissing her, and the desperation in his kiss was wonderful, because it matched her own.

She drove them back to Pasquale's Spaghetti House on North Third, across from the Egyptian Theater, where *Sergeant York* with Gary Cooper was billed with *Maisie Gets Her Man.* The restaurant was closed for the Fourth; the two floors of apartments above the place were the family's living quarters—this was where Michael Satariano had been raised since the age of twelve.

He went up the back stairs while she waited in the car, and returned five minutes later in chinos and a tan crew-neck sport shirt—still vaguely military-looking. They drove around for a while, Patsy Ann staying behind the wheel—she gave him a tour of the modest Northern campus; Michael seemed interested in what classes she had and in which buildings.

When they drove past the modernistic limestone library, she told him she'd been working there part-time. He said he knew that from her letters. She wondered if he knew she'd been testing him.

Reading was a love they had in common, though Patsy Ann preferred the classics—Emily Brontë, Jane Austen and Charles Dickens among her favorites—while Michael's tastes were terribly plebeian, running to pulp magazines and comic books. He had a large collection of Big Little Books, tiny square fat books about comic strip characters and movie cowboys.

Back in high school, she had once teased him for buying a stack of the things at Woolworth's—Tarzan, the Lone Ranger, the Phantom, Dick Tracy.

"Aren't you a little old for Tom Mix?" she'd asked.

They were sitting at the counter sipping nickel Cokes, after school, and he was paying no attention to her, flipping through the pulp pages between the garish covers.

Still paging through, he said, "My brother and I used to read these."

"What brother?"

His eyes tensed; his voice took on an evasive quality. "I had a brother before we moved here."

"What happened to him?"

"He died."

"Oh, I . . . I'm sorry."

"Nothing to be sorry for." His eyes thawed; his smile was warm, too. "It's not your fault I'm a case of arrested development."

You never knew what was important to a person—Michael had taught her that. He never again mentioned this mysterious brother, and yet she always remembered the controlled passion in Mike's voice as he'd spoken about this lost child.

Funny thing—most everyone thought Mike was quiet, even stoic. That was part of what had attracted her in the first place— the mysterious brooding reserve that seemed to mask a reservoir of secrets, of experiences he chose not to share.

But they did talk, Patsy Ann and Mike. In the right mood, he would tell her what he thought—about teachers, about fellow students, about politics and even world affairs. Sometimes they talked about a future together . . . particularly in the afterglow of backseat lovemaking. (Prom night had been the first time.)

Much as she liked to escape to other ages and places through literature, Patsy Ann savored the notion of a simple life here in the Middle West with Michael, where they could both work and, when the time came, raise a family. Neither of them had adventurous yearnings or highflown ambitions—just the hope of being part of a loving family in secure surroundings.

And in a small town like DeKalb, that hope was realized, every day. For one thing, the kind of prejudices you ran into in a big city like Chicago just weren't present; even the three colored families in town were treated fine. That Michael was Italian didn't seem to bother anybody—or anyway hadn't since that time in seventh grade when the school bully called Mike a wop and Mike cleaned his clock.

Come to think of it, that was the day Patsy Ann knew she loved

Michael Satariano, although they didn't start going together till high school, sophomore year. Mike was a star shortstop on the D.T.H.S. baseball team, and quarterback on the football team, all-conference in both instances. Patsy Ann was leader of the cheerleading squad, and secretary of the student body, so a romance between her and the school's star athlete seemed starcrossed.

Even her parents didn't mind—Mike was a good Catholic boy; so what if he wasn't Irish? When they kept dating after high school, she and Mike had been sat down by her father, who let them both know that there would always be a place for Mike at the dealership, if the boy chose not to follow his folks into their restaurant business.

College offers had come along—several small schools offered sports scholarships, and Mike's grades were good—but Patsy Ann's boyfriend had just kept working with his folks at their restaurant, helping out, learning the trade. Patsy Ann had enrolled at Northern, and she and her "guy" had spoken often, about the future—how she would get a job teaching high school lit somewhere in the area and he'd take over his family business.

After driving around till dusk, the couple wound up back at the park, where a dance band consisting of Northern music majors played in the bandshell, the folding chairs gone to make room for dancing. The clear sky glittered with stars and an art moderne-slice of moon made the heavens seem more like the faux-variety you danced beneath in a ballroom.

The other couples were in their teens and twenties, with a few older married folks joining in, on the slow tunes. Michael demurred at jitterbugging, and was amusingly horrified by "The Beer Barrel Polka" and everything it wrought among the dancers. But he seemed happy to hold his girl in his arms for "The Very Thought of You."

They did not stay for the fireworks, preferring to make their own by driving into the country to one of their favorite parking places, a little access inlet to a cornfield, whose tall stalks were brushed ivory in the moonlight, waving lazily in the evening breeze. They necked and petted in the front seat, but it wasn't long before they crawled unceremoniously in back.

━━━━

The sun dress's top gathered at her waist, the dress hiked up, her panties off but the sexy little wedgies on, Patsy Ann lay back, watching as Michael withdrew his wallet and found the little square packet.

"So what if I get pregnant?" she asked.

He thought about it, then, gently, said, "No. We've always been careful. We'll be careful tonight."

Other than that small moment of reality, the lovemaking was wonderfully dream-like; he was always so tender with her, and yet commanding. At first he just looked down at her pale flesh in the moonlight and said she looked beautiful; then he began to kiss her breasts, and was still doing that when he entered her. They came to climax quickly, together, in shudders that looked like pain but weren't.

They cuddled in the backseat in their various states of disarray, the sun dress bunched at her waist, his trousers and underwear clumped down around his left ankle like a big bulky bandage. They had fallen asleep when sharp cracks woke them both—Michael sat up straight, reacting as if to gunshots.

Through the front window, blossoming just above the cornfield, they could see the fireworks, going on at the park right now. They exchanged grins and resumed a cuddly position and enjoyed what they could see of it—not every attempt rose high enough.

Still, they got a kick out of what they did see: a shower of silver here . . . bursting rockets there . . . endless sprays and arrays of red and white and blue sparks. . . .

Finally they got their clothes back on—though all the smoothing out in the world wouldn't hide what the sun dress had been through—and Patsy Ann had Mike take the wheel. He said little as they drove back into town; he appeared distracted.

For what seemed like forever, but was really just four silent minutes, they sat in front of her house, a two-story Dutch Colonial on South Third, a few blocks from the park.

"Is something wrong?" she asked, finally.

"No. Everything's right. Perfect."

But there was something in his tone. . . .

She thought perhaps she understood. "It's difficult for you, isn't it? Just picking up where you left off."

He grunted a little laugh, gave her the half-smile. "You've always been smarter than me. Not that that's anything to brag about."

She saw through the lightness and said, "You can't do anything about it, Mike—your friends in the Philippines. You know MacArthur will go back for them, when he can."

"Dugout Doug," Mike said softly.

"What?"

"Nothing."

"Michael, there are things you can do for the war effort, if you want to."

"Giving speeches?"

"No! I'm sure there must be other things. And—"

"Patricia Ann—it's not just that I'm not over there, doing my share. Not just that I . . . escaped from Bataan, tail tucked between my legs. . . ."

"Mike . . ."

"It's that this life . . . don't misunderstand, tonight was wonderful, like turning a few pages and having years just drop away . . . but I don't know that I can . . . I don't know that I. . . ."

In the moonlight, his eyes looked moist.

"Michael. What's wrong? What is it?"

He shrugged and something gruff came into his voice, a little forced, she thought. "Baby, things happened over there. You waited for me, but I didn't wait for you. I was with ten, eleven prostitutes . . . Filipino girls mostly, plus a couple of nurses."

She recoiled. "Why are you telling me that? You didn't have to tell me that."

He locked onto her eyes; his expression was hard but not unkind. "You need to know these things, so that you can understand that I've changed. I killed hundreds of Japs, Patsy Ann. Hundreds."

"They're the enemy."

"Right. And I was side by side with Filipino scouts who used to be our enemy, too. I'm not sorry I did it—it needed doing.

A soldier does his duty. . . . That's what soldiers do, kill other soldiers."

"Right . . ."

"But they were still people, Patsy Ann. And I killed them. . . . You know the first thing I did when they let me out of St. Elizabeth's Hospital?"

"No."

"I took confession. I sought absolution for killing these people, only . . . I didn't even know how many I killed. How many Hail Marys, do you suppose, for every fifty Japs?"

"Michael . . . it's wartime. . . ."

His eyes widened and the one that wasn't glass rolled. "That's right! . . . but not here in this *Saturday Evening Post* cover, come alive. When I came here, what, ten years ago? I found this sheltered little world comforting. I . . . I had some experiences you don't know about, 'fore I came here, when I was a kid."

"You can tell me."

"No I can't. What I can tell you is, I lived here for ten years and I pretended that I was somebody I wasn't. I pretended that those things never happened to me. That I was a normal kid, like you and your sister Betty and my pals Bobby and Jimmy and everybody else in this jerkwater town."

"You don't have to be cruel."

"I don't mean to be. But on Bataan, something happened: I sort of . . . woke up. Remembered who I was. And then today, tonight . . . I remembered something else."

"What?"

His hands were on the steering wheel—as tight as if he were strangling someone. "I remembered that you can live in a town like this, and think you're safe. And you're not. Everything can get taken away from you, in an instant."

"You're scaring me, Michael."

"I mean to. I still love you, Patsy Ann. But you need to know that I'm . . . having a little trouble. Sorting some things out."

She touched his arm, tentatively. "That's okay. . . . I don't care about those other women. . . ."

He laughed harshly. "I tell you I slept with a dozen whores, and that I killed hundreds of men, and it's the whores you forgive me for?"

She withdrew her hand. "Michael! Please! Stop. . . ."

Again, the hard but not exactly cruel expression locked onto her. "Patsy Ann, if you love me, you'll stay away from me. And because I love you, I will stay away from you."

"Stay away . . . ?"

"Not forever. Maybe just a few days. Maybe a few months. But I need time. Time to work this out."

"I'll *help* you work it out! Please let me—"

"No. You can't help me with this. Do you believe I love you? That I still love you, and have since sophomore year?"

She leaned near him, almost close enough for them to kiss. "Of course I do. And you know that I love you, and that together we can face anything. If only we *trust* each other . . ."

"Then trust *me*—trust me that right now, at this moment, we are not right for each other."

She began to cry; and the worst part was, he did not take her into his arms.

"Some day, maybe," Michael said, raising his hand as if to brush away her tears, but stopping short. "Only, right now I'm not sure I'm fit company for any man . . . let alone, woman."

And he got out of the car and walked away.

She clambered out onto the sidewalk and the prettiest girl in town just stood there with tears smearing her makeup and snot glistening on her upper lip and she cried, "Goddamn you, Michael Satariano! Goddamn you!"

But if he heard, he gave no indication, just walking down the tree-shaded sidewalk, until his silhouette blended with the dark.

2

FOR AS MANY TIMES AS MICHAEL HAD accompanied Papa Satariano to Chicago, the Loop remained intimidating in its size and bustle and sprawl. Of course to the Satarianos, Chicago meant the Near West Side of the Randolph Street Market and Little Italy, where twice a week Papa S. could buy wholesale his vegetables, fruit, virgin olive oil, spices, fish, sausages, ricotta, Parmesan, Romano and Provolone cheeses and other supplies.

Despite the relative nearness of DeKalb, Michael had only been to Chicago a handful of times, otherwise—a high school field trip to the Art Institute, and occasionally taking Patsy Ann to the theater or on some other special date.

Going down State Street the other day,

seated on the back of a Cadillac convertible, waving at the cheering crowds, wellwishers surging toward him only to be held back by police, people hanging out of windows gesturing frantically as a snowfall of torn paper . . . from ticker tape and old phone books . . . cascaded down, that hadn't seemed like Chicago. More like some bizarre dream, or nightmare. . . .

Now, alone in the family's 1936 blue Buick business coupe, Michael felt small as the great masonry buildings reflected off his windshield, magnificent structures ranging from would-be Greek temples to starkly functional modern tombstones. For a boy whose adolescence had mostly been spent in a small town, the crowded rectangle of the Loop—defined by the Elevated tracks— seemed a cacophony of traffic roar and intermittent train thunder, a towering world of thronged sidewalks, mammoth department stores, and giant movie palaces.

The imprint of the war on the city made itself evident from BUY BONDS posters and service flags in storefront windows to horse-drawn wagons that mingled uncomfortably with autos, slowing traffic and providing the streets with an earthy sort of litter. The vehicles didn't have the alphabet of ration stickers Michael had seen on the East Coast, but that would come soon enough. Women on the sidewalks—the city's fabled wind exposing legs sans silk stockings—outnumbered men, at least those roughly in Michael's age group, who when you did see them were often in uniform.

Michael's destination was one of Chicago's most impressive monuments to itself: the Federal Building. On Dearborn between Adams and Jackson, extending to Clark, the massive turn-of-the-century structure—an ornate cross-shaped edifice with a classical dome—served as the Midwestern administrative center of the U.S. government.

Michael was in uniform, because he had been summoned to the Federal Building at the request of Captain McRae, the Army Public Relations officer. Perhaps McRae had changed his mind about switching Michael's military status to inactive duty; that was fine with Michael, as long as he was given something constructive to do—he had no intention of putting up with any more of this P.R. baloney. He was a soldier, not a flack.

He performed a minor miracle by finding a parking place on the street and headed inside. If Michael had felt small before, walking across the three-hundred-foot-high octagonal rotunda, his footsteps echoing like tiny ineffectual gunshots, made him feel infinitesimal. An eyeblink ago he'd been in a steamy jungle; now he was surrounded by polished granite, white and Siena marble, mosaics and gilded bronze.

As imposing as this rotunda had been, the federal facilities themselves proved to be a utilitarian cluster of offices, hearing rooms, and conference chambers. Michael checked the slip of paper on which he'd written his captain's instructions and found the corresponding number on pebbled glass, and knocked.

"Come in!" a mellow male voice called.

Beyond the door, Michael found himself in a small one-room office facing a scarred wooden desk, behind which a man of perhaps forty sat in a swivel chair that was the cubbyhole's most lavish touch. Filing cabinets hugged the left wall and stacks of white cardboard boxes did the same at right, stopping at a window whose whirring fan was aided by an afternoon that was fairly cool to begin with.

In one corner, right of the door, stood a hat tree on which a trenchcoat, dark gray fedora and lighter gray suitcoat were neatly hung; in the other corner, a water cooler burbled. A single wooden chair faced the desk, waiting for Michael.

It was as if the young soldier had entered the office of the guidance counselor at DeKalb Township High.

A six-footer with alert gray eyes and a ready smile, Michael's host—in a white short-sleeve shirt with a copper-colored tie—rose and extended across the desk a hand, which Michael shook, the grip firm but not overdoing it. The man's boyishly handsome face—spade-shaped, faintly freckled—seemed just a trifle puffy. Overwork, Michael wondered, or maybe this was a drinking man?

Possibly both.

Michael had noticed this quietly affable fellow on the periphery of the events in Chicago a few days ago, when the mayor and various politicians and dignitaries had been making their Medal of Honor fuss in front of public and press. Just another vaguely official presence in a fedora and crisp suit and tie, the man had spoken in an intimate, whispering way with both Captain McRae and Governor Green.

Michael had picked up on this, but so much had been going on, it hadn't really registered; the man had seemed familiar, but this was a fairly typical government sort, almost nondescript. . . .

Now, close up, Michael had a sudden jolt of recognition, though he hoped it didn't show.

"Please sit, Sergeant," Eliot Ness said.

Michael Satariano had been named Michael O'Sullivan, Jr., the last time—the other times—he had seen Eliot Ness. And Michael had only been eleven years old.

The first instance had been in Chippiannock Cemetery, in Rock Island, Illinois, in the winter of 1931. Michael's mother, Annie O'Sullivan, and his brother Peter were buried there. Michael's father had gone to the cemetery not only to visit the graves, but for a meeting with Ness, a federal agent working to take down Chicago gangster Al Capone.

Michael's father had arranged the parley to turn over to the G-man key evidence against a crony of Capone's—the patriarch of the Irish Tri-Cities mob, John Looney.

For a dozen years, Michael's real father—Michael O'Sullivan, Sr.—had been the trusted right hand of Looney, who since the turn of the century ruled the Iowa/Illinois Tri-Cities. A hero in the Great War, the pride of the Irish immigrants of Rock Island, Michael's father became like a son to Mr. Looney.

Unfortunately, Mr. Looney already had a son—Connor, or as some called him, "Crazy" Connor . . . having "Looney" as a last name apparently not sufficiently conveying the man's homicidal hotheadedness. It was said Connor Looney resented O'Sullivan getting all the really important jobs, as if Old Man Looney were grooming the lieutenant for a greatness Connor considered his birthright.

When the O'Sullivan family had gone to the Looney mansion at Christmas, just before everything bad happened, the affection the old boy had for Michael's father had been apparent. Looney and O'Sullivan had sung together, arms around each other's shoulders, while Connor, lurking unhappily on the fringes, looked on.

And the O'Sullivans had benefited from the Looney association, no question. Next to Looney's mansion itself, they had the nicest home in town, and the O'Sullivans owed their very good life in those very hard times to the patriarch.

Nonetheless, Michael's father had kept Michael and his younger brother Peter—and their mother—as far away as possible from what the head of the house did for a living. O'Sullivan made it clear that certain questions were not to be asked, and that Mr. Looney's munificence was to be respected and valued.

Michael and brother Peter would talk deep into the night, wondering what their papa did for Mr. Looney, exactly—and why Papa carried a gun—until, on a kind of dare, a few days after Christmas, young Michael stowed away in the backseat of Papa's car, to spy on him, and see what kind of "missions" Papa was going on. . . .

What Michael saw was his father and Connor Looney round up some men into a warehouse. Papa had a tommy gun (that's what they called it in the movies, anyway) and it was like he and Connor were arresting the men. Curious, the lad had gone to a window of the warehouse to watch, despite a driving rain. He saw Connor Looney arguing with a man, and when the argument got nasty, Connor just . . . just . . . *shot* the man.

Murdered him!

The other men used the moment of confusion to go for their own guns, and Michael had witnessed his father emptying the machine gun, killing them all, empty shells raining down harder than the rain itself, and then Connor Looney caught a glimpse of young Michael in the window glass, peeking. . . .

But Michael did not run.

He felt strangely guilty, whether for what he'd done or what his papa had done . . . after all these years, he still couldn't say. And so, sitting in the pouring rain, like a naughty kid banished to a corner, he promised both his father and Mr. Looney's son that he would never tell anybody anything about what he saw . . . and Connor Looney seemed to accept that.

A few days later, Mr. Looney sent Michael's father on an "errand," only the message O'Sullivan was delivering to another Looney associate named Lococo turned out to be O'Sullivan's own death warrant. Not for nothing, though, had Michael O'Sullivan, Sr., earned the sobriquet "The Angel of Death": the trap failed, Lococo and several of his underlings dying in the attempt.

While Michael's father was supposed to be getting himself killed—and while Fate or perhaps God had seen to it that Michael was not home, rather at a church party—Connor Looney came to the O'Sullivan house and shot Michael's mother, coldbloodedly murdering her, then (mistaking Peter for the older boy) killed Michael's brother, too.

Both O'Sullivan and Michael got home too late to do anything but grieve. They paid their respects to Mama and Peter, gathered their things, and slipped into the night. They would flee the Tri-Cities, but first O'Sullivan went looking for Connor and Mr. Looney, though all he found was a lot of Mr. Looney's other soldiers and a lawyer who tried to make a deal. So O'Sullivan, Sr., declared war, leaving a trail of dead gangsters behind. And one dead lawyer.

That night they drove to Chicago; O'Sullivan had done work there for the top gangsters, who had an alliance with Mr. Looney. Michael's papa talked to Frank Nitti (who was second only to Al Capone himself), pleading his case, asking that the Chicago people stay out of this personal matter, and offering to come work for them, when it was done.

When Nitti didn't accept the offer, O'Sullivan declared war on Chicago, as well, leaving a trail of dead Capone thugs throughout their Lexington Hotel headquarters.

It had been O'Sullivan's intention to take his surviving son to the farm of an uncle and aunt outside Perdition, Kansas, for safekeeping; but with both the Looney and Capone forces after them, that became too dangerous, and father and son remained on the road. Eventually, at Chippiannock Cemetery, O'Sullivan was able to turn that key evidence over to Eliot Ness, which led to Looney's arrest.

With the Looney operation no longer pumping cash into the Capone coffers, O'Sullivan decided to squeeze Chicago further, by robbing rural banks where the Syndicate kept its money. Young Michael was the getaway man, sitting on phonebooks, pumping pedals built up with blocks. He had a wonderful time, and grew closer to his sometimes remote father than he ever had before.

Finally Michael's father worked out a deal with the Capone mob: he would cease looting their operations if they would hand over Connor Looney. On a rainy night in Rock Island, in the street in front of the Sherman Hotel, Michael O'Sullivan, Sr., took his revenge on Connor Looney.

And so, finally, Michael and his father reached the farm outside Perdition; but the Capone mob betrayed them: O'Sullivan was shot in the back, ambushed by a contract killer.

A moment later, Michael killed his father's killer. He had killed once before on the road, defending his father and himself, and the only emotions the child felt had to do with his fallen father.

The boy had pulled himself together enough to drive his dying father not to a hospital, but—at his father's insistence—a church, where Michael O'Sullivan, Sr., gave his final confession and received his last rites.

Shortly after that, Michael Jr. again saw Eliot Ness, who discreetly arranged for Michael to disappear into a Catholic orphanage in Downers Grove, Illinois.

As best Michael knew, his adoptive parents, the Satarianos, did not know of his true background; at least, there had never been any indication of such.

Memories flooding through him, Michael took the seat opposite Eliot Ness in the Federal Building cubbyhole office, doing his best to give nothing away.

"Sergeant," Ness said, "I appreciate you dropping by. My name is Eliot Ness—I'm the director of the Division of Social Protection."

Michael had no idea what that was. He said, "You needn't thank me. I was ordered here by Captain McRae."

"I wasn't aware he'd made it an order. I'd hoped he'd indicate the voluntary nature of why I asked to see you."

"I'm up for doing anything for the war effort—particularly if it doesn't involve War Bond rallies."

Ness's half-smile dug a dimple in one cheek. "I hate public speaking, myself. I've had people after me to run for office, for years . . . but I'm sure it would be a disaster."

Michael shifted in his chair, just a little. "I believe I noticed you at the Fourth celebration in DeKalb. And the day before that, here in Chicago."

"Yes. You did. You see, Sergeant, I've taken a kind of . . . interest in you."

"Why is that, Mr. Ness?"

The half-smile bloomed into a full grin; but Ness's eyes were hard. "Well, after all, Michael—we go back a long way."

Michael said nothing.

"I recognized you from your picture in the papers," Ness said. "You haven't changed all that much—and to the degree you have, a resemblance to your father's crept in."

"Most people don't think I look like Papa S. at all."

Ness arched an eyebrow. " 'Papa S.' That's what you call him? Not just Papa?"

"Well . . ."

"Maybe that's because he isn't your real 'papa,' Michael. We both know that. I owed it to your father to make sure you were safe; I got you into that orphanage, and I kept a quiet eye on you."

"You seem to do a lot from the sidelines."

"These days, I do. Of course, I prefer being in the game . . . but this game? You succeed at all, they make you a damn administrator. Guys like you get to have all the fun."

"Guys like me."

"We'll get into that. But it seems to me I owe you a few answers . . . that is, if you have any questions."

Michael folded his arms. "The Satarianos—do they know who I am?"

"No. And don't think I didn't have a twinge when I discovered they'd adopted you. If I'd been on the scene, keeping closer tabs, I might even have interceded."

"Why?"

"Your safety, for one. You grew up kind of close to Chicago, didn't you? Considering who you are?"

"Back when my father and I were on the road, none of the Capone people ever saw me. My picture, maybe. Little kid picture."

"And one little kid is pretty much like another . . . and then of course you sprouted up."

"Listen, Mr. Ness, I . . . I realize I owe you a certain debt."

Ness nodded. "You do. I'm the one who saw to it you went into an orphanage, not reform school. I talked the police into interpreting that crime scene in a way that indicated your father had killed his own killer—that you had nothing to do with it."

"There were stories about us in the true detectives magazines," Michael said. "And they always got that wrong."

"That's because no one likes to think that a kid could be a killer. But you're your father's son. And he taught you well."

Michael's eyes tensed. "Is that an insult?"

"No. But it's not a compliment, either. Who you were . . . those months on the road with your father, learning to shoot, learning to kill, experiencing the euphoria of action . . . that was the school our nation's first Medal of Honor winner graduated from."

Michael said nothing.

Ness leaned forward. "Tell me it didn't all come back to you, rushing back. . . . Tell me in that jungle you didn't wake up to who you are."

". . . So what if it did?"

Again Ness shrugged, gesturing dismissively. "You can't help who you are, Michael. You can't undo the qualities, good and ill, you were born with. And you can't erase the things you experienced." Now the G-man's gaze hardened. "But you can channel them constructively."

"War, for example?"

"When madmen are trying to steal the planet, yes—a man with your skills comes in handy."

Michael laughed once, hollowly. "The army doesn't want me, anymore. I have only one eye, remember, Mr. Ness?"

Ness pointed a finger. "Oh, but Uncle Sam still wants you, Michael . . . if you're willing. And the job I have in mind, you should find very . . . satisfying."

"I'm listening."

Ness's expression was somber as he said, "I need to know one thing, first. If you had an opportunity to do something about the people who killed your father, would you seek justice? Or revenge?"

Michael's eyes tightened, and he sat forward; any sham coolness disappeared. "What?"

Ness rocked back; crossed his arms. "I'm talking about the Capone gang, Michael. Frank Nitti is still in charge, following the directives of Capone himself, who's been calling the shots from his Palm Island mansion in Florida, ever since his release from Alcatraz in '39."

Capone . . . Al Capone . . . the man responsible for his father's death. . . .

Now Ness sat forward, eyes glittering. "And now for the first time, we have them on the ropes. We're in a position to take them all down."

"And . . . I can be part of this?"

"You haven't answered my question, Michael. Justice, or revenge?"

"Well, justice," Michael said.

"Good," Ness said. "Good. . . ."

For an hour Ness filled Michael in about the current status of the Capone mob. They were "on the ropes" because an elaborate extortion scam, relating to their infiltration of various Hollywood movie unions, had unraveled; three major underlings were in custody. Investigations on both the East and West Coasts were under way, with a core group of honest cops helping on the Chicago front.

The movie scam had been one of several schemes Frank Nitti had undertaken to replace missing income after the repeal of Prohibition. Various union takeovers and of course gambling were among the other major mob moneymakers, but in particular prostitution—brothels, roadhouses, strip joints—had come to the fore.

This was where Eliot Ness came in.

"Last March," he said, "I resigned from my job as Public Safety Director in Cleveland to take this on—it's my way of fighting the war."

The Division of Social Protection's mandate was "safeguarding the health and morale of the armed forces and of workers in defense industries." This included educational efforts, like films and pamphlets warning of the dangers of venereal disease; but primarily involved a law enforcement effort to cut back on prostitution in areas close to military and naval bases, as well as industrial areas.

Ness supervised the activities of twelve regional offices; but he had made the Chicago branch his "baby," as it provided him with an opportunity to clean up some unfinished business.

"Al Capone was sentenced on tax evasion," Ness said, "in this very building. We accomplished that with a two-pronged attack— my squad cut off the mob's financial flow while the accountants fine-tooth-combed the books we seized."

Shifting in his chair, keenly interested, Michael said, "And this is a two-pronged attack, as well? While the government prepares the movie extortion case, you hit Capone on prostitution?"

"Exactly right, Michael." Ness leaned forward, hands folded prayerfully. "You and I might be settling up some old scores, here . . . but that's just a bonus. We really would be fighting the homefront war."

Ness laid it out. Chicago was the nation's center for transportation; the Quartermaster Corps had its headquarters here. The Stevens Hotel had been converted to a military training facility and housing center for G.I.s in transit; the Chicago Beach Hotel was now a military hospital, Navy Pier a training facility, universities providing military training. Fort Sheridan, north of the city, remained an army training camp, and the navy had taken over Curtis Air Field.

The city's industrial plants were converting heavily to war production, Pullman switching from train cars to aircraft, the

Electromotive plant turning out tanks. The steel mills were working overtime, and a new Douglas Aircraft factory on the North West Side was producing frames for the C54 transport. The Grebe shipyards, near Riverview Amusement Park, were turning out subchasers.

"All of these locations are prey to prostitution," Ness said. "And, when ration stamps hit the Midwest, we can assume the Capone boys will move into stealing and counterfeiting 'em; and black market meat will soon follow."

"I'm convinced there's a problem," Michael said, "and an opportunity. But what role can one one-eyed soldier play?"

"A key one. You're not Michael O'Sullivan, Jr., to the Capone mob. You're Michael Satariano, the Italian American . . . a Sicilian boy, no less . . . who just won the Medal of Honor. Your heroism tells the public at large where Italian Americans stand on this war."

"And how is that helpful?"

"Do I have to tell you the biggest problem I'm fighting isn't social disease, but corruption? Mayor Kelly is in Capone's pocket, and those legislators shaking your hand the other day? Mob shills. And then there's the police—I have only a handful of local coppers I trust. I need a man on the inside, who can feed me information."

Making sure he'd heard this correctly, Michael slowly said, "You want me to get hired by the Capone Outfit. To work for them."

"And *with* them. Yes. It's an undercover assignment, and it's dangerous. Maybe not as dangerous as facing a hundred armed Japs . . . but dangerous enough."

Michael was shaking his head, doubtfully. "Me being a war hero . . . maybe that gets me in to shake Frank Nitti's hand. It doesn't get me 'inside.' "

"There's a way. There *is* a way."

"I don't see it."

"Your father, Michael."

". . . My father?"

"I mean, Papa S."

"What about him?"

"Ask him to recommend you. Ask him to pave the way."

"What, are you nuts?" Michael literally waved this notion off. "Papa S. is no mobster."

"I didn't say he was. But he is, in his small way, connected."

"Connected? Little white-haired, chubby Papa? You're out of your mind—I mean, no offense, but, hell—"

"Please. Just listen. Your 'father' opened his restaurant in 1924 in DeKalb, as a kind of front; Pasquale was a middle man between Chicago and farmers who provided the hops, malt and corn needed for processing liquor."

Michael said nothing. How could he protest, when he thought back on the core regulars at the restaurant: farmers who brought their families in once a week, and who spoke and joked warmly with Pasquale, like old friends . . . .

"Prohibition was the plague that created the Capones and the Looneys," Ness said. "And the Volstead Act taught honest people like Papa S. that breaking a stupid law like that might be a crime, but certainly no sin."

"Maybe in the '20s," Michael allowed, again shaking his head in doubt. "I'm sure he has no contact with them, anymore."

"Does Papa S. buy his produce and supplies in Chicago? The mob controls olive oil, fruits and produce, and tomato paste . . . just like they do gambling, dope, and prostitution."

Silence filled the room, interrupted only by the whirring of the window fan.

"Now keep in mind," Ness said, lifting a warning finger, "you may be asked by these people, even ordered to do things, that you can't do. Break a law undercover, you've still broken a law."

"I thought this was war."

"There are wars and there are wars. If you think you've gotten in over your head, for God's sake swim to shore."

"And if somebody like Frank Nitti tells me to commit a crime for him . . . ?"

"You must . . . somehow . . . manage not to do it, without tipping your hand. That's the hardest part of your assignment.

You must *seem* to be one of them, without becoming one of them. . . . Do you understand?"

Finally Michael said, "Am I being ordered to do this?"

"I told you—strictly volunteer. You'll remain on active duty, and receive your pittance of a paycheck from Uncle Sam."

"Who will know?"

"I will. So will Lieutenant William Drury—your police contact. And should both Drury and myself be eliminated by the Capone crowd, I'll have left a sealed envelope with Governor Green, explaining everything."

"Can he be trusted? You said those legislators were mob shills . . ."

Ness grinned. "Dwight Green prosecuted Scarface . . . I can show you the courthouse, downstairs. He helped me send Al Capone to Alcatraz."

Just as you, Mr. Ness, Michael O'Sullivan, Jr., thought, *will help me send Al Capone to Hell. . . .*

Ness had been right.

Something *had* awakened in Michael in the jungles of Bataan. That war was lost to him—Captain Wermuth and General Wainwright, right now they were either dead or imprisoned by the Japanese, and out of Michael's reach—nothing he could do for them.

But this old war, the Capone war, could still be waged . . . and won. After all these years, after all this time, the death of his father could be avenged. It might start in Chicago, but it would end in Miami, with Al Capone in Michael O'Sullivan, Jr.'s gunsights.

Or his hands.

His father had put the squeeze on Capone; Michael would squeeze another way.

Michael stood and extended his hand to Ness, who rose, and again they shook, rather ceremoniously.

"Thank you, Michael."

"Glad to help," said the son of the Angel of Death.

MICHAEL SPOKE TO PAPA SATARIANO AFTER HOURS THAT evening, the help gone home, Mama finished in the kitchen and upstairs, Papa having tallied the till and locked up.

Pasquale's Spaghetti House was larger than a hole in the wall . . . just. But while the distressed red-brick interior was narrow, the building went back as far as the alley, with a high decorative tin ceiling, which they'd painted out black a few years ago—Papa S.'s idea of remodeling.

Wooden booths with red cushions lined either wall, a scattering of round tables with red-and-white-checkered cloths between. High on the walls perched framed oil paintings, stripe-shirt gondoliers and commedia dell'arte clowns, acquired by Papa S. at Little Italy street fairs.

The glassed-in area between the dining room and kitchen proper was where Papa and a handful of trusted employees—including Michael, ever since junior high—would toss pizza dough, and feed a hungry oven. The term "pizza" hadn't caught on in the sticks, and on the menu Papa S. called his exotic specialty "tomato pie." Some Chicago pizza parlors made a thick crust in a deep dish, but Papa S. provided a thin, crispy variety . . . and lots of entertainment for those lucky enough to have a seat near that window.

Mama S. did most of the other cooking, and she made the salads, but sauces were another of Papa S.'s bailiwicks. Between them, the smells of homemade-style Italian cooking permeated the place with a distinctive aroma the customers cherished; Michael, living upstairs, had formed his own opinion . . . though after a year on the Philippines, Michael now inhaled the familiar scents with something approaching delight.

At the moment, however, delight was not his state of mind. As he sat with Papa S., explaining what he wanted, what he needed, the old man's obvious discomfort was second only to his own.

"These words," Papa S. said, eyes tight behind wire frame glasses. His face was round, his mustache white and well trimmed. "I hear them. They're comin' out your mouth, son— but they can't be you."

"They're me, Papa."

" 'Papa' is it?" The old man snorted a laugh. "You *do* want this." Now began the elaborate gestures, the sing-song sarcasm. "Usually, it's 'sir,' or 'Papa S.'—you always let me know that *you* know I'm not really your blood papa."

"I never meant—"

Papa raised a palm. "It's okay. You weren't no foundling on our doorstep. We took you in as a grown young man. They told us you had a troubled past. We didn't care. We loved you. We looked at you, and we loved you."

Michael knew why. The Satarianos lost a son, ten years of age, to scarlet fever the year before they'd adopted him; pictures of the boy held more than a vague resemblance to Michael. Funny—he'd almost died of scarlet fever himself; but his father had nursed him to health, on the road.

When he'd found the photo album, with the pictures of the lost Antonio, Michael felt strange—as if he'd been chosen by the Satarianos for wrong reasons. He felt like a brown-and-white spotted puppy picked to replace a dead brown-and-white spotted dog.

Papa S. was saying, "But when you wanted somethin', car keys, night off, advance pay, oh then I was *Papa*, all right."

The words were gruff, and even the tone; but the eyes behind the glasses remained kind. Papa S. couldn't fool Michael. The man was a soft touch. Always had been. Particularly when his adoptive son called him Papa. . . .

Michael leaned forward. "You dealt with these people over the years, didn't you?"

Papa S. reared back. "Who says I did?"

"Oh come on, Papa. You were the middleman between the Outfit and the farmers, right?"

"*Gossip* you're believing now? What if I tell you I never had nothing to do with those kind of people."

"Tell me, then."

Papa S. said nothing. "I'm gonna get some coffee. . . . You wanna pop or something?"

"Coke."

Papa got up and lumbered off; he had bad corns and there was more side-to-side motion than forward movement.

Soon Papa S. was handing a frosty bottle of Coke to Michael; then the old man sat and spooned three spoonfuls of sugar into his coffee.

"Times was different, then," Papa said softly, stirring, stirring. "Twenty, thirty years ago, we were like coloreds. We had no say, nobody to go to. We turn to the Unione Siciliano, because why? Because there was no place else. Colosimo and Torrio, *they* were the government to us."

The same could have been said about the Irish in the Tri-Cities and the Looney mob, Michael knew. Funny—both his fathers had turned to the mob for the only fair shake available to them in America at that time. Only, Pasquale Satariano dealt in produce, and Michael O'Sullivan, Sr., had dispensed muscle.

"Why you wanna work for them, son?"

Michael shrugged, swigged the Coke. "They run a lot of restaurants and clubs. If I get in solid with them, maybe I can manage or own something of my own, someday."

Papa S. gestured around them elaborately. "*This*'ll be your own, someday!"

"Not sure I want to stay in a small town, Papa. Big world out there."

Black eyebrows rose. "You don't think this world, this small town world, is better than a buncha Japs shooting at your skinny behind?"

"You know as well as I do, a kid with a last name like mine needs connections in the big city. You've got them. All I ask is you share them with me."

"Dangerous people to run with."

Michael grinned. "Not as dangerous as a buncha Japs."

A small smile curled under the mustache. "Throw my own words back at me. You've changed. Used to be, you were respectful."

"I still am. I still appreciate everything you and Mama S. have done for me."

"Mama S.," the old man said, grunting it, making a sour laugh out of the words. "All she's done for you is right. This would break her heart, she knew you were with the Mafiosi."

"Don't tell her, then."

Papa S. just stared at him. Then he sipped the coffee. "We could say you're doing war work in the city. Missions for the army. It's . . . what do you say, confidential."

"Yeah. That should do."

"Top secret."

"Right. Like your sauces."

They smiled at each other.

But then Papa S.'s expression turned grave and he shook his head. "You honor your country, your honor your family, then you turn around and—"

"I won't dishonor you, Papa, or my country. You have to trust me in that."

The old man leaned forward, his voice soft, pleading. "You don't need to do this, son. With that medal, you can go through all kinda doors. Even with our last name. You're the first, the very first, Medal of Honor winner! Do you know the pride swells in my chest?"

"I do know. And I appreciate that, Papa. But you have to do this for me."

Papa S. studied Michael, who did not avert the gaze, in fact held it.

Then the old man said, "I'll do this thing for you."

"Thank you, Papa."

"Because I love you. Because your mama loves you. And you . . . you *appreciate* us."

The old man stood and the light hit his eyes; tears were pearled there. Turning away, moving in that shuffling side-to-side gait, Pasquale Satariano headed toward the rear of the building, to the stairs to their living quarters. Michael thought about going to the old man and putting his arm around him and saying, "I love you, Papa, I really do."

But he didn't—he didn't go to the old man, and he didn't love him, either.

Respected, admired, appreciated him, yes. Adored, venerated, prized Mama S., yes. Not love.

Since the deaths of his parents and brother, over ten years ago, Michael had made it a point not to love anybody; puberty had doublecrossed him where Patsy Ann was concerned, but that had been his only slip.

No, Michael O'Sullivan, Jr., had never allowed himself to love the Satarianos.

And it was too late to start now—now that an old hatred had renewed itself to fill him with new purpose.

3

―――――

AT THE TURN OF THE CENTURY, THE ten-story Hotel Lexington at Twenty-second Street and South Michigan had been among Chicago's most stellar. The imposing hotel—with its turreted corners and bay windows and lofty lobby—had played host to President Grover S. Cleveland when he came to town to open the Columbian Exposition in 1893.

But since 1928, the Lexington had become better known for playing host to Al Capone, who controlled the Century of Progress Exposition in '33. For many years the Capone organization monopolized the third, fourth and fifth floors, the latter reserved for women who serviced the mobsters and their guests. A ten-room suite on the fourth had been Capone's—his living quarters and his offices, supplanted with hidden panels, moving walls and silent alarms.

After Snorky (as Capone's intimates referred to him) was sent away by feds like Eliot Ness and Elmer Irey, the Outfit (as they were locally known) scaled itself back, assuming a more low-key posture in the community, their presence at the Lexington lessening considerably. Subtracting Capone's former living quarters, the suite of offices on the fourth floor was halved, the third and fifth floors long since returned to the hotel for its own devices.

As Frank Nitti walked across the black-and-white mosaic tile floor of the Lexington, a pair of bodyguards fore and aft, he found the grand old hotel looking sadly long in the tooth. The overstuffed furnishings were threadbare, the potted plants neglected; only the mob's cigar stand, which was also a bookie joint, seemed prosperous.

Nitti much preferred to do business out of his suite at the Bismarck Hotel, conveniently across from City Hall and footsteps away from the Capri Restaurant, out of which he also worked; the Lexington had outlived its usefulness (of course, as the gangster knew all too well, some might say the same about Frank Nitti).

At five eight, Nitti was smaller than all four men accompanying him. He wore no hat, his hair well trimmed, slicked back, parted at the left, touched with gray at the temples; average of build, he did not appear physically imposing, though he took confident strides. In the perfectly tailored gray suit with the dark gray tie, he looked like the smooth business executive he was, albeit one with a roughly handsome face, lower lip flecked with scar tissue, eyes dark and alert. He was not carrying a gun. The bodyguards were.

The impeccable grooming of the small, dapper man still known to many as the Enforcer reflected a former profession: barber. He had cut hair and provided close shaves in his cousin Alphonse Capone's old neighborhood in Brooklyn, in the early '20s. Occasionally he had not shaved but cut a throat, and—imported to Chicago by Al as a bomber and assassin—Nitti had earned respect for coldblooded violence, though his rise in the

Outfit was due more to his business brains and organizational skills.

Appointed by Capone as chairman of the board, for the duration of Snorky's prison term, Nitti had avoided the headline-provoking brutality of his chief; he had ruled calmly and fairly, and no turf wars to speak of had broken out during his tenure. He considered himself a captain of industry, and had replaced bootlegging with unionism.

Yet here he was, still holding court in the infamous Lexington, whose art-moderne aura spoke of the '20s and '30s, not the '40s, not today. But wasn't that the point? The psychological link to the old days—to Al—that the suite of offices on the fourth floor represented could not be underestimated. And anyway, his Bismarck suite did not include a boardroom.

Half an hour later, Nitti sat at the head of the long well-polished table; several pitchers of iced water were positioned around, and glass ashtrays for the various cigars and cigarettes of Nitti's five guests, who took up only half of the available seats. The room was air-conditioned and, like so many late associates of the men at this table, well ventilated.

On the wall behind Nitti were three oil paintings, two of which had been in Al's office in the old days: George Washington and Abraham Lincoln. The third, over a fireplace whose mantel was decorated by various civic awards for their absent leader's philanthropy in the Depression, loomed a distinguished three-quarters view of Capone himself—without his trademark Borsalino, his scars hidden from view.

Seated at the long dark-oak table were five of the top Outfit *capos* in Chicago.

At Nitti's right hand sat Paul Ricca—pale, thin, white-haired, with high cheekbones, long narrow nose and slash of a mouth in a placid expression belied by dark dead eyes; he wore a crisp brown suit and a blood-red tie, and smoked a cigarette. Nicknamed "the Waiter," after a profession he had rarely ever pursued (other than when filling in "occupation" on a form), Ricca had been Capone's bodyguard and was now Nitti's underboss.

Ricca was famous for killing two guys in Sicily, going to prison for it, then on the day he got out, killing the eyewitness. Theoretically Nitti's top aide, the Waiter (the Enforcer knew all too well) was angling for the top chair.

Next to Ricca sat Charlie Fischetti—stocky, white-haired, handsome, as impeccably attired as Nitti in his own gray suit and a handsigned Salvador Dalí necktie. Fischetti, one of three brothers in the Outfit, oversaw gambling and nightclubs. Nitti trusted Fischetti, who agreed about the need to move into legitimate concerns, encouraging mob investment on Wall Street and in Texas oil.

At Fischetti's right was slender, perpetually smirky Murray Humphreys, in charge of labor unions, cleaning plants and laundries; Humphreys was also a master fixer of politicians. Another spiffy, dashing gangster, Murray the Camel was the Outfit intellectual: he'd graduated high school. The only non-Sicilian at the table, in fact the only Welshman in the Outfit, Hump was valued by all, despite his outsider's inability to become a "made" man.

On the other side of the table, at Nitti's left, sat Louis "Little New York" Campagna, the Enforcer's most trusted associate, a short blocky man in an off-the-rack brown suit, with cold dark eyes in a lumpy mashed-potatoes face with perpetual five o'clock shadow. Imported from NYC in '27 by Al himself, Campagna handled enforcement for Nitti—from those personal bodyguards who'd come up with him in the elevator, to any points that needed making related to any of their business concerns.

Next to Campagna sat Tony Accardo, a roughneck dubbed Joe Batters by Capone for the thug's abilities with a baseball bat (off the diamond, of course). A big man with an oval face, sad eyes crowding a bulbous nose, Accardo wore a blue suit and lighter blue tie, nothing fancy but nicely respectful, coming from a guy who preferred sportshirts and slacks. In addition to running West Side gambling, Accardo was often called upon by Campagna for heavy stuff.

Despite the long table and the boardroom trappings, this was not a meeting of the "board." Around ten gangsters had gambling territories (like Accardo's) and numerous other Outfit associates had varied responsibilities—Capone's lookalike brother

Ralph ("Bottles") took care of soft drinks and tavern supplies; Eddie Vogel had the slots, cigarette machines and vending machines; Joe Fusco had liquor distribution (legal, now); and Jake Guzik remained treasurer. Seldom were all these figures gathered at once.

But these five were key players, and Frank Nitti had summoned them because he had important business to discuss.

"You heard Ness is in town," Nitti said.

"Fuck Ness," Accardo said, and there were nods and grunts of agreement, all around.

Ricca, his gaze on the cigarette in his fingers, said, "Guy's a joke. Got run out of Cleveland on a rail."

Fischetti, gesturing with a cigarette-in-holder, demurred. "Ness was effective for many years in that town. Just ask Moe Dalitz. He was crimping the style of the Mayfield Road boys right up to the end."

"But the point," Ricca said, without looking at Fischetti, or anyone else for that matter, "is Mr. Big Shot has *reached* the end. . . . Jerkoff gets drunk and slams his car into somebody else's, and then doesn't report it? You or me, we'd be in stir for that. Hit and run, pure and simple."

Humphreys said, "As amusing as the notion of an alcoholic prohibition agent may be, my understanding is Mrs. Ness was driving, and she was injured and he rushed her to the hospital. After checking on the other motorist."

Now Ricca cast his hard gaze on Humphreys, and to the Hump's credit, the man did not look away. "Ness resigned in disgrace," Ricca said. "He's nothing now. Not a danger to nobody."

Finally Nitti spoke, softly, reasonably; he had just lighted up a cigar and gestured with it, nonthreateningly. "I disagree, Paul. It's exactly because Ness had to resign in disgrace that he's dangerous to us."

Ricca waved a dismissive hand.

Accardo asked, "Why's that, Frank?"

Nitti's eyes darted from face to face. "Does anybody disagree with Hump about Ness's performance in Cleveland? Just about the best in the country; drove our friends outa there—cleaned up the police force, caused trouble with the unions, with the numbers racket. Gotta hand it to him."

"He's a relic, Frank." Ricca's gaze, cool now, settled on Nitti . . . tellingly. "He's one of them people you hear about that don't know when their time is up."

Nitti frowned at the narrow-faced gangster. "You think Ness's time is up, Paul? He's a fucking *fed* again!"

"Yeaaah," Rica said, sneering. "Makin' sure our boys in the armed forces know that sex is bad for 'em. A dick policin' dicks— what a joke."

"No joke." Nitti looked around at them, and all eyes and ears were his, with the exception of Ricca's. "Is there anyone in this room who doesn't think Al would be sitting where I am, if it wasn't for Ness?"

"Ness was only one of a dozen," Ricca said, and slapped the air dismissively.

"A dozen that included Dwight Green, currently governor of our fair state," Nitti said. "So Ness will have allies. Even a few cops, like Drury. Still, Paul, you're right—Ness *is* down. He's on his damn knees."

"Blowin' G.I.s," Ricca said.

Everyone smiled at that. But Nitti.

Who said, "No one's more dangerous than a champ who's just come up off the canvas, looking for an opening. How does Ness rehabilitate himself, do you think? How does he get his good name back?"

"He doesn't," Ricca said quietly.

Nitti continued: "He returns to the site of his first, most famous victory. He looks at the Capone mob. And he knows that if he can bring us down, he's back on top."

"Not going to happen," Ricca said.

"I know it isn't." Nitti slapped the table and everyone, even Ricca, jumped a little. "Because as of today, we're shutting down all prostitution around military installations and defense plants."

Ricca half-rose. "What the fuck?"

And everyone else at the table seemed stunned.

"Sit, Paul." Nitti motioned at the air with both hands, cigar in the corner of his mouth. "Sit. I'll explain . . ."

"Explain! You know what kinda income that brings in, Frank? Are you nuts?"

"Watch what you say, Paul—I *do* speak for Al."

Ricca frowned; smoke curled upward from his cigarette between fingers. "You talked to him about this?"

"Through intermediaries. You know I don't dare speak on the phone with Al—fucking federal wiretaps. But I'm scheduling a meet for a couple weeks from now, in Miami."

Ricca, eyes tight, sat forward. "*I* want to talk to Al."

"You know that's impossible."

Both Capone and Nitti had homes in Florida; and meetings between them were fairly frequent. But because of law enforcement surveillance, the policy was that nobody visited Capone but Nitti himself.

Ricca was shaking his head, boiling.

Frowning, Fischetti said, "I'm afraid I'm with Paul on this one, Frank. How can we shut something down that's so lucrative?"

"We won't shut it down, not entirely. Just the whorehouses—the wide-open brothels. We'll leave the strip clubs alone . . . good healthy fun for our boys in the armed forces. And we'll have understandings with the girls that if they take the boys home, well, we get our cut."

"Just no houses," Fischetti said, eyes tight with thought, starting to slowly nod.

"Right. No madams. No joints that can be raided. We'll also set up call girls, big-ticket lookers; put 'em in hotels, nice ones."

Ricca still seethed, but the others seemed to be coming around.

"Boys," Nitti said, and he gestured with both hands, palms up, "we're businessmen. We're part of the community." He motioned toward the awards on the mantelpiece. "Al was beloved—he gave to charity, he set up soup kitchens and homeless shelters. Town loved him. Why?"

Accardo said, " 'Cause they was fuckin' thirsty."

Everyone but Ricca laughed.

"Exactly right," Nitti said. "They was fuckin' thirsty. Nobody thought Al was a bad man for helping the average guy buy a beer after work. We didn't have a public relations problem till St. Valentine's Day, and even Al admits that was a mistake. What did we learn? Don't stir up the heat!"

"People also get hungry," Ricca said, "for a whore. No difference. Appetites, either way."

"Big difference," Nitti said, shaking his head. "If we stay with our wide-open houses, Ness will crucify us in the press. We'll look like we're undermining the war effort. Hell, we're already a bunch of Italians, ain't we? You wanna be on a wanted poster next to Mussolini?"

"Awwww," Ricca said, and waved at nothing.

But Fischetti was thinking out loud: "You mean, we need to worry about how we look. To the public. We give 'em gambling, we're pals, helpin' 'em unwind. We give G.I. Joe the syph, we're a buncha un-American dagos."

"Now," Nitti said, pleased, "you're thinking like a businessman."

"Sex is good business," Ricca said coldly.

"It is. So we have the strip clubs, and arcades, on the low end; call girls on the high end. But no brothels. If the public sees us as whoremongers, we're finished. Ness will make us look like traitors . . . and himself a hero."

Ricca turned his dead gaze onto Nitti. "We just invested in that packing plant, and that slaughterhouse. You gonna close that down? Black-market meat, that unpatriotic too, like fucking a whore?"

"Fucking isn't unpatriotic, Paul; pimping is. And I'm all for the black-market meat business. It's bootlegging all over again. People will love us for giving them what they crave. Same with ration stamps, when they start up—counterfeit or stolen."

Accardo said, "And anyway, it's the whores that are Ness's beat, right?"

This got an unintentional laugh, including both Ricca and Nitti.

"That's right," Nitti said. "We don't want to play into that prick's hands. We made him a star once—we ain't gonna do it twice."

Ricca said, "This is immediate, this shut down? I thought you was gonna wait till you talked with Al."

"You're right, Paul. For now, we stay open; but we start plannin' pulling out . . . so to speak."

Again, smiles all around.

The discussion of the brothel situation was followed by updates on the Hollywood union case. Ricca reported that the feds were offering Willie Bioff, George Browne and Nicky Dean reduced sentences if they spilled. So far all three were sitting tight in the federal pen. But everybody at the table was unnerved by the government coming down on them.

"Problem like this makes Ness look like the nothing he is," Ricca said.

"All the more reason," Nitti said, "not to give the feds anything else on us."

With the meeting dismissed, Nitti gave Campagna a look that said, *Stick around,* while Ricca approached.

"I meant no disrespect," Ricca said, shaking Nitti's hand; Ricca's grasp was like holding a dead fish. "I will honor Al's wishes on this."

When Ricca was gone, Campagna said, "Al's wishes. Not yours."

"Al *is* the boss."

"The boss in Miami. The boss in exile. You run Chicago, Frank."

"Not if Ricca gets his way. . . . My office, Louie."

They walked down the hall and into the office through the reception area; though his secretary was still at her desk, Nitti's waiting room was otherwise empty. At one time the chairs lining the walls would have been filled with crooked politicians and shady businessmen, waiting for a few precious minutes of Nitti's time; but Nitti conducted his business in a more discreet fashion, now—either one-on-one, at the Bismarck suite, or working through intermediaries.

The spacious, wood-panelled office, lavishly appointed, might have been a La Salle Street broker's. Another portrait of Capone (in hat and coat with cigar) hung over another fireplace.

Nitti settled in behind a desk no larger than a Lincoln Continental. Behind him was a window with a view onto the South Side of Chicago, long the Capone empire; the swivel chair in which he sat had been Al's as well, a gift from the Chicago Heights boys, its back bullet-proofed.

Campagna, comfortable with his chief, fetched from an ice box a bottle of milk and poured Nitti a chilled glass (ulcers) and then got himself a bourbon on the rocks from the liquor cart. The loyal, lumpy-faced little killer settled into the leather-padded visitor's chair across from Nitti, who had his feet up on the desk, rocked back in the swivel chair, sipping his milk thoughtfully.

"How big a problem," Nitti asked, "do we have with Ricca?"

"Big," Campagna said.

"Who can I trust?"

"Probably everybody but Ricca."

"Who for sure?"

". . . Me."

"You know, the Waiter's been lining himself up with those hot-head kids from the Patch. This Giancana, Mooney they call him? He's got a screw loose."

"He ain't the only one. DeStefano makes Mooney look normal. Mad Sam, they call him."

Nitti sipped his milk. "Isn't DeStefano a solid juice man?"

"Yeah, the best. Who ain't gonna pay up a guy that'd feed ya your nuts, parboiled?"

Nitti nodded; this was a good point. "All these wild youngsters, Ricca's got 'em in his pocket. Couple are on my staff." He frowned. "Louie, can we trust these bodyguards?"

"Far as it goes. Frank, always comes down to, these guys kill people for money. Allegiance ain't what it used to be."

Nitti shook his head. "And in these times, we should have that. We should pull together. Tell you the truth—my preference is, we stay out of the black market. I think it *is* unpatriotic. But I couldn't go that far. Didn't dare."

Campagna nodded. "Good call, Frank. Nixing the whorehouses was drastic enough."

Nitti sighed. He took his feet off the desk and leaned on his elbows. "What I'd give for a reliable goddamn bodyguard."

"You got me, Frank."

"You're too valuable for flunky work, Louie. I wouldn't insult you."

"It'd be an honor."

"Louie . . . I wish I had a hundred of you."

"My Ma says, when they made me? Broke the mold."

"Your ma is right, Louie."

Campagna looked at his watch. "Listen, in about half an hour, that kid's comin' around. That war hero?"

Nitti straightened. "Well, I look forward to that. Congressional Medal of Honor. And he's Sicilian! Now somebody like him, that's what I'm talkin' about."

Campagna shrugged. "Hey, well . . . his old man says he wants to work for us."

"That's this fella . . . Pasquale Satariano?"

"Right. In DeKalb. He was our guy with the farmers. Sweet old Mustache Pete kinda goombah. He makes a gravy worth drivin' out there for."

"I couldn't do that, could I?"

"Drive out there?"

"Involve somebody like that, in our thing?"

"The war hero kid?" Campagna shrugged. "I dunno. Up to you. Up to him. Why don't you ask him?"

And that's what Nitti did, but not at first.

Stiff and polite in a dark brown suit with a brown-and-yellow tie, the young man sat where earlier Campagna had. Campagna was standing over by the fireplace, now. Nitti offered the boy a drink, and he requested a Coke; said he didn't drink liquor. Nitti liked that, considered heavy drinking among his people bad for business.

It also made him feel comfortable and unselfconscious, having a glass of milk in front of the kid.

"You honor us," Nitti said, and saluted him with the glass of milk. "You honor Sicilians like us. You honor Americans like us. God bless you, Michael Satariano. And God Bless America."

Michael toasted Nitti back, with the glass of Coke, and then said, "You were a great friend to my father."

"Your father, Pasquale, he was valuable to us. We still consider him one of us. I understand you'd like a job."

The boy sat forward, his expression earnest. "I would. You see, I lost an eye in combat, so I can't serve any more. And, frankly, after a year on the Philippines, going back to work at my father's spaghetti house . . . well, it seems a little dull. Tossing pizza dough."

"Noble profession. Don't knock it, son."

"I respect my father. And I think someday I'd like to be in that business . . . roughly speaking."

"Roughly, how?"

The boy shrugged. "A bigger restaurant, even a chain. Nightclub . . . or clubs. Not just a hole-in-the-wall in a little college town."

"You're ambitious."

"I'd like to be somebody, sure. That's the American dream; it's what we're fighting for. . . . Just look at what *you've* accomplished, Mr. Nitti."

"Nothing, compared to you, son."

"I'm young, Mr. Nitti. I crave work that's challenging. That might even have a little . . . excitement to it."

Nitti studied the kid. Michael Satariano had such a sweet, almost angelic face, though the dark eyes were unfathomable. This young man had killed over a hundred Japs. That was more kills than all the Mooneys and Mad Sams put together.

Then something flashed through Frank Nitti's mind; something jarring—this kid reminded him of someone. Years ago, another killer had sat across from him at this desk and offered his services: O'Sullivan, the Angel of Death. How Nitti wished he'd taken the man up on his offer, that he'd stood aside and allowed O'Sullivan to kill the Looneys.

In that case, O'Sullivan would have come to work for Nitti; would have been Frank Nitti's loyal enforcer. A smart man, tough but not ruthless, and the bravest son of a bitch who'd ever walked the earth. How Nitti wished O'Sullivan were alive and at his right arm now, an ally as reliable as Campagna and ten times as valuable.

And here was another young killer, a Sicilian boy from the sticks with a vague resemblance to that long-dead Irish hitman. Funny—Nitti had the strange feeling he was getting a second chance. . . .

"If you came to work for me," Nitti said, "the law you would answer to would be our law. Al Capone's law."

"Mr. Nitti, I know all about killing the enemy. Just point the way."

Nitti almost laughed. This sweet kid . . . and yet he knew from the newspapers what this young man was capable of.

"Can you drive, with one eye?" Nitti asked.

"With one eye and two arms and two feet, sure."

"I could use a bodyguard. A loyal man who would die for me. Who would, as you say, kill for me."

"I'm that man, Mr. Nitti."

Nitti glanced at Campagna, who shrugged; but Louie was smiling. He, like Nitti, was amused and impressed.

"Do you have a place to stay?" Nitti asked.

"No. I came up from DeKalb. I can't really commute, with gas rationing coming. Anyway, I'd prefer to live in town."

"We'll put you up at the Seneca Hotel. Lot of our people live there."

Nitti rose. Extended his hand across the expanse of the desk.

The Enforcer and the war hero shook, after which the latter found five hundred-dollar bills left behind by the former.

"Anything else you need?" Nitti asked.

"Not that I can think of," Michael said. "Oh! . . . A shoulder holster would be nice."

4

The "Calumet" of Calumet City, Illinois, derived from the French word for the peace pipe once used by the Indians in these parts, long since displaced by the white people they'd bargained with. Finding something interesting to smoke in wide-open Calumet City these days would likely not be a chore. You could turn up just about anything illegal and entertaining, in this residential outgrowth of Hammond, Indiana, a (mostly) quiet hamlet of twelve thousand souls.

Quiet was how Michael Satariano, at the wheel of a '39 Ford Deluxe coupe, found the forty-minute drive from the Loop. Tooling down Torrence Avenue about dusk, he'd had a pleasant if intermittent conversation with his companion,

Louie Campagna, passing on one side of the road swimmers and boaters on Lake Calumet, and on the other side a geometric gray expanse of industry, steel mills, oil refineries, chemical works, and fertilizer factories, all disgorging dirty clouds steadily into the sky.

Then as they neared Calumet City, open spaces with wild grass greeted them, prairie land suggesting they were indeed about to enter the Wild West.

"You know, kid," Campagna said at one point, after a long silence. "Mr. Nitti likes you."

"Yeah?"

"You come along at a good time for the both of you—there's people who'd like to see Frank retire, the hard way. So somebody he can trust, like you . . . it's a Godsend."

"That's generous of you, Louie."

"Hey. Just sayin', keep your nose clean, please the boss, every reason to think you could go places."

Four days had passed since Frank Nitti had hired Michael as a chauffeur-cum-bodyguard. Nitti had dismissed his other bodyguards—at least the daytime crew—and occasionally Michael was joined by Campagna in duties that consisted primarily of driving Nitti here and there, and sitting outside or sometimes inside one of the crime boss's offices.

Nitti worked out of the Bismarck Hotel more than the Lexington, Michael soon learned; and, on nearby North Clark, held court in a booth at the Capri Restaurant. Nitti's home in suburban Riverside was the final stop on Michael's route. Nitti, whose wife of many years had died last year, had recently remarried and the home was a new purchase; he had a nine-year-old son.

Campagna had commented on that, too: "He worshipped Anna." That was Nitti's first wife. "Hit him hard, last year . . . he was depressed as hell. And some people took advantage of that. But Frank's coming on strong again. Comin' on strong."

Occasionally other stops were made during Michael's daily tour of duty as Nitti's driver, as when the gang lord sat down for a pow wow with Outfit treasurer Jake Guzik, an obese creature who apparently worked strictly from a perpetually food-filled table at

St. Hubert's English Grill, near the Union League Club. Like any executive, Frank Nitti spent his time in meetings and on the phone—that the men he met with were frequently on various public enemies lists did not change the mundane nature of things.

Nitti was friendly but preoccupied, and in four days perhaps ten sentences had been exchanged between employer and new employee . . . until late this afternoon, when the Enforcer had summoned Michael to sit beside him on a couch in the white-appointed, gold-trimmed Victorian-looking Presidential Suite at the Bismarck.

"So much for challenging work, right, kid?" Nitti said good-naturedly. He was drinking milk. An attractive colored maid had provided Michael with a Coca-Cola on ice, already established in the Outfit as the war hero's drink of choice.

"Beats tossing pizza dough," Michael said, the nearness of Nitti unnerving him.

"But soldiering is like that, right? Hurry up and wait? Nothing happens, nothing happens, nothing happens . . . then bang, all hell breaks loose."

"Is it about to?"

Nitti laughed, patted Michael on the leg. "I just wanted to watch you for a few days. Let you get used to me, so's you could see how things go around here."

"And size me up a little?"

"And size you up a little . . . Ready for a real job?"

"Give the orders, Mr. Nitti. I'll carry them out."

Nitti rested the milk glass on a nearby coffee table, on a coaster, then shifted on the couch, his arm on the back of the sofa; the intimate nature of the conversation should have made Michael feel more relaxed, and didn't.

"You see, Michael, because you're Sicilian, you have the potential to go a long way. Hey, don't get me wrong—we ain't biased against nobody. A good earner is a good earner. You met Guzik the other day—he's a Jew, but what the hell do we care? He's smart, so he's one of our top people."

"That's the American way," Michael said, hoping no irony showed through.

"It is. It's what you fought for. Still, blood is blood, and we Sicilians run this business. To be more than an errand boy, though, you need to be a 'made' man."

"I don't understand."

Nitti shrugged. "Here again, it's a blood thing. When you've taken a life, in the line of duty, you'll be in a position to be made. Invited inside. It's that simple."

"Who do you want me to kill?"

Nitti sat there, frozen, for a few moments, then said, "Kid, I was just . . . filling you in. You understand, we don't attract heat no more. One of the reasons Al had to go away was he attracted heat. Too many shootings on public streets, in the subway, red splashed all over the headlines."

"Sounds like it's hard to get 'made,' then."

"It may take time. Years. But we're not the Cub Scouts. Now and then, here and there, the knife and the gun, we turn to them. There are disloyal people who have to be . . . weeded out. There are scores that need to be settled, examples that need to be made. We're just more discreet about it than in Al's heyday."

"How does Mr. Capone feel about retirement? If you don't mind my asking."

Nitti shook his head. "He's not retired, kid. He's still the boss. I run things, but with his approval. Don't ever forget that."

"I won't."

"Now. . . . Like I was sayin', I do have a little job for you. It could get rough . . . I don't think so, but it could, and it's possible things might get messy."

"I'll be fine."

"Any case, Louie will be there to back you up. Also, we have the local cops in our pocket, so even if things get good and goddamn messy, you're in the clear. Understood?"

"Yes."

"You have to go in strong, because this is one of those set-an-example deals I was talkin' about. You ever hear of a guy called Ness?"

"No," Michael said.

"Think back—it was in all the papers maybe ten years ago, early '30s."

"I was just a kid, then. Reading the funnies was my speed."

Nitti grinned; he had large teeth, very white, and Michael wondered if they were real. "Well, if you was readin' *Dick Tracy,* you were close: Ness was one of the feds that got Al on income tax charges; he's a raider type . . . likes to bust up and confiscate property. Costly prick. But dedicated and smart."

"You want me to threaten him? Hurt him?"

"No! Jesus, kid. Settle down."

Nitti explained to Michael that he'd decided to curtail prostitution activities, to head off Ness's vice efforts. But Calumet City—the wide-open little town owned by the Outfit, which catered to servicemen and defense plant workers—was going to be a problem.

"Our partners there," he said, "are kinda cowboys. Whole damn town is like Dodge City or Tombstone or some shit. And I have sent word that the brothels are to be shut down . . . I've made it clear that the strippers can still strip, and can still negotiate fun and games with customers."

"Isn't that prostitution, too?"

"Yeah, but untraceable to us. B-girls, hostesses, not a problem. A lotta girls live in Cal City, and can take guys home to their places, what's the harm, who's to know? But the out-in-the-open whorehouses, they gotta be shuttered."

"Which these cowboys don't want to do?"

Nitti's smirk was disgusted and humorless. "No. Worst of them is a pipsqueak called Frank Abatte. Owns a dozen clubs in Cal City, with us as silent partners, of course. Does just fine with gambling, so he'll make do without the broads. Problem is, he thinks *he's* the boss of Cal City."

"You'd like me to point out that he isn't."

"If you would, Michael. Now, Abatte's got his own crew—couple lads called Vitale and Neglia, both killers, and they can be triggerhappy. . . . You sure you're up for this?"

"Piece of cake," Michael said.

Louie provided the details, explaining a lot about how

Calumet City worked, along the way. The Outfit controlled the town in part because Cal City was in Cook County, but also by political clout. The bartenders, entertainers, taxi drivers, tavern owners, gamblers, prostitutes, strippers, bouncers and so on all lived right there in Calumet City, the riffraff outnumbering the better element.

But even some of the better element voted along with the riffraff, since the sinful two blocks at the extreme northeastern part of town, nudging the Indiana state line, paid the lion's share of the city's taxes by way of high license fees.

This kept property taxes down for those who lived in the neat crackerboxes with well-tended lawns on the intersecting streets of this typical small American town with its city hall, stores, library and churches. The police? Mostly ex-employees of the joints, who spent their time trying not to run over drunks in the town's four patrol cars. The number of Cal City saloons: 308. The number of Cal City cops: fourteen.

Night had fallen by the time Michael and Campagna reached Calumet City's State Street; the sky to the north blazed red, courtesy of the steel mills, which complemented the street's own scarlet hue, countless relentless neons washing the world garish shades of red and yellow and orange. It was as if the city were on fire, names screaming out of the conflagration: *Rainbow, Ron-da-voo, 21 Club, Playhouse, Show Club, Club Siesta, Oasis, Rip Tide.*

Wasn't quite nine and things hadn't started to hop yet, the sidewalks populated but not thronged; uniforms from every branch of the service could be spotted as well as the rough faces and leather and denim jackets of mill and factory workers.

These were ordinary storefronts that had been converted into saloons and clubs, and most had big picture windows through which the activities within—sometimes a little band tearing it up, or comic telling jokes, but also strippers working runways—could be glimpsed as a come-on.

Michael prowled down the street in the Ford, the electric fire reflected on the windshield and bathing both their faces; finding a parking place here was tougher than downtown Chicago.

Campagna pointed out a spot in front of a fire hydrant, and Michael obediently pulled in.

"We don't pay *any* kinda fine in Cal City," Campagna said, getting out into the neon noon.

Campagna wore a wide-lapeled gray suit, presently orange, and a darker gray fedora, scarlet at the moment. Michael's dark brown suit, from Marshall Field's, was a little big for him, to accommodate the nine millimeter Browning in his shoulder holster; later he'd get something tailored. He wore no hat. He too was tinted orange and red.

Right in front of them, through a window, they could see past the bartender into the club, where over the heads of seated patrons, a pale shapely woman on a behind-the-bar runway was removing her G-string, her pasties already off.

"Must be kinda different for ya," Campagna said with a knowing chuckle.

They began to walk down the sidewalk, weaving in and out among mostly male strollers. As they moved past one joint after another, various musical styles asserted themselves: honkytonk; jazz; blues; even polka music . . . here an accordion, there the mournful wail of a clarinet or earthy moan of a saxophone, country shuffles and stripper-friendly tom-toms courtesy of a succession of low-rent Krupas.

"Different how?" Michael asked.

Campagna snorted a laugh. "Well, you musta never seen the likes of this, before. I mean, they don't have this kinda fun in DeKalb, right?"

"No they don't."

But they did in Manila. And Michael wasn't terribly impressed by the strident sinning of Cal City. He was a veteran not only of the war in the Philippines, but of dives with names like the Santa Ana, the Zamboanga, the Circus Club, and the Yellow Den. Joints where Filipina babes were too bored to walk the streets, making the customers come to the bar stools where they sat, and God help the guy who didn't know these doll-like beauties had been taught to use knives since childhood; a town where even the best hotels had prominent signs saying:

FIREARMS ARE PROHIBITED ON PREMISES; PLEASE CHECK GUNS AT DOOR.

Yes, Cal City had wide-open gambling; you could hear the rattle of dice from the street, slot machines, roulette wheels, birdcages, games of poker, right out in the open. But in Manila there was all that plus Jai alai and cockfights and the ponies.

"Yeah, Louie," Michael said, dryly. "Hick kid like me can only say, 'wow.' . . . Where can we find our friend Frankie Abatte?"

"One of a half-dozen places. You wanna get a steak first?"

"I'd rather eat, after."

"He might not be in yet; it's not even nine. This place is barely woke up. Anyway, we oughta chow down before it gets too drunk out, in Cal City. People puking around me takes the edge off my appetite."

This seeming a good point, Michael followed Campagna to the Capitol Bar and Lounge, which had a fancy awning (CONTINUOUS ENTERTAINMENT!) and occupied a defunct bank that looked vaguely familiar. Maybe he and his father had robbed it. Probably the fanciest joint in town, with a number of well-dressed slumming couples in attendance, the Capitol featured an attractive blonde in a black ballgown who played the organ and sang current hits with a nice smile and pitch that nestled in the cracks of the Hammond.

"What's the story on Abatte's boys?" Michael asked.

Both men were eating rare T-bones smothered in grilled onions and mushrooms, with french fries on the side. The blonde was butchering "Blues in the Night."

"Vitale's tall, dark, looks sleepy," Campagna said. "He ain't. Usually kind of duded up. The other one, Neglia, is short and squat. Froggy-lookin' guy, a slob. Dangerous."

"What do they do for Abatte?"

"Rough people up who welsh on gambling debts. I hear Vitale's the one who does the shooting. Neglia, he beats on people, while Vitale holds a gun on 'em."

"Thanks. Always good to know the players."

"Well, Abatte himself's more dangerous than his boys. Time

to time, he makes a point of putting a bullet in a welsher's head his own self, so that word gets around what a hard case he is."

"Nice to know."

Campagna cut into his steak, blood running. "Squirt's got a big sense of himself. Likes to throw his weight around, like little guys do, sometimes."

Campagna himself was on the small side, but Michael said nothing, and managed not to smile.

"Will they have guns on them?" Michael asked.

"Mutt and Jeff will. The boss, he'll have a gun and probably a shiv in his desk. But he likes to wear a tux and act the big shot, and a gun under the arm ruins the cut of a tux, you know. The line."

"Yeah. Fred Astaire hardly ever packs a rod."

Campagna thought about that for a second, then laughed. "Hey, that's funny. . . . Kid—you don't look nervous."

"Should I be?"

"You're puttin' that steak and fries away, just fine."

"Is this a test, Louie?"

"No! No, hell no, kid. It's just, I'd be nervous, if I was thrown into this pit, for the first time. Little slice of hell, like Cal City."

"This isn't hell, Louie. Purgatory, maybe."

They began checking specific clubs of Abatte's; he had offices in the back of all of them.

In the 21 Club, where the decor ran to college pennants, a skinny stripper with an appendicitis scar was bumping and grinding and all the lipstick in the world couldn't hide the horsiness of her face. But the young army trainees sitting along the runway were staring up at her pubic thatch in awe, perhaps just figuring out where they came from.

At the bar, drinking Coke from a bottle, his back to the naked woman, was a little boy of perhaps ten in a plaid shortsleeve shirt and jeans, seated way up on a stool, kicking his legs in boredom.

"Stripper's kid, probably," Campagna said with a shrug.

In the Club Siesta, a little Mexicale combo played for another stripper; at the Oasis, a bigger band, six pieces, offered up swing and boogie-woogie tunes, filling a postage stamp dance floor, the men keeping their hats on because nobody stayed at any one of these joints long—whole point was to go up and down the street sampling sin.

The smell of cheap beer common to all these joints Michael found repellent, and all of them were filled with gray-blue clouds of cigar and cigarette smoke—no wonder the steel mill hands felt at home, here.

Whatever the theme of the club, the ambience was the same: skimpy decorating failing to deliver on neon promises, crude unprofessional murals of pin-up girls often drawn directly on otherwise unpainted walls, cheap wooden tables cluttered with beer bottles and ashtrays, where men sat with women they usually hadn't come in with.

The floozies were not dolled up—they looked like ordinary factory or shopgirls, if a little harder; and Michael could not be sure if these were hookers or just pick-ups. Party girls or pros, Campagna explained that such shenanigans were fine with Nitti— this kind of thing could not be policed by Ness.

In several joints, however, Michael noted women taking men by the arm—sailors and other servicemen, and steel mill hands— and disappearing up back stairways. Each time, Campagna gave his young friend a knowing look and nod.

And in every joint, Campagna asked to see Mr. Abatte and, in every joint, Mr. Abatte was not in.

The Ozark had a three-piece hillbilly band including a balladeering guitarist, with a slightly larger sawdust-covered dance floor. This was a rough crowd, and a bouncer had to break up a couple of brawling steel workers at the bar, fighting over a young woman who seemed bored to tears, blowing smoke rings while they hammered at each other.

This cleared (and knocked over almost) every stool at the bar, at least momentarily, and Campagna seized the moment to approach the bartender, a bald bruiser with a cigarette in his tight lips and a white shirt and black tie.

Campagna asked, "Mr. Abatte in?"

"Maybe. Who wants him?"

"Frank Nitti."

"You're not Frank Nitti."

"You're not Frank Abatte."

The bartender mulled over that conundrum for a moment. Customers were returning to the scene of the brawl, turning stools right side up and climbing aboard.

"I'll let them know you're here," the bartender said, and used a phone down the bar.

Several minutes later, as a courtesy, the bartender brought them draw beers. Campagna nodded to the guy, but neither man drank them. Michael didn't care for the stuff, and he had an idea Campagna feared a Mickey.

Just enough time had gone by to make Michael hope he'd never hear a country fiddle player again when a door to one side of the bar opened. Framed there was a toad-like man in a rumpled light blue gabardine and a dark blue porkpie hat about the same color as his five o'clock shadow.

Michael glanced at Campagna, raising his eyebrows in a silent question that Campagna answered with a curt nod: this was Abatte's man Neglia, all right.

Campagna headed over but Michael put a hand on the older man's shoulder.

His whisper barely audible over the country and western racket, Michael said gently, "Let me lead the way, Louie."

Louie paused, and bestowed another curt nod: Nitti had indeed meant for Michael to handle this.

Unbuttoning his suitcoat, Michael stepped out front. At the doorway, Neglia held up a thick hand, traffic cop fashion. The thug's round head rested on a mammoth double chin atop a neckless frame; but Neglia was more massive than fat, the shoulders and arms powerful-looking.

"I don't know you," the toad-like toady said thickly.

"I don't know you," Michael said.

"But I know him," Neglia said, with a gesture toward Campagna.

"Now that we've established who you know and who you don't know," Michael said, "let's see Mr. Abatte."

"You don't have an appointment."

"He's not a goddamn dentist. Stand aside."

Neglia scowled. "You don't talk to me that way."

"I'm talking for Frank Nitti. Stand aside."

Campagna, behind Michael, said, "What are you, Neglia? The bridge troll? Get the fuck outa the way."

Neglia's sigh came out his nose and mouth simultaneously in a foul wave of garlic. Michael's eyes damn near teared up. Then the toad turned and led them into a short hallway, Campagna shutting the door behind them. At another door, Neglia knocked shave-and-a-haircut.

"Nitti's guys!" Neglia called.

"Okay!" a deep voice responded.

Neglia opened the door, went in first, allowed Michael and Campagna to step inside, then closed it behind them. The room was medium-sized and probably looked bigger than it was, usually, since the only furnishings were an old scarred-up desk with chair, with a chair opposite, the wall behind decorated with framed stripper photos, hanging crooked; but the office was in fact crowded.

Frank Abatte—a small, weasel-faced man with thinning black Valentino hair and wide-set dark blue eyes—was seated behind the desk; as advertised, he wore a tuxedo. A hooded-eyed hood, skinny in a sharp gray pinstripe and pearl-gray fedora, stood just behind his boss, at right; this was obviously Vitale.

Along the left wall stood three more individuals—a dumpy cigar-chewing guy in an apron, a tall blond fortyish man in a black vest and slacks, and a heavy-set woman about fifty in a new polka-dot dress as crisp-looking as she wasn't.

Neglia, grinning to himself, trundled over behind his boss. So both Abatte's muscle boys were at his side, bookending him, now.

Abatte grinned, too; he looked like a ventriloquist's dummy come to life, specifically Charlie McCarthy in that tux, without the monocle of course. The desk was bare but for a telephone.

"You Chicago boys stop by at an opportune time," Abatte said, his voice rich and deep, a big sound for a little man. "We were just havin' a little meeting of concerned Cal City citizens."

"Sorta like the Chamber of Commerce," Campagna said.

Abatte folded his hands like a priest about to counsel a couple contemplating marriage. "My fellow owners share with me an interest in keeping our Cal City business happy and thriving and free of interference from the outside."

"You work for Mr. Nitti," Campagna snapped. "Don't ever forget that, Frankie!"

Abatte's disdain was palpable. "Mr. Nitti's a partner, a silent partner, with all of us. He'll get his share. But I don't work for anybody but *Frank Abatte*, get it?"

Michael sat down across from Abatte, crossing his legs, ankle on a knee. Campagna not taking the chair of honor seemed to puzzle the tuxedo-sporting gangster.

"You're a little young, aren't you?" he asked Michael.

Campagna, positioning himself by the door, said, "His name's Michael Satariano. He's new."

With his limited peripheral vision, Michael could not see if the name registered on the group at left. Neglia certainly didn't recognize it; but Vitale's sleepy eyes wakened, a bit. And Abatte's upper lip curled in contempt.

"The war hero," Abatte said, as if tasting the words and not finding them flavorful. He gestured, a sarcastic master of ceremonies. "Ladies and gentlemen . . . we have a special guest. We're privileged to be in the presence of Chicago's own Congressional Medal of Honor winner."

Michael glanced at the trio—the guy in the apron, the man in the vest, the gal in the polka-dot dress; they were exchanging wide-eyed looks.

"Mighta known," Abatte said. "Nitti's sure as hell been wrappin' himself in the flag lately. Shoulda figured he'd recruit the Sicilian Sergeant York. . . . Did he just enlist you for this one mission, kid? What, is seeing you supposed to shame me into doin' the 'right thing'?"

Stepping forward, Campagna said, "Mr. Nitti does not want wide-open whorehouses and jackrolling and cheating our boys in the armed forces—that'll bring heat down on all our heads. *Capeesh?*"

Through clenched teeth Abatte said, "This street was built on brothels. And the heat is *Nitti's* job—it's what we pay him for."

Campagna turned toward the trio of owners. "These war years will be a boom time for Cal City. Don't botch it. Mr. Nitti appeals to your patriotism, and your common sense. Federal heat is—"

Abatte slammed his hand on the desk and everybody but Abatte himself . . . and Michael . . . jumped a little; the phone made a stunted ringing sound.

"You city boys . . . you can run and hide, if you want." Abatte's eyes showed white all around. "This is a wide-open town here, a good time to be had by all. And we intend to keep it that way. Press us on this, and Nitti won't even get his goddamn pound of flesh."

Michael cleared his throat.

Abatte, who seemed to have forgotten about the young man's presence, looked at Michael with a disdainful expression. "You want something, sonny boy?"

Michael said, "Just the answer to a question."

"Ask me and we'll see if it's worth answering."

Michael uncrossed his legs. Quietly he said, "Who do you work for, again?"

Again Abatte slammed a hand onto the desk; the Cal City big shot's other hand, however, had dropped from view, where the man might access a drawer holding a gun and a knife. . . .

Spittle flew: "I work for me, myself and I! Frank Abatte! And no one else."

Michael slipped a hand inside his suitcoat.

Both Vitale and Neglia lurched forward, and Abatte straightened; but Michael raised his other hand, gently, and said, "Please, gentlemen. I just need to get something out to make a point."

The bodyguards settled back, Abatte relaxed, and Michael withdrew the .45 automatic.

Every eye in the room widened, except Michael's.

Pointing the gun from the hip at Abatte, Michael asked, "Who do you work for?"

Abatte's upper lip curled in contempt. "I . . . work . . . for . . . Frank . . . *Abatte*."

Michael shot him in the head.

Time stopped for Abatte, paralyzed him momentarily, his eyes wide, the red hole in his forehead like a third startled eye; then he flopped forward on the desk, hands asprawl, revealing a splash of gore on the wall, between framed askew photos, and a gaping hole in the back of his head.

Still seated, Michael shot Vitale, who was clawing for his gun under his own suitcoat, in the throat; this Michael did because he anticipated the gurgling gargling blood-frothing horror that would ensue would distract and discourage the others.

He had saved Neglia for last, because he knew Vitale was the more competent of the two; but the toad had a .38 in hand and his teeth clenched, a fraction of a second away from shooting, when Michael fired, another head shot, which knocked the porkpie hat off and splattered blood and brains and bone onto a stripper's picture, straightening it.

Behind Michael, Campagna was training a gun on the owners, who were standing with their hands up and their jaws down.

Without getting up, Michael swiveled calmly in the chair to the trio of owners, who stood against the wall as if they'd like to disappear behind it. He spoke to the man in the apron.

"And who do *you* work for?"

"Frank Nitti!"

"Who do you work for?"

"Frank Nitti."

"Who do you work for, ma'am?"

"Frank Nitti."

"Any questions about the new prostitution policy?"

"No."

"No."

"No."

"Good," Michael said.

He rose and went to the door, opened it, looked out at the hallway, letting in some country swing; the fiddle sounded better to him now—it had a folksy quality he found soothing. No sign that anybody had heard anything over the natural din of the Ozark.

Returning his attention to the owners, he said, "By the week-end, these wide-open whorehouses are past history."

Eager nods, all around.

"By the way—any of you see anything tonight? I hear it gets rough around here, sometimes."

But none of them had heard or seen a thing.

"It's early," Michael said, with a shrug. "Might be some excitement, yet."

The guy in the vest had pissed himself; that was a good sign.

"Why don't you get back to your places of business, then," Michael said pleasantly, nodding toward the door.

They scrambled out—thanking Michael as they went.

He was smiling about that when Campagna said, "That's three eyewitnesses you let go, there, Mike."

"You think any of them's a problem?"

Campagna, who'd been frowning in thought, began to laugh. "No. No, I don't. Joe Batters does the collecting around these-here-parts, and he'll back your play . . . Kid, you're a caution."

Michael re-holstered the .45. "Just so Mr. Nitti doesn't think I stirred up the heat."

Campagna was going to the phone; one of Abatte's dead hands seemed to be reaching for it.

"Hell no," Campagna said, lifting the receiver. "Just let me call the Cal City police chief."

"Why him?"

"Jesus, kid," Campagna said and shrugged. "Somebody's gotta dump these stiffs!"

5

THE COLONY CLUB, AT 744 NORTH
Rush, had two devout neighbors: the
Methodist Publishing House, next door,
and (a block south) Quigley Preparatory
Seminary, where young boys prepared for
the priesthood. The Colony, however,
catered to sinners seeking not salvation but
a damned good time.

And the ultra-ritzy club's pretty hostess, Estelle Carey—a willowy green-eyed
golden blonde who looked ten years
younger than her thirty-one years—saw to
it that the patrons got whatever kind of
good time they might desire.

At the moment that meant Estelle
singing. Perched on a stool in a slit-up-
one-side dark blue gown, bodice covered
in sequins, in a corner of the bar next to a

baby grand, her accompanist Roy tickling the keyboards lovingly, Estelle kept couples at tables nearby enthralled with her small, sweet, smoky voice. Her favorites were Dinah Shore and Ella Fitzgerald, and she sounded a little like both, which was intentional, aided by doing a lot of their hit tunes.

Estelle was a star attraction at the Colony; though various big bands that played in the spacious dining room were national names, locally the name Estelle Carey meant something—something naughty, perhaps, but something.

She'd started out life part of the crowd, with a last name—Smith—to prove it. Daddy Smith died when Estelle was a toddler, and much of her childhood had been spent in an orphanage; she'd left high school early on for waitressing. But her beer-budget background had somehow spawned champagne tastes, and her salary and tips from a Logan Square restaurant had been supplemented by sharing more than just a smile and a wink with male customers.

Estelle had always liked men—liked the power her good looks gave her over these powerful creatures, enjoyed the physical act of lovemaking in a way many girls at least claimed not to. From a junior high teacher she'd seduced at thirteen to every boss she'd ever had, Estelle had improved her life by generously sharing her considerable charms.

Still, she did not in the least consider herself a harlot—she had never made love for money in her life.

On the other hand, she'd never gone to bed with a man without the next morning receiving money to help out her sick mom, or make up a rent shortfall, real or imagined. Now and then, over the years, a steadier boy friend might lavish gifts upon her, from fur coats to rent-free apartments. This was to be expected.

Waitressing at Rickett's on North Clark Street had been Estelle's breakthrough into a better life. Not that Rickett's was posh; heck, it was just your typical white-tile restaurant. But it was open all night and attracted show people and the artsy crowd from Tower Town . . . and even Outfit guys like Nicky Dean.

With his mop of well-oiled black hair, Nicky was like some

smooth George Raft-type movie gangster had walked down off the screen and into her life. Tall, dark, roughly handsome, Nicky looked like a million in a dinner jacket; he had style and charm and clout with the Outfit . . . also a wife, a little chorus cutie he'd married maybe ten years ago, but Mrs. Dean was sickly, and Nicky treated Estelle better than a husband treated a wife.

Still, some would say Nicky made Estelle earn every expensive stitch of clothing and even "pay" the rent on various fancy flats, by putting her to work. Even now, people said that—look at her in the Colony Club, singing for her supper.

But Estelle Carey had never been lazy. She liked to work, and just as Nicky was no one-woman man, she enjoyed other lovers, just not on an extended basis. Nicky didn't even mind Estelle entertaining the occasional Outfit guy, because he seemed to take pride in having them taste a dish just once or twice of which he could partake any ol' time.

What had gotten Estelle into the newspaper gossip columns— and turned her into a local celebrity—was her continuing status as Chicago's most famous 26 girl. She rarely played the game herself these days—the bar at the Colony had half a dozen stations where gorgeous girls took care of those duties.

Twenty-six was a game played all over Chicagoland in watering holes from the lowliest gin mill to the poshest nightspot. At a table or podium, an attractive, well-built doll would shake dice in a leather cup and roll for drinks with a male customer. Though playing for quarters, the customer—who was often drunk—might manage to lose as much as ten dollars.

What had got Estelle into the papers, though, was taking a Texas oil millionaire for an astonishing $10,000 at the penny-ante game. And the guy loved her for it. Always sought her out when he was in town.

Which was what made Estelle Carey the queen of dice, and provided the basis for what she taught her girls: a man needed to feel that a 26 girl was his friend, even a sort of sweetheart, and that the bar was a home away from home.

The 26 girls at the Colony, handpicked, handtrained by Estelle, knew how to spot compulsive gamblers or otherwise potential highrollers, and (earning a nice bonus for each sucker) steer them to the "private" club upstairs—a full casino where many fortunes were lost and only a handful were made . . . Nicky's and Estelle's, among them.

The club had an art-moderne decor out of an RKO musical—chromium and glass and shiny black surfaces. The casino upstairs was less chic—just a big open space with draped walls and subdued lighting, noisy and smoky, rife with the promise of easy money that almost never delivered, and the promise of easy women, who more frequently did.

That had been Estelle's idea, and Nicky told her how Capone, Nitti and others in the Outfit had praised her genius: no one ever figured out a better blow-off for a burnt customer than this. A highroller who'd been stung—often with an off-duty 26 girl on his arm, who'd egged him on at the tables—would be invited up to the third floor, where private suites awaited. After some behind-closed-doors time with a beautiful dame, many a loser walked away from the Colony Club wearing a winner's smile.

Estelle was good to her girls. On slow nights, she allowed them to take a non-highroller up to a suite for fifty bucks; on a less slow night, the price bumped to a hundred (either way, the house got its cut). If the Colony's first floor was largely legit, the second-floor casino and third-floor beauty parlor were definitely not; this meant hefty monthly payments to the cops and politicians, and the Outfit was obviously a fifty-fifty partner.

Estelle was perched on her stool, singing "Fools Rush In," when she noticed that kid again, sitting at the bar, almost looking like a grown-up in a sharp gray suit, pretending not to be watching her as he nursed his Coca-Cola. She hadn't seen him right away—this was Saturday night, so the place was hopping, the tables filled, a fog of cigarette smoke drifting across the bar.

Michael Satariano. The city's celebrated Congressional Medal of Honor winner. And she was pretty sure the kid had a crush on her. Which didn't depress her, not hardly—he was one good-looking boy; the scar near his left eye only gave him character, helping him not seem so goddamn, cradle-robbing young. . . .

Something maternal rose within her, a surprising sensation, all things considered; but part of her wanted to scream at him, *Get away from these people!* What was a kid who had the world by the tail doing hanging out with Outfit goons? She herself'd had no other choice, really; the likes of Nicky Dean had been her best ticket to a better life.

But this kid shook the President's hand! This kid was famous, not just locally, but all across the nation. Wasn't a business in the country that wouldn't give him a job, a good job, a *real* job, and on a damn platter.

And yet there he'd been, three nights ago, sitting next to Louie Campagna at a table in this very bar, after closing; she'd been sitting at that same table, too.

Campagna had explained about Eliot Ness and the crackdown on prostitution; and that Mr. Nitti was concerned about the Colony Club's third floor.

As they spoke in the bar, the lights were up, and two bartenders were sweeping. She and the two Outfit guests sat in a corner near the piano, out of earshot of the help.

Estelle, sitting with a leg crossed, showing her knee, was sipping a Coke. She had noted that the young man with Louie Campagna—Louie was drinking Scotch rocks—had also ordered a Coke.

Rather than respond to Campagna's question, Estelle asked the kid, "You don't drink when you're working?"

"I don't drink at all," the kid said. A nice mellow voice.

"Well, do you smoke?"

"No."

Estelle laughed. "Neither do I. Girlfriend of mine, long time ago, told me I'd look young longer if I didn't smoke or drink."

Without a smile, the kid said, "It's working."

Despite the babyface on him, something smoldered under there. . . .

Louie sat forward, mildly irritated. "Estelle—this is business, here. We're talking about things."

To the kid, she said, "I've seen you somewhere. . . . Louie, he's new. Right?"

"Right. And the reason you recognize him is 'cause he's Michael Satariano."

Estelle snapped her fingers. "Medal of Honor! Yeah!"

This had led to a conversation mostly between her and Campagna, with Satariano embarrassed and Louie actually proud that a war hero like this had chosen to honor his Sicilian heritage by going into business with his *paisans.*

But they had finally gotten to the subject of the meeting, Louie saying, "This club, it's famous. Hell, Estelle, you're famous. A Rush Street landmark—so you got to watch yourself, this third floor."

Polite but cold, she replied, "I would think the gambling would be a bigger problem. That's wide open. What happens on the third floor is . . . discreet."

Louie shook his head. "You ain't listening, Estelle. This ain't about anything except Eliot fuckin' Ness havin' a hard-on against Al Capone and Frank Nitti. Guy's lookin' to make another name for himself, on the Outfit's back, get it?"

"I get it. And gambling isn't Ness's bailiwick."

"No. But whorehouses is."

Estelle lifted both eyebrows. "My girls aren't prostitutes. And I'm not a madam."

Campagna's lumpy face registered skepticism. "Well, do you think that G-man's gonna make whatever-the-hell distinction it is *you're* makin'? Kid yourself all you want, Estelle—you won't kid this Ness character."

Her eyes tightened. "Does this have anything to do with Nicky? With the Hollywood case?"

Since late last year, Estelle had been running the Colony Club herself. Nicky, who'd been Nitti's watchdog over those union goons Bioff and Browne, had been convicted in the movie union extortion case; poor baby started doing his eight years last December.

"Maybe not directly," Campagna said. "Back ten years ago, when the T-men was building their case against Al, Ness was hitting us hard in the pocketbook. So now he hits our brothels, while the other feds build this Hollywood case against us. Same old double-team, Mr. Nitti says."

"But with Nicky in stir, and Bioff and Browne inside, too," she said, "surely the movie-union thing is over."

Estelle had never really understood what the fuss was about, anyway; all Bioff and Browne had done was sell strike prevention insurance to movie moguls, and all Nicky did was mule the money back to the Outfit.

"Word is," Campagna was saying, "the G's trying to build a conspiracy case. Feds're crawling all over town usin' information Bioff and Browne spilled, copping a plea, gettin' a shorter sentence."

"Those two union goons are known liars. Don't they both have perjury raps on their records?"

"That's why the feds are lookin' for real witnesses. And that's why Ness is back. Estelle, restrict the third floor to compin' high-rollers. No exchange of money, honey."

"I hear you."

"Do you? I hope so. Let me spell it out: no fuckin' whoring, Estelle. Should we get that faggelah piano-player in here, so I can sing it for you?"

"No, Louie. I hear every note."

"Good. And I know you got an ear for music."

They had gone, then—Louie and his Medal of Honor winner. But she had noticed that on the occasions when Campagna had gotten either tough or profane with her, the kid had winced, just a little. Like he didn't approve of a lady being talked to in that fashion.

Estelle really liked that.

The next night the kid had come back, alone. Late, on a much slower night. In a sportshirt and slacks, looking damn near collegiate, he sat at the bar, drinking Cokes, listening to her, watching her discreetly, even trading a couple of smiles with her.

On her break, Estelle took the stool next to him. "Hey, hero," she said. "Slumming?"

His smile was boyish, shy. "This is a beautiful place."

95

"It is nice."

"You . . . you sing great."

"Thanks." She laughed a little. "But I think it's more the talking-dog deal."

He frowned in confusion. "Pardon?"

With an elaborate shrug, she said, "They've heard of me, the notorious 26 girl. Gangster's moll. When I sing, and carry a decent tune, and don't screw up the words, they're bowled over. . . . See, a talking dog doesn't have to say anything impressive."

"Just talk," he said, with a half-smile that was wholly adorable.

"That's right. Just talk's enough."

His forehead tensed. "Listen. . . . Louie's really not a bad guy."

"Oh, I know that."

"He had a job to do, the other night. Me, too. This situation with the feds, it's serious. I'm sure he didn't mean any offense."

"I'm sure Louie didn't. Just tryin' to make his point. Is that why you came back tonight?"

"I guess. . . . I was curious to hear you sing. We came in after you were finished, other night."

"Wanted to hear the dog talk?"

He flashed the half-smile again, though his voice had a touch of embarrassment. "Miss Carey . . . a dog you're not."

"Well I can be a little bitchy, at times."

"I doubt that. . . . Anyway, you sing swell. Like Dinah Shore and Doris Day all rolled into one."

"Oooo . . . makes me sound fat."

Abashed, blinking, he said, "Oh, you're not fat."

She kept him wriggling on the hook, saying, "You really know how to compliment a girl."

And now he blushed.

Fucking blushed!

She touched his hand. "You're really very sweet, Michael. . . . May I call you Michael?"

"I'd like that."

"And you'll call me Estelle. . . . Michael, why did you take a job with Frank Nitti?"

He shrugged. "I'm Sicilian. Good opportunity to make a lot of money before I'm very old."

"You may be surprised to learn that a lot of Sicilians aren't mobsters. I'd go so far as to say most aren't."

"I know that." He stared evasively into his Coke. "I just like the . . . charge you get. I was in combat and it's a kind of intense feeling. Adrenaline rush."

"Are you kidding me?"

He looked up at her, something plaintive in his expression. "Miss Carey . . . Estelle. Could we talk about something else?"

So they had chatted about their backgrounds, and how he was staying a few blocks away at the Seneca Hotel. This was no surprise to her, as the Seneca was home to a lot of Nitti's gangsters. Then it was time for her to go back on, and she saw him slip out, during her third number.

Now tonight the young hero was back, sitting at the bar again. That well-tailored gray pinstripe indicated Outfit money had already started to flow for him. But he seemed troubled to her, sitting slumped over that Coke like a boozehound on his twelfth whiskey and soda.

The last song of her set was, "Our Love Is Here to Stay," and the couples at the tables gave her a nice hand. Michael's eyes weren't on her as she slipped onto the stool next to him.

"Back for more punishment, hero?"

"You sing great. Really pretty."

"Thanks. . . . You look kinda blue tonight."

"I guess I'm a little homesick."

"Well, hell, soldier—how far *is* DeKalb, anyway?"

He tasted his tongue. "Real far. Farther every day."

She studied him. "You got a girl back there?"

"You . . . you remind me of her."

Estelle was about to kid the kid about using such an old line on her, but from the pain around his eyes, she knew he meant every word.

"Does your best girl," she asked gently, "know what you're up to, here in the big city?"

His eyes widened with a touch of horror. "Not hardly."

"Then why *are* you up to what you're up to, Michael? Every door in this town, every door in this *country*, is open to you!"

He turned to her, the glass eye as cold and expressionless as the rest of his face; but the good eye, the real eye, was on fire. "I have things I need to do."

For a moment, she felt frightened, and she wasn't sure why. She'd read the newspapers stories about all the Japs this kid had killed, but it had no meaning to her; it didn't seem real—Japs dying in movies were just milk bottles getting knocked down by baseballs at a carnival.

Now, suddenly, she sensed the killer beside her.

And yet she also sensed a sweet, troubled boy.

She put a hand on his arm. "Would you like to go somewhere more private? Where maybe we can talk?"

"I . . . I don't know if I want to talk."

She stroked his cheek. "You don't have to, sweetheart. But you look like you could use some company—and I don't mean Louie Campagna."

He thought for a moment, then nodded.

A self-service elevator off the second floor took them to the third, where she led him by the hand into one of the ten private suites. The spacious single room had a fireplace, light blue plaster walls, white trim, white carpet, modern dark blue furnishings, several framed abstract paintings in blue and white, a large double bed with blue satin spread, a small wet bar, and a window onto the neons of Rush Street, semi-visible through a sheer blue curtain. She went to a table lamp with a translucent blue shade and a dim bulb and switched it on; this was all the light they'd need.

She walked him to the bed and kicked off her heels, nodding permission to him to do the same. His Florsheims off, she helped him out of his sportcoat, and carefully hung it over a chair near the bed. She was mildly surprised not to find a shoulder holster. Then she loosened and removed his tie, and took him by the hand and led him to the bed, where they lay on top of the smooth spread, generous pillows behind them. He was on his back, staring blankly at the ceiling; she lay on her side, chin propped on the heel of her hand, studying him.

"What's on your mind, handsome?"

"Are you Catholic?"

Her eyes widened. This was not a response she'd anticipated. "Well . . . that depends on how you look at it."

He turned his face toward hers, forehead tightened with interest. "How so?"

"I was raised that way, for a while. But I haven't been to mass, for a long, long time."

"Did you ever go to confession?"

"Well, sure."

He sighed. Looked at the ceiling again. "I went today."

"Did you, now."

"I feel kind of sick about it."

"Why?"

"Because I . . . I don't know. I guess I feel like a hypocrite."

"And why's that?"

"It was a big sin."

"Well. I guess sins come in all sizes."

"They don't come much bigger than this. Anyway, I'm not sure I believe, anymore."

"Then why go?"

"Habit. Tradition. A feeling that . . . my father would have wanted me to."

"Listen, don't knock it. You *had* a father. More than I can say. So what if it comes with a little baggage."

"I'm not knocking it." A painful, painfully young earnestness came into his face. "But my father *believed*. He really thought he could do something . . . something really bad, and a few words from a priest could wash it away."

"Who's to say it can't?"

He looked at her again. "But what if you commit that same sin again? What if when you're asking for forgiveness, you know you have every intention of doing that sin again?"

"Well . . . maybe it's sort of one sin at a time. You know, a matter of keeping up with 'em, making the bookkeeping easier, for you and God both, not to mention the stupid priest. . . . I'm sorry you're so unhappy."

■■■■■

99

This seemed to surprise him. "Am I?"

"Well, this, whatever-sin-it-is, is bothering you, isn't it?"

"Not really."

"But you're . . . talking about it . . . thinking about it. . . ."

"Yeah. But I'm not really feeling anything."

"Well, sure you are. You feel guilty, or you wouldn't go to church and confess."

He gave her a mildly annoyed look. "I told you. That was habit or duty or something."

"You don't feel sad? You don't feel guilty?"

He didn't say anything for a while; his gaze returned to the ceiling. "I haven't felt anything, really, not for a long time."

"Oh, yeah? What about feeling homesick? What about that girlfriend of yours?"

He shifted onto his side, leaned his elbow against a blue satin pillow, and a hand against his head. He bestowed her that wonderful half a smile again. "Hell, Estelle. That's just biology."

She grinned, laughed. "How old are you, hero?"

"Twenty-two."

"I'm almost ten years older, you know."

"You don't look it."

"Not in this light, anyway. But I just wanted to make sure you were okay with it."

"With what?"

"An older woman kissing you."

And she did. A soft, slow, tender kiss that he responded to well. They kissed for five minutes; necked like she was as nearly a high school kid as he was. Then they petted, and she found it surprisingly exciting; breathing hard, she slipped off the bed and out of her gown. He was sitting on the edge of the bed, unbuttoning his shirt.

Soon the lamp had been switched off and they were naked under silk sheets, and he was a sweet, gentle lover at first, kissing her face, her neck, her breasts, and she slipped her head under the covers to take him into her mouth, enjoying the shudder she invoked. Finally she climbed on top of him and rode, because she liked to control men, and he seemed glazed, as he looked up at her body washed as it was in blue neon from the street. She came so hard she thought her head would explode, but he restrained himself and let her go there alone; then he eased her off him and onto her back and mounted her, and—displaying an intensity that thrilled and frightened her—brought her to another climax, and himself, collapsing into her arms, where she held him close, patting him like a crying child as his breathing returned to normal.

"Did you feel *that*, cowboy?" she asked.

"I felt that," he admitted.

"But just biology, huh?"

"Where would we be," he said, "without it?"

ELIOT NESS WAS SITTING ON A BENCH IN A MUSEUM studying a massive pastel painting called *A Sunday on La Grande Jatte*, depicting Parisian city dwellers on the bank of the Seine on a Sunday afternoon.

Right now it was Sunday afternoon in Chicago, at the Art Institute, that massive Italian Renaissance-style building with its famous bronze lions guarding broad steps facing Michigan Avenue. On the second floor, in chronologically arranged galleries, were the paintings of masters from the thirteenth century to the present.

Ness was no intellectual, but he found the museum interesting and restful, and this particular painting was at once impressive in its majestic size and soothing in its subject matter. Rounded shapes from the sloping bank to the bustles of the ladies with their parasols pleased his eyes, people strolling, sailing, fishing, lounging; you could look at it for a long time without being bored.

The museum was not busy; people in Chicago were out and about on beaches on this sunny July day, up to the same kind of things as painter Georges Seurat's subjects.

And no one at all was around when Michael Satariano sat next to Ness on the bench.

"In future we'll minimize these public meetings," Ness said quietly. "Just find a public pay phone."

"All right." Michael wore a sportshirt and chinos; he looked like a college boy—undergrad. "I don't think you're going to like what I have to tell you."

Ness was disappointed but not surprised to hear that Nitti was shutting down his brothels in anticipation of the G-man mounting raids. He was also not surprised to hear that he himself was a topic of conversation among the hoodlums.

"They say you resigned from your Cleveland police job," Michael said, "in disgrace."

He shifted on the bench, a little. "It was a matter of politics. I was an appointee of the previous administration."

"Not 'cause of some hit-and-run thing."

"That's an overstatement and over-simplification."

Michael shrugged. "I'm just telling you what they talk about. They think you're trying to use them to recapture a past glory."

"What do you think, Michael?"

Michael's unreadable gaze switched from the painting to Ness. "I think they're a step ahead of you. Frank Nitti is a smart man."

"Very smart. Listen, Mike . . . there's a place on Rush Street called the Colony Club—I want you to check it out. Big-scale prostitution operates out of there."

A faint smile tickled the boy's lips. "Already been there—Campagna and I called on Estelle Carey. I don't think that'll take you very far."

"Why not?"

"First off, it's a high-hat joint. That's one expensive, tony place. I didn't see one serviceman. And it's not exactly a defense worker hangout, either."

"But there is prostitution."

Michael shrugged. "If that's what you'd call it. From what I understand, these 26 girls and some other hostesses just latch onto a highroller, and if he goes bust, give one more free roll . . . in the hay, this time."

"It's still prostitution."

"I'm not going to tell you your business. But you raid that place, you'll make all kinds of enemies. I saw politicians there, and rich people. And with that wide-open casino, you know the cops are protecting them."

Ness said tersely, "Let me worry about that. What's the story on Calumet City?"

Michael told him how Nitti had laid down the law; there'd no doubt be individual girls selling their wares, but the Cal City cathouses were closing down.

"Kinda rough around there, I hear," Ness said.

"I don't follow."

"Don't you? Surely you saw the papers. Frankie Abatte turned up on a roadside outside Hot Springs, Arkansas—nude and with a bullet in his head."

"Wonder what he was doing down that way?"

"Yeah, and without his two watchdogs, Vitale and Neglia. Of course, you probably saw that in the paper, too—how Vitale turned up dead in a sewer, and Neglia was found in a trunk on La Salle Street, also dead."

Michael made a clicking sound in one cheek. "Wages of sin."

"Tell me you weren't responsible, Michael."

"For hauling Abatte down to Hot Springs? And stuffing those other guys . . . what were their names? In a sewer, and a trunk? Hell no! . . . You mean a car trunk, or a steamer trunk?"

Ness studied the blank face, looking for sarcasm, because there hadn't been any in the tone.

"Car," Ness said patiently. "Michael, I told you when we began this undertaking—"

"Poor choice of words, Mr. Ness."

"I told you that your status as an operative does not extend to committing crimes, just to stay credible among these lowlifes."

"I'm aware of that."

"Any crime you commit, if you're called to an accounting, you'll stand for."

"I know." He looked at Ness, his boyish face hard. "Hypothetically, let's say, if I were in a situation where gunmen had me cornered . . . would responding in kind be out of line?"

"In self-defense, you mean."

"Self-defense, let's call it."

"Well . . ."

"Or should I, in such a case, pull the plug on the operation? Go to the police, and explain that I was undercover and had to defend myself?"

". . . If it was self-defense, then . . . well."

"Hypothetically, Mr. Ness."

"Hypothetically . . . I wouldn't expect you to break your cover, no."

They sat and looked at the painting for a while. Michael had to move his head to take in the big painting, due to his mono-vision.

The young man nodded toward the vast canvas. "Lovely, isn't it? It's all made out of little dots."

"Yes. The eye kind of blurs them into colors and shades."

Michael nodded, saying, "But the artist really just made a lot of little points . . . and they added up to something meaningful. That's nice, isn't it?"

"It's a nice painting."

"Just goes to show you. Sometimes you have to make a point, to make an impression."

Ness, not liking the sound of that, moved on to a new subject. "I'm going to be out of town for a week," he said. "Possibly two. I have eleven other offices around the country to supervise, you know. You have Lieutenant Drury's number, if you need something, or learn something."

"Actually, I may be out of town, myself."

Ness frowned. "Oh?"

"Nitti's meeting with Capone, soon, in Miami Beach. He's talking about sending me down there, as a sort of advance agent."

Urgency in his voice, Ness said, "Try to get a good look at Capone. Get close to him."

Michael said, "I intend to. . . . What's on your mind?"

"Nothing, really. Our people down there have seen damn little of him, lately. He's more and more reclusive."

"Don't worry," Michael said, "I plan to get very close to Capone." He rose. "Good afternoon, Mr. Ness."

Ness remained for another five minutes, not wanting to be seen exiting with Michael. He just sat and stared at the huge painting and wished he could walk into it, and feel the sunshine, and hear the lap of the river, and disappear into a simpler time.

6

BEHIND THE WHEEL OF HIS RENTED '39 Packard convertible, heading out the causeway linking Miami with the face-lifted sandbar of Miami Beach, Michael wondered if the salt breeze was conspiring with the golden-white sunshine to make him feel more relaxed than was, under the circumstances, wise.

He was tooling down Palm Avenue, which bifurcated Palm Island—villas on either side, their backs to Biscayne Bay—on his way to the Capone estate, on this three-quarter-mile-long, man-made key the shape of one of Big Al's trademark cigars.

In the company of numerous servicemen, he had arrived on the Dixie Flyer this morning at seven. On Flagler Street, he selected sunglasses in a curio shop, purchased a tropical white suit and panama-style fedora at a department store, at a pawn shop picked up a spare Army Colt .45, bought white wing tips with black toes at a shoe store, and two boxes of .45 ammo at a sporting goods shop.

Michael had a mid-morning breakfast at a one-arm joint called the Dinner Bell, and was relieved to find that the food went down easy. He'd had a little trouble on the train last night, and wasn't sure if it was nerves or just the rattle and bump of the ride.

Not that this job for Mr. Nitti looked at all taxing. Yesterday the ganglord had filled him in at a table in a private dining room at the Capri Restaurant. Other than Nitti, Michael and occasionally the waiter, no one else was there; even Campagna had been left downstairs.

After lunch, Nitti smoked an expensive, sweetly fragrant cigar while Michael mostly sat and listened, arms folded.

"You're going in a day ahead of me," Nitti said, "to make sure the security is up to snuff, for my meet with Al."

"Will they know I'm coming?"

"Of course—you'll report to Al's brother John . . . 'Mimi,' only you call him 'Mr. Capone' until or unless he says otherwise. Mrs. Capone, Mae, Al's wife, lives there with a few of her family members. There's a good fifteen, twenty armed guards working in shifts, protecting Al."

"Sounds sufficient."

"It's mostly just for Al's peace of mind. Ever since he got out of stir, he's been . . . anxious, about somebody out of his past maybe showin' up to settle scores."

"Really."

Nitti shrugged, blew a smoke ring. "I know, I know—it's what the head shrinkers call paranoia."

How did Nitti know that term, Michael wondered; did the gang boss have his own psychiatrist? Campagna said their chief had been depressed after his wife's death, last year.

"Anyway," Nitti said, "make sure the security team's still sharp—that they ain't got fat and sloppy. Been three years since Al's release, you know, with never an attempt of any kind."

"Guys can get lazy under such circumstances."

"Exactly, kid." Nitti leaned forward. Sotto voce, he said, "And you do know I'm also concerned about . . . certain parties. Certain factions."

"Yes," Michael said.

While little direct information had been shared with Michael, he'd gathered from both Nitti and Campagna that Paul "the Waiter" Ricca was contemplating a power play.

"Now I trust Mimi," Nitti said, gesturing with the cigar as if it were a baton and Michael the band. "Al's little brother is a harmless boy. . . . 'Boy,' hell, he must be forty, now. But that's still how I think of him—a damn kid."

"Why's that, Mr. Nitti?"

"Well . . . Mimi never was an achiever. Ran after skirts, mostly . . . but he's got a clean record, and speaks well, so he handles the press for us down there, in Florida. And he supervises the estate . . . and, like me, Mimi cares about Al's welfare."

"Sounds like a good, loving brother."

"He is. But Ricca goes back a long way with the Capones—Al was best man at the Waiter's wedding. So when we put the security staff together, some of 'em came from Ricca's crew."

"I see."

"This meeting I have scheduled with Al, to get approval on my new prostitution policy, among other things . . . that's an ideal opportunity for somebody to take us *both* out."

"And with you and Capone gone," Michael said, "Ricca steps in."

"Not a goddamn doubt in the world, kid. . . . So check out the lay of the land. Talk to people, sniff around, listen to your gut." Nitti clasped Michael's arm. "Report to me when I get down there, and when I do . . . watch my back."

"Mr. Nitti," Michael said, actually feeling a little guilty, "I appreciate the trust you've given me."

Nitti beamed at the young man. "Michael, when I first saw you, I felt like I knew you for years."

". . . I felt the same way, Mr. Nitti."

"If it don't embarrass you, me saying so . . . if I'd had a son, I'da been pleased to have him turn out like you."

Michael frowned in confusion. "But you do have a son, Mr. Nitti . . ."

"Yes, and I'm sure not disparagin' my own fine boy." Though they were alone, Nitti whispered: "He's adopted, you know."

"Oh."

"Anna and me, we never had a son. Or daughter. And my boy . . . you've seen him, he's nine. Smart kid, very smart kid. I don't want him to go into this kind of work. Or if he must, I pray it's when we're one hundred percent legit."

"You think that day will come, Mr. Nitti?"

His eyes tightened. "Under me, it will. Under Ricca? And those crazy wild kids from the Patch? The Outfit'll be peddling heroin on schoolyards."

"I believe that." Michael applied a smile to his face. "It'll be an honor to meet Mr. Capone."

"But you won't," Nitti said, his expression darkening. "At best you'll glimpse the Big Fellow from afar."

"Because he values his privacy?"

"It's more than that. Al developed health problems in stir—his syphilis kicked in, it's as old an enemy of Al's as Ness . . . who's fightin' the syph himself, right?"

"Right," Michael said, summoning another smile.

"Anyway, Al's got his pride. He's put on some weight, hair's gettin' thin—and once in a while he has a little attack, kinda on the order of epilepsy."

"How sad."

"Some convulsive side effect of the crud. Fear of that happening in front of the boys . . . that's what made Al turn reclusive. And become the elder statesman, and rule through me. *Capeesh?*"

"*Capeesh*," Michael said.

"I had my way, you'd sit and talk with him for hours. Got the stories, Al has, still sharp as a tack—just prefers to be remembered as he was in his prime."

"I can understand that."

"You can pay your respects to him, and to me, by taking a good hard look at the Palm Island security."

Which was the job Michael had to do here for Frank Nitti. But he'd also come to Miami to do something for himself, somewhat at odds with the ganglord's goals.

Michael intended to kill Al Capone.

But first he had to tell Capone who he was. He wanted Capone to know that betraying Michael O'Sullivan ten years ago had finally come back to bite him in his fat evil ass. Michael wanted to see in the Big Fellow's eyes the fear and anguish and the realization of just who it was that had come calling.

On the train, thoughts that had danced, tauntingly, at the periphery of his consciousness from the beginning, only now came to the fore, forcing Michael, with the deed a day away, to confront certain realities. . . .

Could he find a way to settle this score without losing his own life? Was there a way to be alive two days from now, with a future of some kind ahead of him? Could he dupe the shrewd Frank Nitti into thinking Michael Satariano had no role in Al Capone's death?

If so, the possibility of a normal life—the smalltown life with Patsy Ann he'd brushed aside for this opportunity to avenge— nagged at him. Wasn't that what he wanted most of all, to replace what had been taken from him, so long ago? A normal life, a family life, with a loving wife and healthy, happy children, in the secure warmth of hearth and home . . . ?

That would have been his dream, at least, if he'd allowed himself to dream it. If he had dared dream it. In a world where men like Capone and Ricca thrived—for that matter a world where the leaders of great nations like Germany and Japan and yes Italy behaved no better than the gangster chiefs of big cities like Chicago—could such a small, mundane dream ever be a reality?

For all the homefront flags and bands and warm welcomes waiting for a "hero" like him, Michael saw around him an America where telegrams announced the loss of a son to loving parents, where a pretty girl of eighteen was a shattered grieving widow, where a high school baseball game was cancelled because last season's star player had been killed in action. And somewhere in the Philippines, right now, his friends and comrades were in prison camps, possibly facing torture, *if* they were lucky enough to be alive. . . .

Michael Satariano—Michael O'Sullivan, Jr.—was a soldier. He could no longer fight the Japanese or the Germans; but he could do his country—and the memory of his dead father, brother and mother—the service of removing from the face of the earth the blight of Alphonse "Scarface" Capone. Who even now, from a distance, ruled the Chicago Outfit, barely having to lift his pudgy fingers.

Little of the mansion was visible from the road, thanks to an eight-foot concrete-block wall. Michael pulled in at the spiked-iron gate before heavy oak portals. No guard met him but, using a house phone on a stucco pillar, he announced himself while still in the Packard, receiving no acknowledgment. He was just starting to think that phone was dead when a slot in one oak door slid open, speakeasy-style, and dark eyes under bushy dark eyebrows gave him the onceover.

The portals swung open, and then the gate, courtesy of a tall, solidly built guard in white slacks and a white shortsleeve shirt, cut by the dark brown of a shoulder holster. Michael waved at the deeply tanned guard and received a nod for his trouble; the Packard headed down the gravelled drive, the doors and gate closing behind him.

To his right was that white concrete wall, to his left an elaborate rock garden; ahead the gravel drive ducked under the archway of a mission-style gatehouse, to curve around to the looming mansion itself. Perhaps a dozen palms surrounded and shaded the impressive beige two-story neo-Spanish stucco structure; the arched windows wore green-and-brown-striped canvas awnings, the flat tile roof also green.

A castle fit for a king—in this case, King Capone.

Michael pulled up into the area where the gravel drive widened to accommodate parking, though only one other vehicle was present, a 1941 aquamarine Pontiac. As Michael got out, a slender dark-haired man in a white suit mirroring his own came out the front door, followed by a colored servant in a black vest and white shirt and dark trousers.

Holding out his hand, the man spoke in a slightly squeaky tenor: "Sergeant Satariano, a delight, an honor, sir. . . . I'm John Capone, but my pals call me Mimi."

Michael's host had an oblong, pleasant face that seemed a more handsome if less forceful version of his famous brother's. His white shirt was open at the neck (Michael had worn a light blue tie).

"Thank you, Mr. Capone," Michael said, shaking hands with Big Al's younger brother, whose grasp was mild despite much enthusiastic arm pumping.

"Make it Mimi, please. This is Brownie, our house boy—he'll get your bag."

Michael nodded to the "boy," who was about forty. Brownie nodded and smiled back.

Mimi slipped an arm around Michael's shoulder and walked him to the side of the house. "Michael . . . is it Michael or Mike?"

"Either."

"Mike, Frank Nitti has nothing but good things to say about you. I was thrilled to get to meet you, and I know Mae feels the same. Medal of Honor! Damn! And you haven't forgotten your Sicilian roots, good for you! . . . I think Sonny's coming over tomorrow to shake your hand, too."

"Sonny?"

"Al's son. He's about your age. He's a mechanic over at the Miami Air Depot—tried to get in the army but he's got a bum ear."

As they strolled along the side of the house—a paved walk and mosaic patios edged it—Michael noted a stocky swarthy tough in a yellow sportshirt and tan trousers; he wore a shoulder holster with a revolver, and was ambling up and down that side of the mansion. Another guard, again in a sportshirt with shoulder holster, sat on a beach chair on one of the patios, reading *Ring* magazine. Another guard, next patio down, sat engrossed in *Spicy Mystery*, a pulp with a naked woman tortured on the cover.

The guards in their casual attire looked like they should be lugging golf clubs on the links, not weapons around the grounds of a gangster's palace . . . though the lawn and shrubs were as carefully tended as any country club's.

Mimi noticed Michael tallying the help and said, "We have five outside, including the gate guard, and two in the house."

"Day and night?"

"Yeah, three shifts. Usually we only have four on the grounds, but 'cause of Frank's concern, I canceled days off. Beefing up, a little."

"Good to hear. Good-size staff."

"Twenty-one guys, all from Chicago. Know their stuff."

Maybe, but every guard was in his mid-thirties or older; in the Outfit, Michael knew, if you hadn't made a mark by your early thirties, you weren't going anywhere. King Capone or not, these were not the first team.

Not that that made them pushovers or any less deadly than any thug with a gun.

And there were a lot of them, with—as Mimi Capone explained—half a dozen living on site, in the gatehouse as well as a two-story Moorish-style cabana, just beyond the endless backyard swimming pool.

"Would you mind pointing out Mr. Capone's room, Mimi?"

"Not at all, Mike—that's it right there."

The younger Capone indicated a second-floor balcony; underneath, on the first floor, was one of those arched windows with its striped awning.

"First floor awnings got to go," Michael said.

"Pardon?"

"Second floor don't matter, but take a look at this."

Michael walked over and demonstrated how he could step on the first-floor window ledge, and hoist himself up on the metal framework of the awning, giving him easy access to Al Capone's balcony.

"Jeez, Mike—I see what you mean."

Michael dusted off his hands as he and Mimi began to walk again. "I want those awnings taken down tomorrow morning, before Mr. Nitti arrives. Okay, Mimi?"

"Not a problem. Of course, Mae won't love it. . . ."

Mimi was a gracious, talkative host, who pointed out all the sights, from a rock pool with tropical fish (Al liked to feed them bread crumbs) and the dock on the north side, which was home to a cabin cruiser (the *Arrow*) and a speedboat (christened *Sonny*). No cement wall encumbered the dockside view of Biscayne Bay— white sunlight careening off white sails, powerboats cutting abstract designs in the blue expanse with their wakes.

Mimi sat Michael down by the pool on one of several deck chairs and went into the cabana to fetch refreshment.

Handing a moisture-sweating bottle of Coke to Michael, a grinning Mimi said, "Frank said you don't drink. He respects that. Me, frankly . . . I think that's plain nuts."

And then Mimi laughed, so Michael laughed, too.

"Beer for me all the way," Mimi said. "Been good to our family. . . . Hey, you know who built this villa? Whose money, I mean, back in the early '20s?"

"No idea."

"Clarence M. Busch of St. Louie!"

"The brewer?"

"None other. When Prohibition came in, one beer baron on hard times had to sell out to another one, on the rise! Ain't life funny?"

"Hilarious," Michael said.

The two men sat there for fifteen minutes, talking, or anyway Mimi talked and Michael listened; the view onto the bay stretched out before them, a soothing presence.

"I have the feeling," Mimi said carefully, "that Frank may doubt the loyalty of some of our boys."

"He didn't say so," Michael lied.

Mimi swigged his beer. "Well, we always keep a tight lid on, when Al and Frank get together. Hell, even I won't be around."

"Oh?"

"Less I know about what's really goin' on, happier I am."

"Don't you live here, Mimi?"

"Actually, no. I got a place down the road."

"Who does, besides half a dozen of your guards?"

Mimi ticked off fingers. "Mae and her sister Muriel, and

Muriel's husband, Louis. Muriel and Louis already skedaddled—
went for a few days' vacation to Fort Lauderdale. Brownie lives off
premises; so does Rose, our maid."

"And of course Mr. Capone lives here."

"Al lives here. And I guess you know the rules, where Al's
concerned."

"I've been told not to bother him. Keep my distance."

"He's uncomfortable with anybody but family. Even the guards
keep ten feet or more away."

"Really."

Mimi nodded. "Al's a cheerful man. Always has been good-
natured. But he came out of prison . . . fearful. You know anything about Alcatraz?"

"Just that it's on a rock near Frisco."

"It was designed for only the most famous inmates. Sort of an
All-Star prison team . . . and some of those guys are psychos—
sick, warped fucks. Al got beat up, more than once. There were
attempts on his life."

"A man in his position makes enemies."

Mimi shook his head, in disgust. "These weren't enemies—
just assholes wanting to take the biggest man in America down.
And enhance their own stupid reputations."

"Must've been hard on your brother."

"You quote me, Mike, I'll deny it . . . but Al's jumpy. Nervous. His greatest fear is some enemy out of his past will come
over those walls and . . . I don't know what."

Michael was already "over" that wall. "You trust your security
force, Mimi?"

"I do. About half of 'em worked for Paul Ricca back home,
you know—and the Waiter ran the toughest crew in Chicago."

Apparently Mimi Capone was unaware of the suspected Ricca
takeover.

"What kind of alarm system do you have?"

"Nothing—just a yappin' terrier that belongs to Muriel. And
the mutt's gone, went on vacation with 'em."

"Mr. Capone's room isn't wired or anything?"

"No. No need. We've got strength in numbers. Firepower."

"You do indeed."

"Security on Palm Island is my job," Mimi said, puffing his chest out. "And I take pride in it. I love my brother. I wouldn't let anything happen to him."

"I hope you don't feel I'm trying to undermine you, in any way."

"Not at all! Frank has a right to check us out before a meet. That was a good catch, those awnings. . . . Ready for the nickel tour, inside?"

The house had fourteen rooms, not counting four baths and a glass-enclosed sun porch. The living room was to the right, as you entered, a banistered stairway to a landing opposite the front door; at left a dining room beckoned.

A large-as-life painting of a somberly attired Capone and a similarly dressed young boy (his son, at a tender age?) loomed from over the fireplace of a cavernous living room. The simple Mission style of the house, with its graceful arches, seemed at odds with the tasteless array of obviously expensive Louis XIV furnishings, complete with scrolls, curved armrests and golden ornamental motifs. The over-upholstered, massive chairs and couches added to the aura of tacky opulence.

"I decorated this myself," a lilting female voice said from beside Michael. Was that a hint of brogue . . . ?

"It's lovely," Michael said, turning to the tall, slim woman who had deposited herself at his side.

The beaming interior decorator responsible for this ghastly living room was as charming as it wasn't; she had big blue sparkling eyes, platinum blonde hair brushing her shoulders, and pert, pretty features. At first glance Michael thought the woman might be in her thirties, but on closer examination, more like mid-forties.

"You must be Michael Satariano," she said, offering a small slender hand bearing a big fat diamond. "Mae Capone. We're so pleased to have you with us."

Michael knew nothing about Mrs. Capone—the gangster had worked hard to keep his wife out of the limelight—and wondered if this striking woman had once been a chorus girl.

"You have a beautiful home," he told her.

"I'm about ready to remodel," she said, hands on hips, surveying the living room; she wore a simple blue-and-white floral-print dress with white belt and white shoes. "I think I overdid it, buying all this junk when we first moved in."

"Oh, no, it's—"

"Pretty gauche," she said, and made a "click" in one cheek. She looked at him, head cocked, half-smirking. "You can take the girl outa Brooklyn, but you can't take Brooklyn out of the girl."

Only the accent that was bedeviling Michael wasn't of the Brooklyn variety. . . .

"Mimi," she said, stepping out to address Michael's tour guide, "would you go upstairs and see if Al needs anything? He hasn't sent down for lunch."

"Sure, Mae," Mimi said, and scurried off.

She slipped her arm in Michael's and gazed at him with those big blue eyes. "Did my brother-in-law offer you lunch? . . . He's a peppy host, but dumber than Dagwood."

Michael laughed at this unexpected (and accurate) observation, and said, "I haven't eaten, but I have my own car. I can easily go and—"

She squeezed his arm and walked him toward the kitchen. "You're our guest. It's not every day we have a Congressional Medal of Honor winner within these walls."

"Thank you, Mrs. Capone, but please don't make a fuss over—"

She gave him a firm, friendly look. "You're going to call me Mae, and I'm going to call you Michael. Agreed?"

"Agreed."

The kitchen was spacious, modern and very white—from the tile floor to the counters and cabinets and the latest appliances; at her direction, he sat at a white-and-black-flecked Formica table. Despite the newness of the surroundings, a pungent odor took him back to his childhood, and not the part spent with the Satarianos . . .

. . . corned beef and cabbage.

She provided a place mat, bread, iced tea with lemon, napkin

117

and silverware, quickly, efficiently; then served him up. She said she'd already eaten, but sat with him and had an iced tea, too.

"This is delicious," Michael said, and it was. "I love corned beef and cabbage."

"So does Al."

"You made this yourself?"

She nodded. "Brownie cooks for the staff, but mostly I take care of Al's meals."

Midway through Michael's meal, Mimi Capone came down to fetch a plate for Al.

When Mimi had again disappeared, Michael said, "May I ask you something, Mrs. Capone . . . Mae?"

"You're my guest. And you're a nice young man. I'm sure you won't overstep."

This was the first indication from Mae Capone that there were in fact boundaries.

"Are you . . . Irish?"

She laughed, a little waterfall of glee. "Yes I'm Irish! Does that surprise a good Sicilian boy like you? That Al Capone would take a bride from the land of the bogs and the little people?"

"Frankly, yes."

Her beautiful eyes took on a distant cast. ". . . That was Carroll Street, for you. The Italian and Irish neighborhoods kind of butted up against each other. And the Irish boys, well, they took forever to marry."

Michael sipped his iced tea. "And the Italian boys got an earlier start?"

"Oh my yes," she said, and laughed again. "We were both twenty, Al and I. . . . We've had a wonderful marriage—does that surprise you, me saying that?"

"No," Michael said, unsteadily.

"My husband was a famous and generous man, when the world was his. And when things went another way—with the imprisonment that those hypocrites brought down upon him—well, I stood by my man, like any good wife, Italian or Irish or otherwise. And now, in his retirement, I'm with him still. He has no other nurse but me, you know."

"Is Mr. Capone ill?"

She rose and took Michael's dish and was clearing it in the sink, when she said, "Prison took a toll." Then she returned and sat again. "But he's still Al Capone. With his friend Frank, he controls Chicago. Even now."

Her pride in the accomplishments of her criminal husband did not surprise Michael; to stay at the man's side all these years, Mae Capone would have long since had to come to terms with who and what her husband was.

Mae showed him the rest of the house, going up the stairs to the landing off of which were various bedrooms, including Michael's own, at the end of the hall.

Finally, at the central bedroom, Mae stopped. "This is my husband's suite. . . . I stay with him if he has a rough night."

"Mr. Nitti indicated I probably couldn't meet your husband."

"I'm afraid that would be impossible. Al did tell me to convey his admiration and appreciation, for your gallant service to our country."

"Well . . . please thank him for me."

"I will. But, Michael, he's a private man. I hope you understand."

"Certainly. Mimi . . . that is, the other Mr. Capone . . . said that there are two guards posted inside the house."

"And that *is* why you're here, isn't it?" she said thoughtfully. "To scrutinize our security."

Surprisingly, she opened the door to the suite.

Michael followed her into a small room, shallow but wide, where two guards sat at a card table playing gin. They, too, wore sportshirts with shoulder holsters. Both were heavy-set, swarthy, dark-haired, though one had a round face and the other a squarish one; veteran thugs, pushing forty or past it. Both were smoking and the room was thick with it.

They stood as Mae entered.

"Rocco, Tony," Mae said, gesturing to Michael, "this is Mr. Nitti's man, Michael Satariano. The young war hero you've heard about."

The round-faced one came over and shook Michael's hand, burbling praise, as if meeting a movie star. The bucket-headed one, his eyes hooded, merely nodded and sat back down; obviously, he wanted to get back to his game.

Michael took the room in quickly: a console radio; a small refrigerator; comfortable chairs in opposite corners with endtables stacked with magazines. A Maxfield Parrish print. That was it.

Mae turned to Michael. "Two men are always on duty here, making sure no one disturbs my husband, and providing any help he might need. . . . Al often gets restless, wakes up around three, and might want something to eat, or maybe sit down on the dock."

The round-faced guard said, "And it's our job to help out, whatever Mr. Capone needs."

"Al spends much of his time in his room," she said, nodding toward the closed door. "Listening to the radio, reading magazines and newspapers."

"He likes to sit by the pool, too," the round-faced one put in.

Mae nodded, and then cast Michael a bland smile that somehow signaled the tour of this suite was over.

"Gentlemen," Michael said with a nod, "sorry to disturb you. Just having a look around for Mr. Nitti."

"Sure," the round-faced guy said cheerfully.

The other guy said nothing.

In the hallway, Michael asked, "I assume these are your top people."

Again Mae nodded. "Only six on staff, our most trusted, sit in that room. People my husband knew back in Chicago."

"Men he feels comfortable with," Michael said.

"Yes. It's probably the same with President Roosevelt and the Secret Service, don't you think?"

That said it all, somehow—that this woman equated her husband with the country's Commander in Chief.

Mae Capone was a charming hostess, but Michael was relieved when she said she'd be leaving this afternoon to join her sister and her sister's husband in Fort Lauderdale.

"I prefer not to be present when business is conducted," she said simply, as they sat on the sun porch, enjoying the view of the expansive backyard and the enormous pool and the bay beyond. She'd already gently scolded him for ordering (but did not rescind) the removal of her "beautiful awnings."

She was saying, "I do apologize for not being here to prepare your supper."

"That is a disappointment. I haven't had corned beef and cabbage like that since my mother made it."

She crinkled her brow. "Your Sicilian mother made corned beef and cabbage?"

Covering, Michael said, "Sure—just like I bet you make a mean lasagna."

"I do! I do."

Early evening, Michael carried Mrs. Capone's bags to her Pontiac—a week's worth for the two-day trip—which she would drive herself. She seemed an independent woman, for having stood in such a large shadow for so many years.

In the same blue floral dress, now with a jaunty dark blue hat, Mae looked at Michael and touched his cheek with a gloved hand. "You're a sweet boy. You remind me of my Sonny. . . . He may stop by to meet you, tomorrow."

"Yes, Mimi said so."

"Sonny was so disappointed he couldn't serve. But he's contributing to the war effort."

"I'm sure he is, ma'am."

"May I ask you something . . . personal?"

"Anything."

"Was your father in this line of work?"

". . . Sort of."

The pretty brow tightened. "Please don't take what I'm about to say wrong. But you seem a fine young man. You've won your country's greatest honor. . . . I say this from experience. Please . . . please consider going down a different road."

Then Al Capone's wife kissed his cheek, and was gone.

FOR DINNER MIMI CAPONE TOOK MICHAEL OUT TO THE Roney Cabana Club in Miami Beach, where the food and service were excellent, though Michael ate very little. Mimi put away a lobster with melted butter, messily, and talked incessantly about celebrities he'd met in the Miami area. The affable Mimi relished the doors his name opened for him; as the "respectable" member of the Capone clan, he had "all the perks and none of the problems."

Michael did not point out to the younger Capone that supervising twenty-one armed guards on a notorious ganglord's estate may not have been the most respectable job around.

Before long, Mimi Capone, a little drunk, driving a sporty '37 Dusenberg convertible, dropped Michael off, loaning his guest a spare key. By eleven o'clock p.m., Michael Satariano—with the run of the place—was alone in the mansion, but for two guards and Al Capone.

Of course, there was a matter of four or five guards outside, and an unspecified number of off-duty guards who might be in their quarters in the cabana and gatehouse.

In the kitchen he got himself a Coke—the fragrance of corned beef and cabbage lingered—and went up the main stairs to the landing off of which were the bedrooms. He stood for a moment, staring at the door to the Capone suite.

Then he went to his own room, with its double bed and nondescript contemporary furnishings fortunately free from Louis XIV touches. He changed from the white suit and Florsheims into a green Army-issue t-shirt, black trousers and black crepe-soled bluchers; then he lay on the bed, atop the spread with only the bedstand lamp on.

He sipped his Coke.

Stared at the ceiling.

The shift change was at eleven-thirty. Had he gotten home earlier, he'd have taken advantage of the tiredness of the current shift of guards; but now he had to wait until the new group had come on and the others were long gone. He could hear, faintly, a radio playing big band music, and wondered if it was Capone listening or his two watchdogs.

She had reminded him of his mother.

Mae Capone's Irish good looks and her cheery manner and her maternal fuss had, inevitably, reminded him of his mama, and there wasn't a damned thing to be done about it. Much as he tried to banish the thought, it kept floating back. The image of a smile that was at once Mae's and his mother's lingered, *goddamnit.*

So what if she was a nice woman? And had a nice son who was doing his bit for the war effort? Who cared that Mimi Capone was a decent, harmless guy, and that their life down here was a placid routine of isolated luxury? *Capone remained Capone*—the man who had betrayed Michael O'Sullivan, Sr., and dispatched a contract killer to cut him down. The same Capone who had aligned himself with the Looneys after the murders of Michael's mother and brother, and who, to this day, conspired with Frank Nitti to rule the kingdom of Chicago crime. . . .

Mae Capone and her son Sonny and their loving husband/father, despite all Al Capone's sins, had enjoyed years together, as a family. They had had birthdays and Easters and Thanksgivings and Christmases. . . . Even with Capone in prison for a time, they'd been alive and had each other.

His hands tensed into fists; untensed. Tensed again.

He stared at the ceiling, not wanting to hurt Mae Capone, but knowing that a few kind words and a plate of corned beef and cabbage were not enough to dissuade Michael O'Sullivan, Jr., from doing what he had come here to do. . . .

A little after two a.m., just below the Capone suite, a guard in a yellow sportshirt banded by a brown shoulder holster bent to light up a cigarette with a Zippo lighter. It didn't spark to flame on the first try and his thumb was poised for a second, when the barrel of a .45 slammed across the back of his skull and dropped him to the grass.

Using black electrical tape, Michael bound the guard's wrists behind him and the man's ankles, too, and dragged the unconscious figure over to nearby bushes, tucking him out of sight before another guard could wander by to notice. Michael confiscated the man's .38 Police Special and stuck it in his waistband, next to the spare pawn-shop .45.

Michael slipped his father's .45 back into its shoulder holster worn over the green t-shirt; then—using the technique he'd partly demonstrated to Mimi, earlier—climbed from window sill to awning frame and hoisted himself up and over the balcony rail.

The sky was clear and starry with a full moon; ivory washed Michael and everything else on the balcony, which was not much: a comfortable-looking deck chair and a little table. The view here was onto the spacious backyard dotted with palms and other foliage, and the substantial swimming pool, the dock beyond; moonlight dappled off shimmering water, both the pool and the bay. No guards in sight.

Curtained French doors led from balcony to bedroom. Automatic in his right hand, Michael tried the handle with his left, gently. . . .

Unlocked.

He pushed the door open and entered the dark room, leaving the door ajar, letting moonlight in. The room was as spare as an Alcatraz cell: two twin beds, one at left, the other right; nothing on the walls, not even a Maxfield Parrish; no nightstands; a chest of drawers; a lounge chair facing the balcony, with a small table next to it.

No radio. No books, or magazines, or newspapers.

Also, no Capone.

One bed, covers rumpled, did indicate a recent slumberer. At his left, Michael saw a closed door with an edge of light at the bottom. Gun in hand, he crossed to that door, tried the knob, went in fast.

Nothing.

Bathroom—shower stall with door closed; oversize toilet; double sink. Many, many pill bottles. Electric razor. Towels on racks and more stacked on a clothes hamper.

Michael opened the shower door and aimed his .45 in at an empty, oversize stall. When he shut it again, ever so gently, metal nonetheless nudged metal and made a sound, and when he moved back into the dark bedroom, a guard in the usual sportshirt and shoulder holster burst in, a small dark frowning

figure, throwing a wedge of light into the bedroom, and pointing a .38 at the intruder.

Michael shot the guard, in the head, and red splashed the
door and smeared into modern art as the man slid down, the
guard's gunshot hitting a stucco wall, making a terrible metallic
reverberation; and then another guard was in the doorway and he
was firing at Michael, who hit the deck and fired up at the
shooter, catching him in the head as well, though the angle sent
the spatter up even as the man dropped down, piling on top of
his crony, doggy-style.

From the open doors onto the balcony, yelling from below—
none of it discernible as words, but the gist easily understood—
discouraged Michael from exiting the way he'd come, and he
figured his best bet was the rental car out front, so he jumped
over the two bodies stacked in the doorway, and as he did, caught
dripping blood from the ceiling onto the side of his face. He
didn't bother wiping it off because it would only make his hands
sticky.

He was heading briskly down the stairway when the front door
opened and three more of them rushed in, eyes wild, guns in
hand, and this time the words were easy to make out: *There's the
bastard! Get him!" "Shoot that fucker!"*

In a flash he realized a tactical error: if he'd made his move
before shift change, these men would recognize him and he
might have talked his way out; but for now he was just a guy in a
green t-shirt on the stairs with a pistol in his hand. And blood on
his face. . . .

He withdrew the other .45 and hopped onto the banister and
went straddle-sliding down, shooting all the way, a regular two-
gun kid, and the men streaming through the doorway fired up at
him, but he was a moving target and they were slowed down by his
gunfire, which was turning them from men into bodies, tripping
over each other as they died.

When Michael got to the bottom of the stairs, four dead men
were sprawled there, one or two of them propping the door
open, and he could see the Packard out there, just waiting . . .

. . . but he could also see three more guards in their

———

sportshirts and shoulder holsters running toward him with teeth bared and eyes wide.

He threw a few shots their way, catching one, and headed into and through the kitchen, corned beef and cabbage taunting him, and hurtled across the backyard, tossing away the spare .45, which was empty, and replacing it with the commandeered .38, from that first guard.

Up ahead was the swimming pool, but beyond that the dock, and a speedboat; that seemed his best, perhaps his only bet. . . .

But as he approached the pool, men came streaming down the stairs of the cabana—four men, two of whom were the round- and square-faced cardplaying guards from Capone's anteroom. They were in their underwear—these were some of the live-in guards—wearing t-shirts and boxer shorts . . . and handguns.

The cardplayer who hadn't spoken this afternoon paused half-way down the steps. "*There!* Get him!"

Michael took the offensive, running right at them, along the edge of the pool, firing up at them with a gun in either hand, and the round-faced guy, who'd been in the lead, caught a couple slugs in his head, which more or less exploded in a bone-and-blood red-and-white shower and then tumbled down, flung onto the steps, and the other three stumbled over him, trying to shoot at Michael, who was doing a better job shooting at them.

Soon they were in an awkward pile of death at the bottom of the steps, as if they'd all gone after a fumbled football, the hard way.

Michael wheeled, looking to see if any more of them were coming up behind him, from the house.

Nobody. Not right now, anyway.

And he wheeled back to the pile of guards in their bloody un- derwear and went over and kicked at them, making sure they were dead; not so long ago, he'd checked the Japs in that clearing much the same way.

Behind him a voice said: "*Nail the fucker!*"

Two guys were running at him, across the backyard, firing wildly, barely more than shapes in the moonlight. The .38 was empty—he flung it to one side—and flopped onto the grass, withdrawing a spare magazine from his pocket and slamming it into the automatic.

Now they were close enough, and he took them down with head shots; one flopped face-forward onto the grass, dead too quick to be surprised, the other caught one in the neck and his hands went to his throat and blood squirted through his fingers as he did a sad short crazy dance before tumbling into the pool sideways, not making much of a splash, then floating there, blood streaming out, diluting itself in the pool water, the red looking black in the moonlight.

Michael got to his feet.

He listened carefully. He could not hear anything but the lapping of the water behind him, the bay beckoning; only now he could afford to head back to the house and use the rental car. Or would others be waiting . . . ?

He was weighing that when another sound drifted across the eerie solitude of the night.

A whimpering.

At first he thought he'd wounded one of them, but the sniveling sound just wasn't right. It was coming from near the swimming pool. Carefully, he stalked over there, .45 ready; and then he saw the figure, down on the cement beside a deck chair.

A big, fat figure, with curly gray thinning hair, rolled up like the world's largest fetus. Wearing a purple bathrobe over cream-colored pajamas; with purple slippers.

Michael almost laughed.

In all the excitement, distracted as he was by killing a dozen or so men, Michael had forgotten what this was about.

Capone.

Al Capone, who right now was a whimpering terrified blob on the pool's cement skirt, and Michael—*his mind's eye filled with the image of his father, dead on the kitchen floor in that farmhouse*—grabbed the figure by the arm and flung him onto his back, though the man's knees pulled up, his eyes wide and confused.

The famous face had a formlessness about it, but this was King Capone, all right—even if those chipmunk cheeks, scars and all, happened to be smeared with tears and snot.

Michael knelt and put the gun in Capone's pudgy neck, dimpling the flesh, and hovered over him, the ganglord on his back, his about-to-be killer on his knees, as if in prayer.

"Look at me, Snorky! Look at me."

Capone looked at Michael.

"Do you know who I am?"

Capone's big eyes registered nothing.

And just as Michael was about to tell the king of crime exactly who he was, Capone asked, in a very small voice, "Where is it?"

Through his teeth, Michael spat: "Where is what?"

"My . . . my fishing rod?"

Michael winced, trying to make sense of this. He got on his feet, looking down at the fat child-like figure. In the moonlight, around them, lay dead bodies—Michael's grim handiwork, all to bring him to this moment.

But Al Capone was rummaging around on the cement like a baby seeking its rattle.

"Here it is!"

With great effort, Capone lifted the fishing rod, which had been on the other side of the deck chair, where he managed to awkwardly seat himself; then he cast the line limply into the water.

It was as if Michael weren't there at all.

The greatest of all gangsters sat fishing in his swimming pool, smiling the smile of a very young and not at all bright child, drool dribbling from plump purple lips as he hummed a tuneless song, oblivious to the carnage around them.

And Michael knew.

He understood. Understood it all: the syphilis had reduced Capone to a near vegetable, and Nitti had hidden that from all but a small select circle, to maintain his own power and the illusion of Capone's.

There would be no revenge upon Big Al, on this or any night; the syphilis had beaten Michael to it, leaving a brain-damaged, befogged husk where Alphonse Capone had once been. Barely forty, this ancient mariner sat fishing in his pool, waiting for a bite he'd never get.

As he processed this shocking news, Michael did not notice

128

the men slowly approaching—three more guards with guns drawn, and behind them Mimi Capone.

Who said, "Put the gun down, Michael."

And Michael tossed the gun on the grass, turning his back on what remained of Al Capone. He fell to his knees and began to weep as the men closed in.

LOONEY DAYS

The Tri-Cities

March 1922

1

ANNIE O'SULLIVAN HAD A STORYBOOK
life and she knew it.

She was twenty-six years old with a
heart-shaped face, reddish blonde hair
bobbed Irene Castle-style, with china-blue
eyes, doll-like features and the fair, faintly
freckled complexion of the Red Irish. Normally petite, at the moment she was a
monster—nine months pregnant in a dark
blue maternity dress whose feminine white
collar made the garment no less tent-like.

The morning had been notably uncomfortable, making her wonder if today
would be the day. But by the afternoon,
the stirrings had settled down, not even a
kick from the anxious resident within her.

She sat reading *The Ladies' Home Journal*
in the living room of the two-story house

on Twenty-second Street in Highland Park, up the hill in Rock Island. Being "up the hill" meant a lot: she and her husband, Mike, had spent almost three years in a shanty in the Greenbush neighborhood below. Now they had one of the nicest homes in town, a two-story white stucco well back from the street on a generous lawn with a detached garage.

Not that the house was ostentatious; there was nothing showy about the O'Sullivans or their home, with its nearly austere interior of pale plaster walls of green and yellow against dark woodwork, softened by curtains of lace.

How exciting it had been to buy all the furniture new (nothing much from where they'd lived before had been worth hanging on to); solid mission oak with straight, unadorned lines—Mike did not care for the fancy new veneers—and her all-white sanitary kitchen, with wood-burning stove, was efficient and modern, a homemaker's dream.

The house and their simple yet not inexpensive furnishings reflected those within. Her handsome dark-haired husband (*Black* Irish, he was) was, for the most part, a serious, dignified man, whose finer qualities emerged in the bedroom, by way of his tenderness, and here in the living room, by way of his love for their son.

Their living room—where she sat in a comfortable, commodious mohair upholstered armchair, suitable to her current size, swollen feet propped up on an ottoman—was as good an indication as any of the devotion Michael O'Sullivan, Sr., felt for Michael O'Sullivan, Jr. The braided carpet on their parquet floor harbored an elaborate electric train layout, the finest Lionel had to offer, from trains and track to signal towers, tunnels, depots and ticket offices.

With his hat literally in his hand, her husband had begged his wife's permission to turn their formal living room into a trainyard, "for just a little while." Young Michael was a precocious three, and though she suspected "a little while" might well prove to be months or even years, Annie had no objections to an activity that would keep their little man's energetic hands, feet and mind happily occupied.

Not that her son had ever been a problem. Michael Jr. had an active mind, and loved to play outside with neighborhood boys and girls; he was in general obedient to both his parents—it was as if he'd been born respectful, or perhaps the example of his stoic but not unkind father had sunk in, early on.

About the only battles that ever occurred were at the kitchen table—her boy was a fussy eater. On the other hand, when meals were served in the dining room, the formality of the surroundings encouraged angelic behavior, even in the presence of brussels sprouts.

Right now Michael was having his afternoon nap. He didn't fuss about it—though the boy did not yet read, he loved books, and would page through picture books (*Peter Rabbit* a particular favorite, and L. Frank Baum's *Mother Goose*) until he fell asleep, whether for his nap or at night.

As for the trains, she took no greater pleasure than to sit nearby with a book or a magazine (neither crochet nor needlework interested her), classical music playing on their new console radio, while father and son crouched and scurried and tended around the edges of their railroad yard. The eyes of both her "boys" flashed with a childish glee that she saw often in her son but rarely in her husband.

She knew her husband, Mike, adored her; he placed her on a pedestal, though he was not shy about removing her from that perch, behind closed doors. A deep passion ran beneath the surface of this stoic man.

The former Annie O'Hanlon had known her husband for several years before they married. He had come to the Tri-Cities from New York, where his late father had been a railroad man; he'd heard that John Deere was hiring and he landed a job as a shop sweeper. She'd met him through church activities at Sacred Heart, and for a time Mike had courted her best friend, Katie O'Meara.

Before long Annie and Mike had become a couple—Katie understood, she'd sensed the attraction between them—and they were talking of marriage when he got swept away into the war by the wave of patriotism encompassing the country. In fact, they'd been together, on the porch of her parents' shanty, when the band had come marching by.

Literally.

The band was made up of college boys—twenty-one members of the Augustana marching band, and they'd enlisted as a unit in the 6th Illinois Regiment. They played a final concert, then paraded through town performing martial marches, from Rock Island to the train station, high-stepping right through Greenbush.

Mike enlisted the next day.

He had returned a hero with a glittering array of medals and a somber, more adult presence that both thrilled and intimidated Annie; he'd been a boy when he left, but things overseas had turned him into a man—things he made clear he would never discuss with her. . . .

Shortly after Mike's return, Mr. Looney had invited him up to his house on the hill, in the Longview Loop area—Rock Island's Knob Hill, rife with doctors, lawyers and old money. Mr. Looney lived on Twentieth Street in a brooding stone mansion in Highland Park, a far cry from Greenbush.

Annie did not know what Mr. Looney had said to Michael, other than a job had been offered. At first Michael called it a chauffeur position, later referring to it as a bodyguard; occasionally, in passing, he called himself Mr. Looney's "lieutenant," as if he were still a soldier.

Shortly after, Annie and Mike had married at Sacred Heart. Over the next several years, her husband's responsibilities and his position grew in the Looney organization. They were invited to events at the Looney home (Mrs. Looney had died in the flu epidemic in 1914, and he lived alone with his son, Connor; two daughters were away at convent school).

And before long the money grew, as well—first the O'Sullivans had a car; then this lovely home of theirs. And along the way, they had their son, Michael Jr.

Of course there were those who shunned the O'Sullivans for their affiliation with John Looney. Briefly the family attended St. Joseph's, near the courthouse, but turned-up noses and whispered remarks among these good Christians put them off, and they returned to the simple church where they had ties.

Many in the Tri-Cities, and not just the Irish, considered the lanky, mustached, handsome John Looney to be a living folk hero, an Irish American rebel and entrepreneur, battling the powers that be. A self-schooled lawyer, Mr. Looney had run for the state legislature as a Democrat but was defeated through trickery by corrupt opponents; he had looked around at the way his people were treated in the Tri-Cities, it was said, and swore he'd provide his own government outside the system, for these disenfranchised souls. He would see to it that "Micks" like Annie's husband got jobs, if not in his own enterprises, then at the area factories, where he had influence.

Some had no real opinion about John Looney—he was just a colorful character who dressed in black like a riverboat gambler and had a flair for theatrics (performing as Irish Catholic martyr Robert Emmet in a one-man play). And of course he was the man who helped the good citizens of the Tri-Cities skirt a bad law, the Eighteenth Amendment, seeing to it a fellow could have a beer . . . which many decent people considered a public service.

But still others saw Looney as, simply, a gangster.

Before they'd moved to this big house, Annie had once risked speaking to Michael about his working for Mr. Looney. She did not refer directly to the bootlegging, brothels and gambling that were as much a part of John Looney's empire as his newspaper, the Rock Island *News*. Nor did she speak of the pistol (brought home with him from the Great War) that Mike carried beneath his shoulder.

All she'd said, serving him coffee in the kitchen after supper, was, "You're respected, Mike. You did your people right proud, over there. You could work for anybody."

"I work for Mr. Looney," he'd said. He lifted the filled coffee cup and said, "Thank you, dear."

She sat. "Some say Mr. Looney makes his money in sinful ways."

Mike had given her a hard look—almost cold. Certainly his words chilled her: "We don't question how Mr. Looney makes his money. It's not our place."

———

On very rare occasions, when she had dared refer to this subject, Michael would speak almost exactly those same words; more often, he would silence her with a look.

And now in this grand house, with a wonderful son upstairs and another baby in the oven, Annie considered herself complicit in whatever her husband and their patriarch did. What was the word, in the newspapers and magazines? She was an accomplice. She prayed for forgiveness, but she never spoke of her conflicted feelings to any priest—how do you confess to things you don't know about?

And don't want to know about?

Yet, the notion that her reserved husband was a "gangster" seemed an absurdity. Surely the whispered stories, the awful rumors, which she heard only the edges of, were gross exaggerations if not outright falsehoods.

This was a man who did not swear. Who did not smoke. Who did not drink (in a rare candid moment, he had admitted to her . . . when she wondered why they couldn't have a simple glass of wine now and again . . . that his father had been a good man who showed a bad side when he drank, and Mike's mother had suffered because of it).

And Annie had a deep and abiding faith in his faithfulness, where their marital bed was concerned, despite the loose women in the world of John Looney.

The smell of corned beef and cabbage emanated from the kitchen—her recipe, but not her doing. Mike had hired help for them, a Greenbush girl. Mary Jane Murphy, a sweet, crude slip of eighteen, cooked indifferently and cleaned lackadasically, but was gentle, even loving with the child.

And in her condition, Annie could not even bend over and pick the boy up.

The girl was skinny, almost scrawny, and looked like a child play-acting in maid's cap and costume. Mike quietly suggested Annie be tougher on the lass, but Annie could not bring herself to do so: she had been a maid herself, for several of the wealthy families, the Baileys with their lumber, the Greggs with their factories.

She had suffered cruelty at the hands of these "upper class" people, overhearing vile remarks that she recalled to this day . . . as when one of Rock Island's wealthiest socialites cattily commented to another that Mrs. Bailey "could surely do better than a little Shanty Irish wench" like Annie.

The socialite said she herself preferred colored help, acknowledging that their service cost more than Irish girls.

No, Annie would not be a strict mistress, where Mary Jane Murphy was concerned . . . at least as long as the wench stayed faithful to Annie's recipes. . . .

Mrs. Michael O'Sullivan did particularly love to cook, but she also took pride in her housework; still, like many women, the enforced relaxation of pregnancy provided a blissful vacation. Mike was insistent that she take it easy—she'd lost a daughter, by miscarriage, last year—and assured her that this time, she'd deliver "right and proper," having been conveyed to the hospital "in good time."

When the labor pains for their first child had come, Annie had been carried by her husband like a bride over the threshold up the hill to St. Anthony's on Thirtieth Street. They had no car at that time, nor phone, and no neighbors did, either. Despite the pain she'd suffered, her memory of the event was a warm one—held in the loving arms of her husband, as he stepped gingerly over the railroad tracks, and strode up the hill, to save her and their son.

John Looney had paid off their doctor's bills. Rumor had it that Mr. Looney, shortly thereafter, contributed to the hospital's new wing, in gratitude for the hospital's policy of never turning away the residents of Greenbush.

Certainly John Looney had been kind to their little family; he was like a grandfather to Michael Jr. (much of the train set had been Mr. Looney's doing) and looked upon Annie with affection, always with a wistful remark about how she reminded him of his late wife. From time to time, they had entertained Mr. Looney in their home, and the patriarch's praise for her cooking was effusive and apparently genuine.

Annie always made a point of inviting Mr. Looney's son,

Connor, but never had Connor accepted. She had noted a certain tension where Connor Looney was concerned, and suspected the man resented his father's regard for her husband. Mr. Looney's son, a little older than Michael, had a snake's smile and awful dead eyes. That he and Michael often worked together gave her many an uneasy night.

Definitely, the pages of her storybook life were frayed, here and there. Just last month, her son had sat in his short pants on the couch, bouncing, kicking his feet up, looking across his trains at his mother, who was seated with a novel by Gene Stratton Porter, her feet up on the ottoman.

"Papa has a gun," Michael said.

"Yes he does, dear."

"Why does Papa have a gun?"

"He protects Mr. Looney."

"What is 'protects'?"

"Keeps him from harm."

"Mr. Looney's nice."

"Yes, dear."

"Nice man."

"Yes he is, dear."

The boy bounced. "At church? Tommy said his mama said Mr. Looney's the boogeyman."

She managed not to smile. "Well, he's not, dear."

"Boogeyman can't be hurt."

"I suppose not, dear."

"So why does Papa need a gun?"

"Play with your trains, dear."

Though amused by this exchange, Annie had also been troubled. She'd spoken about it, after supper, to Mike, who said he would talk to the boy, and make sure his son knew the gun was not a toy.

"You keep that thing under lock and key," she said, in a rare scolding tone, "when it's not on your person."

"I will," he promised.

Mike had been as good as his word, talking to their son, showing him the weapon, comparing it to a toy gun the boy had; and had been extremely discreet about the pistol, thereafter. He wore it to work, and then removed it and locked it away in a bedroom drawer, when he got home.

Occasionally Mike traveled; sometimes he was gone for as much as a week. Nothing was said about why, save for possibly, "A friend of Mr. Looney's needs help." But in his absence, flowers would be delivered to her, the message always the same: "To Annie from your loving husband."

When Mike got home, Annie was still seated in the living room. Tall, broad-shouldered, somber, Mike bestowed a tiny smile upon her—but she could read something in it. A tiny sign of something, if not wrong, then . . . out of the ordinary.

He removed his topcoat and hat, hung them in the front closet. He motioned upstairs, meaning that he was about to proceed with the ritual of disposing of his gun and shoulder holster in their bedroom, and she nodded.

Soon, in his shirtsleeves but with his tie still on, looking like a shopkeeper in his suspenders, Mike deposited himself on the couch where not so long ago his son had been, brimming with questions about "Papa's gun."

Sitting forward, eyes earnest, clasped hands hanging between bowed knees, Mike said, "I'm asking Miss Murphy to stay with you, this evening."

"Is that necessary?"

"I'm afraid I have to go out."

"It's not your poker night, is it?"

"Mr. Looney business."

"Oh." She shrugged. "No need, Mike. We'll be fine, alone. As long as you're not gone long."

"I'm not sure how long I'll be gone. Could be late. You never know with these things."

She knew enough not to ask for a definition of "these things."

"Well," Annie said, "perhaps we would be better off with Mary Jane here. Just in case."

"With you due so soon, I hate not to be here."

"I know, darling."

"If I ever thought I'd let you down . . ."

▬▬▬

141

"You never have and you never will. We'll be fine."

He raised one eyebrow. "Oh, in Mary Jane's capable hands, I'm sure you will be. . . . If you have a problem, call the hospital number. I've made arrangements for an ambulance to come pick you up."

"Don't be silly."

"Nothing silly about it. I don't want anything to happen to you."

Or to our baby, she thought. But it went unsaid.

"Shall we have a walk before dinner?" Annie asked.

"Are you up to it?"

"I have to get some fresh air or I'll die."

"The park is out of the question."

"I know. Just up and down the block."

His smile was mocking, in a nice way. "I could just sit here and bask in the bouquet of your corned beef."

"Mary Jane cooked it."

A week ago he'd have made a face; but Annie had been schooling the girl. "If she sticks to your recipe, we're a cinch for a feast."

They walked down toward the corner, slowly, Annie just trundling along, her gloved hand in his, her fur-collared coat not buttoned around her (that would have been an impossibility), him in his topcoat but without the fedora. In the spring or summer, the street was lushly lined with trees; now, in winter's final days, their skeletal branches silhouetted themselves eerily against a dusk-tinged sky.

"Please be careful tonight," she said.

"It's just business."

A car rumbled by over the brick street.

Then she commented, "We're saving money, you know."

He nodded.

"Nice nest egg," she said.

They were at the corner now. Stopped and looked at each other, breath smoking. "We could go somewhere else," she said. "Live somewhere else."

He frowned slightly, just the faintest hint that her words had hurt him, somehow. "I make a good living."

"Oh, I know."

"Don't you love your house?"

"I never dreamed we could live like this."

He shrugged. "Then let's go home."

Shortly, they were enjoying Mary Jane's corned beef and cabbage, or most of the family was. Young Michael, recently graduated from high chair to oak youth chair, just picked at his food, which his mother had cut into small pieces.

"Too salty," the boy said.

"Just eat half of it," his mother said.

"It's nasty."

Mike looked sharply at his son.

The boy lowered his gaze, which brought his eyes in closer proximity to the corned beef, and he shuddered.

"I can't help it," the boy said. His lower lip extended; his chin crinkled in a familiar preamble. . . .

"If you cry in your food," his father said matter of factly, "you'll only make it more salty. Eat half of it. It'll grow on you."

The boy frowned in horror. "Grow on me?"

His mother covered her smile with a napkin.

"I mean," his father said, "someday you'll acquire a taste for it. You'll like it when you're a man."

"I don't wanna be a man," the boy said, "if I have to eat this."

And he began to cry. The child's stop-and-start wailing agony ricocheted shrilly off the kitchen walls.

His father stood. Pointed. "Go to your room."

Still crying, but obviously relieved, the boy climbed down out of the youth chair with the help of Mary Jane, who walked him out of the kitchen. The boy halted and the maid almost stumbled.

"Mama," he said, pausing in the doorway, looking back at her with red eyes and a tear-streaked face, "will you read to me, anyway?"

"Yes, dear."

"Daddy?"

"Yes?"

"Will you still tuck me in?"

"I'll think about it."

The boy smiled, just a little, through his tears, realizing his victory.

Then the maid and the child were gone. Mike was reaching for his son's plate to help himself to the extra serving when Annie began to laugh.

"What are you laughing about?"

"Cry in your food," she said, "you'll make it saltier."

He grinned. "Well . . . it's what my pop said to me."

"And look at you today, the corned beef fiend."

Mike shrugged and dug in.

Half an hour later, she managed, despite her girth, to embrace her husband at the door; she could feel the hardness of the pistol under his arm. She even managed to get up on tiptoes to kiss him on the mouth. Then she settled back on her sore feet and looked up at him, stroking his face.

"Every time I leave the house," he said, with a funny little smile, "you look at me like . . . like you're trying to memorize this puss of mine."

"Maybe I am."

"Baby," he said, "I memorized your kisser a long, long time ago."

And he gave her a quick smooch and slipped out.

She stood in the doorway and watched him cross to the garage, wondering if he'd avail himself of further weapons from the arsenal out there, kept under tight lock and key.

Annie O'Sullivan loved her life, her storybook life, and yet every time her husband left the house, she had to wonder: how could there be a happy ending, when Mike worked for John Looney?

2

On Twentieth Street's bluff, the formidable three-story structure rose castle-like, with its gabled red tile roofs, ceramic lions, bay windows, sloped turrets, substantial dark-brick walls, and many-pillared porch. The mansion provided its owner a view on the Mississippi River second to none; but also on the mansions below, the homes of high society, his perch enabling the master of this domain to look down upon those who considered themselves his betters.

This had given John Looney no small pleasure, over the years.

The mansion's interior had a warmth to the eye—walnut paneling, mahogany trim, parquet floors, oriental carpets, massive fireplaces—that did not extend to physical reality. The downstairs, with its high ceilings and various cavernous rooms, was prey to winter chill, wind whistling through, turning the place into the haunted house the local children had long ago deemed it. For all its elegance—Victorian furniture, velvet upholstery, stained glass, ornate mirrors, sparkling chandeliers—the mansion was (Looney had to admit it) good and goddamn cold.

Only when a party—holiday festivities or a wedding reception or the occasional wake—brought the warmth of other human beings into the sprawling place did Looney's Roost seem a home, and he'd come to relish such gatherings, accordingly. With Nora gone these eight years, and his daughters off to boarding school, that left only himself and his son Connor to knock around these endless rooms.

When Nora was alive, and the girls under foot, Looney never conducted business in the mansion—would never think of it! He left such things for his law office or the Java House at the Sherman Hotel; or possibly out at Bel Aire, his second, less ostentatious mansion on the Rock River.

Now of course, parties at Bel Aire weren't the family affairs the Roost occasionally put on; they were for men only . . . and a certain type of woman, the kind who fit in with cockfights in the barn, shooting matches in the yard, and drunken orgies upstairs.

Bel Aire was where Looney entertained the Chicago boys, when they came to town. Looney had been aligned with Johnny Torrio for years, though Looney did not have much faith in the chunky scar-faced youth Torrio was grooming for his heir, a hotheaded Sicilian named Capone.

But Looney would have to learn to deal with Capone, and vice versa; as he often said, this business was one of strange bedfellows.

Tonight he'd called a small meeting of a handful of his most trusted associates, and they had gathered at the long table in his library, all seated toward one end. Looney—gauntly handsome, white mustached, in a dark brown suit and gambler's black string tie—sat at the head. On a chair against the wall behind him, not officially a part of the inner circle, was Michael O'Sullivan.

O'Sullivan was Looney's most trusted lieutenant. In some ways, an odd duck (you'd never find him at a Bel Aire orgy), the war hero had earned himself and his boss respect all around Midwestern mob circles. Looney had loaned Mike out to Chicago, numerous times; and somewhere along the line Mike had become a living legend—the Angel of Death, they called him.

This melodramatic sobriquet supposedly derived from O'Sullivan taking no pleasure in killing—it was said he wore a somber, even regretful expression when pulling a trigger.

Though O'Sullivan's relatively lowly duties included bodyguard and occasional driver, Looney trusted the man like no one else in his organization. Someday there would be a place for Mike at this table; someday, perhaps, at its head.

When such a thought crossed his mind, John Looney would wince, feeling he'd committed a small betrayal against his own blood. At the eventual head of the table—the seat he would one day vacate—should be his son, Connor. But Connor was . . . a troubled boy.

Looney did not mind that his son had done poorly in school; the reports that Connor was a bully, and a mean one at that, did not discourage him, either. The family business was a brass-knuckle affair, after all. But Connor had other unattractive traits—he was impulsive and violent; and he drank, and he got emotional over women.

Yet John Looney loved his son; he often paired Connor with Mike O'Sullivan, in hopes Mike's self-control and professionalism might rub off. That Connor and Mike would form a bond, so that O'Sullivan could sit at Connor's right hand one day, and help John Looney's son rule.

Tonight, at the conference table in the booklined room with lamps glowing yellow, Connor sat at his father's right hand. Connor, wearing a gray suit with vest and dark blue silk tie with diamond stickpin, looked sharp indeed; a youthful version of his father, albeit with a longer nose and slightly weaker chin, and minus the mustache. He seemed to be just a little drunk.

At Looney's left hand sat lawyer Frank Kelly, affable and prosperous-looking in a brown suit and red bow tie, a gray-haired fleshy man of fifty with a confident manner. Kelly had been Looney's law partner since the last century.

Next to the lawyer was Emeal Davis, a brawny cueball-bald black man in a light blue suit with his dark blue derby before him on the table like a meal he was contemplating. In his mid-thirties, Davis oversaw the transporting of liquor, guns and whores between Rock Island and Chicago.

Across from Davis, seated next to Connor, was a striking blonde in her late twenties, Helen Van Dale. She wore a tight-fitting black satin dress with lace collar, her hands in white gloves folded primly before her; on the back of her chair was her mink coat (she had not trusted it to the Looney butler). A former whore herself, Helen was the madam who coordinated all prostitution in Looney's realm.

"Let's start with the recall effort," Looney said, hands flat on the table. "Frank, what do you have for me?"

Kelly beamed, leaning back in his chair, arms folded. "We'll have our people all through the Market Square rally tonight. Both speakers, Harry McCaskrin and Ed Gardner, will be demanding the mayor's recall, and—"

"I want you to talk to them beforehand," Looney said.

Frowning, Kelly removed his pocket watch and made a show of checking it. "The rally's in less than an hour, John—what do you want me to talk to them *about*?"

"I've made a decision," Looney said. All faces turned toward him expectantly; what trick did the Old Man have up his sleeve this time? "Several prominent, highly respectable citizens have approached me, and I've decided to accept their draft."

Reactions around the table were varied, starting with Kelly, whose face fell, as he said, "You want to run for *mayor*, John? *Why in God's name*?"

Connor was smirking, Helen Van Dale laughing quietly to herself, her full bosom jiggling, Emeal Davis wearing no more expression than a cigarstore Indian.

"We all know Mayor Schriver has to go," Looney said.

"No argument," Kelly said. "But this recall passes, we can put in a puppet, and—"

"Why not save myself the trouble of pulling the strings? Frank, you know that I came to this town with political ambitions, only to be viciously quashed by the ruling class. Now I'm in a position to take the reins."

"John," the lawyer said, shaking his head, his voice oozing with friendly familiarity, "drumming Schriver out of office is well and good—but a man with your kind of power stays in the shadows . . . not the spotlight."

"Pop," Connor said, "don't you think bein' mayor would be kind of a . . . comedown?"

"I think it's wonderful," Helen Van Dale said, savoring her words. "John Looney has found the ultimate way to spit in Rock Island's eye."

Kelly was shaking his head again, the mop of gray hair losing its shape, locks drooping onto his brow. "John, I don't know if McCaskrin will play ball."

"He's our man, isn't he?"

"Yes, but he's after the nomination for State's Attorney, and he's a Republican. You're a Democrat."

"Thank you for reminding me, Frank."

"Oh, I'm sure he'll say nothing *against* you, and he'll praise you as a good citizen . . . but endorse your candidacy? I think not."

Looney shrugged. "Gardner's a more fiery speaker, anyway. And he'll jump at the chance to ally himself with us."

Connor's eyes and nostrils flared. "Pop! *Gardner*? You can't be serious—the guy's a goddamn *socialist!*"

"We'll need the votes of both the socialists and the Democrats to swing it." Looney turned to O'Sullivan, seated by a table next to a Tiffany-shade lamp, having backed away from its light into darkness. "Mike . . . join us, would you?"

And Looney gestured to the table.

Slowly, O'Sullivan rose and went to the chair next to Davis. Connor was frowning—having this bodyguard invited to the table where insiders made key decisions, surely galled Looney's son. But it couldn't be helped.

"I realize, Mike," Looney said, "that these socialists stick in your craw."

O'Sullivan said, "Not up to me, Mr. Looney."

During the patriotic fever of 1917, socialists like Davenport newspaperman Floyd Dell and his radical writer pal John Reed had led anti-war efforts, preaching peaceful draft resistance and U.S. neutrality. They and other socialists had been treated like traitors by the government.

But along the way, the socialists had become a viable political party, and right now, across the river, Davenport's mayor was socialist, as were five alderman and several other elected officials. In Rock Island, the socialists hungered to gain this side of the Mississippi, greedily coveting the mayor's seat and various city commission seats.

"This has to rub you wrong, Mike," Looney acknowledged, with a somber shake of his head.

O'Sullivan said nothing.

Connor said, "These socialists are a bunch of blow-hard rabble-rousers! Privileged-class intellectuals who never done an honest day's work."

O'Sullivan shrugged. "I can't disagree with that. But could I ask a question?"

"Of course, Mike," Looney said. "I want your opinions and advice—that's why I asked you to sit down with us."

O'Sullivan leaned forward. "Mr. Looney, surely you can't respect a bunch of pacifists, who were against the Great War—can you?"

"Mike me boy, I have no truck with pacifists; I believe a man has to stand and fight for what he believes is right, and that he must redress the wrongs committed against him."

"As do I, sir."

"And I respect you and the honor you brought on the Irish Catholic community with your valor." Looney did not add what he really felt, for fear of truly alienating his top lieutenant: that what went on over there had been England's war, not the war of a "Free Ireland!" rebel like John Looney.

Who said, "I'm a Democrat like you, Mike. And a capitalist—if you haven't noticed by now that I'm a capitalist, then you just ain't been paying attention."

And O'Sullivan actually smiled at that. So did everyone else at the table.

"All around us workers are going out on strike," Looney said. "And the unions're on the rise. That's good for us—we support the working man, because we want him to relax with the diversions we can offer him, *after* work. . . . Right, Helen?"

Chuckling, she said, "Right, John."

Suddenly Emeal Davis, looking sideways at the bodyguard, spoke, in his brooding baritone: "Mike, we make alliances. That's how we can do what we do. And a lot of working stiffs these days vote socialist. Don't kid yourself."

Obviously not liking the sound of any of this, Frank Kelly, pale as a ghost, rose and said, "Well, I better get over there, and make our pitch. Are you willing to run as a socialist, John?"

"No need. It's a recall ballot. My name will be listed, and that will be enough."

Distractedly nodding to everyone, Kelly shuffled out.

Looney gave O'Sullivan a hard look. "What do you say, Mike?"

O'Sullivan said, "Mr. Looney, politics aren't my calling. Anyway—you know I'd follow you into hell."

"That I do know, son."

Connor winced at "son," and Looney immediately regretted using the word. But he was a man who spoke from his heart.

"Tonight, at that rally," Looney said, "we'll build support for my candidacy, and stoke the fires that already rage in Rock Island against this mayor."

"Fueled by the *News*," Helen Van Dale said, puckishly. "I start all my fires with copies of the *News*."

With a small smile, Looney cast his gaze on the madam. "Do you have more information for me, Helen?"

"If I didn't, would that stop you? Wouldn't you just put your most creative reporter in front of a typewriter and let him run wild?"

Helen could get away with this taunting because Looney had great affection for her; and because, next to him, she was the most powerful person in the Tri-Cities.

Much of the information that gave Looney's scandal sheet, the Rock Island *News*, its unique leverage came from Helen, who was in a position (so to speak) to know the sins of various and sundry local men. Looney felt no shame for using his newspaper in a so-called "blackmailing" manner that rival publication the *Argus* had termed "a paper gun held at the heads of his victims."

Looney merely used the naked truth culled from the lives of these hypocrites to sway them to do his bidding, from paying him off for not running a story to cutting him in for a piece of their action. That was how he'd built his empire: bootleggers, gamblers, and whoremongers had a choice of exposure in the *News* or taking on a new partner. Right now, John Looney had over one hundred and fifty such partners, who paid him on average $400 a week in tribute.

"There can be no question that the mayor is feeling the heat," Looney said. "Which is the other piece of news I have for you—I'm meeting with Mayor Schriver in less than an hour. At his invitation."

Connor frowned, and Emeal Davis exchanged worried glances with O'Sullivan.

Davis said, "You could be walking into something, Mr. Looney."

O'Sullivan, sitting forward, asked, "Where is the meeting to be held?"

"Oh, we're quite safe," Looney said, with a dismissive wave. "City Hall! Right out in the open. Above board."

Connor said, "What are you meeting with that clown for, anyway? If you've decided to run for mayor, already."

"If the mayor can convince me he is ready to change his ways," Looney said to his son, "to cooperate with my various requests, to go back to our old arrangements . . . I will consider taking myself out of the recall equation."

Davis was nodding. "That sounds reasonable."

"Emeal, Mike," Looney said, "I want you to accompany me. Connor, we have dozens of boyos in that Market Square crowd. You circulate. Make sure they do their jobs."

"You can count on me, Pop."

Looney stood, motioned with outspread hands, palms up, that the meeting was over.

Connor turned to Helen, and Looney overheard his son say to her, "After the rally, how about I stop by?"

She touched his cheek. "Not tonight, sweetie. Another time."

And the black-satin madam and her mink coat swished by.

Looney went to his son. "What was that?"

Connor's eyes went wide with feigned innocence. "What do you mean, Pop?"

"I told you to lay off that . . ." He turned to make sure Helen Van Dale was gone, but finished in a whisper. ". . . flesh peddler. You find yourself a nice girl."

"I'm just havin' fun. I'm young, yet."

"You'll grow old fast, hanging around with whores. You want to catch something?"

Connor frowned, and nodded toward the other side of the room, and O'Sullivan and Emeal Davis, whose proximity meant they could not have avoided hearing the exchange. The father had unintentionally embarrassed his son.

Looney smiled at Connor. "Ah, I'm just an old woman. You're right, my boy, you're young. . . . Have a good time. Sow your wild oats."

Connor grinned. "Thanks, Pop."

The father raised a forefinger. "*After* you do your work at the rally."

"Right."

Looney patted his offspring on the cheek. "Good boy."

Then the mob kingpin gathered his two most trusted men, neither of which was his son, and headed out for a meeting with Mayor Schriver.

MARKET SQUARE, ACTUALLY A TRIANGLE, WAS THE CENter of rural commerce in this part of Illinois. An open area of hard-packed earth at Seventeenth Street, from Second to Third Avenues, here farmers could sell corn, potatoes and hay, among other produce, the railroad station only a block away, making shipping a snap.

The rowdy buildings surrounding Market Square housed first-floor restaurants, saloons and retailers, with upper-floor hotels for farmers and other transients; on the Seventeenth Street and Third Avenue corner stood John Looney's Sherman Hotel, whose Java House was a wide-open speakeasy and whose upper floors were the bailiwick of madam Helen Van Dale.

At the opposite end of the same block, the stodgy four-story brick *Argus* newspaper building seemed to avert its many-windowed gaze from the indecency surrounding it; this competitor of the *News* had made a crusade out of bringing down publisher Looney, who regularly responded to charges with his own assertions of the rival editor's supposed sojourns at an insane asylum.

At the center of the square squatted an ornate turn-of-the-century pump house with archways and a speaker's platform bearing built-in electric illumination under a gingerbread roof. On this clear, not terribly cold March evening, streetlamps joined with the glow of the speaker's platform to provide plenty of light for the several thousand people, primarily men, who had gathered to hear speakers demand the recall of Mayor Schriver.

The first speaker, Harry McCaskrin, a stocky mustached fellow in bowler and topcoat, had a mild appearance but shook his fists in the air, spouting gloriously invective oratory as he railed against the corruption of the mayor's office, along the way praising the efforts of the editor of the *News*.

"Without the endeavors of John Looney," McCaskrin said, nostrils wide, "Rock Island would be a Midwestern Gomorrah!"

Only half-listening to this as he threaded through the receptive crowd of mostly working-class joes in their caps and coats and heavy work shoes, Connor Looney—in a tan camel's hair topcoat and green Stetson fedora that a month's pay from any of these hicks wouldn't cover—smiled, well aware that everything the mayor was being accused of, Connor's father could match sin for sin.

Cheers and applause met McCaskrin's attacks, and fliers demanding the mayor's recall were circulated by Looney's newsboys, some "boys" as old as Connor. The body odor of these lowlifes got to him after a while, and he paused in his efforts—looking for the Looney shills in the crowd, to encourage them on—to have a smoke on the edges of this madness. Leaning against a feedstore window, he watched as McCaskrin bellowed—these orators could really work up a head of steam—and reflected on the brief conversation between his pop and himself, right before Connor headed over here.

Did the Old Man really think Connor could find an over-the-hill floozie like Helen Van Dale attractive? Sure, by some men's standards, the Van Dale dame still had it; a shape, a nice face, a sassy manner that a guy might go for.

Personally, Connor found it repellent to be with a woman older than himself, and was repulsed by the idea of being with a woman who'd borne a child. To him, only the budding beauties of the early teenage years really appealed. He was no pervert: he wouldn't be with a girl under, say, twelve.

That was about right, he thought, just as they were becoming women—flat chests, round little bottoms, innocent faces, tiny flappers in the making. Such living dolls were his passion; were, in fact, the only females he could achieve excitement over.

Helen Van Dale knew that, and she kept her eye out for him, when a new young thing came on the market. She saved such morsels for Connor, and she never charged him a dime—out of respect. Connor realized Helen knew which side of the bread the butter went on: that he would one day be the boss of the Tri-Cities, and she had best keep him happy.

And he would rule from Looney's Roost one day, though it galled him to see his father cater to that underling, Mike O'Sullivan. No question Mike was a good guy and a real top hand with a gun. But the man was Shanty Irish trash, and Connor was blood.

Sometimes he just couldn't figure his pop—bad enough Mike had been invited to sit at the conference table in the library; must his pop treat that nigger Davis like an equal? Connor understood the coloreds were good customers, and he knew too the likes of Davis had connections that were useful.

But his father let that nigger drive for him—was seen in public with him! And the one time Connor had found the nerve to complain about it to the Old Man, a slap had been his reward. That's what he got, for showing an interest in the family business! The Old Man talked about wanting Connor to be more involved, to think, to express ideas, and then when he did? A fucking slap, like *Connor* was some whore!

A hat was being passed around now—to finance the recall of Mayor Schriver—and between the Looney goons in the crowd, and the strong pro-Looney, anti-Schriver sentiment in this hooping and hollering riffraff, Connor felt sure no fool would try to make off with that money.

As he studied the throng, Connor noted here and there a pocket of better-dressed, obviously educated folk—teachers, lawyers, clerics, doctors—who were likely among the instigators of this socialist flapdoodle. It bothered him that his father would go along with such traitors.

As his eyes were drifting idly over the crowd, he stopped on a familiar figure—a young man of about eighteen, in a shabby shirt and loose pants and shoes patched with tape. He recognized the boy, who had a distinctive birthmark on one cheek, though he didn't know the lad's name.

A week ago, the kid had cornered Connor, who'd been seated alone with a beer in a back booth at the Java House.

The boy had stood before Connor, his face dirty, his light blue eyes wide, his upper lip pulled back over blackened teeth. On his left cheek was a disgusting brown birthmark bristling with little hairs, shaped like a fat *C*.

"I know what you did to my sister," he said.

"What? Go away."

"She went to work for Mrs. Van Dale. She had to do it. We didn't have no money. She didn't ask my mama, she just run off. . . . She come back last week, cryin'. With stories about what Mr. Looney's son did to her . . . in her . . . her backside."

"Get the fuck out of here."

"You have a dirty mouth, mister."

"Well, you're just plain dirty, kid. Beat it!"

"Does your papa know what you do to young girls? Maybe the *Argus* would pay to know. Maybe Mayor Schriver would."

". . . You want money?"

"No! I want to get even for Colleen! You're a bad man, mister. Maybe I'll catch up with you again some day."

But as the boy stood on the edge of the crowd, he merely seemed to be watching the speaker as McCaskrin riled up the rabble further. Or was this kid here to shadow Connor? To take some stupid hick hayseed revenge upon him?

And now Connor had a new mission for the night. He would keep an eye on the kid. Maybe follow him home, to whatever hovel he'd crawled out of—in Greenbush, maybe, or some shoddy farm. If the kid went to the mayor or the *Argus*, that would be embarrassing.

Connor might even get slapped again.

"Mayor Schriver," the speaker was yelling, "is a disease in human form—and he must be eliminated!"

The crowd roared, fists raised, shaking at the sky.

What a buncha rubes, Connor thought, eyes on the boy.

THE CITY HALL, WHICH INCLUDED THE POLICE STATION, was at Third Avenue and Sixteenth Street, a block away from Market Square. The massive three-story brick building, formerly an armory built in the late 1800s, had a one-story jail annex. Because of the rally, Emeal Davis dropped John Looney and Mike O'Sullivan in front, and drove off in search of a parking place.

As they waited, Looney—dapper in a dark topcoat and black homburg—said to his trusted lieutenant, "Maybe His Honor will listen to reason."

"May be," O'Sullivan said.

It was just cold enough for their breaths to plume. They could hear, like nearby explosions, the applause and cheers at the rally.

"Maybe," Looney said, "we won't even have to throw in with these damn socialists."

"Not my business, sir."

Looney put his hand on Mike's shoulder. "How I wish I had a thousand of you." But he was thinking, *How I wish I had one son like you.*

Then Davis returned, saying he'd got lucky two blocks down, and John Looney took the lead with Davis and O'Sullivan right behind him. The police station was on the bottom floor and the entryway fed a short flight of stairs on either side down to the police area, while a wide central stairway went up to the offices of the city government.

The mayor's office was on the third floor; Looney and his two men walked up the metal-plated stairs, their feet making pinging sounds. After hours, free of most employees, the building had a disconcerting stillness, but for some police-station bustle floating up, hollowly. Their footsteps echoed like gunshots off the marble floor; down at the end of the hall, where the mayor's corner suite of offices waited, two uniformed coppers stood guard.

Looney pretended to recognize the cops, saying "Hello, boys," and reached past them for the knob of the pebbled-glass MAYOR OF ROCK ISLAND door. Davis and O'Sullivan fell in line behind him.

In a firm, not quite threatening manner, the cop nearest the door placed his hand on Looney's arm. Looney looked up, eyebrows raised, making sure his expression told the man this act was an affront.

"I'm sorry, sir," the cop said, a young pale lad who was probably Irish himself, "but we have instructions that only you are to pass."

"Is that right?"

"Yes. Your men here need to stay in the hall. His Honor said to inform you he's requestin' a private meeting."

"Oh. Well, then." Looney shrugged to his men.

Davis said, "We'll be right here."

O'Sullivan said, "You don't have to take this meeting, John."

Rarely did O'Sullivan call Looney by his first name; when he did so, it was not out of a lack of respect, rather a show of affection. This was a friend, not a bodyguard, advising him not to go in there.

Looney twitched a pixie smile. "If you hear me holler, boyos, come runnin'."

"Yes, sir," Davis said, smiling wide for the first time that evening, and revealing two gold eyeteeth, which even in this dim hallway found light to wink off.

Looney went into the reception area; behind the counter were several desks for the mayor's secretary and various assistants, all empty at the moment, not surprising for mid-evening. But leaning against the wall, casually, both smoking cigarettes, in rumpled brown suits that mirrored each other, were two plain-clothes men who Looney did recognize—Simmons and Randell. These were the mayor's personal coppers, his bodyguards, really.

Tough birds.

"Evening, fellas," Looney said.

"Mr. Looney," Simmons said, tipping his fedora. He was a big man, six two easily, with a powerful physique, and an impassive homely pockmarked face.

Randell tipped his hat, too, another big man, though only six foot, but beefy; a paunch on him, though his arms were muscular. His face was round and bland with small dark eyes, watermelon seeds stuck in putty.

Looney pushed open the little gate into the private office area, where the two plainclothes men waited, and could feel their gaze on him.

"Should I go on in?" Looney asked, pausing.

"Better knock," Simmons advised.

And Looney went forward to rap on a pebbled glass door labelled MAYOR HAROLD M. SCHRIVER—PRIVATE.

"Come in!" a deep voice called.

Looney opened the door into the mayor's large office, its light-green plaster walls hanging with framed diplomas, civic awards and photographs of the mayor with various dignitaries, local, state and national. No one could say Harry Schriver had a low opinion of himself.

Along the right wall, as if proof work was done here, were wooden filing cabinets; but snugged against the left wall was a well-worn leather sofa with pillows. The mayor's desk was central, a massive ancient oak affair, suspiciously free of paperwork—just a phone, an ink blotter, a pen-and-pencil holder and an ashtray in which a lighted cigar resided, curling smoke. A newspaper, folded, was off to one side.

Shade drawn on the window behind him, in the swivel chair behind the desk, in shirtsleeves and suspenders, sat the would-be Boss Tweed of Rock Island, Illinois.

Stocky Harry Schriver had a disheveled look, due mostly to a pile of graying hair like a pitchfork of straw had been dropped on his head. His eyes were large and dark blue and bulged, giving him a toad-like quality, which his double chin only underscored. His nose and eyes were bloodshot. His Honor obviously did not respect the Volstead Act.

"How kind of you to accept my invitation, John," Schriver said through a big yellow insincere smile.

Looney, hat in hand, took the visitor's chair across from the desk; he slipped out of his topcoat—the radiator was working overtime—and draped it over the back of the chair; then he crossed his legs, resting ankle on knee.

The Irish kingpin said, "My pleasure, Harry. I assume you'd like to reopen discussions about our business affairs."

Schriver's smile was so tight, his skin seemed about to burst; his eyes had a maniacal gleam. "What's this I hear about you supporting this goddamn horseshit socialist recall?"

Looney shrugged, gestured mildly. "Well, that's how America works, Harry. If the people are dissatisfied with their government, they throw the rascals out."

The smile disappeared and Schriver waved a thick forefinger at his guest. "The people of Rock Island are behind me. They're behind me because I'm striking out at lawbreakers like you, Looney!"

Looney merely smiled, folded his arms. "Save your breath, Harry—you're not out on the campaign stump now. These raids you've been having the police make, these charges you've been bringing against my people . . . what can you be thinking of?"

Schriver leaned on an elbow; he withdrew the cigar from the

ashtray and puffed it nervously. "I just think Rock Island would be better off without a certain element."

Looney uncrossed his legs, unfolded his arms; leaned forward. "No, you think you can take over. You think you can run this city and all the vice on top of it. You don't need a John Looney to oversee things."

Schriver leaned back, rocking in the swivel chair, cigar jutting. "Maybe I don't think a city this size needs two bosses."

"You could be right." Looney gestured with the homburg. "That's why I'm throwing my hat in the ring."

The mayor lurched forward, the cigar almost falling out of his mouth. "What?"

"Well, when you're recalled, somebody will have to sit behind that desk. Might as well be the one boss this city needs . . . me own self."

Schriver turned purple; he grabbed the folded newspaper in both hands and snapped it open for Looney to see—the *News*, with today's headline: SCHRIVER'S SHAME, and slightly smaller, NIGHT AND DAY OF FILTHY DEBAUCH IN PEORIA.

"Good to know people in low places," Looney chuckled. "I have the best sources for tips in the Middle West."

"These lies stop *now*," the mayor said, voice trembling.

Looney drew in a deep breath. Calmly, he said, "This is still America, Mayor Schriver. There's a little thing called the First Amendment. Freedom of the Press."

Schriver's upper lip curled back. "There's a little thing called I don't give a shit. *Boys!*"

The door behind him opened, and Looney glanced back to see the two plainclothes dicks enter.

"It's time," the mayor said. To them.

Looney frowned, getting up.

The two coppers were climbing out of their suitcoats, letting the garments drop to the floor; their guns were holstered on their hips.

Patting the air, Looney said, "You don't want to make this mistake, fellas. The likes of the mayor here are a dime a dozen— the John Looneys last a long time."

"Is that right?" Schriver said, but the voice was next to Looney now. "I think you've lasted long enough."

Looney saw the fist swinging but couldn't duck, and his thought, his ironic self-mocking thought was, *Brass-knuckle business is right*, because His Honor was wearing them. The punch shattered Looney's nose, and he would have gone down on his knees, but the two burly coppers were holding onto him.

Blood running through his mustache into his mouth, Looney half-choked as he asked, "What do you want, Schriver?"

The mayor slammed a fist into Looney's belly.

Looney, who had ulcers, felt pain streak through him.

"I want a retraction," the mayor said, "and an apology . . . in print!"

"All . . . all right."

Schriver went back around the desk, opened a drawer, and when he returned, had a length of rubber hose in his hand.

"I . . . I said I'd apologize . . . retract it. . . ."

The mayor whacked the rubber hose alongside Looney's right ear; cartilage snapped like twigs underfoot. "Glad to hear it, John! But that's the last time I want to see my name in your scandalous, blackmailing rag again, understood?"

"Un . . . understood. . . ."

The mayor whapped the rubber hose alongside Looney's left ear. More snapping cartilage.

Looney shrieked, *"You're killing me! You're fucking murdering me!"*

The mayor waved the limp phallus of the rubber hose in Looney's blood-streaked face. "No, John, I'm just warning you. Warning you that your paper will have one more edition, apologizing to me, before you disappear. Before you go out to your New Mexico ranch and hump cattle or cactus, for all I the hell care. Because, John?"

And the mayor kneed Looney in the groin.

Crying out in agony, spitting blood, Looney screamed, *"Help! Mike! Emeal! For God's sake!"*

"They're not available, John. What was I saying? Oh yes, because if I or any of my men see you in Rock Island two days from now, you'll be shot on sight."

Looney, barely conscious, said nothing, held up like a ragdoll by the coppers.

The mayor tossed the bloody rubber hose on the desk and then flexed his hands. "I'm tired, fellas. You work him over for a while. I'll just watch."

And they did, and the mayor did.

3

IN RECENT YEARS, MICHAEL O'SUL-
livan had rarely felt helpless.

He had survived the war, when many
around him in the trenches had not. And
he had returned to America with a new
confidence and a fatalistic outlook that
served him well. Along the way, he had
earned the allegiance of John Looney, even
as he paid Mr. Looney that same respect.

But as he stood in the City Hall hallway,
next to his friend and fellow Looney aide
Emeal Davis, O'Sullivan felt helpless indeed, hearing the cries of his chief, the ag-
onized calls for help, the pitiful shrieking
from beyond the pebbled glass doorway
guarded by the two armed police officers.

"They're killing him in there," O'Sullivan said to the pale young cop, over the muffled yet all too distinctive cries of pain.

"I have my orders," the young cop said; something in the man's voice said he did not necessarily relish these orders.

"Nothing's keeping you here," the other cop said. He was about thirty with a chiseled look and eyes that conveyed a cynical acceptance of his lot in life. He clutched his nightstick in his right hand, tapping it into the open palm of his left, to produce a rhythmic, suggestive thumping.

Looney cried, "*Sweet Jesus!*"

This was not a prayer.

Trembling with rage, Emeal Davis stepped forward and raised a pointing finger. "We're not putting up with that—that's our boss in there!"

The chiseled copper said, "Don't wag your finger at me, nigger. Get the hell out while you still can."

Davis's eyes were wild and O'Sullivan knew the man was seconds away from drawing down on the officers and storming the office and taking back their boss. O'Sullivan grabbed Davis by the elbow, shot him a hard look, and took several steps back, as did Davis, his eyes now hooded and ominous.

Looney's cries continued.

"We can go," O'Sullivan whispered. The two men were huddled against the opposite wall while the coppers eyed them. "And we should."

Davis whispered back harshly: "And leave Mr. Looney in there, to be beaten to death?"

"I don't think the mayor brought him here to kill him. Just to teach John Looney a lesson."

"But the Old Man's health is frail . . ."

"Emeal, he's strong at heart. He's got spine."

Undercutting O'Sullivan's argument, a shrill cry of pain from Looney emanated from the closed office door. The pale young cop swallowed; the older one swung that nightstick into his palm again, harder now.

"You could always go get reinforcements," the smug older

165

cop said, *thump, thump, thump*. "We only have thirty-five, forty fellas on hand, downstairs."

O'Sullivan stepped forward, holding an arm out to keep Davis back. "I know you're just doin' your job, gents."

With a curt nod, O'Sullivan took Davis by the arm and on the first-floor landing Davis glared at his companion. The dark blue derby was at a jaunty angle and the effect, with the intense clenched anger, was almost comic.

Almost.

Whispering, Davis said, "You and me can take those two lads out, easy. Schriver's probably got his bully boys, Randell and Simmons in there, working John over, tenderizin' him like a bad cut of beef. We can take them out, one two, and His Honor'll be shakin' in the corner."

"Can we do that without firing a shot?" O'Sullivan asked. "Without attracting the boys in blue down below?"

Davis's eyes tightened in doubt. "Well. . . . I say we take the risk."

"I say we take Mr. Billy Club's advice."

"What advice?"

"Seek reinforcements."

O'Sullivan took Davis by the arm again and they went quickly down the stairs and out into the night. At the top of the steps, City Hall at their back, the two men could hear the cheers, the applause, the shouts, the intensity of which had grown considerably since they'd gone inside.

"If our triggermen rush the police station," O'Sullivan said, "then every Looney enemy on both sides of the river'll have all they need to end our endeavor, forever."

Davis frowned, his breath steaming through flared nostrils like an angry bull. "Goddamnit. You're right, Mike. Schriver'd be the kingpin of the Tri-Cities. But he's killin' John in there!"

O'Sullivan walked down to the sidewalk, Davis following. "Emeal, if Harry kills John, it'll only be 'cause it got out of hand. He means to take our friend to the woodshed. Take him down as many pegs as pegs there are."

They walked across the street and faced each other.

███

Davis said, "John may not survive."

"That's true. Schriver's risking that—you know how cozy the Old Man is with Chicago. Torrio and Capone would come down on this town with Biblical fire. When the smoke cleared, Schriver would be dead, and some Chicago pawn would have the local throne."

Davis was shaking his head. "Mike—I never heard you talk like this. You always seem like you're just . . . in the background; but you been listenin', ain't ya?"

"I haven't been asleep."

Providing O'Sullivan with applause, the crowd a block over roared.

O'Sullivan began to walk toward Market Square, and Davis put a hand on his friend's shoulder.

"Mike, I parked down the other way."

"Never mind the car. We're going over to the rally."

"Why?"

O'Sullivan flashed the derby-sporting gangster a small nasty smile; put a brotherly hand on the man's shoulder.

"If an angry local populace rushes City Hall, Emeal, seeking release of their champion, John Looney . . . serving that recall on His Honor a bit early . . . then we'd have our way, wouldn't we? And take no blame."

Davis had the expression of a man who'd been slapped; but then he grinned, the gold teeth gleaming. "You ain't been asleep, Mike. Not in the least bit."

CONNOR LOONEY, ON THE SIDELINES, WAS WATCHING the socialist speaker, Gardner, further inflame the flock. A skinny man with a narrow face and sharp features, Gardner wore a black suit with string tie; with his Lincolnesque features, his itinerant preacher air, the orator played the crowd like a god-damn nickel kazoo.

"It is not enough to remove Harry M. Schriver," Gardner was

saying in a spike-edged baritone, "we must look to the fearless newspaperman who has sought to bring our besmirched city back within the bounds of peace, propriety and happiness. The next mayor of Rock Island, my friends, must be . . . *John . . . P. . . . Looney!*"

As fists were raised, shaking wildly, and whistles and squeals and yells swam a sea of applause, Connor revised his opinion of throwing in with these socialists. The speaker was at once a rabble-rouser, full of fiery idealism; and yet just the kind of pushover they could control. The previous speaker, McCaskrin, had towed the Looney line, but stopped short of endorsing the Old Man as the replacement candidate.

This skinny clown had gone all the way, however, due to a whisper (and probably a few bucks) from Frank Kelly, who could be glimpsed hovering near one side of the platform.

Then Connor noted a figure moving through the crowd, against the tide: *it was that nigger Davis!* Seeking out the Looney shills dotted around the square; Davis would pause to speak to each of them, receiving nods in return, and the shills were then moving out through the crowd themselves, animatedly talking to rally attendees as they went.

Connor dropped his cigarette to the pavement, frowning. What was up, anyway?

Then he saw another familiar figure—Michael O'Sullivan—moving through the bobbing heads up near the pump-station platform. Had his father made a last minute decision to speak to this gathering, himself?

But then he spotted that plump leprechaun Frank Kelly going up the side stairs toward the platform, followed by Mike, who stopped the lawyer, whispered to him, Kelly nodding, only to continue on up. Then Mike slipped back down the stairs and was swallowed up by the throng.

Frowning in thought, Connor was watching the stage when he realized Emeal Davis was again moving through the crowd, coming toward him now; Davis had an intense expression and Connor immediately knew something big was afoot.

Quickly Davis filled Connor in on the situation at City Hall, and told him that even now the Old Man was being beaten to a pulp by Schriver and his bully boys.

"Those pricks!" Connor said, hands tightened into balls, face flushed red. "Let's storm the fuckin' place!"

Davis said, patting the air with his hands like a damn minstrel, "Take it easy, boyo—that's exactly what we plan to do. But Mike's got a way to do it, a special way. . . ."

"Mike? Who died and put him in charge? With my pop in custody, that makes me the man who makes the decisions! Haul Mike's ass over here, and I'll tell *him* what to do."

"Connor, it's a good plan . . ."

"I'm not 'Connor' to you, Sambo. It's 'Mr. Looney' or you can get your black ass out of my family's business."

Davis swallowed. "I know you're upset . . . but this plan is a good one, and it's already in motion."

And it was, too: on the stage, Gardner had interrupted his spiel momentarily while Frank Kelly whispered into his ear. Nodding, the scarecrow-esque Gardner raised his hands as if the victim of a holdup; but the crowd, milling and murmuring during the lull in the speech, hushed.

"I am given to understand," the sharp voice said, in crisp single words that shot verbal bullets across Market Square, "that the mayor has taken John Looney into custody!"

A wave of discontent rumbled across the throng. Heads shook in distressed disbelief.

Davis said to Connor, "Just listen and watch."

"Not on any criminal charge, mind you," the speaker went on, "but virtually *kidnapped*—and John Looney is as we gather here in peaceful, lawful assembly being *beaten* behind closed doors at City Hall!"

Cries of *"No! No!"* went up, interspersed with, *"Bastards!" "Sons of bitches!"* and Connor—his opinion swaying—watched with satisfaction as the crowd began to transform itself into a mob. Really quite entertaining. . . .

And now the speaker drove in the final nail: "Yes—just *one block* from here . . ." And he pointed. ". . . your candidate for mayor is being *thrashed* within an inch of his life by *His Dishonor, Harry Schriver*, and his crooked thugs who call themselves police!"

Connor thought, *For a goddamn socialist, this guy takes orders well.*

And now, all around, voices were raised: *"Let's go! Let's save him!"* Still others: *"Save John Looney!"* And (best of all, to Connor's taste): *"Hang Harry Schriver!"*

That these "spontaneous" eruptions came from the Looney men sprinkled throughout the gathering revealed how effective Mike's plan had been, how quickly he and Davis had passed the word and organized this attack. Even Connor could see that.

But he couldn't let Davis know, so he said, feigning displeased reluctance, "Well, it's too late now—we'll go with it! Keep stirring up the shit. I'll do the same."

Davis nodded and disappeared in the crowd, which was already swarming toward the business district between them and City Hall. God, it was great! Connor watched with delight as the crowd of appleknockers and dirty necks turned from shuffling discontent into full-bore hatred and malice.

The ungeneraled underclass army marched, their war cries guttural, nonverbal howls mostly, the injustices they'd suffered at various hands boiling over within them into the rage they'd forced down for so long, and were all too eager to spill. Connor watched with glee as the men found impromptu weapons—bottles, rocks, boards. Still, it didn't seem to the son of John Looney quite enough—not enough to pay Mayor Schriver back for disrespecting the Looneys, and not enough . . . well . . . fun.

"Guns!" Connor yelled, pointing at a hardware store window. "Arm yourselves! There are *cops* in that building!"

A gaggle of rabble surged forward and Connor, laughing to himself, stepped aside and watched as the window shattered under hurled rocks, and the door was battered down. He leaned against a wall half a block away while the unruly clodhoppers poured in and poured out of the hardware store, half-climbing over each other, shouting inanities, armed now with rifles and handguns they were loading on the run from boxes of ammunition they'd looted, and others—once the guns had run out—

found pitchforks and wrenches and other tools easily turned toward destruction.

The example of the hardware store inspired the hurling of bricks and rocks through other retail windows, for the sheer sweet hell of it; rioters were pulling down trolley lines, too, throwing rocks at streetcar conductors. Here and there were stalled automobiles, windows rolled up tight, the terrified eyes of passengers taking in the streaming madness all around. Not all the wrath was righteous, as some rioters began to loot, figures darting into the night with their spoils, away from those swarming toward City Hall.

Market Square had almost emptied out when fate did Connor a favor.

Another figure lurked on the sidelines, just down the street from him, leaning against a building by the mouth of an alley: *that kid with the birthmark and the shabby clothes.* The boy would not likely be a Looney booster, not with what had happened to his sister at Helen Van Dale's. No, the lad had come around out of curiosity, for the big show, and was getting a bigger eyeful than he'd anticipated.

Connor glanced around. A few stragglers were still charging over toward City Hall. A scattering of others around the hard-dirt, brochure-littered area, stood watching, rather stunned, the parade literally passing them by. For the most part, though, the square had been abandoned, as the mob moved on to City Hall.

The boy with the birthmark jumped when Connor stuck the gun in his side.

The boy turned toward Connor, the light blue eyes wide, the mouth with its scummy teeth gaping. "You!"

"Yeah, me, kid. Head down the alley."

"What?"

"Do I stutter? Head the hell down. There's a fence at the end. See if you can make it over."

"What . . . what do you mean . . . see if . . ."

Connor cocked the .38 in his grasp; it was a tiny sound and yet so very loud.

"I'm giving you a chance, kid. Run. Run down that alley and don't come back. Don't never threaten me again."

The boy shook his head, his hands grasped before him, pleadingly. "I was . . . I was just *talkin'*, mister. I was mad about my sister. Wouldn't you be?"

"Run. Hell, you might make it. Do it now."

The boy's face crinkled up, like he was going to cry, and then, from his dead stop, he bolted down the alley.

Connor walked after him—not even particularly fast—and the kid was almost over the fence when Connor fired. The report of the .38 echoed off the brick of walls and paving, bouncing like an ever-diminishing ball; but these were only a handful of sounds, in a night filled with violent sounds, many so much louder.

And the boy didn't make any sound. Well, maybe a whimper. He just slid down the wooden fence, leaving a thin red trail, like a child's crayon scrawl. He lay sprawled with his head against the fence, angled between garbage cans, and there wasn't even a shudder of life leaving him—he'd been dead halfway down the fence.

Connor knelt over the body, just to be sure.

Dead, all right. Right through the pump. . . .

He got to his feet, grunting a humorless laugh. Stupid damn kid. That's what he got, screwing with Connor Looney. Or maybe it was what his sister got, for screwing with Connor Looney. . . .

Connor grunted another laugh, this one mirthful.

Then he turned and had a start—a figure was silhouetted at the alley's mouth.

"What the hell did you *do*?" Michael O'Sullivan demanded, stepping into a shaft of moonlight.

Gun in hand but at his side, Connor walked forward, slowly. "It's personal."

O'Sullivan met him half-way, footsteps clipclopping off the brick. "This was business, tonight. This is about saving your father's life. Or aren't you interested?"

"Just keep it to yourself, Mike. What you saw. You don't wanna know what it was about—trust me."

"Trust you? Sure. Why wouldn't I trust you, Connor?"

"You gonna tell my pop?"

"Tell him what? That while he lay bleeding, you used this riot to cover up some personal score?"

Connor shook his head, forcefully. "People'll get hurt tonight. Shot. This kid may not be the only kill. Who's to know?"

O'Sullivan said nothing.

"Swear you won't tell my pop, Mike!" Connor shoved the gun in the other man's chest.

O'Sullivan swatted the gun from Connor's hand like an annoying fly. The gun hit hard on the brick alley but luckily did not discharge.

"What if your wife knew about things *you* done?" Connor said, backing up. He was afraid and trying not to cry. "Or your little boy, maybe!"

O'Sullivan moved so quickly Connor didn't see it coming, latching onto young Looney's topcoat lapels and slamming him hard into a brick wall, making his teeth rattle.

Nose to nose, O'Sullivan said to the trembling Connor, "Don't ever bring my family into this. Ever. Or I'll kill you. Understood?"

"Y-yes. . . ."

O'Sullivan drew back a step but did not let go. "I won't tell your father because it would break his heart to know what a vicious little coward his son is."

"I . . . I appreciate that, Mike. . . . It's . . . it's white of you."

"I don't know who that boy is or why you cut him down. But you will send ten thousand dollars of your money to his family, anonymous."

"What?"

"That's the price of my silence."

". . . All right. All right—god-*damnit*!"

"I want to see the cash, Connor. I want to see it go into the envelope. I want to see it mailed."

"Okay, okay!"

O'Sullivan took another step back, his hands still on Connor's lapels. "Now . . . if you don't mind, I have to get over to City Hall. Your old man's ass needs saving."

And O'Sullivan again shoved Connor against the wall, and headed briskly out of the alley.

But, as Connor was stooping to pick up the .38, O'Sullivan paused at the alley's mouth to look back and say, "You might want to get over to City Hall yourself and help keep the crowd stirred. Hanging around a murder scene is stupid, Connor . . . even for you."

And O'Sullivan was gone.

Connor picked up the .38, shoved it in the holster under his arm, then bent over and put his hands on his knees and breathed deep, breathed deep again, and again.

Fucker, Connor thought, and smiled. *Got the best of you, you self-righteous fucker. . . .*

Straightening, he glanced back at the crumpled birthmarked boy. "And you, punk. And you."

And Connor, walking with renewed confidence, strolled out across the square, heading over toward City Hall, where it was getting pretty damn noisy.

A DISGUSTED O'SULLIVAN ENTERED THE SHERMAN HOTEL and crossed quickly to the bank of telephone booths along the lefthand wall. Tumbleweed might have rolled between the overstuffed furniture and potted plants, so empty was the lobby.

Behind the check-in desk, the skeletal clerk in bow tie and suspenders looked fidgety, fearing no doubt that the riot would spill inside; the clerk recognized O'Sullivan but said nothing, though his eyes followed the lobby's only other inhabitant. The hotel's coffee shop, the Java House—which served gin in its coffee cups—had shuttered, as had other speaks in the downtown district, afraid of the contagious chaos that had emerged from Market Square.

Inside a booth, O'Sullivan dropped a nickel in and dialed a number that required referring to neither city phone directory nor his little black book (with the names and numbers of politicians and fixers, not skirts).

John Looney's top lieutenant knew the unlisted home phone number of Police Chief Tom Cox by heart.

O'Sullivan listened as the phone rang, going unanswered; he wouldn't have been surprised if the thing had been off the hook, since Cox no doubt knew by now that rioters were at the gates of his castle, and wanted to stay well away.

Tom Cox was a stocky sandy-haired copper who'd come up through the ranks. His reputation as a tough bull and an advocate of the third degree was epitomized by his favorite catch phrase: "Throw the bum in the slammer."

But shortly after achieving the position of chief, Cox became a John Looney associate, receiving a cut from all brothels, gambling and bootlegging. Whores were the man's weakness, and Helen Van Dale had enough on the chief to keep him in Looney's control a few days past forever.

A police chief in Rock Island could serve under any number of mayors; so a longterm relationship with Tom Cox had benefits beyond those of any mere office holder.

Just when O'Sullivan was about to give up, a raspy voice answered: "Yeah, what? I'm busy!"

"Tom, it's Mike O'Sullivan. You know what's going on down at City Hall?"

The response was weary and wry: "Recall rally's gettin' a little out of hand, I hear."

"Laugh it off if you like, Tom. But they broke into a couple hardware stores and helped themselves to guns and bullets. You're minutes away from a shooting war."

"*Christ.* . . . Well, if you think I'm drivin' over there to have a little of it, Mike, you're out of your goddamn mind."

O'Sullivan's voice took on an edge. "Tom—did you know what Schriver had in mind for John?"

"Of course not," the chief growled.

But it wasn't convincing.

"Tom, if you tell me the truth, I'll understand. You're between a rock and a hard place, with your allegiance to John, same time working under Schriver. So just tell me."

"Mike, I didn't know."

━━━

Still not sold, O'Sullivan said, "If you lie to me, Tom . . . I'll be unhappy."

A long silence followed.

Then, a sniveling Cox returned to the wire: "I figured they'd just work him over a little, throw a scare into the Old Man. Only, from what my captain down there says, they've half killed the poor sod."

"If those rioters get inside that building," O'Sullivan said, slowly, carefully, "and see what Schriver and his bully boys have done to John Looney, they'll burn the place down."

"Anarchy. Anarchy. How could it come to this? How could this happen?"

"I have no idea," O'Sullivan lied.

"Mother of mercy, what can we do?"

"Call your captain and have him let me and Emeal Davis in. We'll fetch John."

"Mike, if you haul a bloody and battered John Looney out of there, that crowd'll blow a gasket!"

"Not if you have a Black Maria waiting in the police garage. We'll haul the Old Man over to St. Anthony's. If the rioters do storm your bastille, Tom, well, they won't find a half-dead John Looney inside, to inflame them further."

Another long silence followed.

Then Cox said, "No better plan comes to me. Mike, we'll try it your way. Give me five minutes."

O'Sullivan exited the booth and the hotel, meeting up with Emeal Davis out front, as they'd prearranged. He filled Davis in, heading across the now all-but-deserted Market Square, scattered with discarded recall brochures, toward the hullabaloo. Traffic had disappeared, as if every vehicle in downtown Rock Island had been sucked into the sky.

As the two Looney soldiers approached City Hall, they found Third Avenue and Sixteenth Street clogged with humanity, the full moon conspiring with streetlamps to throw a yellow-ish ivory glow on a surreal urban landscape, the surrounding buildings black against the gray heavens, looming like giant tombstones. It seemed to O'Sullivan that these men had become less than themselves, and more, swallowed up in the breathing, moving organism that was a mob.

"This thing," Emeal yelled into Mike's ear (and yet it was like a whisper), "has got a mind of its own."

"Nothing to be done but live with it," O'Sullivan yelled. "And *use* it . . . for John."

From the stormy sea of bobbing heads and upraised fists—holding weapons, bricks and boards and handguns and rifles—an ongoing rumble of dissatisfaction erupted every few moments into shouted accusations and yelled admonitions. Eyes were wild, gums bared over teeth; the jungle beneath the skin of civilization was showing through.

At the front of City Hall, a short flight of stairs rose on either side to the double doors where Looney, O'Sullivan and Davis had earlier entered; tucked under the porch-like landing were another set of double doors, leading into the police station. From these poured a contingent of cops in uniform, with riot guns, shotguns and handguns, streaming out in twin ribbons of blue, fanning out either way across the face of the building.

This did not go over well with the crowd, separated from them by a narrow strip of brick street. Like Apaches, the rioters raised rifles high in clenched fists and filled the night with non-verbal, animal war cries.

Then, finally, some damn fool pulled a trigger.

The rioters began to fire their weapons—into the air, mostly, some firing at City Hall itself, high over the heads of the row of cops, who were doing their best not to cower, as slugs dug holes in the brick building, spitting back chunks and slivers and flakes to rain down upon the scared-shitless guardians in blue below.

Through this volatile crowd, gunfire snapping in the air like dozens of whipcracks, O'Sullivan and Davis made their way; it took ten minutes to traverse the few yards. While a sporadic barrage of shots continued to emerge from the mob, the coppers out front aimed their weapons but did not fire—which seemed to O'Sullivan a miracle.

Then he and Davis stepped into the no-man's land that was about half of Third Avenue, that brick strip between cops and rioters, and held up their hands as they went, turning their backs to the cops. The gunfire abated, as the rioters—many standing on their toes and jumping up, to see what was going on—reacted to the two men in civilian clothes going across that unofficial barrier toward the enemy camp.

Not completely unaware of the irony, O'Sullivan yelled, "We're Looney men!"

Davis echoed him, and no one from the mob tried to stop them or, better yet, shoot them.

O'Sullivan approached a cop he recognized, Sergeant Bill O'Malley, who was in the midst of the row of armed coppers.

"Bill, your captain's expecting us," O'Sullivan yelled, over the war whoops of the crowd. "I'm here at Chief Cox's behest."

O'Malley accepted this with a nod, and sent them up the stairs, unaccompanied, where they paused on the landing to look out at the teeming force that O'Sullivan had unleashed.

It was one of the most frightening sights of Michael O'Sullivan's life—which was no small thing.

Just inside the door, Captain James Doherty met them, a solemn-faced, redheaded, green-eyed uniformed cop, loyal to his chief. Quickly he escorted the two Looney soldiers up to the third-floor hallway, where the two uniformed cops still stood guard.

O'Sullivan let Doherty do the talking.

"We have a full-scale riot out there," the captain told the two sentries, gesturing toward the muffled popping gunfire. "There's still a shotgun or two downstairs. Position yourselves on the landing, boys—guard the City Hall front gates."

The older smug cop, who'd threatened the Looney bodyguards with his nightstick before, frowned and said, "We have orders from the mayor to maintain this post."

Doherty stepped forward and his face was inches from his subordinate's. "These orders come straight from Chief Cox—this riot situation has developed subsequent to the mayor's orders, and supersedes them. Assume your new assignment, or I'll have you removed and put behind bars."

In an eyeblink, the two sentries had abandoned this post for their new one.

Captain Doherty turned his seemingly placid green eyes on O'Sullivan and Davis and, very quietly, said, "I have to go down to stand with my men. We have under forty to try to hold back a mob of two thousand. . . . I don't know what you intend to do in the mayor's office, and I don't want to know. Neither does Chief Cox. . . . Understood, gents?"

"Understood. The Black Maria is standing by?"

"Yes. I have a driver posted downstairs." He handed a slip of paper with a phone number to O'Sullivan. "Call when you're ready. He'll bring up a stretcher."

Then the captain, too, was gone.

O'Sullivan withdrew his .45 Colt automatic, like him a veteran of the Great War. Davis reached under his baby-blue suitcoat for his long-barrelled .38, slung under his arm in a handtooled leather holster worthy of Wyatt Earp.

"We try not to kill anybody," O'Sullivan said.

"You say so," Davis said, noncommittally.

In the outer office, O'Sullivan slipped out of his topcoat and slung it over the counter, to be less encumbered. Davis wore no topcoat, just that spiffy blue suit with derby. O'Sullivan led the way through the little gate to the door that said MAYOR HAROLD M. SCHRIVER—PRIVATE.

Not knowing whether it was locked or not, O'Sullivan took no chances; the mayor had undoubtedly been informed by phone or otherwise of the impending danger outside and may well have locked himself in. So the rescuer raised his right foot and kicked it open, the door springing off its hinges and the pebbled glass shattering under the impact, chunks falling like melting sheets of ice.

His shoes crunching shards as he entered, O'Sullivan took position to the right of the doorway, leaving the left for Davis, who immediately followed, and both men fanned their guns around the startled tableau within.

John Looney, barely conscious, lay asprawl on his back on the leather couch against the left wall; his white shirt was spattered with blood, the brown suit rumpled, dark dried patches of blood on it, too. The mayor sat behind his desk, leaned back in his swivel chair, and his two bruisers, pockmarked Simmons and round-mugged Randell, sat in a pair of hardback chairs, facing the couch but not close by. All three men were in shirtsleeves, white cloth splotched with blood. The two burly cops were hunkered over, as if exhausted.

"Tuckered out, boys?" O'Sullivan said.

"Takes it out of you," Davis said, "whompin' a helpless old man."

Simmons sneered and went for his holstered gun; the weapon was half out of its hip holster and the plainclothes dick was three-quarters up out of the chair when O'Sullivan's .45 slug took the top of his head off and splashed a covered bridge depicted in watercolor on a 1922 calendar over the file cabinets. Small spatters of blood marked various dates.

The dead Simmons tumbled back over his chair and lay in an awkward V half between the toppled chair and the files.

"Jesus!" the mayor said, on his feet; but he had sense enough to lay his hands flat on the desktop.

The other cop, Randell, remained seated; his bland moon face was largely emotionless, though his left eye was twitching. Slowly he raised his hands.

Davis, near the door, threw his comrade a look that said, *Try not to kill anybody, huh?*, which O'Sullivan ignored, saying, "Got a gun back there, Your Honor?"

The toad-like mayor, trembling with rage and fear, said, "Are you crazy? Out of your minds?"

"We're Looney," Davis said, gold teeth glittering.

Schriver was sputtering, words rushing out: "You don't just waltz in the mayor's office and start shooting the place up! There's forty cops downstairs, you fools! You killed one of their brothers! You'll fry for this."

"Those forty cops," O'Sullivan said, "have their hands full with two or three thousand voters who want your fat ass out from behind that desk. . . . Speaking of which, go stand by the corpse and put your hands up. High."

Swallowing, the now-speechless mayor did that very thing,

revealing the front of his gray pants as glistening wet, which O'Sullivan found gratifying—the two Looney soldiers were making their point.

O'Sullivan got behind the desk and used the mayor's phone to call the number Captain Doherty had provided.

In the meantime, Davis knelt beside Looney, whose face was battered and swollen, decorated with shades of blue, black, orange and red, his eyes almost shut, like a heavyweight fighter in the final round.

O'Sullivan strolled from behind the desk to where the mayor stood; the stench of urine wasn't pleasant.

"Harry," O'Sullivan said, "it's a damn shame a brave officer like Simmons there had to catch a stray bullet in this riot. He'll deserve a commendation."

The mayor's chin was quivering. "You really think I'd cover for you, O'Sullivan?"

"Well, Harry, you best convince me such, right now—or both you and Randell can join Simmons in hell."

The mayor whitened; then he lurched to one side and fell to his knees and vomited.

In a voice that tried to sound calm but had a warble in it, Randell said, "Harry'll cover for you. If he doesn't, I'll kill him for you myself, Mike."

"I believe you," O'Sullivan said. Then to the mayor he said, "Stand up, Harry."

The smell in the enclosed space was awful.

Davis glanced over with his face balled up. "What the hell did you have for supper, Harry? Christ!"

The mayor got to his feet, looking less than dignified in his pissed pants and with puke-stubble around his mouth.

But doing his best, the mayor said, "It's . . . it's sad to lose a fine . . . fine man like Lieutenant Simmons to a . . . a . . . unruly mob."

O'Sullivan nodded. "We're in this together, Harry. You see, I'm doing you a favor."

"A . . . a favor?"

"That's right. That's why Chief Cox paved the way for this."

The mayor couldn't hold back a sneer at word of this predictable betrayal.

"If those thousands rush this building," O'Sullivan said, "and find out what you and your boyos did to John Looney . . . they'll lynch you, sure."

The mayor frowned in the realization of the truth of these words.

"*Both* of you," O'Sullivan said, throwing a glance at the surviving dick. "The way Simmons went out will start to look merciful."

The mayor nodded.

His hands still up, Randell said, "You're right, Mike. For God's sake, get John outa here."

Davis was looking through the open door into the outer office. "John's ride is here," he said.

"Okay," he said to Davis. "Let's you and me drunk-walk John out to the stretcher—no need for another witness to this tragedy. . . . Harry, I'd advise dumping your boy on the street somewhere."

The mayor swallowed and nodded.

Randell said, "I'll handle it personally, Mike. Nobody but us here in this room will know."

"That's how I want it," O'Sullivan said.

Looney's two men, each with a gun in one hand, got on either side of their barely conscious boss and eased him to his limp feet.

From the doorway, as he hauled Looney in tandem with Davis, O'Sullivan glanced back with a tiny smile, and said, "Gents? If you do decide to cross me, make sure you kill me. You wouldn't like bein' on my bad side."

Within moments, Looney was on a stretcher that a young uniformed cop and Davis were bearing down the stairs. The gunfire outside had resumed, but it remained limited to shots in the air and high assaults on the building itself—posturing, so far, not open warfare. O'Sullivan, in his topcoat again, the .45 still in hand, followed as they carted the now unconscious Looney through the empty station to the garage and into the waiting paddy wagon.

Davis rode with Looney, and O'Sullivan sat in front while the young copper drove the bulky black vehicle. The garage was around back, and away from the crowd, so getting out to open and close the door—a chore O'Sullivan handled—was no problem. Pushing through the crowd itself was slow, and rioters banged on the metal sides, making dull clangs; but nobody took a shot, and in five minutes they were clear of the riot scene.

Just before they slipped away, however, O'Sullivan spotted a familiar face at the rear of the crowd: Connor Looney, watching the Maria depart. The Old Man's son was not one of those yelling or waving a gun. . . . In fact, Connor looked eerily calm, a terrible smile glazed on his face.

No man on earth, Michael O'Sullivan decided, had a worse smile than Connor Looney . . . nor was there likely any man who wore a smile more often, at such inappropriate times.

"Where to?" the wide-eyed young cop behind the wheel asked.

"St. Anthony's Hospital," O'Sullivan said.

Unaware that his wife was already a patient there.

4

THE RIOT OUTSIDE CITY HALL ENDED
only when the police began to fire volley
after volley into the mob.

How the coppers had held up so long
was anybody's guess—shots fired over their
heads, bricks breaking windows, stones
tossed their way. Such dangerous indigni-
ties could not forever be withstood.

But they did not fire spontaneously—
they waited for Captain Doherty's orders, which were to shoot to wound, and
thanks to the captain's caution, not one
of the rioters was killed, although
around twenty did go down bleeding.
One malcontent climbed a pole and
tried to cut an electric line, presumably
to plunge the building into darkness, but
a police shot picked him off, an arc light

coming down with him, sputtering to the crowd in a shower of sparks.

Finally the mob dispersed, hauling away their casualties into the downtown. There they lingered, however, roaming and occasionally looting. But by dawn Market Square and the block between it and City Hall were deserted, albeit resembling a battlefield—spent shells, bricks, rocks, shards of glass, chunks of wood, strewn like ominous refuse.

The next morning, the governor—receiving a call not from Chief Cox but from the sheriff—declared martial law and six-hundred militia from Galesburg, Monmouth, Sterling and Geneseo poured in, mobilizing at the Rock Island Armory. Public speeches and meetings were forbidden—groups on the street could be no larger than two. For several days, these uniformed soldiers patrolled the streets with rifle in hand.

But this cavalry arrived after the fact, the rioters long gone. Schriver's police raided speakeasies and bawdy houses, and thirty-four arrests were made. The opening gun of this "clean-up campaign" was closing down the Rock Island *News* on charges of "indecency," with eighteen employees, mostly newsboys, arrested.

Mayor Schriver's efforts to quell John Looney's power of the press were, ironically, seriously undercut by the other Tri-Cities papers—even the archenemy *Argus*.

His face bruised and decorated with bandages, including one around his head that brought to mind the Spirit of '76, John Looney—mid-morning of the day after—held court in his hospital gown from his bed in a private room at St. Anthony's, in the modern wing his money had largely made possible. His eyes almost swollen shut, the publisher of the Rock Island *News* clearly wasn't faking.

An armed bodyguard, Emeal Davis, was posted outside the door; and at Looney's bedside sat the patient's son, Connor, solemn and dressed in black, as if his father had passed away (despite the man's presence next to him). Already the place was filled with flowers; to Connor Looney, it was more like sitting in the winner's circle at the Kentucky Derby than the sick room of a guy who just got the shit kicked out of him.

But Connor was impressed by the crowd his old man had drawn. In addition to the *Argus*, Moline *Dispatch* and Davenport *Democrat*, reporters had come from as far away as the *Register* in Des Moines and the *Trib* in Chicago, driving through the night to get to the scene of a riot that would be reported 'round the world.

"I realize, gentlemen," Looney said through bruised lips, his battered condition well-suited to his melodramatic tone, "that some of us have had our little differences."

Differences like calling the editor of the *Argus* insane, in print, Connor thought, managing not to smile.

"The beating I received at the hands of the mayor," Looney was saying, "shows the disregard this evil mountebank has for freedom of speech, freedom of the press. The bedrock of our nation."

"Three people died, Mr. Looney," a young *Democrat* scribe said. "Including a police officer, killed by a stray bullet through a window. Surely you don't condone the actions of these rioters."

Looney shifted in the cranked-up bed. "Two citizens also died, when the police recklessly fired their guns into a crowd that had assembled because news had spread of my kidnapping and assault. These brave, foolhardy souls ran to my rescue, and I love them for it, even when their judgment failed them. Remember, some two dozen suffered gunshot wounds from police volleys, or so I am told."

An *Argus* reporter asked, "Will you continue to lobby for the mayor's recall? Do you still intend to run yourself?"

"My newspaper has been unlawfully shut down," Looney said. "And until I have my constitutional freedom of speech restored, I can lobby for nothing. That said, I understand the sheriff's office is opening an investigation into graft and corruption in the Schriver administration."

A Davenport *Daily Times* man pressed, "Do you or don't you intend to run for mayor?"

"No. And I never did. I appreciate the enthusiasm of my many friends and supporters in Rock Island . . . but I frankly don't know how that rumor ever got started. . . . In fact, I will be leaving Rock Island very soon, to recuperate from these injuries at my ranch in New Mexico."

The *Argus* reporter dared to ask, "You don't mean to say that the mayor is driving you out of town, Mr. Looney?"

Looney pointed a trembling finger. "Young man, he has threatened to kill me on sight. Ask *him* about that. And see if Harry Schriver dares deny that, while his men pinned back my arms, he brutally bestowed this beating upon me."

A reporter from the *Tri-Cities Worker* asked, "Is the talk true that one of your associates, Michael O'Sullivan, rescued you from an almost certain death?"

Looney managed a smile. "If you remove the word 'almost,' my friend, your statement will be more accurate. And you all know that as publisher of the *News* I insist upon accuracy to the finest detail."

Connor, watching smiles blossom across the little press conference, wasn't sure whether his father was kidding.

"We'd like to talk to Mike O'Sullivan," the reporter persisted.

Raising a hand like the Pope passing a benediction, Looney said, "I'm sorry, no. Mr. O'Sullivan has other more important matters on his mind and hands, at the moment."

The *Dispatch* reporter asked, "More important than the welfare of his employer?"

"Much more, gentlemen. While we have been having our little fun, over these long hours, Mrs. Michael O'Sullivan has been doing God's work—delivering into this cruel city a sweet young citizen."

Connor did his best not to betray the nausea he felt, when his father coughed up such sentimental phlegm. As if the world needed another Shanty Irish brat. As if the existence of another O'Sullivan mattered a whit, in the great scheme of things.

Getting to his feet, Connor said, "That's all, gents—my father needs his rest. You have your story. We appreciate you stopping by."

And Connor rounded them up and guided them out.

At his father's bedside, Connor stood and said, "We need to get you out of here, toot sweet, Pop. Before Schriver has a warrant sworn out, on one trumped-up charge or another."

Looney touched his son's hand; the battered face beamed. "You do care about your old man, don't you, my boy?"

"I do, Pop. You know I do."

And as his father gazed up at him through loving if slitted, puffy eyes, Connor Looney felt a rush of emotion. He did love his father, and his father loved him. Neither one of them was perfect, Connor thought. But then neither was this fucking world.

WARDS WERE THE RULE AT ST. ANTHONY'S, BUT EXCEP-tions were made for the family and inner circle of a hospital benefactor like John Looney.

So it was that in another private room at the modern facility, Annie O'Sullivan held her new son in her arms, the tiny thing slumbering peacefully.

Last night around eight, she'd known the time was nigh; following her husband's instructions, she called the hospital and an ambulance came quickly around. Mary Jane stayed with Michael Jr. and Annie went off to St. Anthony's, into the loving hands of nuns in white who hovered like friendly ghosts, and where hours later, she was joined by a red wee squalling thing whose beautiful ugliness stunned her.

Now she could hardly believe that, barely fourteen hours later, she felt fine. Exhausted, but fine.

Sitting beside her, wearing a silly grin, was the baby's father; dark circles under his eyes, skin a grayish pallor, tie loose around his collar, suitcoat rumpled, he looked like a corpse. But a happy one.

Whispering, not wanting to wake the child, she said, "We haven't spoken of a name, yet."

"Your father was Peter," he said. "Mine David. I vote for Peter David O'Sullivan."

"Lovely. How lovely. It's unanimous, then."

The baby woke and cried just a little—sort of a half-hearted wail, as if only doing what was expected of him.

Annie began to nurse the child, saying "Welcome, Peter. Welcome to the family."

And Mike sat watching, with the goofiest expression.

After a while one of the sisters came and took the child back to the nursery, so Annie could get her rest.

Mike sat on the edge of her bed and held her hand.

"I hear there was a terrible riot last night," she said.

"There was."

"Something to do with Mr. Looney, wasn't it?"

"Don't worry yourself about that."

"So sad."

"Sad?"

Annie sighed. Shook her head. "I overheard two of the sisters talking, this morning. Three died, they say."

"Yes."

"One a policeman."

"So I understand. Annie—"

"One was just a boy of eighteen, running an errand for his mother, taken down by a bullet. In the back. Isn't that terrible?"

How mournful Mike's eyes seemed as he said, "Please don't think of such things, dear."

"Can you imagine? Sending your boy off for an errand, only to have him struck senselessly down like that?"

And then she began to weep.

He climbed up on the bed and slipped an arm around her and lay beside her, comforting her.

"I'm sorry . . . sorry," she said, sniffling. He gave her his handkerchief, and she said, "It's just . . . I'm so emotional right now. Please forgive me."

"You should be happy."

"Oh, I am! I am! But when I think of that poor mother. . . . Never to see. . . ."

And she began to cry again.

Arm still around her, Mike patted her gently, soothingly, as if she were a child herself.

Dabbing her eyes with her husband's hanky, she said, "You have to promise me, Mike . . ."

"What?"

"I don't want Peter, or Michael, involved in such things."

189

"Such things?"

"The kind of work you do. You had no choice. I mean no disrespect, no lack of gratitude. But they must have . . . a better life. Promise me!"

"I promise, darling."

And she could tell by the look in his eyes that he meant it. That he wanted nothing more in life than a different path for his boys.

She fell asleep in the crook of his arm, just as Peter had slept in hers; warmth flooded through her, happiness spreading its glow, with the promise of a shining future for her family, for her children, the likes of which only a great land like America could provide.

BOOK THREE

AMERICAN DREAM

Chicago, Illinois

through March 1943

1

MICHAEL SATARIANO LAY ON THE BED in the darkened room, curled into a fetal position.

He did not know how much time had passed since the carnage at the Capone estate. Although awake, he remained sluggish, and felt certain the hot tea he'd been given, after entering this room, had been laced with a Mickey Finn.

But, whether his captors had doped him or not, he made no effort to emerge from a funk that came largely from within. Something inside him had died, or at least retreated to its own small, private corner, where it, too, rolled itself up, as if the posture of birth somehow welcomed death.

The recent dispatching by Michael of one Capone gunman after another, piling up dead thugs like kindling, filling doorways with bodies, draping stairways with corpses, splashing blood and gore around the grounds like a sloppy child diving into his birthday cake and ice cream, well, it . . . all seemed strangely dream-like now. He could still see in his mind's eye combat in the jungle of Bataan, and himself chopping down Japs with the tommy, summoning gritty sounds-sights-smells reality that, however nightmarish, remained vividly tangible.

But his attempt to shoot his way through an army of bodyguards to carry out his vendetta on Alphonse Capone . . . hours ago, or at most days (*how long had he been held here?*) . . . had already taken on a distinctly surreal cast.

When he woke periodically, in the darkness of the room (*what room? where?*), he would laugh and weep at once, thinking of the terrible irony of it all, Al Capone a gibbering drooling idiot, beyond Michael's grasp, free from the responsibility of his crimes and his sins, an unfit target for the revenge of Michael O'Sullivan, Jr.

Who would die at the hand of these Sicilians, and justifiably: hadn't he for no reason (*no good reason, no real reason*) betrayed their trust to enter a household where he rained death down upon . . . how many men? A dozen? More? Invading the home of their retired, revered leader with the intent to kill. . . .

He had been caught red-handed—literally—surrounded by his pointless homicidal handiwork. And now they would kill him for these transgressions, and his father and his mother and his brother would never be avenged, could never be avenged, because the man responsible was lost in the empty rooms of his mind, waiting unaware for death.

Perhaps in hell Capone would return to cognizance; no doubt Michael would be there, waiting for him. . . .

Mimi Capone, accompanied by two armed men, had walked Michael away from the poolside where Al Capone fished in the deep end while, all around, corpses leeched blood and other fluids into the grass under the moonlight. Michael had a sense of the wide-eyed awe and horror of these tough men who'd rushed onto the scene, shocked speechless by the battlefield they'd stumbled into.

As Mimi ushered him across the backyard, Michael had half-sensed questions, but they'd had a hollow, under-water sound, and though he recognized the words as English, they formed no thoughts or concepts he recognized. Vaguely he remembered being escorted up some steps, and shortly after he entered this small room, this cell-like space with just a single cot-like bed and no table or light or anything else.

Someone had made him sit up and drink the tea—was it Mimi?—and the voice had been soothing, gentle, encouraging Michael to drink.

Which he had. Not that he'd been thirsty, just that he was in no state of mind to refuse. Warmth had saturated his system and, without getting under the covers, he got himself (*or had they put him there?*) onto the bed.

Vaguely he recalled somebody checking on him; had he been walked to a bathroom, once . . . ?

Now, fully awake for the first time, he sensed that his shoes and socks were off; he felt coolness on his legs and arms and realized he was in his underwear, still on top of the bedspread, though the room—which had no windows, at least that he was aware of (he never left the bed to explore his quarters)—was not so cool as to encourage him to crawl under the covers. This would have been far too ambitious an activity for him to attempt, anyway.

Michael's back was to the door when it opened.

He looked over his shoulder: a silhouette framed in a shaft of light. A man. Anyway, a person wearing a man's hat.

"I'm gonna hit the switch, kid," the voice said. "Be ready for it."

Illumination flooded the room blindingly, and Michael, still on his side curled up and facing the wall, shut his eyes and covered them with his hands, as if the glass one were still flesh and blood, too.

Michael heard footsteps and then felt a hand on his shoulder.

"You been out for two days. Go on and sit up."

■■■

Opening his eyes tentatively, Michael took a few moments to get used to the brightness, then he rolled over and sat on the edge of the bed. He touched his face, finding the roughness of stubble there.

Hovering over him was Louie Campagna, wearing a black suit and a black tie and a white shirt and a black fedora. Not very Miami festive—more like Chicago funeral.

"You had yourself quite a party the other night," Louie said flatly. "Made Calumet City look like a cakewalk."

Michael, in his underwear, felt like a vulnerable child. He could think of nothing to say and the notion of nodding was beyond him.

Campagna held some clothes in his arms, shoes in one hand. He thrust them forward. "Put these on, kid."

Then Campagna gave Michael some space, waiting over by the open door. Beyond the door Michael could see a landing looking out over the Capone yard; he was in a room in the gatehouse. It was night out there. Two nights ago, was it, that he'd made his misguided assault?

"They gave you a sedative," Campagna said. "That's why you got the feebles. Shake it off."

Michael got into clothes identical to Campagna's: black suit and tie, white shirt, black socks, black shoes, only no hat. A funeral's star performer didn't need one. Also didn't need to perform.

Campagna gestured to the open door. "After you, kid."

"Where . . . ?" was all Michael could manage; his tongue was thick, his mouth, his teeth, filmy with drugged sleep.

"Car's downstairs. Let's go. Things to do."

Michael swallowed, nodded. He went out past Campagna, onto the landing, wondering if he should make a break for it—a thought he was capable of forming, but not executing. His limbs felt rubbery, his head and stomach ached.

The cool evening air, though, did feel good; and it was another beautiful southern Florida night, grass glittering with the rays of a still nearly full moon. No bodies around—clean-up crew had long since done its work. From here the pool and cabana and the dock could all be viewed, as could the endless shimmer of white-touched blue that was the bay.

Michael clomped down the steps, Campagna just behind him. In the gravelled drive waited a hearse-like black Lincoln limousine. Two burly-looking swarthy guys in black stood on either side of the vehicle, one next to a rear open door. Both had bulges under their left arms—not tumors, Michael thought, though surely malignancies.

"Michael," Campagna said, "you're gonna have to be blindfolded."

Michael turned. Campagna was holding up a black length of cloth in both hands, as if preparing to strangle somebody.

"Not necessary," Michael muttered.

"Sorry. Orders."

Michael did not resist; and when the blackness settled over his eyes, the knot snugging at the back of his neck, he felt almost relieved to be again shut off from the world. A hand on his arm, probably Louie's, guided him.

"Duck your head," Louie said, and Michael did, and was gently pushed inside the vehicle.

Someone climbed in beside him—again, probably Campagna. The door shut. He heard the other men get in, in front, and slam their doors. Then they were moving.

He sat quietly, still as a statue; no one said anything. The sounds were of the limo's engine, other traffic (not heavy), and birds over the bay. His senses were returning to him, and some of his fatalistic lethargy faded and his blood seemed to start to flow again, an urge for survival rekindling.

But blindfolded in the presence of three armed gangsters, Michael had limited options. Still, his hands and ankles weren't bound. He could rip the blindfold off his eyes, throw a punch into Campagna's puss and get to the door and open it and roll out, before either man in the front seat could do a damn thing. The vehicle was not going fast—twenty-five, thirty tops—and unless he pitched himself out into the path of an oncoming car, then he could—

And the limo came to a stop.

The two front doors opened, followed by the sound of shoes crunching on gravel. The back car door to Michael's left opened, and the man sitting next to him (Campagna?) slid out. A hand settled on Michael's arm and guided him out of the car, then steered him across a few feet of gravel and in through a door. Faintly, he detected cooking smells; warm in here, but not hot. Comfortable . . .

. . . except for the part where he was blindfolded in the company of three Outfit hoods.

He was escorted a few more feet, and Campagna's voice, next to him, said, "We're going in a room. You first."

Michael brushed a door jamb as he went through. He stopped, then the hand was on his arm again and he was guided across the room. Not much light was leeching in around the edges of the blindfold, so the room apparently was dim. He heard footsteps behind him, indicating the two thugs had followed, and the door closed.

"There's a chair here," Campagna said, and positioned Michael.

"Sit down, Michael," a familiar baritone voice said.

Michael obeyed.

He felt hands at the back of his neck and the blindfold slipped away, filling Michael's vision with a man seated at a small square white cloth-covered table opposite.

The man was Frank Nitti, also attired in black.

The room was fairly large, but Nitti sat with his back to the wall; of half a dozen overhead light fixtures, only the one directly above the Outfit kingpin was on, creating a spotlight effect. A few framed paintings—landscapes . . . Sicilian landscapes?—hung here and there around the room, but otherwise it contained nothing but two chairs and the small table that separated Michael from the man who had been his benefactor in the Outfit, the man who had trusted Michael and who Michael had betrayed.

On the table were a .38 and a black-handled dagger with a crooked and obviously sharply honed blade. Next to them was a white piece of paper.

Frank Nitti's face was pale and grave. "Michael Satariano," he said. He gestured to the two weapons on the table. "These represent that you live by the gun and the knife, and that you die by the gun and the knife."

So that was what the white sheet of paper was for: a suicide note! Well, he wouldn't write it.

They would have to kill him, Michael thought. He would not commit suicide for them; he was still enough of a Catholic for that to repel. Taking your own life meant hell, for sure . . . as if that mattered now, all the men he'd killed.

But then Nitti flipped over the piece of paper and revealed it to be a color print of the Virgin Mary, a rather florid painting right out of Sunday school.

Michael frowned, not understanding.

Nitti, solemnly, asked, "Which hand do you shoot with?"

Like a kid in class, Michael raised his right hand.

Nitti nodded, his eyes looking past Michael, and Campagna leaned in, took Michael's right forefinger and pricked the tip with a needle.

Startled, Michael managed not to rise up out of the chair as Campagna dribbled drops of O'Sullivan blood onto the Virgin Mary, little droplets of red spattering her.

Then Campagna withdrew to his position behind Michael, as Nitti, standing now, lifted by one corner the blood-dotted picture. With his other hand, Nitti deftly used a Zippo lighter, thumbing it to flame, touching the sheet's opposite corner, and fire ate its way up the Virgin Mary, consuming her, unimpeded by the few beads of Michael's blood.

Nitti held onto the burning paper until the last minute, then dropped it onto the table, where it curled in ashy remains.

Wondering if he'd gone mad, thinking he was still in that darkened room, having a particularly demented dream, Michael watched as Nitti pricked his forefinger and extended its blood-dripping tip across to Michael . . .

. . . who instinctively extended his hand and touched his own pricked fingertip to Nitti's.

The two fingertips withdrew, and Nitti said, "Blood makes us family. But we will burn like that image if we betray each other. Say yes, Michael."

"Yes."

"Repeat what I say. I pledge my honor to be faithful to the Mafia like the Mafia is faithful to me."

"I . . . I pledge my honor to be faithful to the Mafia like the Mafia is faithful to me."

"As this saint and these drops of my blood were burned, so will I give my blood for my new family."

"As this saint and these drops of my blood were burned, so will I give my blood for my new family."

Nitti nodded. "You will answer these questions with 'yes.' Will you offer reciprocal aid in the case of any need from your new family?"

"Yes."

"Will you pay absolute obedience to your *capo* . . . to me, Michael."

"Yes, Mr. Nitti."

"Do you accept that an offense against one is an offense against all?"

"Yes."

"Do you understand that you must never reveal names or secrets to anyone outside the family?"

"Yes."

"Do you accept that this thing of ours comes before all else—blood-family, religion, country?"

"Yes."

"Good, Michael. Understand that to betray the Outfit means death without trial. I am your *capo*. Louie is your *goombah*, your godfather. Is all of that understood?"

"Yes, Mr. Nitti."

Nitti came from around the table and stood before Michael and said, "Get on your feet, Michael Satariano. You are now a made man."

Michael rose and Nitti kissed him on either cheek.

Was this the fabled kiss of death? Michael wondered.

But when Nitti drew away, the ganglord was beaming. And tears glistened.

"Welcome, Michael. Welcome, my son."

And then Nitti embraced Michael.

Awkwardly, Michael returned the embrace.

The three men in black, standing behind the chair where Michael had sat facing the man he had mistaken for his judge/jury/executioner, began to applaud, Campagna saying, "Hey, Mike, you did it, kid! You did it!"

Then Frank Nitti took Michael by the arm and walked him from what the newest made man in the Chicago Outfit now realized was a banquet room, into the dining room of a traditional red-and-white-tablecloth Italian restaurant, the sort of cozy joint Papa Satariano ran back in DeKalb.

His arm around Michael, Nitti ushered him to a corner table, set up just for two, in a section of the dimly lighted restaurant otherwise closed off. Another table nearby was reserved for Campagna and the two bodyguards; but this table was strictly for the boss and his guest of honor.

As they drank Chianti—beginning with a toast to Michael's new life, sealed with a clink of glasses—Nitti effusively answered all of Michael's unasked questions.

"For someone who's been with us so short a time," Nitti said, "it's a rare honor, becomin' a made man. But the service you done the Outfit . . . what you did for me, Michael . . . well, let's just say this is as close to us giving you a Medal of Honor as we can get."

"Thank you, Mr. Nitti."

Nitti, smiling big, shook his head, gesturing with his wine glass. "How did it happen, Mike? Did you come out to find a war going on, raging between Ricca's traitors and our own loyal people?"

". . . Yes."

The ganglord shrugged elaborately. "We can't prove it, of course. But it's obvious, isn't it?"

"It is?"

"That Ricca wanted to kill Al, and strip me of my power. He figures with Al gone, my support'd crumble." Though they were out of earshot of the other patrons as well as Campagna and crew, Nitti leaned forward conspiratorially. "I'm not sure whether Ricca knows the truth about Al or not."

Michael sipped the red wine. "How long has Mr. Capone been in this state of mind?"

"Started at the Rock. They let him out early, it was so severe. But for a couple of years, it was more . . . sporadic, they call it. Sometimes he'd be clear as a bell, other times . . . you saw him. Vegetable. Which is how he is all the time, now."

"And who knows?"

"The staff at the estate is kept away from him, except for an inner group of about six. . . . Four of them are dead, now." He shook his head at this tragedy; then he brightened. "Mae threw in with me—she liked the idea of Al retaining power, and she didn't want the world to know what this great man of hers had come to."

"If Ricca *does* know . . ."

"The Waiter'll back off now. He won't make any more moves, not like this, not for a good long while. He'll credit me with what you done—with anticipating that he was going to hit Al."

"But of course he denies having anything to do with it."

Nitti shrugged again, sipped Chianti, then said, "Actually, ain't spoken to him about it yet. I came down yesterday and met with Mae and Mimi. You know, you left quite a mess there, young man."

"What . . . what was done about it?"

"Let's just say Al's yacht come in handy. The biggest expense will be all the surviving members of each man's family. Part of what we do is look after the families of any fallen soldiers. It's the decent thing. Christian thing. But it's gonna cost." He scowled. "Only it burns me there's no way to know which of 'em were the traitors. You think you could've identified which was which?"

"No. It all happened too fast."

"Figured as much. So the bad get rewarded with the good; such is life. . . . You were in bad shape, Mimi said. Come through unscathed, not a scratch . . . but a nervous wreck. That's why Mimi had 'em knock you out. Let you catch your rest."

"So it didn't get out? The police, the papers . . . ?"

"Never happened. A dozen immigrants and sons of immigrants fall off the face of the earth, and who the fuck cares but us? We're the only government for our people, Michael—even now."

Michael sighed, allowing relief to really take hold. Risked a small smile. "Mr. Nitti, I gotta admit—I didn't know what was going on tonight. I thought maybe *you* thought. . . ."

Nitti waved that off. "Don't be silly."

"Blindfold, black suits . . . I was thinking it was a one-way ride."

With a gruff laugh, Nitti said, "Hey, sorry, kid—didn't mean to throw a scare in you. But these rituals, some people may say they're foolish or silly or Old World . . . but tradition is important. Loyalty. *Omertà*—that's the code, Michael. Our secrets are our secrets."

"I understand."

Once again he leaned forward; he raised a forefinger—the shadow of smudged blood remained. "And speak to no one about Al's mental condition. No one."

"No one."

Nitti leaned back and gestured with open palms. "Now . . . as for your duties, you're officially my number-one bodyguard. My top lieutenant. We're gonna get you a penthouse suite at the Seneca, and you're gonna live like a king. Someday you'll settle down and be a socks-and-slippers man like me, with a wife and kids and house in the suburbs; but for now, enjoy yourself. Be a man about town . . . just be available when I *need* ya. How's a thousand a week sound?"

"Like . . . a lot of money."

"Michael, I've been looking for a sharp, brave kid like you for a long time. Welcome to the family."

Nitti extended his hand across the table and they shook.

A platter of spaghetti and meatballs came, proving to be almost as good as Papa's. They spoke not at all of business after that, and Michael enjoyed Nitti's good-humored company, as they talked about sports (boxing mostly) and movies (Nitti loved Cagney) and Italian food (his late wife Anna's veal scallopine alla Marsala had been to die for, and Michael encouraged his boss to travel to DeKalb for Mama Satariano's version thereof).

Michael felt strangely exhilarated, which was probably mostly his surprise at still being alive. For reasons he could not comprehend, he felt proud that Frank Nitti had thought enough of him to make him a "made" man in the Outfit. What would his father, his *real* father, have felt for his son, Michael wondered—pride? Shame?

On the way to the limo, Campagna fell in alongside Michael. Man-of-the-people Nitti was walking up ahead, chatting with the other two hoodlums.

"Congratulations, kid," Campagna said, a grin splitting the lumpy face. "You're in."

"Better than being out," Michael said, grinning, too.

"Kid, the only way you go out of this family," Campagna said, with a shoulder pat, "is feet first."

Then they drove back to the Capone mansion, where the first person to approach Michael was a tearfully happy Mae Capone, who embraced him and thanked him again and again for the wonderful thing he had done for her husband.

2

AT THE BAR IN THE GLITZY COLONY Club, Michael sat and sipped his Coca-Cola and enjoyed the music.

Estelle Carey leaned against the piano as she sang—perching on a stool was out of the question, in the formfitting periwinkle gown, with its high neck, mostly bared arms, and bodice with tiny glittering stars. Golden hair piled high, glamour-girl Estelle worked her intimate audience of couples, but Michael knew she was singing straight to him.

Right now, her husky second soprano was wrapping itself around "I Didn't Know What Time It Was."

Cigarette smoke draped the bar, which was packed; so was the "aristocrat of restaurants," as the adjacent dining room advertised itself. Michael hadn't been upstairs to the casino yet, but this was a Saturday night and, judging by the ground floor, the Colony Club was hopping. Frank Nitti's new number-one lieutenant was wearing a very sharp dark blue white-pinstriped number, a tailored job disguising the .45 in the shoulder sling; but the majority of the Colony Club patrons were in evening dress (and presumably unarmed).

He'd been back from Miami for barely two weeks, but a lot had happened. He'd moved into the promised penthouse at the Seneca; his relationship with Frank Nitti grew ever closer; and every night he'd slept with Estelle, either upstairs or at his Seneca digs—her own apartment was off-limits, as she roomed with a woman who ran a classy dress shop in which Estelle was partnered.

Now that the publicity over his Medal of Honor had receded, so had his celebrity; rarely did anyone recognize Michael, to ask for an autograph or embarrass him with praise, and he relished this new anonymity.

His state of mind was numb, but not unpleasantly so. He was surprised to be alive, and right now did not feel inclined to swim against the tide. If this was limbo, it wasn't bad—Michael Satariano was, after all, a twenty-two-year-old making a thousand dollars a week, in an easy job, living in a posh penthouse, with a gorgeous nightclub singer for a girlfriend.

Maybe he *had* died back in Miami; maybe Capone's people had shot him full of holes and this was heaven, or possibly a coma he hadn't come out of, and if so, what was the hurry?

With "I'll Never Smile Again," Estelle's set was over—on the weekends, her performances were timed so that while she was on, the orchestra was off, and vice versa. She drifted over to Michael, appearing through the cigarette fog like a materializing dream; she proved her reality by slipping her hand into his and led him into the chrome-and-glass dining room where a table in back waited.

Don Orlando and his Orchestra played rhumbas, the dance floor fairly packed, while Michael ate a rare tenderloin (the modest serving the only sign of wartime shortages) and Estelle a small shrimp salad (anything larger would have shown, in that gown). Afterward they danced—slow romantic tunes, no rhumbas for Michael—in preparation for retiring to the specific third-floor bedroom (the "Rhapsody in Blue" suite) of which Estelle seemed to have sole use.

Michael hoped he was the only other man sharing it with her, now; but he had not yet pressed the point.

In the dim light of Rush Street neons tinted blue by the semi-sheer curtains, the two made love, with the combination of tenderness and urgency that always seemed to characterize the act for them. As usual, she preferred to start on top, her long golden hair undone now, and bouncing off her creamy shoulders, her eyes half-lidded in pleasure, her breasts pert hard-tipped handfuls. *Christ, she was lovely.* . . .

Soon she lay naked next to him, a loose sheet halfheartedly covering the couple, his arm round her, her face against his chest, which was largely hairless ("You're just a boy, you're just a child," she would tease); for a while she kissed his chest lazily, and then she slept, snoring very gently against his flesh, almost a purr.

He felt an enormous affection for this willowy creature with her doll-like features, a girl/woman who had learned to use the softness of her charms in so many hard ways. In a wave of sentimentality, which he mistook for deep emotion, Michael wished he could whisk her away from the Chicago of gambling, whoring and other commercial sins.

She looked so innocent, slumbering against him. So untroubled. So blissfully at rest. But earlier in the week she'd seemed distracted, and on edge.

In this same bed, she had sat up, arms folded over her bare breasts, her brow furrowed. "I may need you to talk to Frank for me. Mr. Nitti, I mean."

Propped on his elbow, he stared at her. "Why, baby? Problem?"

"You see that business in the papers, about those actresses who got burned?"

"Anita Louise, you mean? And somebody else famous, right?"

"Yeah—Constance Bennett. They're in town promoting a new picture."

The robbery of several thousand in jewels from a hotel room of the two visiting Hollywood beauties had made headlines. Seemed like a hard way to hawk a movie.

"Well, they were here when it happened," she said with a humorless smirk, pointing a finger downstairs. "Word is the cops think the heist was planned at the Colony."

"Like somebody kept the girls busy at the club, giving somebody else time to nick the gems at the hotel?"

"Right. But what would *we* have to do with it?"

Michael shrugged. "Unless it was a bartender or somebody else employed here, nothing."

"Right!" she said, hair flouncing. "I mean, what the hell—I can't be responsible for our clientele. We're a popular place; all kinds of people come here."

"How about the cops? *They* come here?"

"Not yet. . . . It's just, I know Mr. Nitti wants to keep things low-key, about now. Mike, I promise I laid the law down with the girls: no exchange of cash. Big rollers get comped with a little affection, but that's it."

"I'll say something to him, if you want."

"Would you?"

She'd seemed fine after that, and by the next day, the MOVIE STAR JEWELRY HEIST had, like his Medal of Honor, faded from the headlines.

And now it faded from Michael's mind, too, as he began drifting off to sleep . . .

. . . *only to have gunshots rudely wake him.*

In half a heartbeat, he was out of the bed in his boxer shorts, snatching the .45 from the holster draped over a chair and heading in bare feet for the door. Behind him, startled to wakefulness, Estelle sat up, fists pulling the sheet to her chin, eyes huge and frightened; but he was in the hallway before she could speak.

Two guys, one skinny, one burly, were barreling right at him. They were in t-shirts and pants and socks, charging down the narrow pink carpet, single file, though he could see them both—and each had a gun in his fist.

The skinny one, at the rear, was firing over a shoulder, three sharp reports, shooting at the stairwell door, punching splintering holes. No one in sight, down there—the door itself seemed to be the guy's target.

He recognized them, sort of: they'd been hanging around the Colony all week; not local, a couple gladhanders who for the last couple days had been hitting the casino hard.

Right now Michael was between them and the elevator, and the burly guy was raising his gun, teeth bared, eyes intense, motioning, motioning, motioning for Michael to move aside.

Instead, Michael walked into the path of the stampeding gunmen and slapped the first guy across the side of the head with the .45.

Then Michael stepped aside—so that the man could go down and his partner stumble over him. Both men lost their guns, identical .38s that went flying.

The burly man Michael had pistol-whipped was unconscious and his skinny partner was piled squirming on top of him, like shower night at Joliet. Before the surprised partner could get his bearings, Michael leaned in and slapped him across the side of the head, too, with the .45 barrel.

The partner slumped on top of his pal, as if in postcoital exhaustion.

Michael was collecting the two fallen weapons when the shot-up stairwell door cracked tentatively. . . .

Then it opened wide, and Eliot Ness stepped out, his own .38 in hand.

Ness, very much his public image in fedora and brown suit, had a spooked expression, not at all like his public image. Clearly the gunshots fired at that door had been meant for him. Seeing Michael, Ness opened his mouth.

Before any words could come out, however, Michael yelled at him, "Who the hell are you? What's going on here?"

Behind Ness, from out the stairwell, came a firm-jawed, dark-haired guy in a homburg and beautifully cut charcoal suit with black vest and red tie. His natty attire might not say plain-clothes cop, but his manner—and the badge pinned on his breast pocket, plus the Police Special in his fist—did. As he joined Ness, a pair of uniformed cops with weapons in hand also emerged from the stairs.

Ness strode up the hall, saying, "I'm Eliot Ness, with the Federal Social Protection Division. This is Lieutenant William Drury, from Town Hall Station."

Drury stayed back, talking to the two cops, sending them into a room down on the right, next to the stairwell.

"These are suspects in a jewelry robbery," Ness said, nodding toward the fallen duo.

"You mind if I get some clothes on," Michael asked, "while you handcuff these boys?"

"Not at all."

Michael rejoined Estelle in the blue suite, where—the bed-side lamp switched on—she'd already put on a simple business-like brown-and-white suit. As he got dressed, Michael explained that he'd apparently just captured the two jewelry bandits for the cops.

"But that fed Ness is along for the ride," Michael said.

Confusion merged with indignation in her response: "What does he have to do with catching jewel robbers?"

"Nothing. He's probably here to try to shut you down."

She followed Michael to the door, but he turned and took her by the arms. "Let me deal with this."

Estelle drew in a deep breath, considering taking issue; then she let the air out and nodded. She sat in a chair by the window, and folded her hands primly in her lap, Rush Street neon wink-ing through the curtains next to her.

In the hallway, Michael saw the t-shirted bandits, too groggy to be pissed-off yet, on their feet and in the process of getting hauled off by the uniformed men.

Michael gave Ness a hard look, indicating it wasn't safe to talk, and said, "I heard the gun shot and ran out into the hall. . . . I have a license to carry."

He patted the .45, snugged back under his shoulder.

"Fine," Ness said. "Come with me."

Michael followed him down the hall and past a shot-up door into a suite done up in whorehouse red, though otherwise identical to the blue room.

Cowering under the covers, wide eyes peeking over their edges, was a 26 girl named Marie, a cute little brunette that Michael knew only to say hello to; apparently the robbers had been sharing her, or maybe one had opted for the sidelines. Neither Ness nor Lieutenant Drury acknowledged her existence, much less her presence.

Drury was standing at the bedstand, where a wallet was open and the detective was thumbing a wad of bills.

"Pretty flush couple of fellas, huh?" Drury said idly.

Ness asked, "Without the jewelry, can you make it stick?"

Drury nodded; he had dark alert eyes, a jutting nose, and, though not particularly heavyset, a double chin that cushioned his firm jaw.

"We have the fence," Drury said, "and we can put both of 'em in the hotel. I think they have an accomplice here, probably a bartender, who called and gave 'em the all clear. We'll see if they give the guy up."

Ness was shaking his head. "Doesn't matter. They're finished here."

Not sure he understood what Ness meant, Michael asked Drury, "What's going on?"

Drury was the police contact Ness had mentioned several times, so he knew damn well who Michael was; but with the little naked brunette witness quivering under the bedsheets, the detective knew enough not to make that evident.

"You've figured out," Drury said, "that we were after those jewelry punks."

"But the robbery warrant gave us entree to the Colony Club," Ness said, "where we've discovered all kinds of law-breaking—including, on this floor, prostitution."

Marie said, "I am not!"

Ignoring that, Ness said, "Anticipating as much, we brought along half a dozen paddy wagons. We've already shut down the casino, though with so many lawbreakers on the premises, we'll have to make a number of trips."

"And about now," Drury said, "my boys will be knocking on doors all up and down this floor—taking johns and whores into custody."

"I am not!" Marie insisted.

Ness said to Michael, "We appreciate your help, sir. . . . We haven't got your name yet, have we?"

"It's Satariano. Michael Satariano."

Play-acting, Drury said, "Oh, Medal of Honor winner! Well, you deserve another one, for nabbing these bad guys."

"They're not local," Michael said. "I've been around the club every night this week, and heard 'em making conversation at the bar. They said they were salesmen."

"Selling what?"

"Judging by who they turned out to be, I'd say selling themselves as salesmen."

Ness nodded, apparently liking that analysis.

Drury asked, "Speak to them yourself, Mr. Satariano?"

"No. They were obnoxious. I kept my distance. But looking back, I can see they suddenly turned into high rollers, after that robbery."

"Thanks for not keeping your distance tonight," Drury said. "We knocked on the door and announced ourselves and they started shooting. We ducked in the stairwell and they ran out and shot some more. We're both lucky not to be ventilated."

"Glad to help," Michael said flatly. "Anything else, fellas?"

"Unfortunately," Ness said, "you'll have to come over to the stationhouse, to make a statement."

"Can't I make that here?"

With unmistakable, nonnegotiable firmness, Ness said: "No."

"Well, I'm down the hall with my girlfriend. I assure you I'm not a john, and she's not a whore."

"Me neither," Marie whimpered, mascara running.

Michael continued: "She's one of the owners and managers of the club."

"Estelle Carey?" Drury asked.

Michael nodded.

"Well," Drury said smugly, "that's handy."

"What do you mean, handy?"

Ness said, "We want to talk to her, too."

MICHAEL DID HIS BEST TO REASSURE ESTELLE THAT everything would be fine, though sounds from the street below—officious yelling by cops, car and paddy wagon doors slamming, the frightened/irritated yammer and babbling of those being rounded up—undermined his efforts.

Finally Ness came around to collect them. Drury was chatting with another plainclothes cop in the hall, a Sergeant O'Connor, who was taking over the supervisory role. Then Michael and Estelle were escorted by Ness and Drury down the elevator and through the downstairs, where a small army of boys in blue were ushering indignant socialites out to waiting paddy wagons on Rush Street, the red and blue lights of police vehicles competing with neons.

Michael and Estelle were driven in an unmarked car to turn-of-the-century Town Hall Station, a formidable red-brick building on the corner of Addison and Halsted. Within ten minutes, inside a small interrogation chamber whose walls and ceiling were acoustically tiled, Michael and Ness sat at a small scarred wooden table.

Michael—his tie off, his collar open—glanced around: the usual two-way mirror was absent.

Noting Michael taking stock, Ness tossed his fedora on the table and said, "It's secure."

"It's not rigged for eavesdropping?"

"No. Some of the other booths are. Like the one Lieutenant Drury's questioning your friend Estelle Carey in."

"You're shutting her down?"

"The Colony Club'll be a memory by tomorrow."

"Won't it reopen? It's a protected joint."

He shook his head. "Tomorrow morning I'm holding a press conference at the Colony. Every paper in town will have pictures of the casino and the third-floor cathouse."

"Sounds like good advertising."

"No. They're done. Something will open to take its place, no doubt—but the Colony's over."

Michael grunted a humorless laugh. "Real blow you struck for Uncle Sam—some serviceman hangout."

"It's the Outfit we're squeezing. That was fortuitous, tonight."

"Me saving your ass, you mean?"

Ness smiled, barely. "Well . . . that, and it giving us a chance to talk privately. You've been something of a stranger, Michael. You don't call . . . you don't write. . . ."

"You said you were going to be out of town."

"I gave you Lieutenant Drury's number. You've been back from Miami for well over a week. What went on down there?"

"Why, what do you hear?"

"Just a few rumblings."

"Such as?"

Ness shrugged. "They've imported some new staff."

Michael shrugged. "Security's an issue, on the Capone estate."

Eyes narrowing, Ness leaned forward, slightly. "Did you see Capone? Talk to him?"

"I saw him."

"What's his, uh . . . mental state?"

Michael fixed a cold gaze on the fed. "You *knew*, didn't you?"

Ness, all innocence, blinked twice. "Knew what?"

Now Michael sat forward. "You manipulated me into infiltrating Frank Nitti's inner circle, so I could finally settle up with the man who had my father killed."

Michael slammed a hand on the table—hard.

But Ness didn't jump. Or even blink.

"And all the time you knew—*knew* 'King' Capone was a drooling imbecile."

Silence held the room for perhaps thirty seconds. Michael felt himself trembling and hoped it didn't show. Ness seemed a statue.

Then finally the G-man said, "We didn't know. We *suspected*— medical projections were made, based upon his condition when he was released, back in '39. But until right now . . . we weren't sure."

"Hell, you oughta put Big Al's puss on a poster and hang *that* up in all the barracks, and show G.I.s what VD really can do."

". . . It's an idea."

Michael snorted a non-laugh and sat back and folded his arms. "So. I've fulfilled my mission, then."

"You have accomplished a major portion of it, at least. You've confirmed my theory that Frank Nitti has maintained his control over the syndicate by perpetuating the fiction that Capone was ruling from afar."

Twitching a smile, Michael said, "Haven't you veered slightly off course, Mr. Ness? Aren't you supposed to be protecting military bases and defense plants from painted women?"

Ness gestured with an open hand—vaguely conciliatory. "Your sarcasm aside, Michael, that is indeed my job—but I'm also part of a coordinated effort by various government agencies to put the Capone bunch out of business."

"You think stopping Frank Nitti is a good idea."

"Don't you?"

Michael shrugged one shoulder. "Nitti's not the worst man in his world."

Ness's eyes at once widened and tightened. "You can't be serious—what the hell *kind* of 'world'?"

Calmly, Michael said, "A legitimate world, within ten years, if Nitti has his way. Get rid of him and you're looking at Paul the Waiter Ricca—and psychos like Stefano and Giancana, mad dogs up from the street. It'll mean decades of gambling and whores and loansharking and narcotics. Capone'll seem like Walt Disney."

The federal agent sat silent, stunned by this onslaught of words, coming from the normally taciturn Michael.

Finally, Ness said, "Your father thought John Looney was the best man in *their* world. And look what it got him."

Michael snapped, "Frank Nitti is not John Looney, and I'm not my father."

"Are you sure?"

Michael said nothing.

Ness looked pale; almost sick. "You've . . . you're not the kid I sent in, Michael. Maybe I made a mistake."

This time Michael's laugh did have humor in it—dark humor. "What, I'm infected now? *You* oughta have access to penicillin, if anybody does."

Still wearing that stricken expression, Ness said, "You need to understand, Michael. Undercover work has unique pitfalls. You can easily become part of the universe you've insinuated yourself into."

"If you don't, Mr. Ness, you get killed."

With a sigh, the fed said, "I know that. I know that." Ness became suddenly businesslike. "So I'm pulling the plug on you, Michael. This relationship is over."

Surprised that he cared, Michael said defensively, "Swell. What should I tell Frank Nitti, thanks for the summer job? Think I'll head back to DeKalb and toss pizza?"

Ness's expression and voice seemed earnest. "Michael . . . you'll find the moment. Ease yourself out. It's not like you're a made man."

Michael said nothing.

Ness's eyes froze.

And when Ness next spoke, his voice was almost a whisper, as if he could barely bring himself to say any of this out loud. "Oh Christ. . . . Then you did kill Abatte, in Calumet City. Self-defense, I know, 'hypothetical,' you said, but . . . Michael, we have to get you out of there."

"And where would I go? Bataan, maybe?"

Ness was shaking his head, looking for words that weren't presenting themselves.

"You said it yourself, Mr. Ness. Our relationship is over. . . . Are we done here?"

MICHAEL SAT IN A WOODEN CHAIR AGAINST A WALL IN the big waiting-room area on the first floor of the station, with four rough-looking juvies waiting for their parents to come take them home.

Finally, Estelle came down the wide wooden stairs, unaccompanied; in that conservative suit, she again looked almost prim, if shellshocked. Gratefully she took Michael's arm as he led her into the cool dark of early morning.

Michael walked her down the block to an allnight diner, where he called for a cab. Then he sat in a window booth next to her, waiting for the ride; they both had coffee.

"What did Drury want?" he asked her.

"He's working with Ness, you know."

"Yeah, I gathered."

In the pretty face, her upper lip curled back nastily. "Hundreds of bent cops in this town, you wouldn't think one honest flatfoot could cause so much trouble."

She meant Drury. But it applied to Ness as well. And without the cooperation of an honest copper like Drury, the G-man could never have executed a raid like tonight's.

Michael said, "They're shuttering the Colony."

"I know. I know." She leaned forward, the anxiety in her eyes terrible to behold; she reached out and clutched one of his hands. "Mike, please talk to Mr. Nitti. Tell him this wasn't my fault. I didn't know anything about those damn jewel thieves, and—"

"It'll be fine, baby."

She shook her head, blonde hair askew. "You don't understand—the feds, they're squeezing me. They want to pull me in as a witness on this movie-extortion business."

"What do you know about it?"

"Not much."

But she didn't sound convincing; she had been Nicky Dean's mistress, after all, and bagman Dean was already doing time in the Hollywood case. Michael had overheard Campagna and Nitti expressing concern the hood might be bargaining for a shorter sentence by singing.

And not in the way Estelle sang at the club, either. . . .

"I'm not going to cooperate, Michael. I told Drury less than nothing. But if the Outfit boys even *think* I might be spilling. . . . *You gotta talk to Frank for me!*"

"I will," he said gently. "I will."

The cab arrived and Michael took Estelle to his suite at the Seneca. In bed, he held her all night long, and she shivered as if she were cold or perhaps had the flu. Only it wasn't cold in the penthouse, and she was a healthy girl.

For now.

3

FOR THE HALF YEAR FOLLOWING
Michael's initiation into the Chicago Outfit, the made man's life proceeded in a
nonviolent, routine manner.

At times he felt as if he'd wandered out
of reality and onto a Hollywood soundstage. After all, his girlfriend looked like a
movie star, screwed him silly on a regular
basis, and made upon him no demands
whatsoever. His apartment—appointed in a
contemporary manner, all browns and
greens—had a bedroom, living room,
kitchenette and a balcony view on the city.
While he worked long hours, he for the
most part sat around, reading magazines
and novels, receiving a two-hundred-
dollar-a-week check, for accounting pur-
poses, and eight hundred cash, for his own.

He dined out at top restaurants, from Don the Beachcomber's to Henrici's, and here at the Seneca Hotel, owned by Outfit investors, his meals, drinks, everything, was (like his suite) comped. A free ride at most nightspots was waiting, too, from the Chez Paree to the Mayfair Room. He wore custom suits from a Michigan Avenue haberdashery attuned to the special needs of the well-armed gentleman about town; and a company car was his on off hours, ration tickets no problem. And like any good American, he bought war bonds.

As he floated through this easy, vaguely exciting life, directionless, empty, yet numbly content, only a few times a day did Michael feel pangs of . . . not conscience, exactly, more like twinges. Twinges of character.

When he read the papers, morning and evening alike, and certain distinctive words popped out at him—*Guadalcanal, North Africa, Stalingrad*—something gnawed at his gut. Gratifying as good news from the Solomon Islands might be, he was frustrated by the absence of Philippines coverage. The government continued to keep the lid on tight, particularly about how Uncle Sam had left behind the boys on Bataan . . . all except Michael Satariano and General MacArthur . . . to twist in an ill wind from the Far East.

But then he'd turn to the funnies, and force such thoughts out, making room for L'il Abner and Dick Tracy.

At night, between cool sheets in a bed big enough for a family of five, Michael would sometimes face sleeplessness. ("It's the caffeine in those damn Cokes," Campagna would say, advising, "You'd sleep like a baby, you drank beer.") Coca-Cola notwithstanding, he slept better when Estelle lay beside him, breathing, beautiful, human, physical company.

But alone, often when he was just about asleep, faces from the past would drift through his consciousness . . . his father, patiently teaching him to drive on a country back road; his mother, serving a plate of corned beef and cabbage with a knowing smile ("I told you you'd grow to like it"); his brother's gleeful laughter when Michael pushed him in the backyard swing; Connor Looney's sick smile at the last Christmas gathering; grandfatherly

John Looney tousling Michael's hair; *his father blasting away with a tommy gun; his mother and brother dead on the floor of their house; his father cut down from behind, by a Capone killer.*

And he would go out on the balcony, even when it got cold, even when he had to kick snow aside, and he would stare at the abstract twinkling shapes that were the buildings of the city. And sometimes the edge of that railing seemed to call to him, inviting him to slip over and take the ride of twenty stories down to a bed where he could sleep undisturbed. . . .

As the months went by, Michael did not hear from Eliot Ness. Nor did Lieutenant Drury make any effort to contact him. Perhaps the two men were embarrassed by the meager payoff of their raid on the Colony Club.

Shuttering Rush Street's most popular nightspot did not make either man any friends, and the embarrassment suffered by captains of industry, politicians and judges, ignominiously rounded up and shoved in the back of paddy wagons, translated into criticism and lack of support in high places for the gang-busting efforts of both men.

Shortly after the Town Hall interview with Ness, Michael received notification he was back on inactive duty; his little paychecks ceased. He was no longer a soldier in Uncle Sam's army, rather a lieutenant in Frank Nitti's.

Within the Outfit, Nitti's decision to walk away from prostitution was generally accepted as a sound one. With the real houses shut down, Ness stooping to raid the Colony as a "brothel" (a stretch) showed the G-man's desperation. And, at the same time, the boys still got their share from the girls—strip clubs and arcades were flourishing with serviceman trade—with the highclass hookers working out of hotels and apartments kicking back, as usual.

Michael was able to convince Frank Nitti that Estelle was loyal; that despite what Drury was claiming in the press—about the Colony's third floor housing wide-open cash-and-carry prostitution—Estelle had strictly used the favors of her 26 girls as a dividend for high-rollers. That no charges were brought against her indicated she was telling the truth.

"If you vouch for her, kid," Nitti had said, as they sat in a booth at the Capri, "that's all I need."

But the landscape was shifting, and in early 1943 the blessing of Frank Nitti did not always seem to be enough.

Though not privy to board meetings, Michael would get the lowdown from his friend Louie Campagna. On a peaceful return trip to Calumet City—where once a month Campagna and Michael strolled around, just to maintain in certain people the fear of God—Campagna had warned Michael that Estelle might well be in solid with Nitti, but other Outfit insiders suspected her.

"She's straight, Louie," Michael said, behind the wheel. "She's a good kid."

"She's a 'kid' ten years older than you, Mike. And her old boy friend Nicky Dean's helping the feds, we think. Plus which, Ricca and some of the others don't view her getting a free ride from the cops same way Frank does."

"How so?"

Campagna, who was cleaning his fingernails with a pocket knife, said, "They think she got a pass 'cause she's cooperating with the feds."

Frowning, Michael said, "Louie—she got a pass because Drury couldn't make that prostitution charge stick!"

"Yeah? What about the gambling?"

"She leased the second floor out to Sonny Goldstone, you know that."

Campagna shrugged. "They coulda nailed her, if they wanted. Had her in for questioning half a dozen times."

"I been questioned, you been questioned. That doesn't make us rats."

The stocky little hood put away the pocket knife, as the car rolled by a steel mill. "I know you like the broad. Who wouldn't? But even if she's as straight as you think—"

"She is."

"Fine. But Ricca suspects her. And maybe you noticed, innocent till proved guilty don't come up much, in our circle."

From his position on the sidelines, right next to the game, Michael could easily sense the tensions. Though gradual, a certain physical deterioration on Nitti's part was inescapable—the man was drinking more wine than milk these days, taking prescription pain medication for back pains relating to an old assassination attempt, and he'd lost weight, giving him a tired, sunken-cheeked look.

To Michael, however, the man seemed no less sharp; and his impeccable grooming, a point of pride for the one-time barber, kept him looking like the top executive he was. Often Nitti and Michael would have lunch together, sometimes joined by Campagna, sometimes not, and Nitti increasingly spoke of business in front of Michael.

Whose status as Nitti's number-two man (after Campagna) was widely known now, and accepted. The story about Calumet City had reached legendary proportions, and his "rescue" of Capone from disloyal bodyguards—though only a rumor, never openly discussed—had inspired the resurrection, from the Medal of Honor press coverage, of the *Demonio Angelico* tag the Filipino Scouts had bestowed him. Spoken in front of Michael, a certain comic tone usually was present; but respect was there, too. Kidding on the square.

Michael, of course, had benefited from Nitti's misreading of his assault at the Capone estate. But the young bodyguard, a novice to Outfit politics, could not foresee the ramifications facing Nitti himself; and by February, the breaking point approached.

In the white-and-gold Presidential Suite at the Bismarck, Nitti, tie loose, sat on the couch, stocking feet up on a coffee table, a glass of wine in hand. Campagna, Michael and their boss had just returned from St. Hubert's where treasurer Jake Guzik revealed overall earnings were up, despite the decreased prostitution revenue.

While Nitti relaxed, Campagna stewed, pacing behind the couch. This had been coming for weeks; even months. Campagna would bring the subject of Ricca up, and Nitti would bat it away. But today the putty-faced consigliere clearly would be heard.

Campagna finally lumbered around to plant himself before his seated master. "Frank, you gotta face this thing."

Nitti's eyes stared into nothing; the glass of wine in his hand was still. "What thing."

"You know what thing. The Ricca thing."

The tiniest of shrugs caused a bare ripple in the wine. "Nothing to face. Profits are up. We stand firm against these charges."

Nitti meant the continuing federal investigation into the Hollywood extortion matter. Any day now, the indictments would fall, hence the anxiety in the air.

Campagna's voice trembled; his hands were balled. "Frank, you know that ain't what I mean. You have to strike back."

"Not the way I do things."

"In the old days it was. Cermak hit you, you hit him. Mayor of the fuck Chicago tries to have you killed, and you have *him* killed!"

"Discreetly, Louie," Nitti said, his free hand raised in benediction, although still his eyes did not meet his adviser's. "Discreetly."

Now Campagna was gesturing animatedly—this was the most worked up Michael had ever seen the low-key hoodlum. "Sure, the papers wrote it off as a botched hit on Roosevelt! But the people who counted, *they knew—our* people, they found out what happened when you try to take out Frank fucking Nitti!"

Finally Nitti looked at his old friend. "Louie, those days are over. Got to be over. Have to be over. We're businessmen. We came up out of the streets, but now we're in skyscrapers. They call us gangsters, but we're really just capitalists, good American capitalists. Unions, restaurants, laundries, nice and legit—plus, yeah, gambling and such—slice it how you want, it's goods and services for the public. Look at how the Colony Club backfired on those fuckin' do-gooders. Drury and Ness made themselves the villains! Not us. We're just businessmen, givin' the public what they want."

This was an extraordinary speech, coming from Nitti, who chose his words so sparingly. Michael, pretending to read *Film Fun*, peered over the edges of a picture of Toby Wing.

Campagna was sitting down next to this man for whom he obviously had so much affection. "I agree with all of what you say,

Frank. You know that. Your vision of the future is my vision of the future."

Nitti patted Campagna's knee. "Good to hear, Louie. Always good to hear."

An edge spiked Campagna's reply: "Well, what I got to say now *won't* be. Frank, what happened down in Florida was too big to contain. People *know*."

"Know what?"

"Well, for one thing, that Al's slipped the trolley. The new boys we sent down there, to replace all them casualties, some of 'em are in Ricca's pocket and they spilled."

"Nobody's said a word to me about it."

Campagna raised his hands as if in surrender, though he was still fighting. "Nobody wants to broach the fuckin' subject, Frank! Nobody wants to accuse you of . . . of . . ."

Nitti frowned—more in disappointment than anger. "Lying? Deceiving my brothers?"

"Well." Campagna swallowed thickly. "It could be viewed like that."

Nitti took his feet off the coffee table; set down the glass of vino. Swiveled to throw a hard gaze at Campagna, all the harder coming out of the sunken sockets.

"How do they know Al's crack-up ain't recent? How do they know that dose of his didn't push him over the edge, just lately? Them diseases are, what-you-call-it . . . progressive."

Campagna gestured with open hands. "That makes sense."

"Of course it does."

"So tell the boys. Call a meeting. You tell them how Al's sick, but not so sick that he ain't had the good sense to leave you in charge."

Nitti turned away from Campagna, reached for the wine, and sipped. "I'll think about it. Think it over. Thanks, Louie. You always been a good advisor."

Campagna was shaking his head. "Frank, Al havin' the mind of a three-year-old retard is only part of the problem."

Nitti said nothing. Had another sip.

"The takeover try in Florida has Ricca's greasy fingerprints all

225

over it. But what's Ricca saying? That he had nothin' to do with it! That he loves Al, that you must have done this thing yourself."

The ganglord looked sharply at his advisor. "Ricca's saying *I* tried to take Al out?"

With a somber, reluctant nod, Campagna confirmed this.

"Then why don't the prick say so to me? To my damn *face*? We sat at the table at the Lex *how* many times since Miami?"

A small shrug from Campagna. "Ricca talks to people one, two at a time. He's like a goddamn missionary, makin' converts."

Nitti mulled this for a few moments, then again turned pointedly to his consigliere. "Has he talked to *you*, Louie?"

Campagna looked hurt. "I don't deserve that, Frank."

Nitti put a hand on Campagna's sleeve. "Forgive me, then. But you seem to know what the Waiter has on his mind."

Campagna clutched the hand on his arm. "Frank, hit the bastard! I'll help you. Michael over there, you don't think he'll help? With a man like Mike, we can take anything they throw at us."

Slowly Nitti shook his head. "We don't do things like that no more."

"Fucking Ricca does!"

"*I* don't do things like that no more."

Shaking his head despairingly, Campagna kept trying. "Frank! Don't you understand? You look weak in this thing! If you don't hit Ricca, and good and goddamn soon . . . you'll be out and he'll be in."

Eyes tight, Nitti asked, "My friends . . . they would turn on me?"

Campagna tried to make the reply matter of fact, but Michael could hear the sorrow: "You said it yourself, Frank. It's business. They'll go with strength."

Nitti smiled gently at his friend; he touched the man's face. "And you, Louie? Where do you stand?"

As Nitti withdrew his hand, Campagna raised a fist and shook it. "Strong—right next to you. Goin' after that prick Ricca. . . . Michael!"

Michael looked up from his magazine, affected an expression as if he hadn't heard a word of this.

Campagna said, "You'll stand with us. You're the ol' *Demonio Angelico*, right? Ricca can throw all the soldiers at us he wants, and you're still with us! Choppin' up the bastards like firewood! Right?"

"I'm with Mr. Nitti," Michael said ambiguously.

Campagna got to his feet again; he clasped his hands, pleadingly. "Say the word. Say the word. Please, Frank . . . say the word."

Nitti said, "I'll think on it."

Campagna looked to be on the verge of tears. "Think *soon*, Frank."

And the little hood gathered his coat and hat and was gone.

As usual, Michael drove Nitti—who sat in front, not liking the pretension of a chauffeured ride—home to the Near West Side suburbs, where so many Outfit bigwigs lived. Nitti's neighborhood was wealthy in an understated way—generous lawns, overgrown bungalows, paved driveways, backyard swing sets. In the Hollywood soundstage of Michael's life, Riverside was the MGM backlot, but the next shooting here wouldn't be an Andy Hardy movie.

Nitti's home was a brown brick story-and-a-half on the corner, plenty of well-manicured yard separating it from the street—new-looking with crisp white woodwork, shrubs hugging the house, patio out back. Mrs. Nitti's black '42 Ford sedan sat in the driveway. A vice president at a bank might live here; or the sales manager of Carson Pirie Scott.

Michael's duties rarely extended to the house; usually he hung around only for the rare evening board meeting in the living room (Michael relegated to the kitchen). Nitti did not have live-in bodyguards, but a pair of men sat in a car all night outside the house; they hadn't arrived yet.

Michael pulled up at the edge of the drive and Nitti said, "Shut the car off. Don't waste gas. There's a war on."

Michael obeyed. Nitti was making no move to get out. Though they'd exchanged not a word on the ride over, the boss now apparently wanted to talk.

His voice casual, friendly, Nitti asked, "What's your take on what Louie said?"

Feeling in over his head, Michael said frankly, "Mr. Nitti—I'm really not qualified to have an opinion."

Nitti smiled; he patted Michael's knee. "You wouldn't be my number two if that was true. You know, Louie's a good man, and smart, but he's no genius. And he's no leader."

"I like Louie," Michael said, pointlessly.

"I know you do, son. But some soldiers ain't cut out to be generals. Now Ricca could be a general, all right; but he's a ruthless son of a bitch, and the soldiers he surrounds himself with are kill-happy young turks. He'll put us into narcotics, he'll start the whores up after the war, he'll squeeze the unions like a buncha pimples."

Michael said nothing.

"Which puts me in a bad place. Because the terrible things this cocksucker is capable of forces me to consider doing the same kind of terrible things. . . . Michael, are you with Louie?"

"I'm with *you*, Mr. Nitti."

He patted the air with a palm. "I know. I know. But should we take Ricca out? You're the one man I know who wouldn't be afraid of the likes of Mad Sam and Mooney."

Michael thought about it. "Maybe it's like the war. Maybe when you got evil men like Hitler and Mussolini and Tojo, you got no choice."

Nitti sighed. "And I shouldn't sit around on my ass waitin' for Pearl Harbor to happen."

"No. You shouldn't."

Nitti looked older than his years—he wasn't even sixty; he seemed small, as if he'd shrunk. "How I wish you weren't so goddamned young. How I wish you were *ready* . . . because, Michael, I don't know if I have the strength, anymore."

"Of course you do, Mr. Nitti."

He shook his head. "I'm not even sure Louie hasn't already talked to Ricca. That's what that was about, you know, this afternoon—our little conversation."

"I don't follow . . ."

"It was about Louie warning me that if I didn't go with him, he would go with Ricca. . . . Michael . . . my boy. You've been a ray of light in this darkness."

Michael didn't know what to say.

"I've tried to hold on, since Anna's death. You know, I had everything for a while, Michael—a family I loved, a prosperous business. And then when I lost my wife, it all crashed down. Nature of what we do, I had to try not to show it. But I had needs. Not . . . not what you might think. A woman is more than the physical; it's support, friendship, loyalty. I thought Toni was the answer."

Nitti meant his second wife.

"She seems like a great woman," he went on. "She's good with my kid—such a wonderful kid I have. See, I knew Toni before. I adored my Anna, she was everything to me; but I'm a man, and when I was younger, I had those other kinda needs. Toni's been around our business for years—secretarial stuff. You heard of Eddie O'Hare?"

"Yeah . . ."

"Well, Toni was Eddie O'Hare's secretary . . . before he got hit? She's been a good friend to me, a lotta years, and she's strong and smart and so I married her."

"I like her," Michael said honestly, though he'd only exchanged a handful of words with the pleasant, severely handsome woman, who did seem to dote on Nitti.

"But now . . . I wonder about her. She makes phone calls. Hangs up quick when she sees me comin'. . . . No, no, she doesn't have anyone else, that's not it. But I start to wonder. Is my own wife in their camp? Did she marry me to keep an eye on me? Did Ricca and them put her up to it? 'Cause they thought I was slipping? After Anna died?"

"I'm sure your wife loves you. You're just—"

"Imagining it?" He grinned like a skull. "So, Michael, am I going mad, like Al? Only without the dose?" Nitti laughed bitterly. "So much I've built up. So many mistakes, from the old days, I put behind us. If Ricca gets in, it's a return to the old ways, but minus the tradition, the honor. Just the violence. The killing."

"What should we do, Mr. Nitti?"

Nitti again patted Michael's leg. "I'm not sure, son. If we had a few years, you'd be ready, to step in. But it's too soon. Too damn soon. And if the feds do nail us . . . all us big boys go to prison for a long time."

"Could that happen?"

"Looking at ten years, lawyers say. We can buy paroles in maybe three, four, five. If the feds do put us away, pray Ricca goes along for the ride. Accardo, he's next in line, after the eight or nine of us facin' this Hollywood thing. He'd take over, in the . . . what's it called? Interim."

"Mr. Accardo wasn't involved with Hollywood?"

"No. Oh, in a minor way—he hit a guy named Tommy Maloy, at the outset. Projectionist union guy. But other than that, nothing. There'll be no indictment for him."

"You approve of Mr. Accardo."

"He's better than Ricca, and imagine where we'd be with *Giancana* in the top chair! If I'm in stir, get next to Accardo, Michael."

Michael's eyes tensed. "You really think it'll come to that?"

"I think so, I do think so. . . . But get this—Ricca's saying *I* should take the rap. That the Hollywood business was all my doing."

"That's not true—is it?"

Nitti gestured dismissively. "I was the prime mover, but we were all in it. Biggest mistake was using a couple of lying untrustworthy bastards like Bioff and Browne as our reps; that's why I sent Nicky Dean out to look over their shoulders."

"And Dean hasn't talked, like the other two."

"No. Thing is, Ricca knows damn well I can't shoulder the blame. It's a fuckin' conspiracy case! Of course, Ricca already knows that—blaming me is just part of him tryin' to undermine me with the boys."

Michael locked his gaze with his chief's. "You want him dead, Mr. Nitti, he's dead."

Nitti looked at Michael with infinite fondness; patted his cheek like a favored child. "You're a sweet boy, Michael. Sweet boy. . . . We'll talk tomorrow. I'll sleep on it. You too."

Then Nitti slipped out of the vehicle and headed up the sidewalk to his cozy home and his beloved son and a wife he no longer trusted.

THAT EVENING MICHAEL AND ESTELLE HAD COCKTAILS in a rear booth of the Seneca's Bow 'n' Arrow Room, where authentic Indian murals and a mirrored ceiling lent the cocktail lounge an atmosphere of spaciousness and warmth.

But about now the world seemed a cold one to Michael, and closing in. He found the irony of his situation bitterly unamusing— in attempting to take revenge upon a villain whom the fates had transformed into an impotent moron, Michael had managed only to set the stage for the downfall of the one man in the Outfit he truly respected.

Her hair styled short and dyed a reddish blonde, Estelle wore a business-like cream-color suit. She'd been spending time at the dress shop she co-owned, though Michael knew her primary business remained brothel-less madam. At Nitti's behest, she'd developed a little black book of customers and call girls, and from her apartment made referrals.

Michael neither approved nor disapproved; such business had been part of Estelle's life long before they'd met. As a gangster's bodyguard, he was not inclined to judge.

Like Frank Nitti, Estelle had been hit hard by the intervening months; beautiful though she still was, she appeared at once haggard and puffy.

"Michael," she said, in the midst of her third martini, "I think maybe I need to move in with you."

"Well, that's swell, baby."

"I don't mean to impose," she said, shaking her head, "or push you into anything—"

"I've asked you to do it, half a dozen times, and you've said no—half a dozen times. Please do. Pack your bag."

She played with a swizzle stick in the now empty martini glass. "I won't lie to you, Mike. It's not about us."

"Well . . . usually, when a gal moves in with a fella, it is about them. Us."

She swallowed; glanced around anxiously. The cocktail lounge did a good business, but their booth was private enough. Paranoia, it seemed, was going around like flu.

"Michael," she said, leaning halfway across the table, "I'm afraid. I'm really afraid."

This was hardly stop-the-presses stuff; she'd been frightened for months.

"So move in with me," he said, touching her face, "and feel more secure."

"I just don't think it's fair to you if . . . I don't *admit* that to you. Admit that I'm moving in because I think you can protect me. Admit that here in the hotel I don't figure anybody'd dare . . . you know. . . . It's sort of their home turf, right?"

"Now I'm not following you."

She shook her head, arcs of hair swinging like twin scythes. "Oh, Michael . . . how can you be you, and still be so naive? These indictments are about to come down. Everybody knows that. And the feds are pressing Nicky. Pressing *hard.*"

Feeling a twinge of jealousy, Michael said, "You're in touch with the guy? I thought that was over."

"It is over. But we're in touch, yeah. Through lawyers. . . . Michael, there's a rumor on the street."

"What rumor?"

Her lower lip trembled, her eyes brimmed. "That I'm going to be made an example. That something . . . *bad*'ll happen to me, to send Nicky a message."

He reached across and held her ice-cold hand. "I won't let that happen, baby. You move in with me. Right away."

She nodded, and nodded some more. "Thank you, Michael. Thank you."

In his penthouse, Michael and Estelle made love with an urgent intensity driven by unspoken-of emotions that left them both spent; nonetheless, he fell prey to the insomnia again, which had never before been the case on nights when she'd stayed with him.

He slipped from her slumbering grasp and out of bed and, in

his boxers, stepped into slippers; tossed a dressing robe around himself, and walked out into the living room. He slid open the glass door and went out onto the balcony. The night was crisp but not cold. Leaning against the rail, he studied the skyline, its luminescent geometry again reminding him of a Hollywood backdrop.

"What are you doing out here?" Estelle said from behind him. "You wanna freeze to death, silly?"

He half-turned to see her at the door, just inside—shivering in her chemise, breasts perked by the chill.

"It's not that cold. Throw something around yourself, and join me."

Soon, a yellow-and-red blanket wrapped around her Indian-style, she was snuggling against him, looking out at the cityscape. "It just doesn't look real, does it?"

Taking it all in, he nodded. "Like something you'd see out a window in a Fred and Ginger musical."

But her eyes had shifted from the skyscrapers to Michael. "You like the movies, don't you?"

"Yes."

"Always reading books, too. Don't you like real life?"

"No."

"Maybe you'd like it if . . . you could start over."

He turned to her with a curious frown.

She was gazing up at him with an oddly tentative expression. "If you could run off with me . . . would you?"

"Well . . . sure."

"I'm not kidding, Michael."

He thought for a moment. "I don't think I am, either."

"What if I told you . . . that I have some money."

"I'm sure you do."

A tiny crinkly smile appeared on the doll-like face. "No. I mean . . . a *lot* of money."

"How much is a lot?"

"Oh—a quarter of a million dollars, a lot."

His eyebrows climbed. "You're not serious . . . ?"

She hugged the blanket to herself and her eyes drifted across the view. "You mean you haven't heard the rumors? How I salted away a couple million from the movie scams, for Nicky and me to make a new life, when he gets out?"

". . . Maybe I have."

"Well, like most rumors . . . it's exaggerated. There may be as much as a million missing, from union treasuries, but most of it went to those two goons, Bioff and Browne."

"But some went to you? And your friend Nicky?"

Now her eyes returned to him. ". . . Suppose it had. Would you come?"

He grinned a little. "I thought I just did."

"Not just tonight, stupe. Every night. Forever till we're dead."

Trying to make it real, he managed, "Wouldn't they . . . chase us?"

"They wouldn't know where to look. Do you know how well you can live on that much money in Mexico? Or certain South American countries? *Very* good."

"We'd just leave. Disappear."

"That's right. You should be contemplating taking a powder, anyway."

"Why?"

"Your angel, your sponsor, Frank Nitti? . . . Hell, he's mine, too. . . . He's on his last legs, Michael. He's on the way out. And where will that leave his fairhaired boy?"

"Don't count Frank Nitti out just yet."

She sneered and huddled within the blanket. "Fuck Frank Nitti. And fuck Nicky Dean."

"Estelle. . . ."

"Matter of fact," she said, but in a different voice, "fuck me," and she dragged him and the blanket back inside and pulled him down on the floor, on top of her, and they did it again, slowly but with that same urgency, the balcony door open, coolness of the night licking at the heat they made.

"Move me in here tomorrow," she said, afterward, clutching his bare back desperately. "And we'll plan it."

"Okay," he said.

In his ear she said, "Not a word to a soul about the money! Not a word. To a soul."

"Okay."

He carried her like a new bride over the bedroom threshold and deposited her gently on the covers. Soon she was snuggling up under his arm, her face against his hairless chest. Both were quickly asleep, legs tangled.

But he dreamed of Bataan, of that jungle clearing, only this time he was blasting away with his tommy gun at faceless Ricca thugs.

Who, unlike the Japs, refused to fall.

4

THE NEXT MORNING CAMPAGNA phoned Michael saying Mr. Nitti was feeling sick and staying home—though he'd remain on call, this effectively gave Michael the day off.

Estelle, as was her habit, had slipped out in the early morning hours. Alone in the penthouse, showered and shaved but in t-shirt and boxers, Michael dialed his console radio to the latest popular tunes; he did not turn up it loud, just providing himself with a little low-key company by way of outfits like Benny Goodman and Harry James and singers like Peggy Lee and that new kid, Sinatra. He fixed himself breakfast—scrambled eggs, toast, orange juice—and then, at the same table, spent close to an hour cleaning and fuss-ing over the .45 Colt automatic that had belonged to Michael O'Sullivan, Sr.

The gun was just about the only possession of his late father's that Michael owned; just that, and a few family photos he and his father carried with them, long ago, on the road to Perdition (and these were in his room at home, that is, DeKalb). He treated the weapon with near reverence, rubbing it lightly with an oil-saturated rag, then drying it with another rag, a fresh one. The bore he purified with a cleaner-saturated patch followed by a dry patch. With a stiff bristly brush he dusted out all the crevices.

When he was finished, he clicked a fresh magazine in and slipped the .45 into the oil-rubbed shoulder holster, currently draped over a kitchenette chair.

Then he returned to the book he was reading, a reprint edition of *For Whom the Bell Tolls*, which he was enjoying, though he was pretty sure it wasn't going to end well for the hero. Propped up with two pillows, he was just starting the last chapter when the bedstand phone rang.

"Hi, hero," Estelle said.

"Hey, I have the day off. Are you home? I can come over any time and move you out."

"I was calling to try to head you off, in case you got ambitious, Mr. Moving Man. Some old friends dropped by—we'll be visiting for a while. Can you make it around two?"

It was just after eleven, now.

"Sure. See you then."

"Michael, I appreciate this. I'm gonna feel a lot better, rooming with you."

"I'm sorta looking forward to havin' you in my bed, myself."

"Naughty boy," she chuckled.

They hung up, and he folded the book open on the bedstand, figuring to go down to the Seneca coffee shop for a bite. He had stepped into a pair of tan slacks and was just shrugging into a brown sportcoat—having taken the time to sling on the shoulder holster, considering the tensions of late—when somebody knocked at the door.

Withdrawing the .45, Michael strode over and checked the

peephole: it was a woman, a blonde (not Estelle, obviously), good-looking it would seem, but through this fisheye view, who could say?

Still, you never knew, so he opened the door carefully with his left hand, snugging his right-gun-in-hand behind him.

For half a moment he didn't recognize her, though she hadn't really changed much if at all. He just didn't expect to see Patsy Ann O'Hara of DeKalb on the doorstep of Michael Satariano of Chicago.

She looked so business-like, so much . . . older. She had on a brown tweed Prince Albert reefer-style topcoat, with wide collar and vaguely military rows of buttons. Purse under her arm, she wore a white scarf bunched at the throat and white gloves and a little side-tilted brown hat with a feather.

"Hey, soldier," she said, clearly a little apprehensive. "Wouldn't care to buy a girl some lunch, would you?"

He'd almost forgotten how lovely she was—the big blue eyes with the long lashes, the pert nose, the full lips with that phony perfect beauty mark that happened to be real.

"Patsy Ann," he said, and warmth flooded through him, and he embraced her, and she embraced him.

Still in his arms, she drew away a little and gazed up at him, clearly wanting to be kissed.

He released her, moved off and made a joke of it, saying, "Hey—I'm not takin' a girl out for lunch with her makeup mussed. . . . Want to see the digs?"

"Sure," she said, forcing a smile.

He stepped inside, gun still behind him, and gestured for her to enter; when her back was to him, he slipped the weapon in its shoulder holster. Then he showed her around, and she seemed suitably impressed, though something behind her pleasant expression seemed stiff, even disapproving.

The day was crisp but sunny—he wore a gabardine trenchcoat—as he took his former best girl on his arm, walking the little area that was so much a part of his world. Rush was an around-the-clock street, and had surprisingly little of the tawdry look such areas often did by day, neon glow replaced by an aura of the avant-garde. Nightclubs and many restaurants were closed, but other businesses flourished in the sun: art dealers, bookshops, florists with blooming wares overflowing onto the sidewalk, chic dress shops, and of course saloons—even in daylight, this was still Chicago.

As they walked arm-in-arm, further linked by their tan and brown clothing, they said nothing. If an underlying awkwardness had accompanied those first minutes, a wordless comfort had already replaced it. They enjoyed each other's company and were resisting bringing themselves up to date, and spoiling everything.

In a roundabout way, they ended up at Little Normandy, a restaurant not so little and which did not keep the implied promise of French food. The old mansion across from the Water Tower was an elegant graystone with a delightful interior—broad open staircase, grand fireplaces, and leaded glass windows, with murals, wood carvings and ceramic plaques designed by a modern artist who lived upstairs. The bold dramatic artwork struck Michael as cartoony, while (had she been asked) college senior Patsy Ann would have termed it "art moderne with influences ranging from cave drawings to Japanese prints" (but no one asked).

The place was crowded as usual but the pretty hostess/manager, Celia, recognized Michael and provided a cozy booth in the Black Sheep Bar. Patsy Ann ordered onion soup (a rare French item at the Normandy) and Michael chose hamburger steak with Roquefort sauce, a house specialty.

He had his usual Coca-Cola and she drank a 7UP while they waited for their lunch. Finally he asked, "What brings you to the big city?"

She leaned forward a little, gloved hands folded on the tablecloth. "Well, you know I graduate in June. So I'm interviewing for teaching positions. There's an opening at a high school in Evanston, and that interview's at two-thirty, and then I have another at Downers Grove, for an elementary. That's at four-thirty."

"Could be a little tight," he said. "Opposite sides of the world."

Nodding, she said, "I know, but these interviews only last about fifteen minutes. It's mostly your grades and letters of recommendation and. . . . Michael, thank you for not being angry with me."

"Why would I be?"

She shrugged, leaned back; she looked awfully sweet in that feathered hat; the dress beneath the topcoat had proven to be a smart brown corduroy suit.

"You didn't want to be crowded," she was saying. "You made that clear . . . but you have to admit . . ." And now she leaned forward again, and gave him a bold little smile. ". . . you did leave the door open."

". . . Patsy Ann, you know you'll always have a special place in my heart."

She frowned. "What a horrible thing to say."

"What?"

"*That* sounded like the door closing. Slamming."

Her gaze was boring through him. He transferred his attention to the glass of Coke and sipped it, offhandedly saying, "How did you find me?"

"Papa Satariano. . . . Now don't be mad at him—I know you made him promise not to tell anybody where you were. But I wore him down, Michael—took months to do it. . . . Why haven't you gone home to visit? Even once? It's not that far."

How could he explain how vast the distance was?

"I write once a week," he said.

"To them. Not to me. Some things never change—it's like you're still at war."

Now she'd stumbled onto it.

He took one of her gloved hands. "I'm involved in something that I . . . I don't want to have touch any of the people I care about."

She swallowed; her frown had worry in it. "You mean, because of these . . . gangsters you're in with."

He frowned. "Papa S. told you that?"

"Eventually. . . . He says you want to get in solid with them, so that someday you can have a restaurant or a nightclub. He says these people control businesses like that—show business, too. Is that true?"

"True enough."

She put her other hand on top of the one holding hers; she squeezed. Her eyes were urgent. "What if I said I didn't care?"

"What?"

"What if I said I didn't care that you were in with gangsters. You think I didn't see you put that gun away? When was I ever stupid?"

". . . Never."

"Why do you think I'm looking at schools around Chicago? I have an offer at DeKalb Township."

"I would imagine you get . . . a lot of offers."

He wasn't talking about teaching jobs.

Her chin crinkled as she drew her hand away from his. "I do. I always have had. I can still snap my fingers and get any man on campus."

"Why don't you?"

"Because I love you, you selfish son of a bitch."

Their food came. They picked at it in silence.

Finally she said, "Not enough, huh?"

"What isn't?"

"Selling my soul to be with you. In books, that's all it usually takes."

Michael waved a waiter over to remove their plates. No dessert. Check please.

Then he leaned toward her and said, "Do you remember, a long time ago, when I told you I had a brother who died?"

"Yes . . . of course. But I respected your privacy and—"

"I was adopted, Patsy Ann."

". . . I didn't know."

"We didn't advertise it. If I tell you something, you can't repeat it to anybody, not even Papa S., 'cause even he doesn't know."

Eyes tight with interest and concern, she bent forward. "Know what?"

"That my brother was killed. That my mother was killed. That my father was killed."

Her eyes froze as she repeated the word, as if it were foreign: "Killed."

"Murdered," he said, offering a synonym the lit major might be familiar with. "By gangsters. My real father was one of them, and he tried to keep us separate from what he did. But it . . . spilled over. And my mother was killed, and my brother, and when my father went after the ones responsible, he was killed, too."

Her eyes were huge and shimmering. "Oh, Michael . . . oh my God, Michael."

He shrugged. "So now I'm in that life. Following in my father's footsteps. But I'm not going to make the mistake he did. I'm not going to risk those I care for."

"*Why*, Michael?"

"Isn't it self-evident?"

She shook her head, blonde locks bouncing, frustrated with him. "No. No, why are you . . . following in footsteps like *those*?"

"That I can't go into. I promise you the reasons were good ones. But things . . . they've gotten a little out of control."

She reached across and took his hand again in both of hers. Her grip was surprisingly strong; so was her gaze. "Walk away from it, Mike. With me."

How he could tell her he was thinking of doing that very thing with another lovely blonde . . . only, one who was—like him—damaged goods? He couldn't risk such a life with a good person like Patsy Ann. Even if she would sell her soul for him.

Which *was* a nice gesture, but still he said, "No. You need to move on. I've gone down my own road, and you don't want to even consider taking that turn."

He paid the bill, grabbed her by the hand and walked her out to the sidewalk. "Where's your car?"

"On the street, near the Seneca."

"Let's go."

Almost pulling her along, he escorted her to that same Buick in whose backseat they'd made love by a cornfield under fireworks in the starry sky, eons ago, last year.

She was angry now, and the question of whether to grant her a goodbye kiss—which might betray how difficult this was for him—became a moot point. In a nonpatriotic squeal of rubber, she was gone.

Out of his life for good this time?

For her sake, he hoped so.

DRIVING THE NAVY 1940 FORD SEDAN HE FREQUENTLY ushered Nitti around in, Michael headed toward Estelle's on West Addison. Because Estelle shared the place with her partner in the dress shop, Michael had seldom stayed over there, though he did have a key. Her apartment house was a large one in a battery of such buildings in a quiet, upper middleclass neighborhood in the shadows of nearby lake shore skyscrapers.

Today, however, West Addison was not quiet, the sidewalks on either side lined with gawkers, from proper-looking businessmen to women in curlers and housecoats. A small fire engine was barring passage, though clearly the handful of black-slickered firefighters—moving with no urgency whatsoever—were wrapping things up, literally and figuratively.

Michael parked by a hydrant—they didn't seem to need the thing anymore—and walked quickly down to the fire truck, approaching the helmeted men.

"What's happened?" he asked.

The firefighter, a young one, said, "You got here in a hurry."

Immediately Michael understood that, thanks in part to his trenchcoat, he'd been mistaken for plainclothes police.

Manufacturing a half-smile, Michael said, "Hell, the station's only two blocks away. Buddies are right behind me. What do we have?"

The firefighter gestured with a heavily gloved finger. "Third floor flat . . ."

Estelle's flat was on the third floor!

". . . fire was contained to just the dining room, and we've got it out; ready for you guys to take over. One victim, and that's why we called you."

"Go on."

Slickered shoulders shrugged and the helmet nodded toward the apartment building. "See for yourself. I may be new on the job, but that's no fire fatality. That's a goddamn murder."

Hiding his alarm, Michael nodded thanks, and went quickly in. The building had multiple entrances, stairs leading up to landings where apartments faced each other across the stairwell. The acrid smell of smoke filled his nostrils as he took the stairs three at a time.

The door to her apartment was open, the smoke stench issuing its nasty invitation. . . .

He braced himself and went in. The living room was in disarray, though the firemen could have caused that. He moved on through into the dining room and there she was.

Bracing himself had not been enough. It couldn't have been.

A chair had been positioned centrally; she lay nearby. The two adjacent walls were black and dripping wet, from the firefighter's successful effort to stem the blaze. Much of the carpet was also black, a broken whiskey bottle on the floor apparently having fed the flames. The acrid stench was almost overpowering.

Wearing only a red silk robe, she lay on the plush scorched carpet, on her back, in a Christ-on-the-cross sprawl. The robe was charred from the waist down and her legs were burnt so badly that from the knees down, the limbs were cinders.

Michael knelt near the upper half of her, as if praying that this battered, burnt corpse was not the woman he'd shared his bed with the night before. But he knew such prayers were useless, because this clearly was not the roommate, rather Estelle herself—the welts and bruises and cuts could not disguise the fact, nor the ragged slash through one eye nor the punctures on her cheeks; not her bloodied broken nose nor the smashed pulp of once-lovely lips. Not the frightwig hair, clumps yanked or cut from her scalp. Not even the ear-to-ear slash on her throat, which was not what had killed her, too superficial, merely part of the torture that had preceded her murder.

Her head tilted to one side, eyes blankly open. Her hands

were puffy with burns—had her torturers tossed the whiskey on her, set it aflame, and allowed her to try to put it out with her palms?

Forever till we're dead, her voice whispered in his memory.

Somehow he got to his feet. He staggered into the next room, the kitchen, where he found signs of struggle even a one-eyed man couldn't miss: a broken drinking glass on the floor; blood-smeared cabinets; scarlet spattering the sink. On the floor, a bloodstained breadknife, a bloody rolling pin, and the blood-tipped ice pick that no doubt had made the punctures on those pretty cheeks. Also, a bloody blackjack, as if the kitchen hadn't given up enough impromptu weapons.

On the maple table where he'd on several occasions shared breakfast with Estelle sat the unlikely meal of a flatiron, also bloodsmeared, obviously utilized as a battering instrument. Blood splatter dotted the table, chair and floor underneath. A glass ashtray with a number of smashed cigarette butts signaled the time the process had taken, and one had lipstick on it. Estelle did not smoke. Had not.

On the stove, milk was simmering. On the counter nearby, three cups with powdered cocoa in the bottom. He recalled what she'd said on the phone: *some old friends had dropped by.* She had turned her back to these friends—*who had been with her when she'd called Michael*—and they had done this to her. . . .

In his mind his own voice, speaking to Patsy Ann, over the cozy lunch they'd had while Estelle was being tortured to death, said, *I'm not going to risk those I care for.*

Feeling weak-kneed, he wanted to sit; hot in the trench coat, he wanted to strip it off and fling it somewhere. But he dared do neither—evidence was scattered from one end of the five-room apartment to the other, and he didn't want to disturb any of it, on the off-chance an honest Chicago cop caught the case.

As if that had been his cue, Lieutenant William Drury—the most famous honest cop in town, despite that camel's hair topcoat—appeared at the mouth of the kitchen.

"What the hell are *you* doing here?" Drury asked.

Michael began to scream and rushed the cop, who backed

into the room where Estelle lay. Throwing a punch that almost connected, Michael met a punch of Drury's that did.

Then he was on the scorched carpet, sprawled next to Estelle's vacant-eyed corpse, her ghastly white/purple/black/red face turned questioningly his way.

Hands jerked him to his feet, but Michael pulled away, shoving past Drury and fleeing to the kitchen where he flung himself over the blood-spattered sink and lost the meal he'd shared, not long ago, with his other best girl.

And when the cuffs were snapped on, he had, mercifully, already passed out.

5

MICHAEL WOKE IN A SMALL ISOLA-
tion cell. Sun filtered in through a high
barred window; he judged it morning—
maybe ten. He knew where he was: Town
Hall Station, only two blocks from Estelle's
apartment.

He had slept deep and long and
dreamed a delirium of faces and events
floating but never congealing into even the
incoherent, surrealistic narrative of a
nightmare—more a review of Michael
O'Sullivan, Jr.'s life as Michael Satariano . . . faces and places from Bataan,
Captain Wermuth, General Wainwright,
the clearing full of Japs, the Zero dipping
down over that jungle roadway . . . scraps
of memory from DeKalb, Papa and Mama
S., school friends, bits and pieces of that

last Fourth of July . . . a drooling Al Capone, bodyguards with guns streaming at Michael, that guy Abatte from Calumet City, standing on the sidelines, grinning at him only with a hole in his head, Frank Nitti patting Michael's shoulder, spouting reassuring gibberish . . . Estelle whispering words of love in bed on top of him at the Colony, transforming into a terrible scorched and beaten and dead Patsy Ann, grinding on him and murmuring her love through battered, cut lips. . . .

He jerked upright.

Shook his head, dispelling the images; swung his legs around, to sit on the edge of the cot in the small cement chamber, which had an open toilet bowl and nothing else. He was in his t-shirt and pants, his belt gone; he was shoeless, though he'd been left his socks. His wristwatch was missing, but checking the time would be meaningless, as he was unsure what day it was.

He had that same drugged, sluggish feeling as when he'd woken in the cell-like bedroom at the Capone mansion. But he knew where he was and why he felt that way—he had a blurred but undeniable memory of attacking uniformed cops in this cell, when his cuffs were removed. He'd assaulted them for no particular reason, other than his grief-driven rage needed somewhere to go.

And another memory—of a doctor with a gladstone bag entering and sedating him—was not blurred at all, as distinct as the needle that had plunged into his arm. The only surprise was waking up in this isolation cell, and not in an infirmary, though considering he'd attacked both Drury and those other cops, maybe the bars made sense.

Clarity and a peculiar calm came to him quickly. He had been adrift of late, purposeless; but his reason for living had returned, as did the deadly stoic surface he'd inherited from his father. And at the core of his being glowed something red hot.

A guard came checking on him, and Michael convinced the man sufficiently he was no longer a threat. Lunch was brought to Michael, and the information that a day had passed came casually.

Eventually he was ushered to the same windowless, sound-proofed interrogation booth as before. Three chairs waited at the small scarred table, and he took one. Before long Lieutenant Drury came in, in shirtsleeves and a vest, tie loosened, his creased pants looking crisp, even if the detective did not.

Drury took one of the remaining chairs. He sat and stared at Michael, who got tired of it quickly and transferred his attention to the wall. For an eternity this went on—a full minute, at least—and then a third party joined them.

Eliot Ness sat across from Michael. The G-man's suit was rumpled but not as rumpled as the G-man. Ness looked terrible—older, puffy, eyes circled; the smell of liquor was on him. His physical deterioration reminded Michael of somebody, vaguely . . . and then it came to him: Frank Nitti.

Drury said, "Are you going to take another swing at me?"

Michael said nothing.

Ness said, "Your fingerprints are all over the Carey woman's apartment."

Michael said nothing.

Drury said, "We don't think you killed her. From what we understand, you two were an item."

Michael said nothing.

Ness said, "Why do you think she was tortured?"

Michael said nothing.

Drury said, "It's no surprise the Outfit had her killed. You know what happened yesterday? It was on the radio."

Michael said nothing.

Ness said, "Grand Jury returned indictments in the Hollywood shakedown. Against Frank 'the Enforcer' Nitti, Paul 'the Waiter' Ricca, Louis 'Little New York' Campagna, Rosselli, Gioe, D'Andrea . . . all of 'em, short of Accardo."

Michael said nothing.

Drury said, "Killing Estelle sends a message to Nicky Dean."

Michael said nothing.

Ness said, "Maybe putting Estelle through hell was part of the message."

Michael said nothing.

Drury said, "Or maybe they were after something—money, maybe?"

Michael said nothing.

Ness said, "There's over a million missing from the stage-hand union retirement fund."

Michael said nothing.

Drury said, "But that might be bullshit. Was there ever really any money? Could the killers have found it in that apartment?"

Michael said nothing.

Ness said, "We say killers, Michael, because it seems to be a man and a woman. Lipstick on a cigarette. People she trusted. 'Friends.' She was fixing 'em cocoa when they started in on her."

Michael said nothing.

Drury said, "Anybody could have sent them. Nitti or Ricca or any one of the other seven indicted. Or the whole damn bunch. You're the little mouse in the corner, Michael. What did you hear?"

Michael said nothing.

Ness leaned forward, desperation in his eyes. "Help us. Tell us what you know. That's why we did this in the first place, Michael—remember? That's why *you* did this. To help me get these bastards."

Michael said nothing.

Drury said, "If we can add murder to extortion, the Outfit is finished; this whole hierarchy will go away for a long, long time, and all the bribe money in the world won't spring 'em loose."

Michael said nothing.

Ness said, "It's not too late for you, Michael. With that medal of yours, I can get you a job with my department. Or with Treasury; Christ, even Hoover wouldn't turn you away. Michael, the Mafia doesn't kill FBI agents!"

Michael said nothing.

Drury slammed a hand on the table. "What is this, that fucking *omertà*? You're a made man, now—on *their* side? The side of those who tortured and killed that poor girl?"

Michael said nothing.

Ness said, "You have to choose, Mike. Are you part of the

problem, or part of the solution? You become one of us, openly, and you'll be protected."

Michael said nothing.

Drury said, "It's your best option, kid. What if we leaked the truth? That you went into Nitti's organization, undercover, for Eliot Ness? How long would they let you live?"

Michael said nothing.

Ness looked at Drury and shook his head. Drury, lowering his gaze, sighed heavily. The G-man got up slowly, took one last mournful lingering look at Michael, and went out. Drury, his expression disgusted, was half-way out the door when Michael finally spoke.

"Interesting interrogation technique," Michael said.

Drury, startled, said nothing.

"Don't hit the suspect with a rubber hose," Michael said. "Hit him with everything you know, and see if it breaks him down. . . . Do I get my phone call now?"

Still poised in the doorway, Drury sighed. "You don't need it. A lawyer's already been around. Should be here with your writ of habeas corpus any time now."

"Your friend Ness looks like he's been drinking."

Drury stepped back in; shut the door. His tone shifted to conversational. "He's had a tough go of it lately. Washington thought he was spending too much time in Chicago; been running him ragged all 'round the country. Only reason he's back in town now is some joint workshop with the FBI."

"America's most famous Prohibition agent . . . a drunk?"

"Eliot's no drunk. He's still a good man . . . and he's concerned about you. You should let him be your friend. You should let *me* be your friend."

It sounded genuine enough, but Michael knew what both men wanted was to use him.

"I'll think about it," Michael said.

"All I ask," Drury said.

Then the cop slipped out, and a uniformed cop ushered Michael back to the cell.

Less than an hour later, Michael was on the street, in his

251

military-style gabardine trenchcoat over the brown sportcoat and tan slacks—same as for his dates yesterday with Patsy Ann and Estelle. The .45, returned to him by the police, was back in its shoulder sling; he was, after all, licensed to carry a concealed weapon.

He found the Ford sedan where he'd left it, parked by the hydrant, wiper wearing three parking tickets; at least it hadn't been towed. He was about to get in when a car behind him honked.

Glancing back, he saw Louie Campagna at the wheel of a dark blue '41 Chevy. The lumpy-faced little hood curled a finger.

Michael got in on the passenger side, shut himself in, and wondered if this was a one-way ride. He said, "Did you arrange for that mouthpiece, Louie? Thanks."

"Actually, I didn't. Guy that sprung you was Bulger."

Michael frowned. "Joe Bulger? He's Ricca's attorney!"

"I know. Things are . . . upside down. I'll fill you in."

The heater was on in the car and the stocky gangster was not in his topcoat, nor was he wearing a hat, exposing his thinning black hair. He looked awful, pasty white and baggy-eyed—not as bad as Ness and Nitti; but bad enough.

"Sorry about the Carey dame," Campagna said, but his mind was obviously elsewhere.

"Yeah. Thanks."

"We need to talk. Diner down the street."

Within minutes they were in a booth and, as they waited for coffee, Campagna asked, "You hear about the indictments?"

"You were expecting it, right?"

Campagna nodded. "But it's like death, kid—you can't get ready for shit like this, even when you know it's comin'. . . . Something bad happened last night. At Frank's. Counsel meeting."

Michael leaned forward in the booth. "Tell me they didn't vote to have Estelle killed."

"No! No. Hell no. I figure that was Ricca."

"Not Mr. Nitti."

Campagna smirked mirthlessly. "Does it sound like him?"

Michael had already thought this through; he knew a murder of this kind was against everything Nitti believed in, where public opinion was concerned.

Still, he said, "Lot of pressure on him lately, Louie. Ricca breathing down his neck. These indictments."

Campagna shrugged, as if they were discussing baseball scores of not very important games. "Word I get is it was a couple, a man and wife, old friends of hers. Named Borgia."

Michael raised an eyebrow. "As in Cesare and Lucretia?"

"No, I think their names are John and Olivia. John's a small-timer, on the fringes of the Outfit, worked with Nicky Dean at the 101 Club. Olivia was a 26 girl, there."

"Is this solid, them doing it?"

"No. Just talk. But John's got ties to Ricca." Another shrug; Campagna seemed vaguely annoyed to be talking about such a trivial matter.

A waitress brought coffee and, after a sip, Michael asked Campagna, "You still up for a little preventative medicine, where the Waiter is concerned?"

Campagna sighed. Shook his head glumly. "I think we missed our moment."

"Why do you say that?"

"I *said* somethin' bad happened last night."

Campagna described the counsel meeting in the living room of Nitti's Riverside home.

Ricca took over the meeting, out of the gate. He reminded Nitti and the others that hiring squealers Bioff and Browne had been Nitti's idea; that Nicky Dean was also Nitti's man. That Nitti had "masterminded the whole scam and it went sour."

"No point in all of us goin' down this road," Ricca had said. "Al took the fall for the rest of us and went on trial alone. You can do the same, Frank—you plead guilty and we'll take care of things. Till you get out."

"I've told you, Paul," Nitti said wearily. "It's conspiracy. Nobody can take the fall for the rest of us—we gotta stick together, and try and beat the thing."

Sipping his coffee, Campagna told Michael, "It got heated, then—harsh words, back and forth. Thought it might come to blows . . . or worse. Finally Ricca says, 'Frank, you're askin' for it.' "

Michael frowned. "What did Mr. Nitti say?"

"Nothing. He . . . Mike, I ain't proud of this . . . Frank looked around the room at us and . . ." Campagna had tears in his eyes. ". . . we all looked away. Nobody stood up for him."

"Not even you, Louie?"

"No. Mike, there was one strong man in that room. One leader. And it sure as hell wasn't me. But it also wasn't Frank."

"What did Mr. Nitti do?"

"That was the worst of it. He got up, went to the front door, opened it, and pointed to the outside."

"What was so bad about that?"

"Ain't you Sicilian, kid?"

Without missing a beat, Michael said, "Sure I'm Sicilian . . . a Sicilian raised in DeKalb, Illinois. What was so bad about what Mr. Nitti did?"

"In the old country, when you open the door on your guests, indicating you want 'em to leave . . . it's a breach."

"Breach."

"Of Sicilian peasant rules of hospitality. It's like Frank spit in all our faces."

"But mostly," Michael said, "he was answering Ricca."

"When Ricca said Frank was gonna get it, you mean? Yeah. Yeah, that was the main meaning."

"How did Ricca react?"

Campagna gestured elaborately with both hands. "It was so . . . so goddamn *dramatic*, that we all just got up, got our hats and coats and went out into the cold. Without a word from Frank. Without a word from us."

"So, Louie. Where do you stand?"

"I wish I knew, kid. Do you know?"

Michael said nothing. Then he took the check, and paid at the register. Campagna tagged along.

"Kid—where *do* you stand?"

"Take me to my car, Louie. Would you?"

Campagna sighed. "Sure. Sure, Mike. Right away."

LIKE FRANK NITTI, PAUL RICCA HAD MOVED TO A SUBURB, RIVER Forest; but the Waiter's heart, Michael knew, remained on the Near West Side where many workers in various legit and not-so-legit Outfit enterprises made their homes. Sluggers, drivers and (yes) waiters lived in these well-maintained two- and three-story tenements, in a neighborhood of cast-iron porches, broad sidewalks and no lawns. Here, in this longtime breeding ground for Outfit soldiers, Ricca could court the Young Turks coming up.

Bella Napoli was a corner building, a one-story brown-brick structure with a row of narrow, shuttered windows extending around its sides; during Prohibition, these windows had been blackened, no doubt, whereas these days (in summer and spring, anyway) window boxes of colorful flowers offered a friendly, family feel. In the gravel parking lot in back, Michael left the Ford among a few other vehicles, one a 1942 black Pontiac sedan he recognized as Ricca's.

Michael had been to the Bella Napoli restaurant once before, with Nitti and Campagna, for a tense meeting with Ricca, whose favorite hangout this was. The Waiter made a point of lunching at this old-fashioned Italian joint, rather than in the Loop with politicians and reporters.

The only entrance was around front, double doors beneath an unlit horizontal neon. Stepping inside, Michael was pleasantly assaulted by the rich aroma of spicy tomato sauce, taking him immediately to Papa S.'s spaghetti house in DeKalb, although the resemblance ended there.

This was a neat, open dining room punctuated by dark woodwork but with an overwhelmingly bright ambience: tables wore white cloths, walls bore murals of ancient Rome under blue skies, and decorative wine bottles were everywhere, shelved above doors, lining the red button-tufted booths. The lunch crowd was thinning—it was after one-thirty—but perhaps half the tables were inhabited.

Michael raised a hand to forestall the hostess and walked toward the rear, where at a table with his back to the wall sat Paul Ricca. On his either side were Sam "Mad Dog" DeStefano and

Sam "Mooney" Giancana, the most notorious of the Young Turks aligned with this Outfit elder statesman.

Knife-blade thin, his short hair as white as the tablecloth, Ricca—in a beautifully tailored charcoal suit with a lighter gray tie and lighter-yet gray shirt—had pushed away a small plate with half a cannoli on it; he was sipping espresso and had a cigarette going. With his high cheekbones, narrow nose and mouth like a cut in his face that refused to heal, Ricca had a visage oddly reminiscent of an American Indian's. Obviously he saw Michael approaching, but he reacted not at all, his dark brown eyes unblinking.

At right, Giancana—in a well-cut chocolate suit with orange tie—sat back in his chair, arm slung over it, smoking a cigar. His dark eyes hooded, small, nondescript-looking, with severely thinning black hair, Giancana had a bland oval face that took on a vaguely sinister aura when a sneer formed, as it did upon his seeing Michael.

At left, DeStefano—bigger than the other two, by far—sat wolfing down a dish of spumoni with a spoon. If he'd noticed Michael walking toward them, he was hiding it well. Fleshy but not fat in a black slept-in-looking suit, a red-and-blue food-stained tie loose at his collar, DeStefano had a cantaloupe-shaped noggin with a full head of hair thick with Brillcream yet still as unruly as a bucket of worms. The tiny close-set eyes, nose like a wad of clay a sculptor stuck there (and hadn't got 'round to finishing yet), and thin-lipped permanent scowl all suited him perfectly: he was widely considered to be the biggest lunatic in the Outfit, surviving only at the whim of Ricca.

Both of these Young Turks were graduates of the street gang, the 42s—vicious punks who stripped cars, held up stores and raped high school girls. Giancana was currently Ricca's bodyguard and chauffeur. DeStefano was a loan shark, but was also Ricca's personal assassin. According to Campagna, Ricca would just turn to DeStefano, point to somebody, and say, "Make him go away."

And that somebody would go away.

If there hadn't been so many civilians present, Michael

might simply stride up and shoot the two punks right at the table, to make a point with Ricca and to save himself the trouble, later.

Instead, he just walked up to the empty chair opposite Ricca and stood there expectantly. DeStefano, ice cream dribbling down his chin, finally noticed Michael and his natural scowl exaggerated itself into something that would have been comic, had it not been worn by a psychopath. Giancana leaned back, smiling a little, as if he found Michael mildly amusing.

Both men, Michael noted, wore shoulder holsters: he recognized the cut of their coat (most of the Outfit guys used the same tailor). Ricca appeared unarmed.

"Sit, Michael," Ricca said genially, gesturing with a cigarette-in-hand.

"Thank you, Mr. Ricca," he said, and sat.

"You show a good deal of courage, coming in here. Of course, a Medal of Honor winner like you, small potatoes, right?"

DeStefano seemed frozen, his brow grooved deeply, as if a thought trying to form had curdled there; spumoni in its various colors dripped down his chin like a messy flag.

"I take you very seriously, Mr. Ricca," Michael said, nodding toward both men. "*And* your friends."

Nodding gravely, Ricca said, "Respect is an important thing, Michael. . . . Sam, wipe your face. We have a guest."

DeStefano hung his head and picked up a napkin.

Michael said, "May I speak frankly?"

Ricca raised a hand in "stop" fashion, like a traffic cop. "I prefer you and I speak in private, Michael."

"I would like that."

DeStefano, his face wiped clean of spumoni but not confusion, said in a rough baritone, "Mr. Ricca, you want Mooney and me should move over a table?"

"No, Sam. Mr. Satariano and I are going to speak in the back room. Alone."

Giancana sat forward so quickly, Michael thought the little man might lose his balance. "Boss—you're not gonna go off with that . . . this . . . *Demonio* fucker by yourself?" The nasty little hoodlum curled his upper lip as he said to Michael, "Everybody knows you're Frank Nitti's lapdog."

Michael said, "And whose son of a bitch are you?"

Giancana was half out of the chair when Ricca reached out and gripped him by the arm. "He's my guest, Momo," Ricca said, using another of Giancana's nicknames. "He showed us respect, we must do the same."

"He didn't fucking show *me* respect!"

Ricca made a gesture with an open palm. "You insulted him. You were in his place, wouldja've ignored such an insult? Of course not. Now, you two boys sit here and behave yourselves. Sam, order some more spumoni if you like."

DeStefano seemed to like the sound of that; but Giancana was frowning, his eyes locked on Michael like unfriendly magnets.

Ricca got up and this time Giancana was the one who reached out, gripping his master's arm. "At least make him leave his biscuit behind."

By that, Giancana meant Michael's weapon.

Michael met Ricca's gaze and shook his head: *no way will that happen.*

Ricca nodded, then said to Giancana, "I don't think the management would appreciate it if Mr. Satariano were to display his 'biscuit' in public."

"I think that's wise, Mr. Ricca," Michael said. "There's always a chance it could go off."

Giancana's sneer was in full bloom as he said, "War hero. Remind me to piss myself, when you scare me."

"I won't have to."

DeStefano started to giggle, and Giancana glared at him.

"So sue me, Mooney," DeStefano said, through sniggers. "Funny's funny!"

Ricca stepped around the table and gestured toward the double doors into the kitchen. Michael, walking sideways to keep an eye on the two young lunatics, followed him through. A number of bustling cooks, under the supervision of a chef, were hard at work, steam rising, pots and pans clanking, and again the restaurant smells triggered memories in Michael, who followed Ricca into an office off the kitchen.

It was just a cubbyhole with a small desk and a file cabinet; the only decoration was a framed photograph of the restaurant on opening day. Despite a chair opposite the desk, and one behind it, neither man sat.

Ricca, hands on hips, stood perhaps two feet from Michael and cast a hard unblinking stare at him. "Why did you come here, Michael? After what Frank Nitti did last night, this could be viewed as enemy territory."

Michael was thrown by Ricca's manner. The man's voice was flat, uninflected, and the ganglord seemed unafraid, though Michael could easily have withdrawn the .45, shot Ricca, and then run out through the kitchen to the parking lot, where he could position himself behind the Ford and pick off the two Sams as they came after him. . . .

"*Is* there going to be a war, Mr. Ricca? Have the battle lines been drawn?"

"Yes to the second question. The first question I can't answer yet."

Michael frowned. "That doesn't make sense."

Ricca smiled enigmatically. "It will."

Frustrated, Michael snapped, "Why the hell did you bail me out?"

"Technically, I didn't bail you out. That wasn't necessary. Mr. Bulger merely delivered a writ of—"

"You know what I mean."

"I had my reasons."

"Obviously. What were they?"

Ricca sat on the edge of the desk; he folded his arms and smiled gently up at Michael. "Let me tell you why you came around here. You think I had your girlfriend killed. . . . Well, I didn't."

"Really?" Michael gestured with a thumb toward the restaurant. "Your resident Frankenstein monster, Mad Sam, is known for torturing his victims before he kills them. He's a sadistic bastard."

"Yes. But he's *my* sadistic bastard, who does what I tell him. And I didn't tell him to kill Estelle. I liked Estelle."

"I suppose you want me to believe Frank Nitti ordered it done."

Ricca shook his head. "No. It's not his style. We both know that, just as you know that I'm not a fool, and I know you're not a fool. . . . I'm afraid I have disappointing news for you, even though in a way it's good news."

"Disappointing how?"

A tiny shrug. "I know what makes you tick, Michael. It's revenge, isn't it? That's your whole reason for living."

The back of Michael's neck tingled. "Estelle was my girl, like you said—I want to even the score."

"Oh I know you do. I'm afraid that's the disappointing part. You see, a couple named the Borgias were responsible."

Michael's eyes tightened. "I heard that from Louie Campagna. Where can I find them?"

Ricca lifted his hands in mock surrender. "Let's not get ahead of ourselves. First, these two were freelance; just a couple of greedy lowlifes who were after Estelle's money. You know—the money Nicky Dean embezzled and left with her? It had nothing to do with anybody Outfit making an example of her. Notice I'm not trying to pawn this off on Nitti—this is the truth, Michael."

A sense of urgency was pumping through him, fueled by the notion of getting his hands on these murderers. "All right. Suppose it is. Where can I find them?"

An open-handed shrug now. "Somewhere under Lake Michigan."

"You're saying they're . . . dead."

"Well they aren't holding their breath. . . . I think one of Frank's people took care of it. Oh, I can see how disappointed you are."

"How do I know you're—"

"Telling the truth? Not lying? Because I'm your friend. Or I'm going to be." Ricca folded his arms again and bestowed that enigmatic smile. "Michael, I could have ruined your life months ago, had I wanted to."

"Really."

"Oh yes. *Really.* You see, William Drury is an honest cop—boringly, stupidly, pointlessly honest. You know—like your friend Ness."

It was as if cold water had been splashed in his face. "My—what?"

"Eliot Ness, Michael. Not every cop at Town Hall Station is as honest as Bill Drury—almost none of 'em, in fact. That's how I was able to hear a wire recording of the conversation you and Ness had there, the night the Colony Club was raided."

Michael whipped the .45 from under his shoulder and pointed it at Ricca.

Who did not blink. Did not react an iota.

Rather, merely said, "I know who you are, Michael. You're Michael Satariano, yes. But you're also Michael O'Sullivan, Jr."

The words hit him like a physical blow.

"I knew your father. He was the best soldier ever lived. What I would *give* for a man like that . . . a man like you, Michael. A clown like Mad Sam has his uses; and a cunning little shitheel like Mooney, too. But an angel of death . . . a demonic angel . . . why, they come along only once in a lifetime."

His hand gripping the gun trembled; he tried to stop it from doing that, unsuccessfully. "You . . . if you know who I am . . . why . . . ?"

Ricca's smile widened and turned ghastly in the process. "Why not expose you? After all, you are, in a way, an undercover cop . . . or anyway, you were. Only, your loyalties shifted from Eliot Ness to Frank Nitti many months ago. That was clear in the conversation I heard, from Town Hall. Also from your conduct."

Mind reeling, Michael managed, "Why didn't you tell Nitti about me?"

Ricca's eyes popped. "And have a good man killed? The son of the Angel of Death? Do I look like a fool? As I said, I know what makes you tick, son. I know that it was you—a one-man army—who rained all that blood down upon Palm Island. You discovered . . . and made it possible for me to discover . . . that for fucking *years* Al Capone has been a feeble-minded figurehead for Frank Nitti."

A numb Michael asked, "You knew that . . . and still you didn't. . . . I don't understand."

"You will. I said, *I know what makes you tick.* Like any good bomb. . . . Oh, lately you've lost your way, maybe more than just your way—you lost your purpose. You went to Miami to kill Al Capone. Why?"

"You seem to know everything."

"To avenge your father's death. Your father made a deal with the Outfit—he would stop robbing their banks, the war he waged against them would end . . . *if* they gave him the Looney kid. And they did. Connor Looney died in the street in Rock Island. I know. I was there."

"You were *there*?"

He folded his hands on his skinny belly. "I was one of the bodyguards who sent Connor out to meet his fate that rainy night. His 'fate' being your father. . . . Your father kept his end of the bargain, but he was betrayed. Only . . . that wasn't Al Capone's doing."

"*What?*"

"The man who made the bargain with your father was the man who broke it. Oh, I'm sure he had Al's blessing or at least tacit approval. But your father's betrayer, Michael . . . was Frank Nitti."

Again, the words punched Michael like a fist.

"No," Michael said, shaking his head. "I don't believe you. . . ."

"You don't *want* to believe me . . . but it's true. And when you think it through, you'll know I'm not lying."

Emotions, conflicting and confusing, surged through the young man; it was all he could do to steady the gun.

"And, Michael? To get back to what we were talking about, before? . . . There doesn't have to be a war. Not if Frank Nitti dies."

Michael swallowed thickly. The .45 in his hand felt so very heavy. . . .

Ricca slid off the desk to his feet and he put a fatherly hand on Michael's shoulder and smiled at him.

"And who better to carry out this execution, than his trusted right hand—Michael Satariano? Just as what more fitting end could there be for Frank Nitti, than at the hands of Michael O'Sullivan, Jr.?"

6

TWO MEN IN A GREEN 1940 CHEVY
were parked outside Frank Nitti's suburban home. Michael did not know them,
other than to exchange nods with—they
were bodyguards who usually worked the
graveyard shift, keeping an eye on Nitti
and his house after dark. That they were
here in mid-afternoon indicated the
heightened security following the disastrous counsel meeting of the night before.

The man behind the wheel, dark,
small, was named Jimmy the Rat Rossi, his
name reflecting rodent-like features that
his toothpick sucking somehow accentu-
ated. He wore a dark suit and tie, his hat
off to reveal dark hair given way to a
monk's bald spot.

In the rider's seat, also in dark suit and

tie, reading *The Racing News*, was stocky, bucket-headed Tony "Pocky" Licata, whose claim to fame was a single pockmarked cheek; his hat was off, too, his prematurely gray hair cut close to the scalp. Both men were in their thirties and neither were live wires—just your standard-issue Outfit muscle.

In his military-style trenchcoat, Michael stopped alongside the Chevy, tapped on the window—the car wasn't running, but it was cold enough to keep the windows up—and leaned in as the Rat rolled it down.

"Anything unusual?" Michael asked.

"No, Mr. Satariano," the Rat said. "Quiet as a mouse."

The minor irony of the statement seemed to escape the man who dispensed it.

Pocky looked up from the racing rag to say, "Mrs. Nitti left about fifteen minutes ago."

Michael glanced over at the empty driveway.

"Okay," he said. "I'm going up to the house. I have a little business with Mr. Nitti."

The Rat nodded, not giving a shit, rolling the window up. But unlike his partner, the Rat wasn't reading on the job; he seemed to be attentive to the effort, almost as much as to shifting that toothpick around.

Michael crossed the street to the unpretentious brown-brick home. It had snowed yesterday afternoon, lightly, and while the city showed few signs, out here in the suburbs, the brown of the short-trimmed yards had a dusting of white that somehow took the edge off the dreary, chilly weather.

On the stoop, Michael paused to collect himself. He felt calm; in fact, he felt as if he were sleepwalking.

He was about to ring the bell when the door opened and there was Nitti, poised in the doorway in a brown fedora and brown plaid overcoat, blue-and-maroon silk scarf loose around his neck, coat open to reveal a snappy gray checked suit.

Startled, Nitti—his face going in an instant from bland to savage—yanked a .32 revolver from his pocket and thrust it toward Michael.

But before Michael could react—had time to react—Nitti's expression just as quickly changed to relief, and he slipped the little black revolver back in his topcoat pocket.

"Jesus, kid," Nitti said, and chuckled, an ungloved hand on his chest. "Give me the scare of my life, there."

"Sorry, Mr. Nitti. I was about to ring the bell."

"I was just going out for a stroll. Toni went to church to light a candle or two, all this shit goin' on. Frankly, I, uh . . ." He stepped out onto the little porch with Michael. ". . . drank a little too much vino, this afternoon. Thought I'd walk it off."

The smell of wine was on him, all right. Like the smell of booze had been on Eliot Ness.

"That's not like you, Mr. Nitti."

Nitti put his hand on Michael's shoulder and smiled. "I'm not proud of it. . . . Do I seem drunk to you?"

"No." It wasn't exactly a lie.

"Walk with me?"

"Sure."

From the sidewalk, Nitti made a "no" motion to the bodyguards in the car, not to follow along. In the rider's window, the Rat nodded, rolling his toothpick.

They turned right, Nitti saying, "We'll just walk around the block. Get a little of this nice fresh air."

While the weather wasn't chilly exactly, a brittle edge made it just cold enough for their breath to smoke; neither man wore gloves and kept hands in pockets. Of course Michael was aware that Nitti had that .32 in his righthand one.

The shrunken-looking Nitti had been fairly diminutive to start with, and seemed much smaller than Frank Nitti had any right to be. But the ex-barber's hair was freshly cut and, vino or no, he seemed alert. He was lifting his face into a crisp breeze and relishing it.

"Spoke to Louie," Nitti said, as they turned the corner. He flashed a sideways, chagrined grin. "Sorry about letting you sit overnight in the jug. I honestly didn't know you was in there."

"You had a right to be distracted."

Nitti shot him a sharper look. "So, Louie's filled you in on the situation?"

"Kinda sounds like you threw the gauntlet down to Ricca, Mr. Nitti. That surprised me."

"Did it? Why?"

Michael, hands still in his pockets, shrugged, walking. "You're usually more careful than that. Why stir up enmity with Ricca, right now?"

Nitti shook his head, his mouth tight. "I didn't stir it—he did. He's taking advantage of this moment to try to bring me down. . . . A kid who uses a term like 'enmity' probably knows what a coup is, right?"

"Sure."

"Well this is what the politicians call a bloodless coup. If Ricca can convince the rest of the counsel I'm a selfish fuck-up, un-willing to fall on my sword for 'em . . . then he slides into my chair."

"And he figures you won't move against him."

Nitti nodded. "And I won't. We're facing a trial that's gonna get big play in the press. But what's it over? Buncha Hollywood nonsense. Union stuff. Compared to war news, it ain't nothing. Public yawns and flips to the funnies." The little ganglord stopped cold. "But we start shooting at each other, acting like gangsters? Then we get way too much attention from John Q. Public."

Nitti calmly walked on. They turned the corner, to the right. They had the sidewalks to themselves; it was a school day, Friday, and cold enough to keep housewives inside. The tree-lined streets twisted through an idyllic world where the dwellings, if less than mansions, were nonetheless spacious and distinctive; noth-ing cookie-cutter about the homes of Riverside. Despite the white-brushed lawns, a consistent peppering of evergreens threw a little color into the landscape.

"Kid," Nitti said, and his expression was grave, "I'm sorry about that girl of yours."

"Thanks, Mr. Nitti."

"I liked Estelle. She was as smart as she was pretty. Good earner for us, too."

"Who do you think did it?"

"I know who did it, and a guy who does work for me, time to time, took care of it." Nitti stopped again and so did Michael; the older man put his hand on the younger one's shoulder. "I know you'd like to've been the one who took 'em out, but it's better this way."

Michael nodded.

They walked along.

"Their name was Borgia," he said. "If you know your history, you see how fitting that is. They probably were sent by Ricca either to throw a scare in her—afraid she'd talk, in the trial, y'know—or maybe to kill her, and send Nicky Dean a wake-up call."

"Would Ricca do that?"

"Sure. But I doubt even the Waiter's reckless enough to attract the press that torture killing got. Stupid. Now, that's just what I'm talkin' about—look at the *fuck*-ing field day the papers are having over Estelle Carey! It puts the goddamn spotlight right on us. All of sudden, we're mobsters again, not businessmen."

"I don't think Ricca thinks of himself as a businessman—at least not the way you do, Mr. Nitti."

"Probably true. Probably true. Or else he wouldn't surround himself with sick-in-the-head killers like Mad Sam and Mooney." Nitti sighed. "Only good thing could come from this is Ricca going away. I have confidence in Accardo."

Once again Nitti stopped. This time, he put both hands on Michael's shoulders. Speaking with great emphasis, he said, "While we're away, Joe Batters will be capo."

That was another name for Tony Accardo.

"He's a good man. You can trust him. Stand by him, Michael. Serve him."

"Yes, Mr. Nitti."

Nitti's hands returned to his pockets. They walked on.

Michael said, "No way you can beat this rap?"

"No. And though I can't take the fall, I must bear some responsibility. Trusting Bioff and Browne, that was stupid. But the nature of what we do is risk. Decisions can come back to haunt you."

"Bad decisions?"

"Even good ones. We make hard choices for the greater good."

"Like that guy, what did they call him? The Angel of Death?"

They were at the end of the block. The residential area gave way to undeveloped lots; across the street a row of skeletal trees mingled with shrubbery, behind which a wire fence defended a patch of prairie, high dead grass and brush cut by intersecting tracks of the Illinois Central. In the distance, beyond the dead brush, and the tracks, was a complex of brick buildings, a tuberculosis sanitarium.

Michael knew as much because Campagna had mentioned the fence, which had a gaping hole in it, as a security issue in guarding Nitti. In these days of gas rationing, neighborhood employees of the sanitarium had clipped a hole in the wire barrier, to be able to walk to work.

Having stopped again, Nitti frowned in thoughtful surprise. "Angel of Death . . . haven't heard that phrase in ages. O'Sullivan. Looney's man."

"Right."

Nitti grunted a laugh. "Haven't thought of him in ages, either."

"Looney or O'Sullivan?"

"Take your pick." Hands still in pockets, Nitti rocked on his heels. "Old man Looney's still in stir, I hear. But O'Sullivan—he was something. Best soldier I ever knew." Nitti's eyes narrowed. "How the hell d'you ever hear of him, son?"

"It was written up in the true detective magazines."

Another grunted laugh. "Buncha bullshit, most likely. Although, with that O'Sullivan—you wouldn't have to exaggerate what *he* did, make a good yarn."

"I thought he was your enemy."

Nitti shook his head. "No. Looking back, I wonder if I shouldn't've taken him up on his offer—he came to me, wanted me to step aside and let him take his revenge on Looney. But we had a business relationship with Rock Island, and . . . well."

"What had Looney done to him?"

Nitti shivered, possibly not from the cold. "It wasn't what Looney did—the Old Man's kid, a lunatic like Mooney and Mad Sam—killed O'Sullivan's wife and son."

"I thought our families were off limits."

"They are. They are. But these weren't our people, Michael—these were a bunch of crazy micks, killing each other."

"Ah. Why did Looney's kid kill the mother and son?"

Nitti shrugged, still rocking. "Oh, the reason isn't impor-tant. But he did it, and when I wouldn't back O'Sullivan's play, he hit us hard, in the pocket book. Kinda like Ness! What a man that mick was."

"But you had him killed."

Again Nitti shrugged. "I had to. To allow one man to inflict such damage to our business, and get away with it? Some things you just can't abide."

"I can grasp that."

Nitti cocked his head, giving Michael a curious half-smile. "What makes you so keen on ancient history, son?"

"I have a vested interest."

Curious, Nitti smiled. "Really? What kind?"

Now Michael shrugged. "Well, you see, my real name isn't Michael Satariano. I was adopted."

"Yeah?"

"Yeah. I'm the kid who helped rob those Outfit banks. The driver? . . . I'm Michael O'Sullivan, Jr."

It took a while for Nitti's smile to fade, as if Michael's state-ment were some colossal joke.

"You . . . you're *O'Sullivan's* kid?"

"Yes, and I got next to you so I could kill Capone. I thought he was the one responsible for my father's death. But now . . ." And Michael slipped his right hand under the trenchcoat and withdrew the .45 and, holding it close to his body, pointed it at Nitti. ". . . now I know different."

Nitti raised his hands, just to waist level, more a reasoning gesture than one of surrender. "You . . . you should know, then, that what I did was business. You heard me just now! How much I respected your father."

"I can understand that, Mr. Nitti. You can respect a man you have to kill."

Eyes narrow, Nitti was shaking his head as pieces slipped into place. "All of that . . . in Miami . . . *your* doing. Ricca wasn't behind it."

"Wasn't Ricca at all. When I saw Capone, fishing in his pool, I couldn't squeeze the trigger. Would've been like shooting a little kid."

The smile returned, bitter now. "But you can shoot me, right, Michael?"

"I think so."

"You aren't sure?"

Michael let out a tiny humorless laugh. "It surprises me, but . . . the rage. I can't summon the rage. All I feel is . . . disappointment."

And in a flash he recalled when he'd last felt like this: it was when he witnessed his father shooting those men in that warehouse, when he knew his brave war-hero father had not been on missions, but was just a gangster, a thug, a killer. . . .

Nitti put his hands down. "It would be . . . foolish to say I'll try to make it up to you. But Michael, I've come to look at you as a son . . ."

"Don't say that."

Nitti's eyes tightened; he wasn't exactly pleading. "You could be my successor. You have the guts and the mind and the heart to take this Outfit where it needs to go! And leave all the illegitimate shit in the past where it belongs. Listen to me, son. . . ."

"Don't call me that!"

Nitti nodded. "I understand . . . I understand. But I know . . . *no matter what you say,* I know there's a bond between us."

"Stop it."

Slowly Nitti shook his head. "You don't want to do this. You've already lost your father, the rest of your family. If you do this thing, you'll burn in hell, and you won't even have to die to get there."

"*Satariano!*"

Without taking the gun off Nitti, Michael whirled to one side and he saw the two bodyguards, Rat and Pocky, heading toward them, guns in hand, down the sidewalk.

Michael swung the .45 toward them, when Rat called out: *"We know you're with Ricca, Mike!"* Toothpick tumbling from his lips, Rat added, *"Get down, the fuck down!"*

Nitti, eyes and nostrils flaring, shoved Michael, knocking him to the cement, and ran pell-mell across the street toward the row of trees and bushes, topcoat flapping. Gunshots rang in the afternoon air, hollow little sounds, like the firing of a starting pistol before a race.

Which was apropos, because the shots had missed Nitti and he was slipping between the trees, stepping over bushes, crawling through the gaping hole in the fence. The ganglord had the revolver in hand now, and paused to turn and throw one sharp shot their way.

The bullet flew well over Michael's head: he lay on the sidewalk, .45 in hand, and Nitti's shot seemed intended for the two approaching on-the-run bodyguards-turned-hitmen.

Rat paused to help haul Michael to his feet. "You want in on this, come along!"

And then Michael was standing on the corner, watching Rat and Pocky pick their way between trees and brush and through that hole in the fence.

Things were happening fast, and reflection was not an option; but somehow he knew, no matter what Frank Nitti had done ten years ago, that he could not allow that man to be brought down by these traitors.

As he ran across the street, cutting between the trees, bursting through the fence, .45 in hand, Michael was unsure whether he was acting so that he could kill Nitti himself, or to protect this man, about whom his feelings were decidedly mixed . . .

. . . but he fell in behind Rat and Pocky, who were up ahead about fifteen yards, wading through waist-high grass, the way slowed by clumps of shrub brush and wild skinny trees that leaned like modern dancers in the gentle wind.

As if chasing through mud they went, Michael at the rear, the bodyguards up ahead, the pair throwing rounds at the fleeing Nitti out in front, their shots cracking the air, sounding firecracker-small under the big gray sky.

Nitti only paused one more time, to toss a wild shot back at his pursuers, and then the man was slicing through the dead undergrowth toward the train tracks, where the grass and brush had been cut back to accommodate passage. Michael knew at once what Nitti was up to: the dark buildings of that sanitarium loomed, and the tracks went right by there, meaning the fugitive could find refuge among a wealth of witnesses; taking this road also allowed the little gangster to run faster, the topcoat flying behind him like a cape.

But Nitti also made himself a better target for his bodyguard pursuers, and two shots took the fedora right off him, sending it flapping away like a wounded bird.

Michael stopped running, planted himself and aimed at the back of the Rat's head; he squeezed the trigger and the bodyguard stopped dead, literally, his head coming apart in red and white and gray chunks.

Pocky, who was just a few steps behind Rat, almost fell over his own feet, coming to an astonished stop as he saw the corpse of his partner do a final limp bow, as if seeking applause before curling up awkwardly in the grass, just another dead animal.

Startled but enraged, Pocky wheeled and saw Michael coming and ran right at him, shooting the revolver. Michael fell face down on the grass and when Pocky ran over to check the body, the "corpse" reached up and shot him in the head.

Pocky's face, with wide surprised eyes, one pockmarked cheek, and a single new red pock in his forehead, was haloed in his own prematurely gray hair and a mist of scarlet.

Then he too dropped, swallowed by weeds.

That left Nitti, about twenty-five yards up ahead, on the railroad tracks. He was clearly winded, and staggering along, not making much headway.

Michael quickly cut over to the tracks and was coming up behind the man when Nitti glanced back, saw him, and cut off the tracks, running through the grass to the deadend of more wire fencing.

Breath heaving, his back to the barrier, Nitti raised the revolver as Michael pushed through the grass, slowly now.

"Stop, Michael! Right there. Stop."

Michael kept moving, brushing aside the prairie jungle. The .45 in his hand was held waist-high.

"I'm not going to let you do it!" Nitti said, his eyes wild, the little revolver pointing unsteadily at Michael.

"Mr. Nitti . . ."

Nitti laughed. "So respectful. Respectful to the end." And Frank Nitti raised the revolver to his temple. "I don't want to see you in hell, son. *Understand?* Okay?"

"Mr. Nitti!"

Nitti fired the .32.

Only a small spray of blood exited his left temple, and he slid like a cloth doll down the fence and sat slumped there, chin on his chest, the revolver loose in his hand.

Michael stood staring for several long seconds, then, shaking his head, said, "I wasn't going to. I wasn't going to. . . ."

A clanging and a whistle and engine noise signaled an approaching train and, keeping low, Michael rushed through the grass as voices rose above the wind-whisper, two voices, back and forth, coming closer all the time, a flagman and a switchman, hanging off a forward-moving caboose:

"*Shot himself!*"

"*You're tellin' me? I saw him do it!*"

Retracing his path, more or less, Michael stayed low as he headed for the hole in the fence. He'd already slipped the .45 in its shoulder holster when he stepped through, to find a breathless Louie Campagna waiting.

"What the hell happened, kid?"

"Nitti's bodyguards turned on him."

"Pocky and Rat?"

"Yeah. They're out there in the weeds, dead as hell. I made them that way."

Michael felt sure Louie knew all about the turncoat bodyguards—else why was Campagna here? But he kept that to himself.

Together they walked across the street, back to the corner where Michael had revealed himself to Nitti. The neighborhood remained quiet, the sidewalks empty; it was as if the world had ended.

Campagna asked, "What about Frank?"

"He thought they had him cornered. Didn't know I'd taken care of it. Turned his gun on himself."

Shaking his head, genuine sorrow on his lumpy mug, Campagna said, "Aw. Ah hell. Ah Frank."

Michael pointed toward the fence. "Cops'll be here soon. Better have some men pull those stiffs out of the weeds, or this'll get uglier than it has to."

Campagna nodded, patting Michael on the back. "Done. You get the hell out of here, kid."

Michael nodded.

He was just heading off when Campagna stopped him, with a hand on his arm.

"I know how you feel, kid."

"What?"

Campagna swallowed thickly. "He was a great man."

Michael didn't know what the hell Campagna was talking about until, behind the wheel of the Ford, he saw his face in the mirror.

Saw the tears streaking his cheeks.

7

MICHAEL SATARIANO AND PATSY ANN
O'Hara sat on the same stone bench in
Huntley Park in DeKalb, Illinois, as last
July Fourth. The cement-and-boulder
bandshell was bare, and the park itself seemed
abandoned. On this chilly afternoon in
late March, under a sky as gray as gun-
metal, Michael and Patsy Ann were rare
sweethearts holding hands here.

They looked young, but then she was a
college student and he wasn't much older.
He wore a brown leather jacket and chinos,
she a soldier-blue wool coat and lighter
blue slacks. Neither wore a hat, and an easy
wind ruffled Patsy Ann's blonde hair without really mussing it.

Michael sat staring at the empty bandshell. Frank Nitti was in the ground—

hallowed ground, for this good Catholic who'd condemned himself to hell; on earth, at least, the fix was in. He'd left behind a loyal wife—who conveniently was at church, praying, during the killing—and a nine-year-old son he adored. Paul Ricca considered Michael to have been responsible for Nitti's demise (officially suicide), and Louie Campagna had informed Michael—with a smile that said just how quickly Nitti had become yesterday's news—that "the Satariano star" was rising.

This was the same Campagna who'd told Michael the way one leaves the Outfit, after the blood oath over dagger and gun: feet first. Nitti had left that way. His bodyguards, too, though they hadn't even made the papers—Campagna's Sicilian clean-up crew had quickly stowed them in the trunk of a car and, before any cops showed—or honest ones, anyway—whisked them into eternity. The pair were in a landfill by now (Mad Sam was in the garbage trade), or maybe at the bottom of Lake Michigan making it a foursome with Estelle Carey's "friends," the Borgias.

Michael knew all too well that Ness's offer to help him parlay his Medal of Honor into some kind of government badge was no real option. Despite the Outfit's reluctance to kill cops, particularly feds, a made man who became a G-man would surely be an exception.

Michael Satariano was one of them now. Like it or not.

At the Bella Napoli, Michael had sat with the Outfit's new top capo at a rear table, just the two of them. Michael's peculiar tastes were honored with an iced glass of Coca-Cola, while Paul Ricca again sipped an espresso. Bodyguards were on either side, at their own tables.

"Mr. Ricca," Michael said, hands folded respectfully, "I am weary of bloodshed. I had my fill overseas, and found more awaited me here."

Ricca's eyes were hooded, though their dark brown seemed oddly gentle, in the angular, cruel face. "I understand. But a soldier goes where his general bids him go."

"This I know . . . have I earned the right to ask a favor?"

Ricca nodded.

"As soon as possible, I would like to leave Chicago. My father . . . in DeKalb . . . is in the restaurant business. I spent years around that trade. A restaurant, a nightclub, perhaps something in show business would please me."

Ricca nodded slowly. "Like your late capo, you prefer the legitimate. The whores, the juice, the gambling, narcotics, none of these things appeal to you."

"They do not. I say this in respect."

He sipped the espresso, then, conversationally, said, "You know, Michael, Nitti's the only one who'll beat this federal rap. We'll be gone, many of us, perhaps as long as five years. While we're away, Tony Accardo will hold my chair. I've recommended you to him."

Not relishing these words, Michael nonetheless said, "Thank you, Mr. Ricca."

The gash in Ricca's face that was his mouth formed something that could be called, charitably, a smile.

"Michael, when I return, I'll grant your request. We'll send you to Vegas or possibly Hollywood. . . . Despite this setback, we still have interests out there."

"Thank you, Mr. Ricca."

"Until then, here in Chicago, you serve Joe Batters."

"I am honored."

Ricca lifted a lecturing forefinger. "Now, Michael—do not mislead yourself. You can be in a passive part of our business and still be called upon. With your talents, from time to time—this will happen. This . . . *will* . . . happen."

"I know."

Ricca, lighting a cigarette with a silver lighter, studied Michael. He drew on the cigarette, exhaled a wreath of gray-blue smoke, then said, "You need to live your life."

"I . . . I'm not sure I understand, Mr. Ricca."

Ricca snapped shut the lighter. "We will not speak of your parents . . . your real parents again . . . but I will say now that you must not let what happened to them stand in the way of your living a normal life. You're an American hero, Michael—you deserve the best."

278

"Thank you, sir."

"Go out and find a good wife and raise little micks who'll think they're Sicilian—okay? And someday get yourself a mistress. You'll need the outlet. Believe me."

Michael nodded.

Ricca reached out and patted Michael's folded hands. "We don't bother each other's families. When you're made, we don't fuck your wife, let alone kill her. *Capeesh?*"

"*Capeesh,*" Michael said softly.

"Do what I tell you. Wife and family. House in the suburbs." Ricca shrugged elaborately. "It's the American dream, my son."

And now Michael was next to Patsy Ann on a park bench. The sky was bleak and the air was cold, but he handed her the little black box, which she opened, and the two-karat diamond ring in the silver setting on the velvet bed sparkled so brilliantly that Patsy Ann saw nothing but brightness.

He helped her on with it and then she did that thing women do—outstretching her hand, as if making sure the diamond was big enough to be seen at a distance—and finally she hugged him and kissed him and kissed him and hugged him. . . .

With her in his arms, he stared into her lovely blue eyes and said, "You don't have to sell your soul for me, baby. I'm gonna work in strictly legit areas."

She touched a forefinger to his mouth. "Loose lips sink ships," she said.

And those same eyes told him that she would not ask him about his work, nor would she judge him for it; she loved him. No strings. No small print.

"All I ask is that you always love me," she said, not smiling now, her voice trembling, "and our children. Promise me that— and that our children will be safe."

He drew her closer. "I promise you, baby. These kiddies are gonna have a better life than I ever did."

Kissing her again, tenderly, slowly, lingeringly, he did not tell her that keeping such a promise should not be difficult. Not when the standard was *his* life. . . .

But he did promise himself he would protect her and their

kids-to-be. They would have a happy and prosperous life, and nothing would touch them; he would not let it. If some small voice of reality spoke from the recesses of his mind, he batted it away—he had once thought he could never put at risk those he cared about; but he now knew he could not face a life without those he cared for around him.

And right now, this smart, painfully pretty college coed, who was foolish enough to care for him back, was the only person on earth that he loved. Not the only person he cared for—but the only one he loved. . . .

At Pasquale's Spaghetti House, they showed his parents the ring, and told them of their decision, and the Satarianos were beside themselves with joy, fat old people bouncing like babies. Patsy Ann called her parents, who dropped everything and, with sister Betty in willing tow, came over to the restaurant, where they all sat at a big table and the two families, about to become one, had mountains of spaghetti, and plenty of vino, too.

Patsy Ann said that she had three good offers in the Chicago area for teaching jobs, and hoped Michael wouldn't mind if they waited a while to start their family.

"You can support me forever, if you want," Michael said, gesturing with a wine glass. "You're a modern woman, I'm a modern man."

He told her they would live in Chicago for a few years, but that he'd been promised a position out west, mostly likely in show business.

"Oh, Michael," Patsy Ann said, clutching his hand with her newly diamond-adorned one. "It's like a dream come true. Is it terrible to be so happy, when the world is at war?"

Papa S., across from them, lifted his wine glass and said, "Wars don't last forever. And in the post-war world, everything will be possible."

Patsy Ann's burly, handsome father raised a glass and made a toast any Buick dealer in the USA might well have made: "To the American dream!"

Voices all around the table echoed: *"To the American dream!"*

Only Patsy Ann noticed that Michael hadn't joined in. He was remembering Ricca using the same phrase: *It's the American dream* . . .

. . . *my son.*

He only prayed he would never wake up screaming from it.

A TIP OF THE
FEDORA

DESPITE EXTENSIVE SPECULATION, supposition and fabrication, this novel has a basis in history. Many historical figures appear under their own names, including John and Connor Looney (and their minions and contemporaries in early twentieth-century Rock Island, Illinois) and of course Frank Nitti and Al Capone (and their minions and contemporaries in mid-twentieth-century Chicago).

Michael O'Sullivan, Sr., is a fictional character grown out of several estranged lieutenants of ganglord John Looney. As with my original graphic novel, *Road to Perdition* (1998), I have taken the liberty of moving up the Looney activities a few years; and time compression has been used in both the Looney section and the two longer Nitti ones.

283

Eliot Ness did head up the wartime Federal Social Protection Division, and was concentrating on the Chicago area when Frank Nitti decided to cut back on prostitution. From these two obscure facts I have spun a central conflict of this novel. Similarly, my notion that Frank Nitti downplayed Al Capone's mental incapacity to shore up his own power has some basis in reality.

Before I acknowledge my two stellar research associates, I must state that any errors here, historical, geographical or otherwise, are my own.

On the Chicago Outfit sections, I was abetted by George Hagenauer, my longtime research assistant on the Nathan Heller historical detective novels. We drew upon research material which had pertained in particular to the first three Hellers—*True Detective* (1983), *True Crime* (1984) and *The Million-Dollar Wound* (1986), known collectively as *The Frank Nitti Trilogy*—specifically, photocopies of Nitti-era newspaper accounts. I have never lived in Chicago, whereas George was born and raised there, and spent much of his life in that great city; any sense of the town that I've achieved derives from George's counsel and input. In addition, George gathered much of the Bataan material, and offered many good ideas on how to utilize and organize it.

For the John Looney section, I turned to Rock Island historian, BJ Elsner. BJ's book *Rock Island: Yesterday, Today & Tomorrow* (1988) was indispensable; also, this fine writer (and Rock Island native) provided many pages of background material, a welcome combination of history, ideas and insights, making a major contribution to this work.

Other Looney references include the late Jim Arpy's lively six-part article, "The Lawless Looney Years," which ran in the *Quad-City Times* in 1979; and "Smashing Rock Island's Reign of Terror" by O. F. Claybaugh in *Master Detective* (December 1930).

Thanks to my cousin, Kris Povlsen, for hooking me up with Stephen J. Bigolin, who generously shared his encyclopedic knowledge about DeKalb, Illinois. Thanks also to my old rock-bandmate, Rob Gal, for a reason he'll understand, should he ever read this book.

I have already mentioned in passing the graphic novel, *Road to*

Perdition (1998). I am not sure if a prose sequel has ever before been written to a graphic novel (i.e., a long narrative told in comics form). Since *Road to Perdition* was essentially a comic-book spin-off of my historical approach (and of the Chicago Outfit material explored) in the Nathan Heller novels, returning to prose form for this sequel seemed natural and even necessary to me.

Obviously, *Road to Purgatory* came about because of interest in the film adaptation of *Road to Perdition* and, to some degree, might be considered a sequel to my novelization of David Self's fine screenplay, which was based in turn on my work. Unfortunately, my movie tie-in novel—of a length similar to this one, and filled with backstory, history and additional scenes—was published in a severely truncated manner, leaving only material directly paralleling the film. It is my hope that someday either my original version of the movie novelization or a new prose work grown out of the graphic novel will join this book (and its forthcoming sequel, *Road to Paradise*) to complete the trilogy properly. In any case, I direct readers who have not read the graphic novel to seek it out, as the true precursor of this sequel.

Which leads me to Richard Piers Rayner, my Brit "brother," the graphic novel's gifted illustrator. I wish to acknowledge and thank Richard for his wonderful work on *Road to Perdition*; his stunning art had much to do with the warm reception our graphic novel received, both in Hollywood and among readers worldwide.

And I would like to thank several others who made the original graphic novel (and the DreamWorks film based upon it) possible: Andy Helfer, the editor at DC who provided both the opportunity and shrewd counsel along the way; Daniel Ostroff, the Hollywood agent (now successful producer) who saw potential in the graphic novel; Dean and Richard Zanuck, the father and son producing team who made the film version happen; Steven Spielberg, who gave the project its green light (and liked my ending better); Sam Mendes, the director who—with writer David Self, cinematographer Conrad L. Hall and composer Thomas Newman—captured on film the spirit of *Road to Perdition*;

and the amazing cast of actors, including Tom Hanks, Paul Newman, Jude Law, Jennifer Jason Leigh, Stanley Tucci, Daniel Craig and Tyler Hoechlin, who made my characters live and breathe (and, often, die).

In addition, I would like to acknowledge a number of books and their authors from whose work I drew information and inspiration in writing *Road to Purgatory*.

A particularly helpful reference, which was key in the early Heller novels, was *The Legacy of Al Capone* (1975) by George Murray; also the following excellent biographies of Al Capone: *Capone: The Life and World of Al Capone* (1971), John Kobler; *Capone: The Man and His Era* (1994), Laurence Bergreen; and *Mr. Capone* (1992), Robert J. A. Schoenberg. Also consulted was the full testimony of Paul Ricca and Louis Campagna from the 1950 Congressional Investigation of Organized Crime in Interstate Commerce.

Other helpful books on the Chicago mob include *Accardo: the Genuine Godfather* (1995), William F. Roemer, Jr.; *Captive City* (1969), Ovid Demaris; *Crime in America* (1951), Estes Kefauver; *The Don: The Life and Death of Sam Giancana* (1977), William Brashler; *Double Cross* (1992), Sam and Chuck Giancana; *The Mafia Encyclopedia* (1987), Carl Sifakis; and *Syndicate City* (1954), Alson J. Smith. The latter book and *The Valachi Papers* (1968), Peter Maas, were the chief sources for the Mafia initiation ritual in this novel.

Several sources above include material on the Estelle Carey murder. Readers of the Nathan Heller novel *The Million-Dollar Wound* will recognize the Carey case—and the downfall of Frank Nitti—as major elements of that book. I have attempted here to look at the tragic "26" girl's death (and Nitti's suicide) from a different vantage point without contradicting that earlier narrative. While each book obviously stands on its own, my intention is that these stories take place in the same world.

I have written much about Eliot Ness in the Heller novels, but even more in four novels about Ness's Cleveland years—*The Dark City* (1987), *Butcher's Dozen* (1988), *Bullet Proof* (1989) and *Murder by the Numbers* (1993); considerable research went into that quartet, and many sources that helped form my take on the famous Untouchable can be found in bibliographic essays at the conclusion of those novels. Two nonfiction accounts of the life of Eliot Ness have subsequently appeared, which I'd like to credit: *Eliot Ness: The Real Story* (1997), Paul W. Heimel; and *Torso* (1989), Steven Nickel.

Chicago references included *Chicago Confidential* (1950), Jack Lait and Lee Mortimer; *Dining in Chicago* (1931), John Drury; and *Vittles and Vice* (1952), Patricia Bronté. The WPA guides for both Illinois and Florida were also helpful.

The Bataan section of this novel drew upon numerous books, including *Bataan: Our Last Ditch* (1990), John W. Whitman; *The Battle of Bataan* (1992), Donald J. Young; *But Not in Shame* (1961), John Toland; *Crisis in the Pacific* (1996), Gerald Astor; *Eagle Against the Sun* (1985), Ronald H. Spector; *The Great Battles of World War II, Volume 1: The Pacific Island Battles* (1985), Charles E. Pfannes and Victor A. Salamone; *The Greatest War* (1999), Gerald Astor; *Hero of Bataan: The Story of General Jonathan M. Wainwright* (1981), Duane Schultz; *I Saw the Fall of the Philippines* (1942), Colonel Carlos P. Romulo; *I Served on Bataan* (1943), Juanita Redmond; *Bataan: Our Last Ditch* (1990), John W. Whitman; *MacArthur and Defeat in the Philippines* (2001), Richard Connaughton; *MacArthur and Wainwright* (1974), John Jacob Beck; and the particularly helpful *They Call It Pacific* (1943), Clark Lee.

Other World War Two references were *Baa Baa Black Sheep* (1958), Gregory "Pappy" Boyington; *No Name on the Bullet: A Biography of Audie Murphy* (1989), Don Graham; and *Since You Went Away* (1973), Donald I. Rogers.

Perhaps the biggest thanks must be reserved for two editors: Trish Lande Grader, who saw the potential in my proposal for prose sequels to *Road to Perdition*; and Sarah Durand, whose insightful input guided me to a stronger book. I must also acknowledge my friend and agent, Dominick Abel, who recognized movie potential in *Road to Perdition*. My entertainment lawyer, Ken Levin, has similarly been my champion on this journey.

Finally, I have to thank my wife, Barbara Collins. Having a talented writer in-house to read and edit work-in-progress is a blessing, of course; but Barb did more, aiding in research and helping me talk through plot points and characterization concerns. I could ask for no better partner than Barb, to accompany me down my criminal road—even if she does frequently comment unfavorably on my driving.

And Nate—without you, son, I could not have conceived this *Road* trip. You and your late grandfather—Max A. Collins, Sr.— are this saga's spiritual co-authors.

MAX ALLAN COLLINS, a Mystery Writers of America "Edgar" nominee in both fiction and nonfiction categories, has been hailed as "the Renaissance man of mystery fiction." He has earned an unprecedented twelve Private Eye Writers of America "Shamus" nominations for his historical thrillers, winning twice for his Nathan Heller novels, *True Detective* (1983) and *Stolen Away* (1991). His other credits include film criticism, short fiction, songwriting, trading-card sets, video games and movie/TV tie-in novels, including the *New York Times*–bestselling *Saving Private Ryan*.

His graphic novel *Road to Perdition* is the basis of the Academy Award–winning DreamWorks 2002 feature film starring Tom Hanks, Paul Newman and Jude Law, directed by Sam Mendes. His many comics credits include the *Dick Tracy* syndicated strip (1977–1993); his own *Ms. Tree*; *Batman*; and *CSI: Crime Scene Investigation*, based on the hit TV series for which he has also written a bestselling series of novels.

An independent filmmaker in his native Iowa, he wrote and directed *Mommy*, premiering on Lifetime in 1996, and a 1997 sequel, *Mommy's Day*. The screenwriter of *The Expert*, a 1995 HBO World Premiere, he wrote and directed the award-winning documentary *Mike Hammer's Mickey Spillane* (1999) and the innovative feature, *Real Time: Siege at Lucas Street Market* (2000).

Collins lives in Muscatine, Iowa, with his wife, writer Barbara Collins; their son, Nathan, is majoring in computer science and Japanese at the University of Iowa.